HAROLD ROBBINS

Books by Harold Robbins

The Stallion
The Raiders
The Piranhas
The Storyteller
Descent from Xanadu
Spellbinder
Good-bye, Janette
Memories of Another Day
Dreams Die First
The Lonely Lady
The Pirate
The Betsy
The Inheritors
The Adventurers
Where Love Has Gone
The Carpetbaggers
Stiletto
79 Park Avenue
Never Leave Me
A Stone for Danny Fisher
The Dream Merchants
Never Love a Stranger

HAROLD ROBBINS

THE Stallion

POCKET BOOKS
New York   London   Toronto   Sydney   Tokyo   Singapore

This book is a work of fiction. Names, characters, places and incidents are products of the author's imagination or are used fictitiously. Any resemblance to actual events or locales or persons, living or dead, is entirely coincidental.

POCKET BOOKS, a division of Simon & Schuster Inc.
1230 Avenue of the Americas, New York, NY 10020

Copyright © 1996 by Harold Robbins

All rights reserved, including the right to reproduce this book or portions thereof in any form whatsoever. For information address Simon & Schuster Inc., 1230 Avenue of the Americas, New York, NY 10020

ISBN: 0-671-87294-X

First Pocket Books printing January 1997

10 9 8 7 6 5 4 3 2 1

POCKET and colophon are registered trademarks of Simon & Schuster Inc.

Cover photo by Barnaby Hall

Printed in the U.S.A.

For my wife, Jann

The last shall be the one and only.

FOREWORD

One summer day in 1939, in a park in Detroit, sixty-one-year-old Loren Hardeman met eight-year-old Angelo Perino. Hardeman was in a wheelchair, being pushed through the park by a nurse. Angelo was pedaling a kiddie-car replica of a Bugatti that his grandfather had had specially made for him in Italy.

Loren Hardeman observed that the car didn't work very well—that is, it couldn't achieve any speed on a slight up-slope, no matter how furiously the little boy pedaled. Maybe, Loren said, he could fix it; and he grabbed a sketch pad and drew the design of a variable transmission for the little boy's toy car.

Angelo had no idea that the man in the wheelchair was in fact the chief executive officer of Bethlehem Motors, the nation's number four automobile manufacturer. He had created the company, and he governed it like a fief. He was the same kind of man the first Henry Ford was: an inspired tinkerer who had built his first car with his own hands, with no education in engineering, then built his own manufacturing company with his own hands, with no education in management. He resembled Henry Ford in other important respects—he, too, was arrogant, arbitrary, and capricious.

FOREWORD

It was Loren Hardeman's caprice to spend $11,000 of his company's money to build a concatenation of chains and sprockets and levers that made the best use of little Angelo's pedaling and gave the car speed and power.

As the years passed, Loren Hardeman grew sicker and more bitter at the hand God had dealt him. He had only one son and was unfortunate in him. He had only one grandson and was unfortunate in him, too. The world came to call the three Hardemans Number One, Number Two, and Number Three. Number One never trusted Number Two or Number Three with the power to run his company.

Angelo Perino grew up to share several of Number One's characteristics. He was as vigorous and lusty as the old man. Like Number One, he was obsessed with automobiles: designing them, building them, racing them. Like Number One, he almost always got what he wanted. First, he wanted to race. In 1963 he was the world's number-two-ranked Grand Prix driver and would have been first if he had not climbed the wall at Sebring and nearly died in a flaming crash that broke his body and scarred his face.

Number One had designed a new transmission for Angelo's kiddie car bacause he was bored. He loved to *do*, to *build*, to *achieve*. The venerable Sundancer, the design that had made Bethlehem Motors a power in the industry, was a bland family car. In 1969 he decided to build a sports car. He told his teenaged great-granddaughter, Elizabeth Hardeman, he would name it after her: the Betsy. The girl pronounced the idea "cool."

To design and build the Betsy, Number One called in a man he knew he could trust—a race driver but also an automotive engineer, Angelo Perino. He ordered Angelo to have a plastic surgeon repair his face, claiming he couldn't have a top executive of his company looking like a movie monster. Angelo agreed and had the surgery done in Switzerland. Number One installed him in Detroit, with ample powers to build the Betsy.

But there was a problem. Number Two was dead, and Loren Number Three believed the future of Bethlehem Motors was in making appliances, not cars, and he was determined to have his way. He fought Number One and tried to take the company away from him, using tactics that were sometimes legal but always dirty. He'd be damned if any wop—let alone the grandson of a mafioso bootlegger—would diminish his authority as heir to the Hardeman business and fortune. He even went so far as to have Angelo beaten by thugs.

But Angelo Perino could fight, too, and the beating did not frighten him; it only angered him. In a confrontational stockholders meeting, he defeated Loren the Third and saved the old man's control of his company.

Number One savored the victory Angelo had won for him, but even so, he didn't like it. He had not meant for his grandson to be defeated and humiliated. He was *family*, after all, and blood was thicker than water. The old man abruptly fired Angelo and ordered him off the company's premises.

But the story of the fateful link between Angelo Perino and the Hardeman family was hardly over.

I

1972

1

Angelo's father, Dr. John Perino, raised a glass of dark red wine—dago red the Hardemans would have called it. He stared around the table, over a serving platter heaped with pasta. The others took the cue and raised their own glasses: Angelo's mother, Jenny Perino, Angelo, and Cindy Morris.

"To a brighter future for you and Cindy, Angelo," said the doctor. "I thank God the old man fired you. You've lost enough time with the Hardemans. Nothing can ever redeem that family. The grandson, Loren the Third, is just as bad as the grandfather, the one they call Number One."

"Worse," said Angelo as he joined the others in a swallow of wine. He had to sip it through the right corner of his mouth, because the left side of his jaw was still wired, and his lips on that side of his mouth were still hugely swollen.

"Another toast, please," said Cindy quietly. "To you, Mother and Father. I call you that because Angelo and I agreed this afternoon to be married."

Jenny Perino drank the toast with tears in her eyes, and they flowed down her cheeks as she filled the plates. All of them understood she could only have been happier if her future daughter-in-law were Catholic. They also knew she

1

had learned to love and respect Cindy and was pleased that her son was marrying so fine a girl.

According to family tradition, she served each person more than any of them could possibly eat. In addition to the homemade pasta covered with a thick meat sauce, she served a tossed salad from a huge wooden bowl. A platter of garlic bread was passed around the table.

"We'll have a big wedding," said Jenny.

"We want to do it quickly," Angelo said gently. "We're leaving for Europe soon. I'm going to see Dr. Hans again so he can fix whatever is broken, and then try to put me back the way I was. I mean the way I was before the other plastic surgery."

Three years ago, Number One had insisted Angelo go to Switzerland and have the famous plastic surgeon remove the burn scars he had suffered in his final Grand Prix crash. The surgeon had done more than that. While he was at it, he had given Angelo a new, more youthful face. Angelo had joked that very few men got a second face; but it really was a second face because it made him look like a twenty-five-year-old when he was in his forties. Now, with the injuries he'd sustained in the assault, he looked grotesque again. He had to see Dr. Hans again, but this time he was going to ask the doctor to put him back together more like the mature man he was.

"A lot of big changes in one year," said Dr. Perino. "I am sure they will all be for the better."

"Some of the changes may not suit you very well," said Angelo. "We are not going to live in Detroit. Cindy and I talked a long time this afternoon, in the hotel room. We are going to live somewhere else."

"We can visit you often?" his mother asked.

"And we'll be here often," said Cindy. "Often enough to make you tired of us."

"You'll have children?" Jenny asked with a smile that widened as she asked.

"Six or seven," said Cindy.

"You don't like Detroit?" asked Dr. Perino.

"It's grubby and dangerous," said Angelo.

"That will change," said the doctor. "As the blacks take

over and make it *their* city, they will want to save and improve it. Since it never belonged to them, they never cared what happened to it. Now—"

"There are two other reasons," said Cindy. "First . . . Well, I'm sorry; it's your hometown. But frankly, when you've seen one boonie, you've seen them all. I want to live in New York."

"The other reason?" asked Jenny. "You said there were two."

Cindy smiled wryly. "If we stayed here, we'd be forced to associate with horrid parvenus like the Hardemans and the Fords. I really couldn't tolerate it. God forbid I had to go to a country club dance and dance again with that clumsy, pawing, two-bit drunk Henry Ford the Second. I think I'd vomit."

Angelo grinned. "We're going to get out of here. You think I could talk her out of it?"

"You don't want to," said his mother. "And you shouldn't. Do you remember your grandfather, Angelo?"

"Yes, of course."

"It is too bad you couldn't have gone to Sicily to see him. Now you will not see him until you join him in heaven. But maybe you should go to Sicily and see—"

"No, Mama," interrupted Dr. Perino. "Maybe someday Cindy should meet Uncle Jake. But go to Sicily? No. Our family does not keep up that connection."

"My grandfather was deported to Sicily," Angelo explained to Cindy. "He was reputedly a Mafia don."

"My great-grandfather Morris was a robber baron," said Cindy, grinning. "How else did I get so much money? It's only rarely obtained by earning it."

"She has a cynical philosophy." Angelo shrugged.

"Never mind philosophy," said Jenny Perino. "It is time you fixed your mind on what's important, Angelo. You got a good education. But you race cars—and get yourself hurt and almost killed. You try to manufacture cars—with other people's names on them. You get all mixed up in a fight to help an old man control his company—not *your* company, *his* company—and you get yourself hurt and almost killed. Now you are out of it. Stay out of it! Marry this lovely girl.

3

Have a family, Angelo . . . and Cindy. That's what's important."

2

"Jesus Christ!" cried Betsy van Ludwige as she gazed at Angelo in her Amsterdam apartment. "They really worked you over, Angelo."

"There were some very strong emotions involved, Miss Elizabeth." He leaned farther back in the sofa and put his arm around Cindy, who was sitting next to him.

"If you call me Miss Elizabeth one more time, I'm going to throw something at you. You built a car for me: the Betsy. Why can't you call me Betsy?"

"I don't know. I guess because I think of Betsy as the name of a car."

"It's *my* name, Angelo. Please . . ." She shrugged. "Anyway . . . Switzerland?"

Cindy spoke up. "Dr. Perino says everything has to heal before the plastic surgeon can start again. We stayed in London a month. We'll be in Amsterdam two weeks, then we'll go to the Riviera for a while. After that . . . the surgery."

"I hope it works out very well for you," said Max van Ludwige.

Betsy had not wanted to marry Max, and he had not wanted to marry her. But the Hardemans—Number One especially—had insisted that her baby have a name. Everyone but Betsy—whose wishes didn't count for much—had agreed that Max's wife would divorce him quickly. He would marry Betsy in order to make the child legitimate, then Betsy would divorce him, and he would remarry his wife. Money lubricated the arrangement.

Knowing all about it, Angelo was surprised to find that Max van Ludwige seemed to be a very decent fellow. The baby was his, after all, and he had wanted to do the right thing. His wife remained in the family home, and he and Betsy shared a handsome apartment on the fourth floor of a house that dated from the seventeenth century and overlooked a canal.

Seeing Max established here with the extraordinarily

beautiful twenty-year-old Betsy, Cindy wondered if the last element of the arrangement would ever really be carried out.

She had seen enough of Betsy to know that Betsy lived in style, wherever she was, no matter the circumstances. The apartment's white plaster walls were decorated with Dutch paintings—no Rembrandts or Vermeers, nothing that grand, but bright, airy paintings of city and country scenes, painted three hundred years ago. School of Rembrandt, school of Vermeer—that sort of thing. Her home was fragrant with cut flowers, which filled myriad vases and bowls.

They paid the obligatory visit to the nursery to see the two-month-old Loren van Ludwige, the child Betsy already called Loren the Fourth. An English nanny had already been employed and was with him. Having admired the baby, they returned to the living room for drinks and a sampling of Dutch cheeses.

"I hope you will enjoy the restaurant where we have booked a table tonight," said Max. "Dutch food is very good, but if you haven't visited a rijsttafel, you should."

3

The rijsttafel was a Balinese restaurant where close to one hundred dishes were served. An immense bowl of rice was set on the table. After they had loaded their plates with rice, they added as much variety as they wished from almost a hundred tiny bowls of spiced meats, vegetables, and fruits, hot and cold, that were brought to the table on serving carts.

Angelo had never experienced this kind of meal before but was immediately glad he had come. On Max's recommendation, they ordered glasses of the mild Dutch gin, genever; and they ordered a bottle of Burgundy and one of Chablis.

"What are you going to do, now that you are no longer in the thrall of the Hardemans?" Betsy asked Angelo.

"Well, I have several options," he told her. "In the first place, my stock in Bethlehem Motors is worth six million dollars. I may sell."

"Please don't," Betsy said simply. "Or if you must, sell it to me. I'll come up with the money somehow. You paid *one* million for it."

"You know that," said Angelo dryly.

"My father nearly split a gut when he found out. Number One never transferred his stock outside the family."

"He needed seed money for the Betsy project. Your father tried to squeeze him out of the idea by holding back company money. That was before Number One set his foot down again and recaptured absolute control."

"What are your other options, Angelo?" Max asked, obviously anxious to turn the conversation in some other direction.

"I can also go with the competition," said Angelo. "I've had offers."

"I can't imagine you doing that," said Betsy. "In spite of everything."

"We'd have to live in Detroit," said Cindy. "And that's out of the question."

"We don't have to decide for a while," said Angelo. "We're not going back to the States until after the surgery and the recovery and—"

"If you're going to be in Europe so long, please plan on stopping by and visiting us again," said Max.

"Max and I may no longer be together," Betsy announced flatly. "We are going to carry out the agreement, of course."

"But not in the next two or three months, surely," said Max.

"I suppose not," Betsy conceded. "Not in the next two or three months anyway, but before you get me in Dutch again."

Angelo grinned. "You . . .? Forgive me. I shouldn't ask."

"Better with Max than with somebody else," said Betsy. "I'm not going to go without."

When they left the restaurant, Cindy said she wanted to see the famous Amsterdam red-light district. It was within easy walking distance, and Max led them there. The district ran on two parallel streets, the Oudezjids Voorburgwal and the Oudezjids Achterburgwal. Many of the girls strolled along the streets or lounged in doorways, typically in raincoats; but many sat in lighted show windows in various stages of undress.

The business was conducted with surprising decorum. "Every fourth or fifth man you see is a plainclothes police officer," Max explained. "They enforce the rules strictly. The girls are not allowed to approach men, either by word or gesture. The man must initiate the conversation. But if you ask one of them what time it is, she is likely to respond, 'Fifty guilders.'"

Because they were two couples, no one so much as looked at them. It was understood that they were tourists, as were many of the people on these streets.

While Angelo and Cindy, Max and Betsy walked through the district, a light rain began to fall. The girls on the streets opened folding umbrellas or pulled rain hats out of their pockets. None of them left their stations.

Max walked beside Cindy. Betsy walked with Angelo, and she slowed down so they could drop back from the others.

"I thought maybe you'd wait for me," she said quietly.

"Wait . . .?"

"Little Loren should be *your* son."

"Betsy . . ." Angelo hesitated, then said, "The whole Hardeman family would have gone into orbit."

"Don't you care as little about that as I do?"

"You'd better care about your great-grandfather. Number One is capable of . . ."

As he hesitated again, she finished the sentence. "Murder. But it's my father who'd go into orbit. I heard him call you the grandson of the bootlegger who supplied Number One's liquor during Prohibition. He doesn't seem to comprehend that we Hardemans are new money. Number One was a bicycle repairman. He built a car, just the way the first Henry Ford did. The two of them were inspired tinkerers, nothing more. Where does my father get off thinking he's better than the grandson of the man who supplied liquor to his father? By the way, is it true?"

"It's true. My grandfather supplied him. Good stuff, too. Number One never missed a sip in all those years."

"That's what he hates most about what happened to him," said Betsy. "It's not the wheelchair. It's being unable to drink his Canadian whisky."

"I can sympathize," said Angelo.

She took his hand for a moment. "You *are* married, aren't you? I mean, really. Is she pregnant?"

"No. Not yet. We don't think so, anyway."

Betsy shook his hand and then let go. "Angelo Perino, I'm going to have a baby by you. I've decided. You just wait and see if I don't."

"Whatever Betsy wants, Betsy gets," he half sang, essaying the tune from *Damn Yankees*.

"And, little man, Betsy wants you," she finished the line.

"Well, to paraphrase FDR, you'll have to clear it with Cindy." He laughed.

4

This was his third face. He'd grown up with one, and it had been shattered and burned in the racetrack crash. He had never been satisfied with the second, which Dr. Hans had given him and thugs had broken up in a Detroit alley. That one had seemed false because it had been too youthful for a man his age. Now he had a third face, his second reconstructed one in a little more than three years.

Cindy insisted on being in the room when the bandages were removed, even though Dr. Hans and the sisters had warned her he would not look right at first. She gasped. "He looks like he's been out in the sun too long!"

"Yes," said the surgeon calmly. "It is red, as we told you it would be. In a week . . ."

In a week he was a third man. He did not have the same face he had had before the crash; reconstructing his original face remained an impossible feat for the plastic surgeon. But he did not have the sham young face he had worn for the past few years. His Roman nose had not been restored; it was straight, Teutonic: what Dr. Hans considered correct and handsome. His broken cheekbones had been restored, partly with bone taken from his pelvis. Another piece from his pelvis replaced a hunk of his chin that had been destroyed by the men who had worked him over. The best thing about his new face was that people would not turn and stare at him anymore.

THE STALLION

"I like it," said Cindy.

Which to Angelo was all that counted.

5

In London, in Amsterdam, and on the Riviera, Angelo and Cindy had accepted only one telephone call that was not from a member of their families—a call from President Nixon, congratulating them on their marriage and wishing them well at the Swiss hospital. He said a man like Angelo might want to consider a position in government and asked him to call when he was fully recovered.

During the weeks they spent at the hospital, Angelo and Cindy dealt with some of their correspondence and accepted a few telephone calls. He had a call from Lee Iacocca at Ford, who expressed sympathy about his beating, wished him a complete recovery, and suggested he phone him when he came home. Henry Ford the Second sent flowers to the hospital, with a note inviting Angelo to call when he came back to Detroit. The Ford flowers were delivered on the same day as a wire from Bunkie Knudsen warning him to keep his distance from Ford. Ed Cole at General Motors called to suggest they meet. To Angelo's complete surprise, he received a wire also from Soichiro Honda.

The most interesting call was from Robert McNamara at the World Bank. He suggested that Angelo consider becoming a consultant in the field of automotive engineering and design. People on the Street, he said, constantly sought insight from people who could offer them sound information and advice about the state and the future of the industry and the corporations in it. He could become an industry analyst.

Since it was the kind of amorphous enterprise that appealed to both Angelo and Cindy, they determined to explore the idea.

6

Returning to the States, they went to Detroit and made their duty calls. The Perinos pronounced themselves happy with Angelo's new face and forever grateful to Dr.

9

Hans. ("But may the good Lord forbid he should ever have to do it again," Jenny prayed.) They had lunch with Lee Iacocca, dinner with Bunkie Knudsen, and cocktails with Ed Cole—all of whom applauded Angelo's decision to become an industry analyst rather than join another company and try to build another new car.

"I understand you've got a great new car coming out," Angelo said to Iacocca. "What are you going to call it? The Mustang?"

"You'll make a fine analyst," said Iacocca wryly. "You know what you're not supposed to know."

"But what will it do for you?" Angelo asked. "Will Hank Ford be grateful and give you academic tenure?"

Iacocca shrugged.

"You know better than that," said Cindy. "If the car's a success, he'll convince himself it was *his* idea. If it's not, it was *your* idea. By today, Loren Hardeman the First is sure he never wanted to build the Betsy. And Loren Three is absolutely certain Angelo shoved the idea down the company's throat."

"I'm not quite as cynical as you are, Cindy."

She smiled at Iacocca and put her hand on his. "Lee, let's come back here for lunch five years from now. You will no longer be with the Ford Motor Company."

Lee Iacocca grinned. "And you, Mrs. Perino, will be the wife of the president of Bethlehem Motors."

In New York, they moved temporarily into a suite in the Waldorf until the Manhattan apartment they had leased could be made ready.

One evening Cindy came into the bathroom and found Angelo, who had just taken a shower, standing naked at the mirror, staring at his face. "Do you know what happens to men who stand too long in front of their mirrors and study their faces?" she asked. "Staring at your face distracts you from what's *really* important." She reached around him and grasped his penis in both her hands.

"Well . . .," he said. "That part's not very useful in business."

"It's useful in fucking," she said. "What's more, it's passed the test."

"What?"

"The doctor says—I'm pregnant as hell."

"Cindy!"

"Well, don't play like you're *surprised*. What'd you think would happen when I stopped taking the pill and we went on doing it?"

Angelo turned around and drew her into his arms—cautiously, as a husband just learning of his wife's "delicate condition" always does.

She embraced him tighter. "Hey! I won't break. *It* won't break. When the time comes to back away, I'll let you know. Right now, I want it!"

Angelo grinned. "Like you always do."

II

1973

Loren Hardeman Number Three knew he was a lucky man. He'd fallen into shit and come out smelling like a rose. In more ways than one.

He was in control of the company. His grandfather, Number One, had gone back to Palm Beach; and though he was still the persistent meddler he had always been, he left the day-to-day management of the company to his grandson and the other officers and directors. He insisted that the company continue to manufacture automobiles, so they continued the venerable Sundancer. But one day . . . well, there would come a day.

He was free of Angelo Perino. Perino didn't even come to Detroit much anymore. He was out; but more than that, Number One had told him not to interfere in the affairs of the company. Unfortunately, you couldn't altogether ignore a man who owned two hundred thousand shares, but Perino was smart enough not to buck the old man.

Number One was smart and tough. Always had been. He'd *used* Perino and made that Italian son of a bitch like it. He'd made Perino understand that blood was thicker than water; so even when he, Loren, had fucked up, he was still

12

family and counted for more with his grandfather than a rank outsider could ever hope to count.

But none of this was the chief reason why Loren thought he was a lucky man—that was business. He was lucky at home, which was more important.

Alicia, his first wife, Betsy's mother, didn't bug him anymore. She lived in Connecticut and apparently was content with golf and sailing—and probably a boyfriend. She owned 5 percent of Bethlehem Motors and had written him a harsh letter complaining about the lowered dividend and the declining value of the stock, but with 5 percent there was nothing much she could do about it.

Bobbie, Lady Ayres, his second wife, had her divorce, and she hadn't cost him much. During a furiously angry exchange between them one night, she had confessed she'd fucked with Perino. ("That lying wop son of a bitch swore to me he never fucked my wife!" Bobbie had laughed. "He never did. He fucked your girlfriend, before we were married.") She didn't hate him. She scorned him, which was worse. Anyway, he was well rid of her.

That marriage had ended at the most opportune time. Within a month after he met Roberta, he was free to marry her. And she was the best thing that had ever happened to him.

Anyway, good times had returned. Though he was a little wacky in some respects, Nixon made a fine president who stood foursquare for the values that made this country great. Loren had taken to wearing the American-flag lapel button, as Nixon did; and he was glad, too, that Nixon had repopularized the vested suit. Loren liked vests because he thought they disguised his paunch. Also, it was acceptable to wear a hat again, and because his hair was thinning, Loren was glad to cover his head. He was a thickset man, not as big as Number One had been, but bigger than his father. With a little more exercise and a little less drinking he could be a handsome man, he judged. He'd rather be a contented one.

He sat in the rear seat of a Sundancer, being driven home by a chauffeur. His bodyguard sat beside the chauffeur. Ever since he had arranged the beating of Angelo Perino, he'd had to keep a bodyguard employed. Sooner or later that wop son of a bitch would look for his revenge, if not personally then through one of the hoodlums that adhered to the Perino family. His mistake had been in not ordering Perino beaten to death. If any other occasion arose, he wouldn't make the same mistake twice. Perino was dangerous.

Roberta would not have let him make that mistake.

The most unfortunate aspect of being president of Bethlehem Motors was that he had to ride around in a goddamned Sundancer. He'd thought about introducing a luxury line, the company's Cadillac or Lincoln, maybe called the Loren; but he knew Number One would come down hard on that idea. Anyway, the dealers would never take it. They were having a hard enough time selling Sundancers.

This Sundancer, his personal automobile, was the only one of its kind the company had ever built. Everything about it had been modified to conceal a luxury car in a Sundancer body. The Sundancer engine had been removed and a powerful, high-compression Mercury engine installed in its place. A four-speed Hurst transmission—called a shifter—made best use of the new engine power. To carry the extra weight and withstand the strains of the new acceleration, the chassis had been reinforced and the suspension system entirely replaced. Loren drove it occasionally himself, and he enjoyed surprising the drivers of Mustangs and Chargers when his Sundancer burned rubber.

Mostly he let the chauffeur drive. The interior of the car was what he enjoyed most. No vinyl showed anywhere. All of it had been replaced with leather and polished walnut. Instead of the Sundancer's array of rectangular gauges and too-late lights, this car's instrument panel included a full array of real engine gauges. The rear seat was in effect two comfortable leather chairs, separated by a bar.

The car had cost Bethlehem Motors $550,000. Number One had never seen it and never would. The $550,000 had been hidden in various accounts: R & D, advertising, machine replacement, and so on.

Just now he had opened the bar and poured himself a Scotch. A small refrigerator had proved really impracticable, so he had settled for a little ice chest. One of the chauffeur's duties was to see that the chest was always full of ice—also to be sure the correct brands of Scotch, gin, and brandy were always in the bar in good supply.

He was being driven home—to Roberta's home, actually, since he had moved in with her almost three months ago. They had agreed not to marry until they were more sure of each other, but they had been sure enough to decide to live together, and they told each other they would either marry or separate before the end of the year.

Her name was Roberta Ford (not of *that* Ford family) Ross. Harold Ross, her husband, had died two years ago. He had been an architect and builder and had accumulated a handsome fortune before his death. He had left Roberta well off. He *should* have left her well off. Without her, he would not have been the success he was.

Roberta held a master's degree in business administration from Harvard—one of the first women MBAs. Her specialty was marketing, and she had gone into real estate. Before she married Ross at age thirty-one, she had been for five successive years a member of the Wayne County Realtors Million Dollar Club, meaning she had sold more than $1 million worth of property in each of those years. She had earned more than $75,000 a year in four of those five years. When she accepted Ross's proposal of marriage, she put aside a plan she had been working on to establish her own brokerage.

Within a year after marrying Ross she discovered that Kirk, one of his partners in Duval, Kirk & Ross, was embezzling heavily from the firm. Duval and Ross were willing to forgive and forget. Roberta was not. She took the case to the district attorney. The embezzler spent three years in the penitentiary, and Roberta insisted on the lawsuit that recovered forty cents on every dollar he had stolen.

After that she assumed management of the firm. Duval and Ross did the design work and the building, and Roberta ran the business. Duval gratefully retired at sixty-five. Roberta incorporated the firm and gave stock options to young architects to recruit them. Ross & Associates, Incorporated, became one of the biggest architectural firms in the Midwest.

Then Ross died.

Roberta offered her stock—and full control of the business—to the young architects. She offered a purchase plan under which they would buy the stock by handing her a percentage of the firm's gross revenues. She insisted that the firm be audited by Touche, Ross, and she paid occasional visits to the offices to examine the accounts. Her income from the business exceeded half a million dollars a year.

She was a formidable woman, in every sense.

She was as tall as Loren, actually half an inch or so taller. If not for the work of her hairdresser, she would have been a dishwater blond. She did not want to be that, yet she did not want her hair stripped. She insisted on, and got, a golden color with a wholly natural look. At a time when piled-up hair was in style, she had hers cut short: clipped on the sides shorter than most men wore theirs, then abundant but not piled up on top. Her eyes were vivid blue. Her nose was too big to be thought ideal, but she had never considered letting a surgeon scrape cartilage out of it. Her mouth was narrow, her lips thin.

Roberta's figure was robust. She had broad shoulders and strong arms, and long muscular legs. Her hips were narrow for a woman her size, but her breasts left no doubt of her womanliness. They were large.

She met Loren at the door and kissed him lustily. "Day?" she asked.

"Same old shit," he said. "They're talking about raising the price of plastics again. You know. Goddamned Arab oil embargo. It'll cost us eight dollars a unit on refrigerators, a hundred forty-something on a Sundancer. How the hell can we compete when—"

"Isn't everybody getting hit with the same increase?"

"Well . . ."

"Then you'll compete," she said. "Anyway, you'll figure out a way to overcome it. I know you, Loren. You're one shrewd bastard."

He tossed his briefcase into the closet and hung up his raincoat. He always swore he would work on the papers in the briefcase during the evening, but he never did. Bethlehem Motors had problems, big problems, but he hired people to work at night; he didn't have to do it himself.

Roberta was stunning, as she made it a point to be when he came home evenings. She was wearing tailored gray flannel slacks, cut more tightly than such slacks usually were, to cling to her backside and legs. She also wore an off-white cable-knit turtleneck sweater. For some reason she liked to go barefoot in the house, so she wore no shoes.

"Had anything to drink?" she asked.

"A Scotch in the car."

"Scotch now?"

"Sure."

They walked through the living and dining rooms to a family room at the back of the house. The room was exquisite, as in fact were all the rooms, though this one appealed to Loren more than any other. It was furnished with a baby grand Steinway, which Roberta played, and with English-country-house furniture: two overstuffed couches and two fat chairs, upholstered with colorful floral prints. When the drapes were open, a picture window in the rear wall opened on a densely planted rock garden. A big Persian rug covered most of the oak floor. Paintings of Thoroughbred horses and frolicking spaniels in country settings dominated the walls. Three brass lamps filled the room with warm light.

Roberta brought two drinks to the couch where Loren had sat down. She sat down beside him, saluted him, drank, and then kissed him.

"I just washed, mister," she said curtly.

Loren took a second swallow of Scotch. He nodded. "Good," he said.

He stood, put his drink aside on the coffee table, and began to take off his clothes.

As he stripped naked, Roberta slipped down her slacks and her panties, leaving them around her ankles.

She scooted to the end of the couch, beyond the coffee table. Loren, entirely nude, knelt before her. He lifted her sweater and kissed her on each breast, pausing to suck on each nipple. Then he pushed her knees apart and shoved his face into her crotch. He used his tongue to find what he knew she wanted him to find. He flicked the tip of his tongue over it. Then he licked it. Then he backed away a little and began to lick her entire furrow with his flattened tongue.

If someone had told him a year ago he would do this—and a great deal more that Roberta had taught him—he would have laughed. He, Loren Hardeman, naked on his knees eating a woman's cunt? Well, he was doing it. And not only that, he liked it. He didn't know why he liked it. He couldn't explain it to himself.

Roberta arched her back and moaned. Loren returned his tongue to her clit and gave it all his attention. He worked until with a shriek she achieved an orgasm. Then he licked all up and down again. She came again before he even returned to her clit. Working on it once more, he brought her a third time.

She shoved him back.

"Was it good?" he whispered.

"You've done better," she grunted.

"Do you want to punish me?"

"A little."

Loren picked up his trousers, pulled his belt out of the loops, and presented it to her. He turned over on his hands and knees and presented his backside to her.

"Do it, darling!" he whispered hoarsely.

She flogged him with the belt, half a dozen strokes, raising angry red welts. Then abruptly she threw the belt aside, dropped to the floor beside him, roughly turned him over, and gobbled his erect organ into her mouth. He climaxed within half a minute. She swallowed his ejaculate.

He remained on the floor naked as she pulled up her panties and slacks. She handed him what was left of his drink and picked up hers and gulped it down.

She went to the bar and poured them two more drinks. Glancing at her watch, she said, "We've got exactly eighteen minutes to get to the Farbers'. And Jesus Christ, you've sweated again. You'd better trot up to the shower toot dee sweet. I'm going in what I've got on. Your camel jacket and dark brown slacks would be right."

Loren tossed down half his Scotch. He bent down and

kissed her feet before he trotted away toward the stairs and the bathroom.

He ran his fingertips over his backside and felt the welts. They hurt—really hurt—but goddamn! he was a lucky fellow.

III

1973

1

Anne, Princess Alekhine, whoever she had once
been, however she had been born, was a princess by
anyone's definition. Prince Igor had made her so. Or maybe
she had always had a regal nature, and marriage to Prince
Igor had only afforded her an opportunity to blossom.

She *looked* like a princess: tall, slender, exquisitely graceful. The beautifully tailored pink suit she wore would have
made almost any woman look genteel, but Anne would have
looked aristocratic naked.

In any event, she was acutely aware that the Hardemans
were nouveaux riches and rude Americans. Money, she
observed once again as she sat at Number One's dinner
table in Palm Beach, did not buy breeding.

The old man was not supposed to drink anymore. But he
did. Canadian whisky. Only one or two, but that one or two
he heaved back like a peasant, obviously more interested in
the effect of the alcohol than in the taste of what he drank.

She had sent one of Number One's servants out to buy a
bottle of Tio Pepe. Another princess, much older, with the
name Esterhazy, had remarked to her one day that one
served guests only one sherry, Tio Pepe, and served it only

20

in Murano glass, preferably goblets with crystal stems and milk-glass bowls.

Number One had been the kind of savage who would have thought it the height of sophistication to throw his glassware into the fireplace. Wheelchair bound, he was much subdued, but still he was a savage. She remembered him as a big man. It was impossible for a man really to shrink, but he was probably forty pounds less heavy than he had been the last time she'd seen him. His trouser legs hung loosely over legs long atrophied. His shoulders appeared narrower. He sat with them hunched, his earlobes all but touching them. His face was deeply wrinkled. Even at table he wore a panama straw hat to conceal his liver-spotted bald pate.

Princess Anne had become a snob. She had so intended, and she reveled in it.

Number One was not allowed to eat most of the food that was served to his guest. "What the hell am I *supposed* to eat? Nothing that tastes good. But you know something, Anne? I've been under the so-called care of these medical butchers for more than thirty-five years, and I've outlived most of them. Mostly by not doing what they say I have to do. You know what? I'm ninety-five goddamned years old. Anne, honey, don't live to be this old. It isn't worth it."

"No?"

"No. Think of what you lose! Jesus, Anne, do you realize Elizabeth has been gone forty-four years! My son has been gone more than twenty years. Now your mother . . ." He shook his head. "Sally was a wonderful woman. She was a good wife to my son—"

"A good mother to me," Anne interrupted.

"Yes, of course. That's why you came to see me, isn't it? To share memories of—"

"No," said Anne with brutal severity. "I came to find out if after all these years you would admit the truth."

"What truth . . . ?"

"You're not my grandfather, you egregious old liar."

"Anne!"

"You're my *father,* damn you!"

"Anne, for God's sake—"

"When people are dying, they tell the truth. Even the law of evidence acknowledges that." She reached for the bottle and renewed her glass of Tio Pepe. "When she was dying, my mother told me about you and her. Loren Two knew he was not my father, and he never told me. *You* never told me."

"Don't judge us, Anne," the old man pleaded. "You know what my son was. You found out during the stockholders meeting, thanks to that rotten goddamned—"

"Thanks to Angelo Perino," she interrupted, "whose word is better than yours."

"You can't understand," said Number One tearfully. "Sally was so beautiful, so wonderful, and Loren Two was so incapable of—"

"So you solved the problem in the most direct way," said Anne coldly. "And to be altogether frank, it's a matter of indifference to me. I made a life for myself outside the orbit of this corrupt parvenu family. But it would have been nice to know I was *your* daughter and not to have believed all these years I was the daughter of a weakling who killed himself. All these years I've had to wonder, and Igor has had to wonder, if there wasn't something evil in my genes, a predilection for self-destruction. It would have been nice to know I was not *his* daughter. That would have been nice . . . Dad."

"You must not talk about this," said Number One. "In the first place, no one will believe you."

"I suppose Loren Three doesn't know," she said. She smiled and shook her head. "That worthless little man turns out to be my nephew, not my brother."

"Loren is *not* a worthless man," said Number One, his face rigid with anger.

"Your male descendants do you no honor," she said coldly. "You should rely more on your female ones. I'm a far better person than Loren. And so is Betsy. Betsy and I would not arrange to have a man beaten half to death. That's what Loren did. He's lucky to be alive. Angelo Perino is *connected,* you know. He could have Loren swatted like a fly."

"Don't overestimate the wop. And don't underestimate

what you call a parvenu family. I built a multibillion-
dollar—"

"And didn't learn anything in the process, *Dad*. You're
still a bib-overalls machine-shop tinkerer. And my nephew,
as he turns out to be, is a thug."

Number One's face reddened. "Oh? Well, *you*, my dear
Anne, are an *ornament*. That's what you are: an ornament
purchased by a noble family, in the same way they purchase
art and lovely furniture and fast cars. And Betsy is . . . a
nymphomaniac. She's got a stronger sex drive than any
man."

"As strong as yours?" asked Anne.

2

When Number One first saw Cindy in a dress he
didn't recognize her. He hadn't seen her often, but when he
had seen her she had been a racetrack groupie and a test
driver, invariably wearing faded, ragged jeans with a sweatshirt as often as not smeared with grease. She had been so
fascinated with racing that she had carried a hi-fi around
with her and played tapes of Grand Prix cars roaring on
straights then lowering to gurgles as they were shifted down
in turns. She had been asked to leave hotels because she
played those damned tapes so loud. She played them when
she was making love, and the roars of racing engines helped
her to achieve fiery orgasms.

When Angelo walked away from racing, she walked away
from him: abruptly and completely.

Last year, after his beating and his dramatic confrontation with the Hardeman clan, she had walked away from
everything he'd thought had mattered to her just as abruptly
and completely as she'd walked away from him. Suddenly
she wasn't interested in automobiles anymore, not in the
racing kind or any other kind.

Only then did he discover that she had a fine classical
education. Her time in the racing world had *been* a fling: a
four-year fling after a rigidly respectable upbringing and
schooling. His gamine racetrack groupie was actually a lady.

During their prolonged European wedding trip she had

led him through famous galleries and introduced him to the
glories of art. Angelo had been in St. Peter's twice before,
but he had never been guided through by so knowledgeable
a guide as his wife.

She had her own money, of course, and from time to time
she shipped a painting or sculpture home. These were in
their Manhattan apartment now, and Angelo had seen the
chief art critic for the *New York Times* study for minutes on
end one or another of her pieces and then pronounce it "an
exceptionally fine example of" whatever.

Their apartment was an exceptionally fine example of
gracious living—Manhattan style. It was on East Seventy-
fourth Street and had in fact once been two apartments.
Sometime in the forties a wall had been removed and they
had been joined together. Angelo and Cindy had leased the
place before they'd left for Europe so the work they required
could be done while they were away. The oak floors had
been stripped and refinished. All the walls had been painted
white. Track lighting had been installed on the ceilings of
the living room and entrance hall so spots and floods could
be hung to light the art Cindy expected to display.

The big windows to the east overlooked the FDR Drive
and the East River. Drapes could be opened and closed
electrically. When they came back from Europe they lived
in the Waldorf for four weeks while they chose furniture and
had it delivered. It wasn't what he would have chosen, but
he was content with letting Cindy select what she liked: lots
of fine wood, stainless steel, and upholstery of tan-and-
black leather.

Shortly after they moved into their apartment, Cindy
began to entertain, and Angelo discovered he needn't be
concerned about leaving her alone while he was on business
trips; she would not *be* alone. Many of her friends from
college lived in New York. Some of her sorority sisters even
lived close by. They were transfixed by Cindy's stories of her
years at the tracks. Her experiences were beyond their
imagining.

They were curious, too, about the man she had married: a
big, handsome Italian *seventeen years her senior,* a onetime
championship race driver—number two in the world in
1963—now an automotive engineer. One of them was

playfully forward enough to ask Cindy if she'd been pregnant when she married him.

"No," said Cindy. "But I am now."

"Pretty good is he?" the woman asked.

"Shirley, with his brains, he's an engineer. With his cock, he's an artist. Every fuck's a masterpiece."

The husband of one of her sorority sisters told Angelo he had been at Sebring when Angelo climbed the wall and was burned. The husbands were interested in his new business. Some of them were with brokerage houses and could use competent industry analysis. He made friendships with these men, which would be useful to him as he built his business. One of them proposed him for membership in the University Club, and he joined and took many of his lunches there.

Cindy bought a Leroy Neiman lithograph. It was called *Sautatuck* and was an honest nude: a girl comfortably reclining with her legs apart, wearing one red stocking and one green. The owner of the gallery who sold it to her came to the apartment to help her hang and light it. She was heavily pregnant and did not want to climb on a ladder to install a spotlight in the track. When Angelo came in, that is where the man was: on the ladder.

"Angelo," said Cindy, "I want you to meet Dietz von Keyserling—more formally, Dietrich von Keyserling. He sold me the Neiman."

"I'll shake hands when you come down," said Angelo. "It would be something of a challenge to your balance, I'm afraid."

He examined the lithograph and decided he liked it very much. Although the subject was decidedly immodest, the artist's technique made it modest. It was erotic only in a restrained and subtle way.

Von Keyserling adjusted the light and came down. He was a tall, slender young man, about Cindy's age, which was twenty-five, and he was handsome, though Angelo found him a little too . . . pretty. He was blond. His cheekbones were high and pronounced. His lips were full and a little redder than most men's. He wore a double-breasted blue blazer with gold buttons, a white cotton turtleneck, and crisply pressed gray slacks.

"It is very good to meet you, Mr. Perino," said von Keyserling. "Correct me if I am wrong, but I believe you drove a Porsche 908 in the Nürburgring in nineteen sixty-eight. I was there. I saw you drive, did I not?"

"You saw me," said Angelo. "It was in the twilight of my years. I managed not to slam a wall and nearly burn myself alive; but that was about all I accomplished that year."

"He's modest," said Cindy. "He's one of the great drivers, and he was still a driver the others feared in nineteen sixty-eight."

"They called the 908 the Short-Tail, did they not?"

"You know something about racing," said Angelo. "The 917 was faster but not handy, not maneuverable like the 908. I loved that car."

"You drove a number of marques. Was it your favorite?"

"Well, Porsche . . . Ferrari."

"Brandy?" asked Cindy. "At this stage, I'm not having any, but that's no reason why you two shouldn't."

The two men nodded their assent, and Cindy brought a bottle of Courvoisier and two snifters.

Angelo raised his brandy and saluted. "I am happy to have met you, Mr. von Keyserling."

"Please. In America everyone calls me Dietz. I am Dietrich Josef Maximilian von Keyserling, but I enjoy American informality and like to be called simply Dietz. It is what my mother called me. I am, incidentally, Austrian, not German. From Vienna."

"Dietz—okay. I'm Angelo."

"Dietz and I have been talking about a business proposition," Cindy said to Angelo. "If we can work out terms he might sell me a partnership in his gallery."

"The terms," said von Keyserling, "would be that we would work together. She is going to be a young mother, and I would not expect her to devote much time to the business at first. But as the gallery is now a sole proprietorship, I do not feel I can take a holiday. Cindy could cover for me when I need to be away, especially on buying trips in Europe."

The young man spoke virtually flawless English, which he had obviously learned in England and which so far had been only slightly modified for the States. Occasionally a word or two betrayed him—as, "we would vork togedder."

"I think both of you must look to lawyers for advice," said Angelo. "A contract. And I don't think a partnership is a good idea. You should incorporate the business and own shares."

"Ah. I looked to you for good adwice."

"I won't object, of course," said Angelo. He smiled. "As if I could."

"I assure you, Angelo," said von Keyserling, "I would not enter a business arrangement with your wife without your consent. I am maybe old-fashioned that way."

IV

1973

1

First class or no first class, 747 or no 747, the flight to Tokyo was long, boring, and tiring. Now, on top of that, the taxi ride from the airport was going to take an hour and a half and cost maybe a hundred dollars. Japan would never be a tourist trap, Angelo judged. Just a trap.

He was in an evil frame of mind as he sat in the back of the little car and endured the ride. No wonder Chrysler had sent him first class.

That's what they'd said: first class all the way. He was traveling for Chrysler, which had hired him as a consultant to visit Japanese automobile factories to see if he could discover how the Japanese manufactured automobiles that ran reliably and economically and required almost nothing more than scheduled service.

He had written in an automotive newsletter that the secret was quality control—

The last time I took delivery of an American-manufactured automobile (for charitable reasons, I'll omit the name), the salesman handed me a small notebook and asked me to keep it in the glove compartment. "Just write down any problems you have," he

28

told me, "and bring the car in after a month or so and get all the warranty work done at once." When I went in after two months, the agency had to keep the car for three days to do the warranty work. The windshield leaked. It still does. The passenger-side door could not be locked and occasionally swung open. Sometimes the starter would not engage and just spun around without turning the engine. Gasoline consumption was outrageously high, the result, it turned out, of a leak from the carburetor. (Need I say what might have happened from gasoline dripping on a hot engine?) The wheels were out of line. The radio failed intermittently—and still does. When I drove through puddles on a rainy day, water dripped from under the dashboard and wet my shoes and socks.

The point is, this car had left Detroit with all these defects. It was not a lemon, particularly. Tens of thousands of car buyers report these and worse problems every year.

An American who buys a Honda takes it back to the dealer after six thousand miles to have the fluids changed and filters replaced. Usually that's all it needs. Some Americans may think a Honda looks like a four-wheel motor scooter or a road-running power mower, but the car is built to standards of quality control American manufacturers do not match. The automotive industry in this country is losing billions of dollars on warranty repairs and will in time lose customers because its cars leave Detroit defective and not ready to give reliable service.

Chrysler wanted to know how the Japanese did it. Many reports had come back, most of them citing a native work ethic that could not be matched in American plants because the unions would never allow it. Chrysler wondered and sent Angelo Perino to Japan to find out.

When he finally reached his hotel, he quickly shifted to a better frame of mind. Service was complete, efficient, and obsequious. He was ushered to a luxurious suite on the eighteenth floor, from which he had a view of one quarter of the city and Tokyo Bay. The suite included a tiny kitchen, where he found bottles of Johnnie Walker Black and Beefeater gin, also vermouth and beer. A card by the bottles read—

IT IS OF THE INNKEEPERS PLEASURE THAT ADDITIONAL
  LICORICE GOODIES ARE AVAILABLE.
PLEASE TO TINKLE THE ROOM KEEPER.

Vases of chrysanthemums stood in each room, including the little kitchen.

The centerpiece of the bathroom was a sunken marble bath almost as large as a small swimming pool. It was exactly what he wanted. He loved Jacuzzis, and this bath promised strong jets from a strong pump. He downed one drink and carried another into the bathroom with him. The jets were as strong as he'd expected. He lay back in streaming, bubbling water and felt the tension go out of his body.

When he had soaked for ten minutes or so and was about to go to sleep, the bathroom door opened and a smiling little maid stepped in. She brought towels and more soap. She nodded and murmured something, maybe a word of apology, as she leaned across the tub to put the soap in its place. She was exquisite, probably no more than sixteen or seventeen. As she straightened towels on their bars, she laid a lingering and obviously appraising stare on his crotch. She smiled widely, bowed, and backed out of the bathroom.

Angelo shook his head and reached for his glass of Scotch, which by now was streaming condensation. He had been briefed on the protocol of dealing with Japanese businessmen and judged it would be taken as faintly less than courteous if he telephoned anyone on the day of his arrival. He decided he would go out on the Ginza early in the evening, then return to the hotel for dinner. The food in a place like this couldn't be bad.

"Room service!"

Now what? Had he left the door unlocked, or had the maid done it? He switched off the water pump and reached for a towel. He didn't have to let this one see him. She sounded more mature.

The bathroom door swung back.

30

It was Betsy!

"Turn the jets back on, Angelo," she said. "There's room in there for two."

No matter that he shook his head and said no. In a quarter of a minute she was naked and in the water with him. She pressed the switch to set the jets streaming again and turned on the tap to bring in more hot water. Then she crawled up Angelo and kissed him so fervently that she brought blood to both their lips.

"The man I always wanted," she murmured as she kissed his neck, his ears, and his eyes.

"How the hell—?"

"I read in *Automotive News* you were coming to Tokyo. I'm staying two floors down. I've been here a week and have traveled all over Japan. I'll still be here another week after you leave. But for the next two weeks—"

"I'm going to be very busy."

"If you're too busy to come back to this hotel and sleep with me for two glorious weeks of nights, I'll tell tales out of school. I'll send back word that I'm here, that *we're* here, together."

"Betsy—"

"If you become the first man to turn me down, I'm going to conclude you are queer."

"I don't think I have to prove anything about that."

She lifted his penis in her right hand. "At least I give you an erection. I guess you're straight. So what're you going to do, Angelo?"

He wasn't sure what he was going to do. He'd only been married a year. He loved Cindy, and they had a baby boy. But Betsy . . . She was twenty-one years old, and she was perfect. "Well . . .," he muttered.

" 'Well, what the shit?' Is that what you're thinking? Even on those terms I'll take you. You know, I've spent a goddamned *fortune* to be here with you. Listen, this place has got great room service: Japanese food and American. Let me order for us. I've gained a little experience in the past week. You know from sashimi?"

"Raw fish," he said, wrinkling his nose.

"You never had it till you had it with Betsy van Ludwige sitting naked at the table with you."

"I have a feeling . . ." He paused and drew a deep breath. "I'm not going to get you pregnant, Betsy. If you're not on the pill, then—"

"I'm on the pill, damn it. I don't want to get pregnant again right now, not even by you. Pregnancy is no damned fun, you know? It ruins your figure."

He ran his hands over her breasts, which were still youthfully firm, even though she'd had a baby. "Didn't ruin yours," he murmured.

"Bingo! That's the first affectionate thing you ever initiated with me. C'mon! Play with my titties. Put your fingers other places."

"We can't do it in the water," he said. "Believe me."

"We don't have to do it this instant. Just make me feel good. Then, in a little while . . . Listen, I've got some delicious scandal for you. Guess what? Number One is not Anne's grandfather!" She stopped to laugh. "He—"

"What are you telling me?"

"She's his *daughter*. Before my grandmother—Sally— died, she told Anne that she and my great-grandfather had an affair, of which Anne, Princess Alekhine, is the result. Can you imagine that? That horny old bastard!"

"Not so old. He'd only have been in his fifties when Anne was born."

Betsy shrugged. "Whatever."

"How do you know this?"

"Anne told me. Number One tried to make her promise not to tell anyone, but she called me as soon as she got back to France. I was still in Amsterdam, tidying up, closing the house, and so on."

"Does your father know this?"

"He does now. Want to hear a man choke on the telephone? Anne is not his sister. She's his aunt. She figures she's senior to him in the family."

"I don't imagine Number One sees it that way."

"No. But Number One is ninety-five years old, and how he sees things isn't going to count much longer."

"Be careful, Betsy. He can do a lot of damage in the time he's got left. If you and Anne have some kind of idea you can wrench anything out of his grasp . . ."

Betsy laughed. "All I want in my grasp right now is your cock, Angelo."

2

Cindy switched off the television set and returned to the couch to sit down beside Dietz von Keyserling. They had just watched the announcement of the resignation of Spiro Agnew as vice president.

"I will never understand American politics," said Dietz.

"Don't try."

Dietz wore what was all but a uniform for him: double-breasted blue blazer and white turtleneck. In the privacy of her home, Cindy wore soft and faded old jeans and a gray sweatshirt stained with automotive grease—a relic from her racetrack fling.

He picked up his drink, a snifter of Courvoisier. "Do you agree about the realists?" he asked.

"Whether I like them or not, they will sell," she said. "There is always a market for that kind of art, particularly the nudes. I do like the Pearlsteins."

"You could hang several Pearlsteins here and have a dinner party. Who knows? Philip might even come. Inviting the right people, you could almost certainly sell a painting or two."

"That's why I decorated the apartment this way: to be able to use it as a gallery."

Dietz frowned. "I will have to borrow the money to pay my share of the cost of doing the realist show. I am assuming the bank will be no problem. Sometimes they ask for security."

"Why borrow from a bank?" Cindy asked. "I'll lend you enough for your share."

"Would you do that for me?"

"You give me a note, secured by the art we buy. If you don't repay, I'll own the whole show."

Dietz grinned. He put his snifter aside and leaned toward Cindy to kiss her. She had allowed him to kiss her before, and she did now, in fact returning his kiss. He reached for her left breast and caressed it gently. As he had guessed from looking at her, she was wearing no bra, and quickly he ceased to caress and began to fondle. She had never allowed him to touch her before, but she did now.

For a minute or more he fondled her breasts, squeezing and lifting them.

"You have just changed the nature of the relationship," she said to him quietly.

"Should I be sorry?"

"Not necessarily. But we had better define what the new relationship is."

"You are irresistible, Cindy," he said. "I want you. I want everything."

"Everything—I am not sure what 'everything' includes. Let me tell you what it can include and what it can't. It can include recreational sex. It can't include any kind of emotional commitment. I am married to Angelo, and I'm going to stay married to him."

"If he found out, he would kill me," said Dietz soberly.

"No, and he won't kill me either. I am not so naive as to suppose he's over there in Japan keeping celibate. The first time a Japanese businessman offers him a cute little bedmate, he'll accept her. I know him. And he knows me. He doesn't expect me to be any more chaste than he is. What he does expect—and I expect it from him, too—is that we don't damage our marriage. If he had any reason to suspect otherwise, we couldn't go on being partners in the gallery. Do you want to risk that?"

"I must," said Dietz simply.

"We can't be together on a regular basis," she said. "Probably not even frequently. Only when circumstances are just right. When he's out of town and the nanny has gone for the night."

"I accept those terms." He began to slowly lift her sweatshirt. "May I?" he asked quietly. She did not respond to the question, and he bared her breasts.

"My God," she said quietly when she saw his male organ. "I never saw one like this before." It was small, and it was not circumcised. She twiddled his foreskin between her thumb and index finger.

He gasped. "In Europe," he grunted, "the barbarous mutilation of the male organ is not common. My grandfather saved his life by showing his uncut *Glied* to an SS *Scharführer* who took him for a Jew. Being intact, he could not be a Jew."

She bent down and licked his balls to see if that would make his penis grow.

"It's not very big," she said frankly.

"It performs its office," he said. "I get no complaints."

He was right. When he left, an hour or so later, she had no complaints.

V

1974

1

"What can I say to you?" Cindy asked Angelo. "All I can say is, it'll be costly if not fatal. Jesus Christ, man! Hasn't the time come when Number One can't *summon* you anymore?"

"Well, he wants to talk to me, and he can't come up here. He's a fragile old man. He'll probably never leave Palm Beach again in his life."

"Tough shit," grunted Cindy as she walked to his office window and looked down on Third Avenue. Rain was pouring hard on the streets of New York.

"Overnight," said Angelo. "I'll fly down and have dinner with him."

She glanced around his office. She was pleased with it. She had bought the furniture, and the three paintings hanging on the walls were loans from VKP Galleries—von Keyserling–Perino. Angelo was peripatetic. He didn't spend much time in his office, but when he was here Cindy was glad that he could enjoy a handsome, well-thought-through design.

"You *will* be here for the opening of the realist show? And the dinner."

"You've got a lot tied up in that."

"Want to make a little bet that I get my money out of it, and a nice profit?"

"If you and Dietz think so, I have to think so."

"You'll *be* here . . .," she insisted.

"God willin' an' the crick don't rise."

2

"Just who the hell do you think you are?" Number One shouted at Angelo. "I demand you keep your nose out of my company's business!"

"I don't give a damn what you demand," said Angelo. "I flew down here—at your expense—without much enthusiasm for it, without much interest in ever seeing you again; and if you think you can intimidate me or that I'm going to sit here and take abuse from you, you can go straight to hell."

The ninety-six-year-old Loren Hardeman the First glared at Angelo, but there was no force in his glare. What Angelo faced in that armchair across the dining table was a stiff suit not at all filled by a crumpled old man. The brim of his panama hat shaded his eyes. Betsy was at the table. Her eyes glittered as she watched and listened to the exchange between Angelo and her great-grandfather. Loren Number Three was there, too, a little drunk and a little sullen.

"Do you remember how I reengineered your Bugatti?" Number One asked, the anger gone from his voice. "Remember that?"

Of course Angelo remembered. That was when he'd first met Loren Hardeman the First. Even confined to a wheelchair, Loren Hardeman the First, in 1939, had been a big and obviously powerful man. Angelo had not immediately understood how powerful. Later he would understand only too well. There were giants in Detroit in those days, and the first Loren Hardeman was one of them. For decades he had believed that if he could get up on his feet he could be a giant again—and not just among midgets. He never surrendered that idea.

"I think you owe me a little respect," said Number One quietly.

"And you owe me a little, old friend," said Angelo.

"You're not associated with the company anymore," argued Number One.

"Exactly," said Angelo. "That's what I said in the first paragraph of my analysis. I said I still own two hundred thousand shares of stock in Bethlehem Motors, but I have absolutely no other relationship with the Hardeman family or the management of the company."

Betsy's brows rose skeptically, and she cast an amused glance at Angelo that the two Hardeman men did not see and could not have understood.

"You say we are losing money on the Sundancer. Why do you think so?"

Angelo turned to Number Three. "What about it, Loren? Are you losing money?"

"That's inside information," Loren replied testily.

"You say we're losing market share," said Number One.

"I don't have to have inside information to know that," said Angelo. "Do you deny it?"

"We don't have to affirm or deny anything, Angelo," said Loren.

Angelo shrugged and spoke to Betsy. "Common knowledge."

"I don't know what makes you an 'industry analyst,'" said Loren, "but your damned report caused the price of our stock to go down. Worse than that, we lost eight dealers."

"Do you pay any attention to what I write, or just bitch?" Angelo asked.

"We shouldn't be manufacturing automobiles at all anymore," said Loren the Third.

Number One slammed his hand on the table. "I don't want to hear it! As long as I am alive, Bethlehem Motors will make cars. Period."

"Then you had better make ones you can sell," said Angelo.

"The Sundancer—"

"Was a fine car, in its time and context. Bethlehem Motors didn't capture any of the market Ford captured when Lee Iacocca shoved the Mustang up Henry the Second's ass. You missed that market. Now you're going to miss another one if you don't get out in front."

"I read your goddamned analysis," said Number One. "It's easy to be a genius when you don't have to *do* what you write about."

"I read it, too," said Betsy. "It says the Sundancer—which I agree was a fine car in its day—is now thought of as a dinosaur, a gas-guzzler—"

"Oh, come on!" Loren the Third interrupted. "George Romney thought he could sell fuel-efficient cars. You can't even find a Rambler in a *junkyard* today."

Betsy picked up from where she had been interrupted. "When George Romney called 'Detroit iron' dinosaurs, gasoline sold for thirty-five cents a gallon. Now it sells for a dollar, and we'll see it selling for a dollar and a half. Why do you think Volkswagen sells ten times the number of cars it sold ten years ago? Because it gets thirty miles to the gallon, compared to twelve for a Sundancer. The VW is ugly and uncomfortable, but—"

"It also *runs,*" said Angelo, "and doesn't require days of warranty work."

"So what's *your* solution, Angelo?" asked Number One. "Transverse engines driving the front wheels—"

"No long drive shaft," said Angelo.

"Four cylinders," Number One went on. "Who's going to buy a car with a four-cylinder engine?"

"The people who buy Volkswagens, Hondas, Toyotas—"

"Oh, sure," laughed Loren the Third. "Chuggety-chug. Noise. No pep. No acceleration."

Angelo shrugged. "The MG has a four-cylinder engine," he said. "So does the Porsche 911. Chuggety-chug, Loren?"

Betsy pointed at her father and laughed. "Gotcha there!"

Loren the Third shot an angry glance at his daughter.

Number One reached inside his suit and drew out a clipping. It was Angelo's report to New York securities dealers on the condition of Bethlehem Motors. He read, " 'Bethlehem lacks the facilities to build four-cylinder transverse engines and their associated drive system, and it cannot within any reasonable time retool and begin to manufacture them.' So, young man, we can't, hey? What's your solution? You say, 'A number of Japanese manufacturers have that manufacturing capacity in place, have extended experience in engineering and producing such power trains, and have in fact surplus capacity. They are ready, willing, and able to supply American manufacturers with these fuel-efficient, powerful little engines. Companies like Bethlehem Motors could do worse than enter into negotiations to import them.' So . . . a bastardized car, half American, half Jap. That's what you want us to build, Angelo?"

"It could save the company," said Angelo.

"All my life," said Number One, "the phrase 'Made in Japan' has stood for cheap and shoddy."

"Like Sony television sets and Nikon cameras?" asked Betsy.

Number One slammed his hand down on the table. "While I live," he said, "no automobile made in my plant will have a goddamned Japanese engine!"

Angelo smiled. "That's what Hank Ford told Lee Iacocca. And, frankly, I don't give a damn what you do. There's the truth, whether you like it or not. I'm not asking you to take my recommendations. I didn't make them to you. I made them to the securities boys in New York. Try raising money, my friends. Try floating a bond issue or a new issue of stock."

"Ever consider that you might get sued for libeling a company?" Loren the Third asked.

Angelo ignored his question. "Your ratings are down. Your stock has 'sell' recommendations from the major analysts. Bethlehem Motors has a limited life expectancy."

"So do I," muttered Number One. "Eat your goddamned soup before it gets cold."

3

Angelo knew Betsy would come to his room. He knew it would be more dangerous to lock her out than to let her in. Besides, he didn't want to lock her out.

"You and I are perfect together," she whispered to him after they had made love. She reached for the snifter of brandy she had brought to the room and took a small sip before she held it to his lips and let him sip. "There's got to be more to it than this—more, I mean, than sneaking a night in this house. Oh, God! Leave her, Angelo! Give her a nice settlement and come to me."

"She's the mother of my son," he said simply.

Betsy took the snifter back, took a bigger swallow, and put it aside on the night table. "Anyway, I suppose you love her. You love her, don't you?"

Angelo nodded.

"I'm sure she's a good wife for you," said Betsy. "I'd have been better.'

"You were married when I married Cindy, if you remember."

"You knew the arrangement," she said. "You could have waited."

He shook his head.

"They're feeling murderous," she said. "I mean the old bastard and my father. I'm not exaggerating. They'd gladly kill you if they thought they could get away with it."

Angelo shrugged. "I haven't hurt them. Not really."

"It's not what *you've* published. They figure you're the source of what *Thurman* wrote in his big exposé. You know what I mean."

Angelo surely did. Guy Thurman had published a twenty-page article on the Hardeman family in one of the major newsmagazines—

The qualities that make fathers great men are rarely inherited by their sons. In fact, those very qualities tend to suppress similar qualities in the sons. So it has been with Loren Hardeman, founder of Bethlehem Motors. His son and grandson were also named Loren Hardeman, and the custom grew of calling the eldest man Number One, the son Number Two, and the grandson Number Three.

Number One would come to wonder what Number Two might have been had he not been so completely overshadowed by his domineering father. As it was, he became a weak and vacillating man and a closet homosexual who was blackmailed. In 1952 he committed suicide. Number Three turned out to be a jealous, manipulative man who has tried more than once to take control of Bethlehem Motors away from Number One.

Looking around for a man who could build a Bethlehem Motors sports car, to be called the Betsy for his great-granddaughter, Number One settled on a young man he had known since that young man was a child— Angelo Perino.

Angelo Perino had the engineering degree and he had the same commitment to building automobiles that Number One had. What was more, he had guts. He had spent five years as a racing driver, had once ranked number two in the world, and had nearly died in a crash. He also had money of his own and was willing to take risks.

To build the Betsy, it would be necessary to overwhelm the angry opposition of Loren Hardeman III, who would do anything to frustrate the project—out of jealousy, yes, but also out of a conviction that Bethlehem Motors must sooner or later get out of the automobile business and concentrate on the business that made far more money for the company: the manufacture of appliances.

The battle raged for three years. When Number Three saw he was losing, he went so far as to attempt to sabotage the experimental car. When that tactic failed, he actually hired thugs to beat up on Angelo Perino. . . .

Number Three had sued Thurman, but the case had been quickly dismissed, which left him to pay the legal fees.

"Thurman tells too much not to have had an inside source of information," said Betsy.

"That doesn't make it me. I swear before God I never met Thurman, never talked to him, never corresponded with him."

"You'll never make them believe it. Watch out for them, lover. Never turn your back. They . . . ." She shrugged. "To hell with it. We've got better things to think about."

Betsy got up on her hands and knees and straddled him. She dangled her breasts over his crotch, swinging them back and forth against his cock. "Turn over on your face," she urged in a throaty whisper.

He did. She spread his hinder cheeks with her hands, shoved her face into his anus, and began to probe with her tongue. He drew all the breath he could contain. The sensation was not orgasmic, but what her tongue reached tingled with a pleasure that became more and more intense and yet was not orgasmic. She worked at it for five minutes or so, then reached between his legs, found his rigid shaft, and began to stroke it. He came within half a minute: a deep, riotous, sustained orgasm.

"So . . .," Betsy whispered. "I bet she never does that for you."

Angelo smiled fondly at her and shook his head. He lied. Betsy didn't need to know that Cindy did it, too.

VI

1975

1

     VKP Galleries was located on Park Avenue a few blocks north of the Waldorf and on the west side of the street. On a Monday night in April, Cindy and Dietz presided over the opening of a one-woman show for Amanda Finch, a young artist Cindy had discovered through her sorority contacts.

Amanda Finch had never been a sorority girl, but Mary Wilkerson had. Mary, who lived in Greenwich, was enrolled in art classes at the Silvermine Guild, where Amanda was a figure model for classes in sketching, painting, and sculpture. The two women became acquainted when Amanda walked back among the easels to see how the students were portraying her. When Amanda offered a suggestion about Mary's painting, Mary learned that Amanda was herself an artist and was posing as a figure model to earn a living in a nondemanding way that allowed her to devote most of her time to her own painting. Mary saw some of Amanda's work and immediately invited Cindy to come to Connecticut and look at it.

Amanda Finch's work fit into the realist category that VKP Galleries was still promoting. She painted with meticulous attention to detail, so that her paintings could, from a distance, be mistaken for finely focused photographs. The stamens and pistils in her flowers were scrupulously reproduced, as were the veins in the petals. Her portraits were reminiscent of Rembrandt's in that they resembled greatly enlarged color photographs of faces and hands, that precisely depicted a subject's varying skin colors, including blotches and scars. Eyelashes and eyebrows seemed to have been painted with single-hair brushes.

The most impressive of her works were her nudes. Having been unable to pay models for the long hours it took to paint so realistically, she had modeled for herself, standing before a tall mirror. In two of the paintings she was standing. In the third she was sitting on a wooden stool with her feet hooked behind the legs. This pose spread her legs, and her rendition of her intimate parts was as finely detailed as her paintings of stamens and pistils.

It was obvious to everyone in the gallery that the diffident young woman in gray tailored skirt and white silk blouse— clothes to which she was clearly unaccustomed—was not just the artist but the model. The painting of her spread open sold the first night of the show for $7,500.

Angelo met her on the second night of the show. He had flown in from Chicago too late to attend the opening. She was an attractive but certainly not ideally beautiful young woman. She made it apparent that she had better things to think about than how she looked. Her dark brown hair hung as it would. Her eyebrows were heavy. Her brown eyes were myopic behind a pair of little round gold-rimmed glasses— they, too, were meticulously reproduced in the paintings. Her mouth was wide and thin. Her figure was as her paintings showed her: ordinary. Apart from her eyes swimming behind thick lenses, the only really distinctive things about her were her hands, which were extraordinarily large, too large for the rest of her, like the hands of Michelangelo's *David*.

"I owe Mrs. Perino a debt I'll never be able to repay," she said to Angelo. "This show is everything I ever wanted in my life. If I die tonight, my life has been fulfilled."

Cindy had overheard and came up to embrace the girl. "Would you accept fifteen hundred for the violets?" she asked. "And we've got a possible three thousand for the glads."

"Oh, my God!"

"We've got a bid of four for one of the other nudes. I'm not accepting it yet."

"My God . . ."

"Plan on spending the next six months starkers in front of that mirror of yours," said Cindy, grinning.

Cindy was pregnant again, not yet heavily, but it was visible when she was unclothed. "Except for your condition, I'd commission her to paint *you*," said Angelo.

"It's a beautiful condition," said Amanda with quiet simplicity.

Angelo stared at Cindy for a moment. "To be hung in a private room in our place," he said. "Not here."

So it was agreed. Beginning in July, Amanda moved into the Perino apartment. Cindy posed four hours a day, and Amanda painted six.

The result was a painting that Angelo thought was the most beautiful work of art he had ever seen in his life. Standing in profile so that her distended belly would be dramatized, Cindy was quietly proud. Her eyes were on it, staring as though she could see the life within her. One hand rested on her belly near her navel. The other rested on her hip. Posing on summer days, she gleamed faintly with sweat, and Amanda captured that, too, as she did every other detail of Cindy's body, with the consummate skill of an artist, not an illustrator.

The portrait was in fact hung in Angelo and Cindy's bedroom, but a few trusted friends were invited to see it. Dietz, of course, saw it. So did Mary Wilkerson.

Angelo paid Amanda $15,000 for the painting and commissioned her to do a portrait of him as soon as he could find the time to pose.

2

Number One took a swallow of the Canadian Club that was forbidden to him. He sat in his wheelchair on the lanai, looking vaguely out at the Atlantic. Loren the Third sat on a chaise longue. Roberta, now Mrs. Hardeman, sat in a wooden chair upholstered with vinyl flower-pattern cushions, drank Scotch, and smoked a Chesterfield.

"The stock closed yesterday at eighteen and three quarters," said Number One. "Two years ago it sold at sixty. We're all poorer than we used to be."

"It's the economy," said Loren. "They drove Nixon out of office—"

"We're holding on to barely two percent of the automotive market," said Number One. "And the refrigerators aren't selling well either, in spite of hiring that expensive broad to open and shut the doors on television."

"The price of plastics went up," said Loren.

"Went up for everybody," said Number One.

"They squeeze out the smaller companies," said Roberta. "It's always that way. Basic economics. General Motors and General Electric can achieve economies of scale that we can't. It's a fact of life."

Number One noticed the "we." He raised one eyebrow slightly. "I competed effectively for many years," he said. "How do you explain that?"

"You built an automobile people wanted to buy," said Roberta. "So did Studebaker. So did Packard. So did Hudson and Nash. People could always buy a Ford or a Chevy, but some people wanted a Sundancer. The fore-and-aft Studebaker was a funny-looking damned car, but it appealed to a lot of buyers. It was distinctive. So was the Sundancer."

"Yes, and by God we survived them," said Number One. "You can't buy a Studebaker today, but you can buy a Sundancer."

"We lose money on every unit we produce," said Loren.

"We lose money on your goddamned refrigerators! Don't tell me again to get out of the automobile business. I'm not getting out."

"The company will go under," said Loren sadly.

Number One looked at Roberta.

"No, it won't," she said. "Between the two of you there's enough smarts to air-condition hell." She reached across to Loren and patted his shoulder. "I've got confidence in this man, Mr. Hardeman."

Number One lifted off his hat for a moment and used it to

fan his bald head. "Son," he said to his grandson. "Get this idea of surrendering the automobile business out of your head. Concentrate on making our cars sell. I know you can do it."

Loren stared at Roberta, and she nodded. "Grandfather, I hate to say this . . . but I'm afraid we have to face the fact that Angelo Perino is right. The Sundancer is too big. It burns too much gas. We've got to build cars—"

"With fuckin' transverse engines!" Number One yelled. "And what they call 'power trains' instead of transmissions. And . . . and you're going to tell me next that we can't build them."

Loren shook his head. "No. We can't build them. Oh, sure, we can build anything, given enough time and investment. But the competition is already ahead of us. If we buy the power units in Japan—"

"And build half-breed cars—"

"It's our last chance," said Loren bluntly.

"All right, son," said Number One quietly. "Tell me. Make a flat statement. Tell me we have to build these half-Jap cars to stay in the car business."

"Grandfather, we have to build these half-Jap cars to stay in the business," Loren recited grimly.

"We have the *people*?"

"We'll find them."

"I don't have to tell you who we need."

Loren shook his head. "No. No, by God! No! That wop son of a bitch—"

"We *need* him, goddamnit! On an understanding. He works for *you*. Haven't we taught him that lesson: that when he works for us, he *works for us*?"

"He won't come."

Number One smiled. "I can get him. I'll get him down here in twenty-four hours. And between the two of us, we'll make him fuckin' dance to our tune."

3

Number One went to bed early, immediately after dinner. He had placed a call to Angelo Perino in New York, but the secretary said that Mr. Perino would not be in New

York until sometime tomorrow. Loren and Roberta stayed at the dinner table after Number One was wheeled away. They talked about going out but decided instead to take a walk on the beach and then go to their suite.

It was ten o'clock before either of them mentioned the name Angelo Perino.

Roberta was by then wearing a peach-colored negligee, semisheer for the most part except for a panel of completely sheer material at the level of her armpits that exposed her ample breasts to easy view. She smoked a Chesterfield and had a Scotch within reach.

Loren was naked. He sat on the floor at her feet, bending down from time to time to lick her toes.

"The secret is to use Perino while keeping him under control," said Roberta.

"Yes, of course. But how do I do that?"

"Your grandfather will help you. And so will I."

"I don't know . . ."

"Have confidence in yourself, Loren," she said sternly. "The old man swore he'd never allow a Japanese engine to be put in a Bethlehem Motors car. You won that battle today."

"Angelo Perino hates me. Well, shit . . . I suppose he has good reason."

She reached down and stroked his cheek. "You made a mistake," she said gently. "Everybody's entitled to a mistake, even a big one. But you won't do it again. Mama'll be watching over you and won't let you."

He pushed the skirt of her negligee back and licked the insides of her legs.

"Anyway," she said, "the old man's on your side now."

"He oughta be," said Loren bitterly. "Imagine . . . my grandfather fucked my mother! What the hell is Anne to me, anyway? My half sister or my aunt?"

"Both," said Roberta. "But what's the difference? She stays in Europe with the prince and doesn't meddle."

"Also, Perino fucked my second wife."

"Only before she was your wife. You can't hate him for that. Do you hate my late husband?"

"It's different. Perino knew I cared for Bobbie and was planning—"

"*Forget it, Loren.* You've got other things to think about."

"I won't let that wop son of a bitch screw me again. Roberta, I *hate* Angelo Perino. My grandfather is going to *beg* him to come back with the company. I wish his plane would crash on the way down here. I could arrange something like that maybe, sometime."

She smiled and shook her head. "I think we'd better do something for your frame of mind." She stood and hiked the skirt of her negligee up around her hips. She sat down again and spread her legs wide. "C'mon," she said. "And do it good, so Mama doesn't have to put any new welts on your ass."

4

Cindy had at first felt a little awkward about posing nude for Amanda. There was no way she could do it without being seen by the au pair. Also, of course, Angelo wandered in and out. The baby, John, saw her, of course, but was too young to see anything significant in his mother being the only naked person in the apartment.

She was posing when Angelo came in with the news that he'd had another call from Number One, who wanted him to come to Florida for a brief visit.

"Your master's voice," said Cindy. "Are you going?"

"I feel that I have to. It may well be that he wants to say good-bye. He's ninety-seven, you know."

They had become accustomed to discussing all but the most private matters in the presence of Amanda, and Cindy sneered and said, "He'll live until somebody shoots him in the heart with a silver bullet."

"He's got a goal, he's often told me, of living to be a hundred."

"What if he offers you something?"

"Like what?"

"Control of the company."

Angelo shook his head. "He won't do that."

"He'd better. The company is going under."

Angelo glanced at Amanda. She seemed not to have heard anything, but obviously she had. Clearly, too, she knew what they were talking about.

"He can't depend on Number Three," Cindy continued. "That's obvious. He's calling you in to bail him out. And if you do, you're a damned fool. He tried to kill you once. How the hell can you forget that?"

Angelo glanced at Amanda. "I'm going down there to see what he wants. I won't make any commitment until you and I talk again."

VII

1975

1

    Sitting on the lanai, they faced a hissing rain that obscured the view even of the beach, much less of the sea. It was one of those tropical rains that sometimes fall in Florida: straight down out of a dark overcast sky, driven by no wind, and not intruding inside the screens. It was cold, though, and Number One sat wrapped in a knit shawl hung around his shoulders by his nurse.

"Which king was it?" he asked, "who was wrapped in blankets with virgins to give him heat in his old age?"

"David," said Angelo. He smiled. "If you don't require virgins, we might be able to find somebody."

Number One managed a faint smile of his own. "When you reach that point in life," he said, "when it would make no difference whether the girl wrapped up with you was a virgin or not, the time has come . . . Oh, hell. I swore I'd make a hundred, and I'm afraid I'm going to. Don't make promises to yourself. You may have to keep them."

Angelo had not come straight from the airport. Anticipating a confrontation, he had checked into a motel, affording himself a retreat if he needed one. He wore a madras jacket over a white polo shirt and a pair of Sandhurst-tan slacks.

Loren was there, so conspicuously filled with tension that

Angelo wondered if he hadn't been taking something. No matter what he wore, Loren the Third was always tense and self-conscious, like a kid who had worn his Boy Scout uniform to school only to discover that Boy Scout Week was next week. The golfing clothes he was wearing now looked out of place in the presence of Number One.

The interesting one was Roberta. Angelo had heard of her but had never met her. Her string of names was Roberta Ford (not of *those* Fords, she was quick to tell you) Ross Hardeman, and she was a striking woman, no doubt of that, though he wished he could think of a better word for her. He had rarely seen a woman with as much brash self-assurance. Number One would not have allowed Loren's other wives to sit in on what promised to be a confrontational business meeting, but he was allowing this woman to do it. She was not the kind of woman Angelo would have expected to see attached to Loren.

Apart from her unalloyed self-assurance, she was a physically imposing woman. He was interested in how she'd styled her hair: clipped bristly short to the tops of her ears, then feathered into longer hair above. She was not beautiful, but she did the best she could with what she had, and she was definitely attractive. She was wearing formfitting cream white pants stretched tight by stirrups and a raspberry polo shirt filled with a formidable bust.

"I suppose you still believe in that funny-car you want us to build," said Number One.

Angelo lifted his chin a little. "There'd be a good name for it," he said. "The F-Car."

"Fucker," muttered Number One. "You come here to make jokes or to talk about a car?"

"I came here to pay you a social call," said Angelo. "I didn't come to talk business."

"Loren," said Number One. "See to it that Angelo gets a check for twenty-five thousand dollars within the week. A consulting fee. So we can talk business."

"I didn't offer to talk business, not for any price," said Angelo.

"Don't be stubborn," said Number One. He turned to Roberta and said, "You see what we have to contend with

53

whenever he's around? Let's not play games, Angelo. We want your input."

"What's this? You want my input? When did this come about?"

Number One turned and stared at the pouring rain for half a minute, while the others wondered if he had lost track of the conversation. "Do you remember the time I asked you to be my legs?" he asked Angelo.

"Then fired me when I did the job too well."

The old man's hand fluttered impatiently. "Never mind that. Talk to us about how to build this car."

"Time has passed," said Angelo, "since I told you what you had to do to save Bethlehem Motors. GM has been working on a fuel-efficient car with a transverse engine. So has Chrysler. You're late at the starting gate, Mr. Hardeman."

"Yes, yes. I read your Wall Street reports. I know what you think. The question is, what do we *do*?"

Angelo glanced at Roberta, who he guessed was listening to him with a more open mind than Number One or Number Three. "It's very simple," he said. "You can't build the car now. By the time you design the car, engineer it, and tool up the plant to make what it needs, your competition will have taken the market away from you. But there's a way you can do it."

"Tell us," said Loren, unable to subdue the scorn in his voice.

"The engine and drive train you need is being manufactured by Shizoka. It's a beautiful unit, manufactured to the highest quality standards. They don't sell many cars in the States because . . . well . . . the Chiisai is too small or, depending on how you look at it, too large. The American market right now is for two kinds of cars. They want family cars—the idea still being that you should be able to cram six people into an automobile for a Sunday-afternoon drive—or 'pony' cars, ones that leave rubber on the road. With relatively little work, the Chiisai can be reengineered to carry a body into which five, and maybe even six, American-size people can be squeezed. If that body is cleverly designed, it will look good—that is, racy, romantic."

"I know the Chiisai," Loren said impatiently. "What has it got to do with Bethlehem Motors?"

"You form a partnership with Shizoka," said Angelo. "Maybe even merge the two companies, though I don't think that will be necessary. Jointly, you design, manufacture, and sell one car. In Japan it's whatever Shizoka wants to call it. In America it's whatever *you* want to call it. In Europe maybe it's called something else. But it's always the same car: medium size, peppy but not overpowered, solid, manufactured to high standards of quality control—"

"Partnership!" Number One yelled. *"Merger!* With the fuckin' Japs? I'd rather the company went under."

Loren smiled tolerantly. "C'mon, Angelo. For a twenty-five-thousand-dollar consulting fee, surely you can come up with something better than this."

"Stick your money up your butts, Hardemans," said Angelo. "I don't need it, and I don't need you."

"You were never as smart as you thought you were," grumbled Number One.

Angelo shook his head tolerantly at the old man. "My dear friend," he said. "In nineteen thirty-nine, when you rebuilt my kiddie car, you were alive to ideas and possibilities, in spite of the fact you were already in a wheelchair. Your trouble is—and I can't blame you; you've lived too long too painfully—that you've been dead to anything since . . . well, since nineteen thirty-nine. Your company won't survive you, because all the juice has gone out of you. And you never passed any along to your son and grandson."

Number One stared at Angelo for a moment. His face was bland, showing absolutely no emotion or thought. Finally he nodded. "Good-bye, Angelo," he said softly.

2

Angelo checked the airline schedules. He could have flown back to New York that night, but it would have involved a rush to the airport, a change of planes at Atlanta. No, he decided to enjoy a restful evening after a good dinner.

He called Cindy and told her she'd be glad to hear he'd had no offer from the Hardemans. He'd said good-bye to

Number One, and he guessed he would never see the man again.

From past visits to Palm Beach, Angelo knew you could eat much better off the premises of Casa Hardeman than you could seated across that grim dining table from that ever-grimmer old man. He sat at a table overlooking a crashing surf lighted by powerful floodlights and drank piña coladas, then ordered a big lobster with a bottle of white wine. His waitress said she'd seen him drive at Daytona. She said she had a Pontiac Firebird in the parking lot and would love to be a passenger with him driving. He thanked her and said he'd be glad to take her up on that sometime when he hadn't been drinking.

He had a bottle of Scotch in his room but had had enough to drink. He took off his clothes and stretched out on the bed. A pro football game was on television, and he punched up the pillows and began to watch.

He'd watched less than a quarter when he heard a knock on the door.

"Who is it?"

"Roberta Hardeman."

Angelo was taken aback, but he called, "Hold it a minute. I've got to get dressed."

She was dressed as she had been on the lanai: in the stretch pants and full shirt. "Can I come in? I need to talk to you."

Angelo nodded and stepped aside from the door. "Where's Loren?"

"Sleeping the sleep of the innocent," she said. "Or to put it another way, he's sleeping one off. He never knows what he misses."

Angelo nodded toward the couch, but sat down in the chair. "What do we have to talk about, Mrs. Hardeman?"

"The first thing is that I'm Roberta, not Mrs. Hardeman. Can you offer me a drink? Or should we go to the bar?"

"I've got Scotch. No ice."

"It's a cardinal sin to put ice in Scotch," she said.

"Water?" he asked.

"A teaspoonful."

"Admire my crystal ware," he said as he handed her a

drink in a plastic glass. He had poured himself one, too. "Cheers. Now, what can we talk about?"

"Can you believe that I love Loren Hardeman?"

"No."

"Okay, I know why you would think so. I know what he did to you. Even having heard the story from his point of view, I think it was a despicable thing to do. But . . . I didn't marry him for his money. I have money of my own."

"Good for you. You may need it," said Angelo coldly, taking a sip of Scotch.

Roberta stared into her glass for a moment, then drank. "Whatever you think of him—and are entitled to think of him—you don't want to kill him. Am I right?"

Angelo shrugged. "Don't worry. If I ever had any thought of calling my friends of the Honored Society to get rid of him, that was a long time ago. I healed. I have a new life."

She smiled and nodded. "So does he."

Angelo looked her up and down, unsubtle in what he was doing: making a crass and intimate appraisal. "I bet he does," he said.

"You appreciate," she said quietly.

"Sure."

"Another subject, for a little later," she said. "Right now, what I want to talk to you about is Loren. I know what he did to you: that he had you beaten up, hurt, scarred. That's the price *you* paid for Number One's unconscionable manipulations. The old man used you. You know he did. He used Loren, too. Do you have any idea what price *Loren* paid?"

"Tell me."

"He was emasculated. The old man left him in charge of the company, but first he cut off one of his balls. That's what he did to Number Two—only both balls, as you well know. The old man is *evil,* Angelo."

Angelo shook his head. "Old, frustrated, unhappy . . . yes. Evil? I don't think so."

"You really care about him, don't you?"

"I admire him," said Angelo. "He outsmarted me. I have to have some respect for a man who can do that. That's why I have no respect for your husband. He could never outsmart me. He might try to have me killed, but he could never outsmart me."

"Your modesty is overwhelming," she said, tossing back her Scotch. "Can I have some more of this?"

He got up and took their glasses to the bathroom, where the bottle waited.

"Angelo," she said while he was still in the bathroom. "Loren is going to be castrated again. Do you understand?"

"I can't say that I do. Or that I care."

"The old man gave him control of Bethlehem Motors—"

"Family," said Angelo as he returned with their new drinks. "However deficient he was, Loren was a Hardeman."

"But he wasn't Number One. Nobody is ever going to be Number One. The old man won't let that happen. *You're* as good a man as he is, and he knows it. That's why he fired you. Loren is a safe bet. He'll never be a big enough man to put the founder's name in shadow. So—"

"So?"

"So he gave Loren control of a failing company. Number One built Bethlehem Motors! Number Two wasn't man enough to run it. Number Three—Loren—is going to preside over the collapse, which cuts off his remaining testicle."

Angelo shrugged.

"Did you ever *fail,* Perino? Really fail? Do you know what it's like? I doubt you do. It never happened to you."

"So what do you want me to do? Why'd you come here, Roberta?"

She stood, walked to the window, parted the drapes, and looked out on the busy highway that passed by the motel. Abruptly she pulled the raspberry shirt over her head and turned to face him, showing the imposing bra it took to imprison and mold her.

"Uh-uh, Roberta," said Angelo. "We—"

"Okay," she said. "Not us. Not written in the stars. But let me be comfortable, for Christ's sake." She released the bra behind and let her boobs fall loose: the biggest he had ever seen that were not freakish. Hers were flesh, not just fat. They hung. They did not droop. "You have any idea

58

what it feels like when you've worn a harness like this for twelve hours?" She picked up the shirt and pulled it on again. "You have to wear a jockstrap, Angelo?"

He went to the kitchen, picked up the bottle of Scotch, and put it on the table between them. He had not been attracted to Roberta while she was firmly shaped by nylon and rubber, but those tremendous tits moving freely inside the raspberry-colored shirt caused an erection.

"Your question was, why did I come here?" she said. She reached for the bottle and poured herself another drink. "I came here hoping we might be able to save Loren."

"I can't save him, even if I wanted to. And why should I want to?"

"You can save the company, Angelo. The old man knows you can. He knows you're right about the transverse engine and the deal with the Japanese company. Loren knows you're right. And they're going to ask you to save Bethlehem Motors. And when you do, you'll have emasculated Loren as effectively as the old man has done. You will do what *he* couldn't. His father killed himself. Loren is capable of it."

"I should care?" Angelo asked.

"You're not that hard a man, Angelo Perino. You'll help me save my husband's life . . . if I beg you."

"I don't want you to beg me, Roberta."

"Good," she said. "I'd rather make a reasoned business proposition. Mutually beneficial. To you and me."

"And Loren?"

"Depends on how much of a man Loren can prove himself to be."

"I fail to see anything beneficial to me in getting myself mixed up with the Hardemans again."

"You want to build a car, don't you, Angelo?" she asked. "You're like the old man that way. You can be a consultant, you can be this, be that, but nothing lights a fire in your gut more than building a car—the way the old man built the Sundancer, the way Lee Iacocca built the Mustang. That's why Number One won't let Loren quit building cars. A dozen virgins under his blankets wouldn't warm him the way building one more car would do."

"He's got a funny way of saying so."

"You and I don't give a damn what lights a fire in the old man's gut," said Roberta. "You're interested, I'm interested, in what lights one in *Angelo's* gut. Automobiles are your *life*, Perino. Bethlehem Motors is the only company you can get your hands on. You can—"

"The old man—"

"Will be dead in eighteen months, if not before," she said.

"And Loren . . ."

"Will do what I tell him to do," she said.

"So how do we avoid emasculating him?" asked Angelo. "If I care."

"We work it," she said. "You give me ideas. I'll feed them to him, on the pillow. He'll show up at the office filled with enthusiasm for *your* idea."

"He's that big a fool?"

She smiled. "You've known him longer than I have," she said.

"I feel like I'm . . . being sucked into a whirlpool."

"There's a good word," said Roberta with a wicked smile. "'Sucked.' Sucked you're gonna get. And more." She pulled off the shirt again and this time tossed it across the room. "We'll seal the bargain between us—the one nobody but us knows about."

"Roberta, I—"

"Don't make an enemy of me, Angelo. I want you to build your car. I can help you or I can block you. The Mustang was not called the Lee, and your new car won't be called the Angelo. But everybody'll know who did it."

She continued to undress and was naked in a matter of seconds.

"This isn't a necessary part—," he started to say.

"This is an important goddamned bargain," she said. "And it can't be written down. What would you have it on, a handshake? No. Hey—you remember how they used to mark survey lines in medieval England? They'd take a boy out to an essential point on the line, and there they'd take his pants down and beat his ass bloody. That way they could be sure he would never forget the place. It wasn't just something shown to him; it was the place where he'd got his ass whipped, and he'd never forget. Well, you're not going to forget tonight, and neither am I. We're not going to forget what we agreed to on the night when—"

Angelo nodded. "It'll be memorable," he conceded.

"Just to be sure it is, come here to the couch. I'm going to lie across your legs, and I want you to spank me until my butt gleams pink."

"Roberta . . ."

"I mean it, Angelo. Until I cry and beg you to stop. Then we'll remember our deal. Then we'll do two or three other things that will reinforce our memory. *Fancy* fuckin', Perino. Not the usual stuff."

She turned her head around and laughed at him after his first slap on her behind. She winced after the second and clenched her teeth and grimaced after that. In time she began to cry, but he did not stop because she had not begged. Then she did. She was still sobbing as she knelt and sucked his penis between her lips. She worked on him so hard he was not sure he would be able to do what she promised was next.

In bed she grunted under him and emitted little squeals. "Ohh!" she cried gutturally. "Angelo's a *steel-drivin'* man!"

3

He awoke the next morning to the ringing of the telephone. It was a secretary at the Hardeman house, saying Mr. Hardeman would like to see him before he caught his plane for New York. Would that be possible?

The plane left at 10:10, so he had time to drive to the beach and meet the old man once more.

It was not the old man who met him. It was Loren. He waited on the lanai, with a breakfast of coffee, Danish, and fruit laid out.

The weather had cleared, and the early-morning sun was red over a gentle surf slip-slapping on the beach. Stranded Portuguese men-of-war died slowly as the water at low tide failed again and again to reach them.

"Number One is asleep," said Loren.

"At his age, he's entitled."

"I'll be brief, Angelo," Loren continued. "Number One and I would like to call you wrong about the new car, but we know you're right. We also have to acknowledge that you're right about making the deal with Shizoka. Obviously, Number One isn't designing any more cars or negotiating any more deals. My own skills don't lie in automotive engineering or in negotiating with Japanese businessmen. We need you. So there. Did you ever think you'd hear me say that?"

"I don't need you, Loren."

"Hell, you never did. You're the kind of guy who'd be a success in whatever you chose to do. But I'm gonna make a guess. What really lights a fire in your gut is the idea of building a new car, something very different. Lee Iacocca was responsible for the Mustang. His name's not on it; it's a Ford, not an Iacocca; but everybody knows he built it."

Roberta's words almost exactly, Angelo thought. She'd come home from last night's performance, wakened Loren, and fed him everything she'd said—unless she'd primed him with it before. Whichever, Loren was speaking *her* words like a ventriloquist's dummy.

"What lights a fire in *my* gut is seeing this company survive and prosper," Loren went on. "Angelo, you have good reason to hate me. Hell, man, I have some reason to hate you. But let's put all that behind us, can't we? You want to build the car you believe in. GM, Ford, and Chrysler aren't going to give you the chance. We will. Number One and I need a guy who can build the car that will save the company. Hey, this isn't easy for me, but I'm asking you. Come back, man. Build the car."

"Vice president for research and development," said Angelo. "Not as an employee, as a consultant. A five-year contract. If it doesn't work out, you have to pay out my five years. A stock option. In writing. A further understanding not in writing—that *you* keep hands off, Loren. You'll get credit for having been smart enough to hire Angelo Perino. I'll get credit for having built you a car."

"You put things bluntly," said Loren.

"You have any amendments to the proposal?"

"I buy it. How much money?"

THE STALLION

"Say half a million a year. How's Number One going to take it?"

"Angelo, how Number One takes anything isn't going to count for much. How much longer can he live? Short of that, how much longer before he lapses into a coma? Angelo, it's you and I. That's how it can be. We don't need Number One anymore."

VIII

1977

1

During the course of his five visits to Japan in 1976, Angelo came to like the country better than he had on his first visit. Twice he took Cindy with him. She entered into a deal with a Japanese art dealer to open a one-man show in her New York gallery for Cho Sei-ichi, a sculptor who made exquisite small bronzes of birds, animals, and flowers. She was unable to accompany her husband on his first trip there in 1977 because she was expecting their third child within the next few weeks.

Their son, John, had been born in 1973 and their daughter, Anna, in 1975. Staying home during the last few months of her third pregnancy, Cindy had begun a search for a home in Westchester County or across the line in Connecticut. Angelo expected she would take him to look at houses as soon as he returned from Japan.

Although he had an office at the plant in Detroit, he spent no more than two days a week there. The other days he worked out of his New York office. It was part of his understanding with Loren that he would not be expected to spend all his time in Detroit and that he would not move his family there.

Every time he arrived in Tokyo alone, he had to wonder if Betsy would come knocking on his door. She kept track of him. One night she'd come to his room in Chicago and another night to his room in Dallas.

The negotiations with Shizoka had gone more slowly than he had expected. They were finished now, and the deal was set. The problems that had to be solved now involved the modification of the Shizoka power train to fit into the new car (problems to be solved in Japan) and building a chassis and body that would suit the modified power train (problems to be solved in the United States).

He had made an effort to learn Japanese but had quickly given up on the idea of speaking the language with his new associates. He discovered that the Japanese would rather hear him speak English than anything but perfect, idiomatic Japanese. More and more he understood what they were saying to each other, but he was careful not to let them know it.

Keijo Shigeto was a thirty-nine-year-old mechanical engineer, a major contributor to the design of the Shizoka engines. He had been seven years old on August 6, 1945, and lived in the town of Matsuyama, about fifteen miles across the Inland Sea from Hiroshima. He remembered an intense, enduring flash of pink light, then a strange cloud boiling up in the north, looking to him like a palm tree, not a mushroom. To his child's eyes it was filled with lightning and must have been the center of a huge storm. His mother rushed him inside their house, and when he saw the cloud again it was breaking up and drifting west.

He was a handsome man, with traces of gray already appearing at his temples. He was proud of his English, but he welcomed correction. When Angelo essayed a few sentences of Japanese, Keijo could not suppress his laughter.

During one visit Keijo invited Angelo to dinner at his home. Angelo could not be sure if the dinner was formal or informal, but he accepted the invitation to undress as much as Keijo did—that is, to his underwear—and to wear a silk kimono. He removed his socks as Keijo did and put on white ones instead.

Angelo, Keijo, his wife, Toshiko, and their son and daughter sat cross-legged at a low table. The two children, age eleven and thirteen, spoke perfect American English. Toshiko, a diminutive and beautiful woman, wore traditional Japanese dress. She spoke no English but had many questions about American habits and customs.

Keijo translated, and each question began, "Mrs. Keijo would like to know . . ." Each answer was received with a nervous little giggle. Angelo understood that the giggle was a polite way of acknowledging his answer and thanking him for it.

The meal, served for the most part by a bowing servant girl, was delicious.

Several months later Keijo took Angelo to a geisha house. The dinner there was much more formal. The geishas played little stringed instruments, sang in artificial, doll-like voices, and made light conversation. The one assigned to Angelo spoke English of a sort. She was beautiful, of course—in the formal style of the geishas, which was a little off-putting to Angelo.

"You like Jack Kerouac?" she asked brightly.

"I haven't read any of his books."

She frowned as if shocked, then recovered, smiled, and said, "Yes. Is not so good. Which is favorite?"

"To tell you the truth, I'm old-fashioned enough to like Mark Twain better than any other American author."

"Ah! Yes. Yes. Is much favorite in Japan. You like *beisuboru?*"

Baseball. Yes. He said he liked that.

"Ah! Like Sanders Kewfack?"

"Sandy Koufax. Yes."

Her restrained smile brightened. "Have you see kabuki theater?"

"No. I want to."

"This you must do," she said. "Is beautiful."

When the time came, he and Keijo left. Geishas—*these* geishas, anyway—did not continue their entertainment past dinner and sake, songs and conversation. Keijo asked him in the taxi if he needed a woman for the night, and Angelo said he didn't.

2

      He didn't because Betsy was waiting for him at the hotel.

Betsy had become a problem, for her family and for him. Set loose from Max van Ludwige, utterly contemptuous of her father, almost as contemptuous of her great-grand-father, she seemed to aspire to become one of the beautiful people. Besides some Hardeman money that had been willed to her by her grandmother Sally and the allowance paid to her monthly by Number One, she had a generous settlement from Max van Ludwige. She considered herself independent, and if she was careful about how much she spent, she could remain independent.

Truman Capote wrote of her—

Far more beautiful than Doris Duke ever dreamed of being, but less stylish and definitely less rich, apparently she seeks to make a place for herself by keeping company with people beneath her dignity—some of them beneath anyone's dignity. She has been seen, for example, in the company of the Greaseball Junkie. (That's Elvis Presley, if anyone didn't know.) Better is what may have been a brief affair with William Holden. The lady drinks heavily, travels much, and is reputed to have the scruples of Lucretia Borgia. All of this makes her an exceptionally interesting twenty-four-year-old. If she will just stay out of the company of Budweiser drinkers, she may have a fascinating future in her future.

She maintained a home in London, where the five-year-old Loren van Ludwige saw her surprisingly often, considering the lifestyle Capote had described. Mommy traveled, true, but Mommy came home and stayed home for weeks at a time, during which time she was devoted to him. She rarely went out until after he was in bed, and during the day she took him for long walks in the London parks and on cruises up and down the Thames. When she was invited aboard Richard Burton and Elizabeth Taylor's yacht, moored in the Thames a little upstream from the Tower, she took him with her. She called him Loren Four and suggested to interviewers that he would succeed her father as chief executive officer of Bethlehem Motors.

She played blackjack in London clubs and annoyed the management by winning. She was hailed before a magistrate for driving under the influence and lost her driving license—after which she sold her car. The tabloids loved her. They loved her low-cut dresses, her high-cut skirts, her skimpy bikinis, and her willingness to pause for a moment and smile for the cameras.

Number One knew little of this, but what he did know infuriated him. Loren turned livid when stories came in from London.

Sometimes she disappeared. Right now she had managed that very feat, and neither the tabloids nor the Hardemans knew where she was. She was in Tokyo.

3

"Geishas haul your ashes?" she asked when he entered the suite. She sat on the couch in the living room, naked but for a pair of sheer white bikini panties studded with rhinestones.

"Doesn't seem to be a part of the service," he said.

"I've heard they insert razor blades in their cunts, so if a guy actually does get in—"

"Betsy!"

She shrugged. "Probably isn't true."

He poured himself a Scotch. Pulling off his tie and jacket, he sat down beside Betsy and began to fondle her breasts.

"Do you really do business over here?" she asked. "Or do you just come to have a good time and make occasions for us to be together?"

"I really do business here," he said.

"Tell me about it," she said. "I need to know. I'm not going to be stupid about the business, the way my mother was, the way Anne is."

"Well," he said, "one of the first things we have to think about is converting Bethlehem Motors to metric. For a while I thought we could build the power trains to match bodies put together on English measurements. The complexities of that proved too much. Shizoka wouldn't even think of converting to inches. There was no point raising the subject with them. So everything about the new car will be metric. Fortunately, we don't have to retool the whole Detroit operation, because the engines and everything between engines and wheels will be built in Japan. But we do have to retool the equipment that makes chassis and bodies. The next question is, where do we get the money?"

"Where?" she asked.

"I put in some of my own. I took stock for it. Loren and Number One weren't happy about that, but I wasn't going to make a gift to the company. I talked a New York bank into putting up some more. The company is stretched thin. In terms of personal finances, you'd say the company is strapped."

"What's this car going to look like?" she asked.

"Like nothing ever built in Detroit before. Compact, but not compact like a Falcon or a Corvair. The longtime emphasis on curves is going to be replaced with emphasis on angles. The hood will slope down in front. The backs of the rear seats can be folded forward to make a trunk that runs all the way to the backs of the front seats. Oh, it's going to be a different car."

"How are the old man and my father reacting?"

"Number One keeps sending the drawings back. He uses a French curve on them and rounds off the angles."

"My father?"

"Is keeping hands off, as he promised to do. And he's seething, I have no doubt. I watch my back all the time."

"Don't trust him, Angelo. Remember how he schemed before. Remember what he did to you. He hates you. I promise you he does. Also, he's got that woman now. Roberta. She's smarter than he ever dreamed of being. And tougher. She's got him completely under her thumb."

He smiled. "I take it you don't like her."

"There's an inheritance at stake, Angelo. Anne's, mine, and my son's. My great-grandfather has talked about leaving all his remaining shares in Bethlehem Motors, plus everything else he owns, to a Hardeman family trust. My father would of course be a trustee, and he'd have enough stooges as additional trustees to assure him complete control, even if Anne and I were also trustees. I wouldn't be surprised if Roberta were named a trustee."

"I'm only interested in building cars, not in Hardeman family problems," said Angelo.

"You won't be building cars if my father gets complete control of the company," argued Betsy.

"He won't let the company go under," said Angelo. "And that's what would happen if he backed out of the deal he has with me. The bank let the company have money only because *I'm* running the show."

"His capacity to be devious has been multiplied dangerously by his marriage to Roberta," said Betsy. "I'm not sure he wouldn't let the company go under if he could drag you down with it. He might look like a failure, but in *his* mind he wouldn't be."

"I'll keep what you say in mind," said Angelo, dismissing the subject.

"Now you're going to make love to me," she said.

"Yes. I can't resist you, Betsy. I want to, but I can't."

"You know why?" she asked quietly.

"Why?"

"Because you know I love you. Sure, I've got a beautiful bod, but so do lots of other women you've had and will have. But I love you, you know I do, and you can't push me away."

He sighed and nodded. "You're right. I can't. And I can't leave my wife and children and—"

"Let's not get into all that again," she said. "We don't have enough time together to talk about all that. Let's go take a shower together, 'cause there's something I want to do."

He stood and pulled her to her feet, then gathered her into his arms to kiss her. "What is it you want to do?" he whispered in her ear.

She began to unbutton his shirt. "When you were a horny little teenager, did you ever hear of something called Around the World? I mean, did you ever fantasize having a girl lick every inch of you, front and rear, from your ears to your toes? That's what I'm going to do for you. I've never tried it, and maybe my mouth will dry up before I'm finished, but I'm going to do it as long as I can. Also, remember where I put my tongue sometimes. I wonder how that would feel if I dipped my tongue in brandy first."

"I dipped my cock in brandy once. It burns."

"But up your ass it might just burn deliciously. Let's find out."

He nodded. "Let's find out."

4

On the final full day of his trip to Japan, Angelo traveled with Keijo Shigeto on a fast train, in the comfort of a first class compartment, to Nagoya, which was miles from Tokyo. Keijo had offered to show him something he very much wanted to see.

"We cannot use this in the car we are now building," said Keijo, "but in a future model . . . I think you will be impressed."

The chauffeur who picked them up at the train station drove them out of the city and to the track where Shizoka tested its cars. It was, of course, a secluded place, surrounded by a tall, guarded fence, inside which grew thick, thorny hedges.

A car that looked like an ordinary Chiisai was speeding around the track. It looked like an ordinary Chiisai. Angelo had seen hundreds of Chiisais, but this one was equipped with sensors that were feeding information to recording instruments in the garage. He could not identify all the Japanese gauges, but he could read enough to see that the Chiisai was moving on the straightaways at something over 200 kilometers per hour, a little more than 120 miles an hour. It seemed to be entering the curves too fast, and Angelo wondered what the test driver had in mind.

Keijo called the car in. The driver got out and took the occasion to go to the bathroom.

"You see? It has not an alarming appearance," said Keijo.

Angelo walked up to the car and put his hand on it. Then he rapped it with his knuckles. He could tell from the feel and sound that the body was not made of steel but of epoxy resin. Each component of the body of the car had been built by stretching a fabric over a frame, then applying several coats of epoxy resin. When the part was finished it was removed from the frame, which could be used to make another, identical part.

Keijo stepped up to the car and struck a door panel with a large ball-peen hammer. The panel yielded under the blow, then immediately recovered.

"The main body is made of the same material," said Keijo, "but it is reinforced with a steel frame. The material can be drilled and parts can be fastened together with rivets or bolts, but most parts are attached to one another by epoxy cement."

"Which test are you running now?" Angelo asked.

"I think you know," said Keijo with a broad smile.

"Stress," said Angelo. "Running into curves too fast and stressing the frame and body."

Keijo nodded, the movement originating at his waist and looking more like a short bow. "I show you one we test-crashed," he said.

In a corner of the garage was a car that had been run into a wall. It was as nearly intact as any car could be after that kind of impact.

Keijo took a screwdriver and gouged out a scratch on the rear fender. The scratch was all but invisible; the material was the same color all the way through. He picked up a loose front fender and handed it to Angelo. The material was light.

"Too costly now," said Keijo. "But the technology can be developed to make it far less costly. We hope our American partner will join us in that investment."

Angelo didn't tell him that Bethlehem Motors wouldn't be able to invest in anything unless the car they were now building captured a respectable market share and earned a handsome profit.

IX

1978

1

It was difficult for the Hardeman family to decide whether to mark the one-hundredth birthday of Loren Hardeman the First, Number One, with any kind of celebration. He was weak and obviously sinking slowly into his long sleep. On the other hand, he was still capable of anger and might direct it at anyone he could identify as insufficiently deferential to him and insufficiently interested in his centenary.

Roberta made the decision. They would celebrate with a family dinner, to which only the immediate family would be invited—Loren and herself, Princess Anne Alekhine, Betsy, and her son, Loren van Ludwige. Princess Anne did not so much as respond to the invitation. Betsy flew in from London. She could not bring little Loren because he had contracted measles. The family group that assembled around a table in the late afternoon consisted of Number One, Number Three, Roberta, and Betsy.

The old man sat at the table in a stiff gray suit, white shirt, red-and-blue striped tie, with his panama hat on his head. Betsy had played tennis a little earlier and had not changed out of her tennis whites. Roberta wore her favored stretch stirrup pants, this pair cream white, and a long-sleeved silver lamé top. Loren looked uncomfortable in a blue blazer and white duck pants.

Bethlehem Motors had circulated a news release, reminding the world that Loren Hardeman the First, the founder of the company, would be one hundred years old on Tuesday. Two bushel baskets filled with congratulatory wires and letters sat on a side table. Number One shrugged at them and declined to read any of them.

Loren read one to him. It was from the White House, from Jimmy and Rosalyn Carter. Number One listened, his head bobbing, and when Loren handed him the engraved and embossed card, he waved it aside and said, "Peanuts."

He wouldn't let Loren read the wires from executives of the automobile industry. "Boring bullshit," he muttered. "Pro forma. I've outlived their grandfathers."

He drank Canadian whisky, as he'd done in the old days. "What's the difference now?" he asked.

The birthday dinner was catered. So many foods were off-limits to Number One that he had not employed a cook for years and just ate the bland meals his nurse set before him. Tonight, however, he was treated to a hearts of palm salad and pompano, with a chilled Rhine wine.

When they had finished and the dishes were cleared away, brandy was served, and only then did Number One wave the bottle away.

"I have something I want to say," he said. He pushed his wheelchair back and glanced around the table, letting his eyes settle for a moment on each member of his family. "I guess it was Maurice Chevalier who said the only thing worse than living to a ripe old age is the alternative. If you have ambitions to live to my age, curb them. It's not worth it.

"Loren, that car Perino is developing is a piece of shit. It's gonna look like a fuckin' strawberry box. It's gonna look like a Model A. Maybe it'll run okay; I keep reading about how good the Jap engines are. But it won't sell because it won't have a modern look. Remember this—you can't buy a Studebaker or a Packard or a Hudson anymore, but you can buy a *Sundancer*. That's because I've always kept some of the smart young boys in line. I was building cars before Perino's *father* was born.

"Roberta, you make sure Loren keeps his backbone stiff. I know you keep his other bone stiff, but I'm talking about his backbone.

"Betsy, I have something to say to you, but I want to say it in private. You give the nurse fifteen minutes to get me into bed, then come up. I want to talk to you."

Loren watched the nurse wheel Number One out of the room, then turned and spoke to Betsy. "He's gonna give you shit."

Betsy reached for the brandy. "Maybe not.

2

Number One sat propped up against four big pillows. He wore blue-and-white striped flannel pajamas. Betsy could see now why he wore the panama hat. Only a sparse fringe of white hair circled his liver-spotted pate, which made him look older and frailer even than his hundred years.

Her short white tennis skirt and her tennis shoes were entirely out of place in what was conspicuously the old man's deathbed room. But she squared her shoulders and drew a deep breath and planted her hands on her hips.

Number One pointed at a machine that sat on a table beside his television set. "You think you can make that thing run?" he asked.

Betsy looked at the machine. She had seen two or three of them before. It was a machine that could tape television shows and play them back. She studied the controls for a moment, then said she thought she could run it.

"Good. Pull that big dictionary out of the shelf over there."

She did. Behind the dictionary was a tape cartridge.

"Play it," he said.

She mounted the cartridge on the spindles on top of the big, heavy machine and shoved forward the switch marked PLAY.

A picture appeared on the television screen. It was of an empty bed. Voices began to sound—

"Goddamnit, you shouldn't have come here! You *know* you shouldn't have come here." Angelo's voice.

"Why not? The old fart's asleep. My father is sleeping one off. So's Roberta. Anyway, I *want* you. You can't believe how much I want you." Her own voice.

They came into the view of the camera, she busily pulling off her clothes. The light was dim, and the focus was not precise, but no one could have doubted who they were and what they were doing. She threw herself on the bed and spread her legs. Angelo pulled down his slingshot underpants but did not take off his white T-shirt and he mounted her.

"Four years ago, that was. I've watched the tape a good many times," muttered Number One. "You are a true slut, Betsy! I wish I'd known you fifty years ago."

"Was Sally any better?" she asked.

"Sally—your grandmother—was a lady."

"And you were a gentleman . . ."

The old man shook his head and grimaced. "Angelo Perino," he grumbled.

"You and I are perfect together," whispered Betsy's image on the screen—whispered hoarsely enough for a hidden microphone to capture. She drank brandy and handed the snifter to Angelo. "There's got to be more to it than this— more, I mean, than sneaking a night in this house. Oh, God! Leave her, Angelo! Give her a nice settlement and come to me."

"The best is yet to come," Number One interjected.

It was. After another minute or so of urgent, whispered conversation, Angelo rose on his hands and knees and presented his backside. Betsy buried her face in it and— though the camera had seen only the back of her head—it was obvious enough that her tongue was as deep in his anus as she could push it. Their grunts were further evidence of what she was doing.

"You can turn it off. That was the most interesting part. I do wish I'd known a woman of your ilk even forty years ago. No woman ever did that for me."

"I can't *believe*—"

"Would you like to see your father with Roberta?" asked Number One. "Would you like to see her tan his backside with his belt? She puts welts on his ass. Would you like to hear him tell her how great it is and beg for more? Surely you don't believe, child, that I would allow people to plot and scheme and fuck and lick ass in my house and not make a record of it? Is that like me? How do you think I managed to live a hundred fuckin' years and fuck every son of a bitch that—"

"I was going to call you an evil old man," said Betsy. "You were evil before you became an old man. When did you become evil, Great-grandfather? Was it when you fucked my grandfather's wife and fathered Anne? Or earlier?"

Number One smiled and shook his head. "I've fathered a brood, haven't I? My son was a fairy and killed himself. My grandson . . . well, there's hope for him. At least he's devious and has the capacity to hate."

"Why did you show me this?" she asked, nodding toward the tape machine.

"It will be handy as evidence against you if you try to break the new will my lawyers are drafting—which I'll sign before the week is over. You've been calling your son Number Four. Dream on, you little slut. Your son will never so much as *share* in the control of Bethlehem Motors. I'm leaving everything I own to a trust. You and Anne will be trustees, but you'll be outvoted by Loren and my other trustees."

"You'll have to fight Roberta."

"I've made a deal with Roberta. I've already put a big chunk of cash in trust for her, and I'm getting rid of her. She manipulates Loren like a puppet master, and she's gonna tell him he needs an heir and she can't give him one. As soon as she can find the right girl for the purpose, she will divorce Loren, let him marry the girl, get her pregnant, and produce the *real* Number Four, who will be a Hardeman. When that happens, the trust pays out the money to Roberta."

"Have it all figured out, don't you, you old piece of shit?"

Number One grinned. "I take note that you begged Angelo four years ago to leave his wife and come to you. Since then he's fathered two more children by her."

"Got it all figured out . . ."

"I think so. The lawyers will be here with the new documents before the week is over."

"You overlooked something, Great-grandfather," said Betsy.

"Did I? What?"

"Me," she said.

She jerked one of the pillows from under his head and jammed it down on his face. He struggled, but he was a weak hundred-year-old man, and she was twenty-six and strong enough to have played three sets of tennis that afternoon without getting winded.

Something good happened—good for her. She felt him stiffen and guessed he was having a coronary. Maybe he wouldn't die of the pillow denying him breath. Maybe . . . She held the pillow in place, just the same, for five minutes. When she removed it, he was turning blue, and his eyes were staring lifelessly at the ceiling. To be certain he was gone, she sat beside him for another ten minutes, holding the pillow gently over his face so as not to bruise him.

3

She removed the tape cartridge from the VCR and wiped her fingerprints from the control switches.

He had not made this tape himself. Someone in the house, or someone elsewhere, had done it for him. It would not do for investigators to find missing only the tape showing her with Angelo. She began to move books. Sure enough, she found half a dozen more tape cartridges. She would have liked to see if one really showed Roberta beating her father's naked ass, but she could not stay here and play tapes, and she could not risk keeping them.

She stepped onto the balcony outside Number One's bedroom. The house was silent and mostly dark. She stood for a while, watching to see if anyone was outside. Detecting no one, she tossed all the tapes onto the lawn.

Outside, a few minutes later, she gathered them up. She walked to the edge of the beach. Then, inspired, she took off her tennis dress and panties and walked onto the sand stark naked, clutching the tape cartridges. If anyone saw her and wondered why she was moving so furtively, the explanation would be that she had decided to take a walk, nude, on the beach.

If she couldn't find the remains of a fire, she would sit down and pull all the tape out of the cartridges. Then she would tear it to bits and scatter the bits in the surf.

But a hundred yards south she found what she had hoped she might find: the final glowing coals of someone's fire. At the edge of the tide there were bits of driftwood, and palm frond. She gathered a little fuel. Keeping the fire low, she pulled the tape out of the cartridges—her own first—and laid it on the flames. The tape burned quickly, with a little more flare than she would have liked. When she had burned all the tapes, she let the heat melt the cartridges. She covered the melted mess with sand to cool it, and after a few minutes carried it out into the surf. She cast it out as far as she could, walked out of the water, and started back toward the house.

4

     No one screamed. When she came downstairs in the morning, Roberta intercepted her before she reached the lanai and told her Number One had died in the night of a massive coronary.

"Well, he made his hundred years," Betsy remarked. She had nothing more to say.

It was noon before the formalities were concluded. Even so, word had gone out over all the wires: Loren Hardeman the First was dead.

A telegram arrived from New York—

SHOCKED AND DISTRESSED TO LEARN OF DEATH OF LOREN
HARDEMAN I. MY PERSONAL SYMPATHY TO ALL MEMBERS
OF HIS FAMILY AND ALL HIS MANY FRIENDS, AMONG WHICH
I INCLUDE MYSELF. HE WAS A GIANT OF THE AUTOMOTIVE
INDUSTRY, WHICH WILL NEVER BE THE SAME WITHOUT
HIM.

                           ANGELO PERINO

X

1978

1

Amanda Finch, who had painted her nude, drove
Cindy down the sloping main street of Greenwich, Connecticut.

"I don't know. I guess I've kind of fallen in love with this
town," she said. "There are a lot of artistic people here.
Some celebrities. Sports figures. Entertainment people. The
town is laid-back, easy to get along in. I think you'd like it,
too."

Cindy had decided she and Angelo had to move out of
New York. They loved their Manhattan apartment, but they
agreed it was not where they wanted to raise their children.
Little John was five years old now and needed more of the
outdoors than walks in the city's parks. Anna was three and
restless. Morris was a loud and active toddler who showed
signs that he would soon resent the confined space of an
apartment. Cindy had looked at homes in Westchester
County and in New Jersey. This was her first venture into
Connecticut.

"You can buy anything here, from an apartment to a town
house to a little frame house on a quarter of an acre to a
million-dollar-and-up estate," said Amanda.

She herself was living in a penthouse apartment atop a

five-story brick building situated on a shady street of
Edwardian buildings. She drove Cindy there, and they went
up in the elevator. The main room of the apartment was a
greenhouse on the roof of the building. That served as
Amanda's studio. Besides that, there were two bedrooms,
one of which she used as her living room, a kitchenette, and
a bath. She started a pot of coffee and led Cindy into the
studio and offered her a seat on a couch.

With a glass roof and glass walls on its east, north, and
south, the studio afforded an artist ideal light. Amanda had
installed sheer curtains on the east wall to prevent people in
the taller building across the street from having a view of
her models posing. From the other sides, no one could see
in. Through the windows that faced south she had a view of
Long Island Sound and the north shore of Long Island. The
studio was cluttered with easels, palettes, brushes, boxes of
squeezed tubes, cans of rags, magazines, newspapers, empty
pizza boxes, and burger cartons.

Amanda offered herself to be kissed, and Cindy kissed
her. "I do wish you'd move here, Cindy. I really do."

Cindy stood and looked at the unfinished painting on the
easel: an adolescent male nude in Amanda's unsparingly
realistic style.

"That's Greg. He'll be here any minute. He's a student at
Greenwich High School, and as soon as school's out—"

"He looks awfully young," said Cindy.

"He's sixteen. His parents gave me written consent to
paint him. His mother sometimes comes with him and sits
here while I work. She prefers that he make his spending
money as a model rather than by delivering newspapers or
bagging groceries. He won't pose for classes, though, and I
doubt I want to do more than two or three pictures of him."

Amanda moved behind Cindy, put her arms around her,
and caressed her breasts. "If you lived here, you could
model for me again. I could change your face a little, so no
one would recognize you."

The gallery had sold six more nudes that Amanda had
done of herself. At the moment she was the world's most
famous artist's model, more famous as a model than she
was as an artist. A huge mirror stood on a big wooden easel
in a corner of the studio.

"I'm not sure I want to take my clothes off in front of you again," said Cindy. "You're horny enough as it is."

Amanda kissed the back of Cindy's neck. "I love you," she said simply.

They talked this way to each other, but Cindy was sure that Amanda didn't really mean what she was saying. She did not believe Amanda was in love with her in the romantic sense, only that she was attracted to Cindy and considered her not just her benefactor but her best friend. She had allowed Amanda to kiss her breasts and her belly when she was posing for her, but she had never allowed her to put her tongue in her furrow—nor, for that matter, had Amanda tried to. When they had a moment alone, she returned Amanda's kisses, including wet kisses on Amanda's proffered nipples; but she had never done anything more.

The coffeepot coughed, and Amanda went to the kitchen and returned with steaming mugs of her favorite strong black coffee.

"I see in the news that Mr. Hardeman has died: the *original* Mr. Hardeman."

"Good riddance," said Cindy.

"A massive coronary," said Amanda. "I suppose at his age he was entitled."

"He took his time about it."

"I remember your saying one day he'd live till somebody shot him with a silver bullet."

"His death gives us a much better chance of getting our new car on the road," said Cindy. "He promised not to meddle, but that's exactly what he was doing all the time. He wanted the new car to look like what *he* thought a car should be: like what he built thirty years ago. I think he'd have put fins on the rear fenders if he could have had his way."

"As soon as the new car appears, I'll buy one," said Amanda innocently. "I—"

The doorbell rang, and she went to a button and pressed it to unlock the lobby door.

"That'll be Greg."

"We can't talk about the Hardemans or the car or

anything in front of him," said Cindy. "I'll leave in just a few minutes. He won't want to pose—"

"No problem. Greg's a grown-up kid."

She introduced him as Gregory Hammersmith. The young model shook Cindy's hand and said he was glad to meet her. "Amanda told me she is a friend of yours. I've heard of Mr. Perino, though I never saw him drive, even on television."

"Greg," said Amanda, "do you mind posing with Mrs. Perino here?"

"That's okay." He spoke so insouciantly that for a moment Cindy wondered if his next words might be, "The more the merrier." But without saying anything more, he began to undress. He kicked off his shoes, bent to take off his socks, pulled his sweatshirt over his head, and lowered his jeans. Without hesitation he pushed down and stepped out of his underpants. Naked, he stepped up onto the low model platform and assumed the pose that showed on the unfinished canvas. He was solemn but nonchalant.

Cindy tried not to stare too intently, though it made really no difference since his pose required him to stand with his face turned away from her. He was an adolescent, his chest and shoulders still narrow, though hard muscles on his arms and legs suggested he was athletic. His skin was pale. He had no body hair whatsoever, except a little coarse, light brown hair in his crotch. She could not tell if his part was entirely flaccid or semierect. Notably long but boyishly thin, it hung in a shallow curve down over his scrotum.

"I like Amanda's painting," he said to Cindy without turning his head. "Knowing you're posing for a really good and serious artist makes it easier to do this."

"I know. I posed for her, too."

"Like this?"

"Like that."

The boy's jock stirred a little, as if his mental image of her naked generated an incipient erection.

"Greg," said Amanda, "you live in backcountry, don't you?"

"Well, there's backcountry and there's backcountry. We don't live on one of the grand estates."

"The Perinos are thinking of moving to Greenwich."

"My uncle is a realtor," he said.

"We'll give her his name," said Amanda.

"The schools are good here," said Greg soberly.

Cindy went to the kitchen and refilled the coffee cups. As she looked through the kitchen door at the busy artist frowning over her canvas and the nonchalant teenager posing nude with his parents' consent, she decided that if this scene in any way characterized the place, she wanted to move to Greenwich.

2

It wasn't so easy, and within two weeks Cindy had decided she didn't want to live there. By then Angelo had decided they, by God, *would* live there.

Greg's uncle, the realtor David Schroeder, received the Perinos in his office and began to show them books of listings. Greenwich real estate was expensive, and they soon learned that they would have to spend a minimum of a quarter of a million dollars to buy a home that would suit them.

After they had looked through the realtor's listing books he suggested he take them to see two or three houses. A tall, handsome man with thick white hair and a flushed face, he drove a silver gray Mercedes and was elaborately polite to Cindy as he held the back door open and offered her his hand to assist her in getting in.

He drove them to a part of town called Cos Cob, and after passing through several unattractive commercial streets, they entered a residential neighborhood. The houses he showed them were attractive enough, though anything but imposing. The neighborhood had well-tended green lawns and well-maintained houses, but Cindy noticed that many houses had as many as five cars in open garages, in the driveways, and parked at the curbs. Some of the vehicles looked old and were in bad shape. There were also pickup trucks in some of the driveways.

"I can't believe that all of Greenwich is like this," Cindy said. "I've heard of backcountry. I've heard of Riverside. Let's see houses in those neighborhoods."

David Schroeder pulled the Mercedes to the curb and

stopped the engine. He turned so he could talk to Angelo in the front seat and Cindy in the rear.

"We could encounter a little problem, Mr. and Mrs. Perino. I have to be perfectly frank with you."

"What's the problem?" Angelo demanded.

Schroeder drew a deep breath. "It's embarrassing to talk about, and I wish I didn't have to say this, but there's a determined effort in Greenwich—not uniformly successful—to keep people of Mediterranean descent in the Cos Cob area."

"Meaning Italians," said Angelo darkly.

Schroeder nodded. "Also Spanish people, even French. I'm terribly sorry. I didn't create this idea, and I don't support it; but I'm stuck with it."

"Meaning what?" asked Angelo.

"The first problem," said Schroeder, "would be in finding an owner who would sell to you. The second would be that the board of realtors would ostracize me if I arranged to sell you a house outside of Cos Cob. In any event, the banks would find some fault in your loan application, for sure."

Angelo turned to Cindy and smiled. "Well, well, well," he said. "Frankly, Mr. Schroeder, until now I didn't really give a damn if we lived in this town or not. But, by God, we're *going* to. Wanna bet on it?"

3

Cindy's elder brother, Henry Morris, was the president of Morris Mining. After their marriage ceremony and before they'd left for Europe, Angelo and Cindy had visited him and his wife at their home in Pittsburgh. Since then they had seen him and his wife half a dozen times. The Morrises sent generous gifts to the Perino children on their birthdays and thoughtful gifts to the whole family at Christmas.

Henry had a lively wit. "I admire your new face," he'd once said to Angelo. "I do hope, though, it is the final version."

Henry had inherited his place in life, but he had done so far more gracefully than Loren Hardeman the Third. He held a degree from the Colorado School of Mines and had served as a lieutenant, United States Marines, in Vietnam. He had deplored but had not resented Cindy's fling as a racetrack groupie. He was thirty-nine years old, so his little sister was married to a man nine years his senior. Angelo was sure that Henry would have preferred a different brother-in-law than himself, but he seemed to have accepted him and come to respect him.

Henry Morris was about the same height and weight as Angelo. In fact, the two men resembled each other. He was a little more formal than Angelo, invariably wearing a suit except for when he was on the golf course. He still smoked an occasional cigarette, having cut down from two packs a day to half a pack or less. He drank wine and beer, no hard booze. Angelo found him a little too serious, but if that was the only fault he could find in a brother-in-law, he thought himself lucky.

Over dinner in their New York apartment, Angelo let Cindy tell her brother about their Greenwich experience.

"It is a tragedy," Henry commented, "that there are still people who think like that. If you are determined to live there, there are federal laws about housing discrimination. A suit in federal court—"

"My idea is to tackle it more directly," said Angelo. "You'll have to excuse me, but I've done some research. Morris Mining does all its banking with Consolidated Pennsylvania Bank. Consolidated holds thirteen million dollars in notes from Byram Digital Equipment, Incorporated, which is slow in paying. The CEO of Byram is one Roger Murdoch, who happens to be the chairman of the Greenwich Republican Party, the president of the Greenwich Historical Society, last year's chairman of the Greenwich United Way campaign, et cetera, et cetera, et cetera. Now, a word in the ear of the bank's chairman, resulting in a word in the ear of Byram Digital, might produce an anxious call from Murdoch to the president of the board of realtors. You follow? I'll take them into federal court, sure as hell, but I prefer faster methods."

Henry Morris smiled. "I wouldn't like to find myself opposing you, Angelo. I can do more. The president of the board of realtors will also get a call from Governor Ella Grasso."

Angelo lifted his glass. "If the Morrises and the Perinos can't break a small-town board of realtors, what good are we? Particularly when our cause is just."

4

"Mille grazie, Signor DiCostanzo," said Angelo. *"Questo è per Lei."* He handed the old man across the table a small case. When the old man opened it, he found a gold wristwatch inside.

They were sitting in a small diner in the Cos Cob section of Greenwich. Their entire conversation was conducted in Italian.

Signor DiCostanzo smiled but pushed the watch back across the table. "You do not need to do this," he said. "You are a man of honor, doing honorable work."

Angelo shoved the case back toward the old man. "It is my honor to recognize your inestimable contribution," said Angelo.

"Our people can live anywhere in town now," said Signor DiCostanzo. He chuckled. "The board of realtors put their cocks on the anvil, and we slammed the hammer down." He lifted a glass of wine. "We accepted your suggestion."

Angelo nodded and drank. "I figured it out. The Wasps take the trains to New York every day. The wops stay home and run the town. When you had the building permit denied for the—"

"The *fourth* application for a building permit," said DiCostanzo. "The rules are so complex and detailed that *nobody* can file an application that *must* be granted." He laughed. "We can leave them buried in their own trash, too. We haul every ton of it."

"Signor," said Angelo. "I am buying a home on North Street. My wife and I will be honored if you and your family—and such friends as you wish—will be our guests at a very early date."

The old man smiled. "Well, Angelo, you may want to think about that."

"My grandfather was a bootlegger, Signor. He sold liquor to the first Loren Hardeman. Now I am a vice president of Bethlehem Motors, and the grandson of his bootlegger dominates Number One's company. As soon as we are in the house, we will have a great party! I value friendship, Signor DiCostanzo. I do not turn my back on my friends after I have enjoyed the benefits of their friendship. Do you?"

5

As Cindy had noticed before, Greg did not cover himself during his breaks. Usually he walked around the easel to see what Amanda had been doing. He accepted a glass of Coke from Cindy, as he had done before.

She was struck by the realization that she was far more unsettled by looking at a naked sixteen-year-old boy than he was by being looked at by a thirty-year-old woman. A couple of days ago she had been painfully embarrassed when it had become obvious that he had noticed her staring at his crotch. He hadn't seemed to care, but he'd acknowledged what he'd seen by smiling faintly.

"Cindy," he said now—she had encouraged him to use her first name—"I'd like to know what you did to my uncle. Whatever it was, I like it."

"We didn't do anything to him," she said. "We did something to some people who were doing things to him."

"He says Greenwich will never be the same."

"Let us fervently hope so," said Amanda.

Greg left at five o'clock.

"I've got to quit looking at your teenage model," said Cindy. "It's getting to me."

"He gets to me," said Amanda simply.

"Jesus, hon . . ."

"Let's quit playing around," said Amanda.

When the downstairs doorbell rang a little after six, Cindy fled into the bathroom to dress and repair her makeup before the elevator arrived, bringing Angelo.

Angelo accepted a brandy and studied the painting on the easel. "Interesting . . .," he said.

"I think I'll buy it," said Cindy.

XI

1978

1

A week before Christmas, Angelo went to London to meet with a group of British bankers and automobile dealers who were interested in possibly selling Bethlehem Motors' new car through a chain of English and Scottish franchises. The meetings were protracted but progress was made toward an agreement.

"Tell us something," one of them said over a luncheon at the Café Royale. "What will the name of the new car be? Please tell us it won't be Sundancer."

"It won't be Sundancer. That I promise you."

"What, then?"

"We have a group working on it," said Angelo.

Yes, they had a group working on it. Loren liked to work through committees. He acknowledged that he knew little about automotive engineering, but he fancied that he knew a great deal about marketing, and he had appointed a committee to come up with a name for the new car—*assuming* the new car would in fact be built, a matter that had not yet been settled.

The call was Loren's. With Number One gone, he controlled the company. Angelo had heard talk that the old man had changed his will to disinherit Betsy and her son, Loren, and to settle control firmly in Loren the Third's hands; but the will that came to probate contained nothing surprising. Betsy inherited. Princess Anne Alekhine inherited. Control rested, even so, in Loren, who would vote his own stock, and in the Hardeman Foundation, which would vote its stock. A majority of the trustees of the foundation would vote with Loren.

That meant that Loren also controlled the board of directors, which he now reduced to five members: himself, Roberta, Randolph and Mueller of the foundation, and Congressman Briley. If he were fool enough to do it, he could dump the new car project and focus the company, as he had always wanted to do, on manufacturing appliances. Or he might sell off the company's assets and retire. He could say—he *would* say—that Number One had left him a failing company no man could save and that it was better to cut his family's losses and live on what they had left.

Angelo was aware that the death of Number One left him with no appeal if Number Three decided to bail out.

After the luncheon at Café Royale Angelo had accompanied two of the bankers back to the City for an additional meeting. Shortly before five he caught a cab and returned to Regent Street. It was a rare man, he thought, whose spirits could not be lifted by the Christmas decorations on Regent Street, so he decided to walk from there to his hotel. In London in December, it was already dark by five o'clock, and the decorations gleamed against a black sky.

He left Regent Street and started west on Piccadilly. When he reached the Burlington Arcade he walked in and began to look through the windows of shops.

He saw her. Roberta was there, buying something in a shop that featured cashmeres and Scottish woolens. She had said she would be in the arcade at about five and would shop there until he came.

He knew he shouldn't be seeing her. But he had his reasons. She was devious. She was a liar. But she was also ambitious. Maybe he could use her. She hadn't quite taken his full measure.

2

She was staying at the Hilton and made a point of being there early in the evening to receive the telephone call from Detroit that invariably came at six o'clock. So far as Loren was concerned, she was in London for Christmas shopping and the theater. Maybe he knew and maybe he didn't know that Angelo was in London, too. In any case she always told him she had shopped all day and was going to a show, after which she would have a late dinner and be in bed by one. That would be eight P.M. in Detroit, and she could be confident he would be too schnocked by then to call again.

Angelo was staying at Dukes Hotel on St. James's Place: a small, very old, and very traditional hotel, which he wouldn't have known about but for the recommendation of Anne, Princess Alekhine. He'd arrived on Monday, a week before Christmas day, and would fly home on Thursday. Roberta had been here since Friday and would fly home on Friday. They had three nights.

"I bought you a present," she told him as they walked out of the arcade.

She handed him a box. They stopped in the entrance to the arcade while he opened it. A Burberry raincoat. He didn't know its exact price, but he knew a Burberry coat cost more than $500. Quite a present indeed.

"I've got to go and take my call from the moron," she said. "Early dinner, right? We do have some business to discuss. I want to cover all of it over dinner, so we can fuck all night."

That was the arrangement already agreed to, and Angelo nodded. "All night," he said.

While she went to her room in the Hilton to take Loren's call, Angelo sat in Harry's Bar in the cellar of the Park Lane Hotel, drank Scotch, and waited for her. He tried on the coat. It fit. He'd have to declare it at customs at Kennedy Airport and then of course explain at home that he'd bought it for himself, on impulse.

He didn't like this relationship with Roberta. What he had going with Betsy was altogether different. Roberta was a vigorous, noisy piece of ass. How noisy she'd get if he turned her out was a question. He didn't trust her.

As he sat sipping whisky, he thought about going to a telephone and calling Cindy. He had found out something she didn't think he knew: that she'd diddled von Keyserling. Well, what could he say? Betsy. Roberta.

Roberta was a piece of ass. She might be useful. No. It was useful not to cross her. Betsy was . . . Jesus! She was more. How could a man say no to Betsy? But Cindy. Cindy, for God's sake, was the mother of his children. More than that. He loved her! Goddamn, he loved her! That was for sure. And she loved him, which was also for sure; and if she played around with Dietz, it was that: playing around and nothing more. He left her alone too much. What could he expect?

Roberta had changed, probably bathed, too. She swept into the bar as if she owned the place. She swept into every place as if she owned it. She'd bought two of the Burberry coats, apparently; she was wearing a woman's version of the one she'd given him. When she took it off and tossed it casually over a chair, she revealed a tight black knit dress adorned with a heavy gold chain around her neck.

She lifted the chain and grinned at Angelo. "My late husband gave me this. It had a cross hanging on it." She laughed. "Can you imagine?"

She sat down beside him, close to him, her hip firmly touching his.

"Glenfiddich?" he asked.

"Whatever Harry recommends."

There were few people in the bar at that hour. Tourists were at dinner or on their way to the theater. Angelo signaled the bartender.

"You know something?" Roberta asked. "I'm by-God hungry."

"How adventuresome are you?" he asked.

She rumbled with a throaty laugh.

"Willing to eat lambs' balls?"

"If you eat 'em, buddy, I'll eat 'em."

When the bartender brought the drinks, Angelo asked him to ring up the Lebanese restaurant on Shepherd Market and book a table for him and his lady.

3

Angelo requested one order of lamb testicles as an appetizer for the two of them. Westerners who ate them did it more for the adventure than because they tasted good. They were in no sense nauseating, but they were definitely an acquired taste. Other parts of the lamb would be served as the entrée.

Otherwise, they ate hummus spread on crisp Lebanese bread, lots of wrinkly Greek olives, black and green, tomatoes, radishes, and carrots—all with two bottles of excellent Lebanese red wine.

"Business," said Roberta when she had eaten two lamb testicles and was cleansing her palate with olives and wine. "Loren would like to kick your ass."

Angelo glanced at the two Middle Eastern men at the next table, which was so close to theirs they could no doubt hear everything they were saying. The two men had been talking in Arabic, and if they understood what "kick your ass" meant, they showed no sign of it.

"I'd like to kick his, but what specifically is going on?"

"He has it in mind to oppose the new car," she said. "More to screw you than for any other reason I can discover."

"Fine. I'll do it with somebody else. I don't need Bethlehem Motors."

Roberta seized his hand and gripped it tightly. "I don't need to watch two rams butt heads. If it came down to that, I know who'd win. Eventually, after a lot of shit. Lover, you can defuse Loren. You can get what you want and use his company to do it. Use your head and not your machismo."

Angelo glanced around the room. "This is a rather public place to talk about this."

The restaurant was brightly lighted and bustling. Waiters scurried around the dining room. With brisk efficiency the sommelier opened bottles of wine. Two thirds of the clientele were Middle Eastern. The rest were tourists. The big windows looked out on a street where London's most conspicuous hookers plied their trade.

"You know you'll win," she said. "The only question is whether you care enough about me to leave my husband sitting up and taking nourishment."

"Be specific, Roberta."

"All right. The whole key, as I've said to you before, is to make him *think* he's important. What's the *name* of the new car? If Loren named it, he'd—"

Angelo grinned. "I know what I want to call it," he said. "Okay. Let Loren propose the name. I'm tired—I think the public's tired—of cutesy-pie automobile names. Mustang. Pinto. Charger. Starfire. New Yorker. Duster. Impala. Hey! I once heard a salesman tell a customer, 'This *isn't* a Chevrolet. This is an Impala!' Toronado. Regal. Roadmaster. God, there's no end to it! The new car . . . I'd like to call it the 1800. The engine displacement is eighteen hundred cubic centimeters."

Roberta frowned. "The *what* 1800?" she asked.

"Oh, yeah. The BM 1800. Bethlehem, Pennsylvania, crap! Number One named his car company after his hometown, where nobody ever manufactured an automobile. The name has hung around the company's neck like a goddamned albatross. Loren wants to look like he's the guy in charge? Let him propose to the directors that the name of the company be changed to BM and the name of the new car be BM 1800."

Roberta ran her tongue over her lips. "No way. I might agree with you about cutesy-pie names, but the American public isn't ready for a car called just 1800. It's got to have a name."

"Like what?"

She smiled, at first just amused, then the smile spread into something wicked. "Hey! *Stallion*. For my Italian stallion. I'll get Loren to suggest that name, and he'll never guess what it means. It'll be our secret, and every time we hear it we can laugh."

"If he guesses, if he even gets the least suspicion in his mind, he'll scuttle the project."

"Believe me, he won't. Leave that to me. Hey! It's the kind of thing that makes him look big in his own eyes. He names the car. He renames the company. That's the kind of thing that massages his ego. And believe me, he's a man whose ego needs massaging."

"Doesn't take much, does it?"

"Don't think that Loren is a total idiot."

"Only fifty percent idiot," said Angelo. "Hell, not even that. Just a guy who was shit on by his grandfather, who was an unparalleled expert at shitting on people."

4

The elegant little room in Dukes Hotel had a fireplace, in which logs had been laid. All Angelo had to do was touch a match to the kindling underneath the logs, and the fire would catch and burn.

While he did this, Roberta threw aside her black dress, her bra, and her panties and waited for him in a black garter belt holding up dark stockings.

"I want to do something we've never done before," she said. "I want to give you something you've never had before. What would that be, Angelo? Is there something you've *dreamed* of doing but never did?"

"I guess I'm kind of a square guy," he said. "I like the regular stuff best."

"Remember the night you spanked me?" she asked. "Did you like that?"

"Well . . ."

"Don't give me 'well,' you bastard. You blistered my bottom. You better by God have enjoyed it! So, tell me. Did you like that?"

"Roberta . . ."

She grinned. "Except for the fact that they'd last and I'd have to explain them to Loren, I'd let you put welts on my backside—with your belt."

"I'd rather fuck you, Roberta."

"And *you better*! But I was thinking of starters to get you up good and stiff."

"I'm good and stiff now."

"And all covered up. Let's see." She reached for him and began to open his clothes. "Oh, my God, you are, aren't you?"

She helped him until he was naked, standing with his engorged phallus standing almost horizontal.

"Lover, how would you like to put that in my rear?"

"Have you ever done that, Roberta?"

She shook her head. Her face was flushed, and beads of sweat appeared on her forehead.

He shook his head. "No good," he said.

"Why not? You think I can't take it? I—"

"I'm sure you could take a fire extinguisher. Not the point. We do that, we can't fuck."

"Oh . . . You mean—"

Angelo grinned. "The microbiology that grows in that part of the human body is not suitable for another part of the body I'm thinking of. It causes vaginal infection. My father is a doctor. He used to say to me, 'Angelo, whatever you do, don't . . .' My mother used to wonder if I might become a priest. My father knew that would never happen, so he gave me some practical advice."

Roberta laughed. "You lie down on your back, lover," she said. "I'm gonna climb on top. That way I can take you in deepest, and I'm gonna have you up to my belly button. After that, I'm gonna suck you dry, until you can't come again and beg for mercy—even if you come fourteen times. You're gonna remember Roberta as the best piece of ass you ever had. And I've got a notion I'm not the only woman named Hardeman you ever had."

XII

1979

1

    "This meeting of the board of directors of Bethlehem Motors, Incorporated, will come to order," said Loren sonorously.

    Angelo had counted votes—idly, knowing it was not necessary. The directors were Loren; his sister/aunt, Princess Anne Alekhine; his wife, Roberta; James Randolph, the director of the Hardeman Foundation; Professor William Mueller, administrative director of the foundation; retired congressman Alexander Briley; and Myron Goldman, vice president of Continental Detroit Bank, which held enough corporate notes to break the company if it called them.

    Loren controlled the board. Besides his own vote, he could count on the votes of Randolph and Mueller for sure. Briley was an old political hack who lived on his congressional pension and the fees he received as director of half a dozen corporations, and he would vote as Loren suggested. That was four, a majority. Sometime Roberta might vote against her husband, but it wasn't going to happen today. Anne would vote against him, if she felt like it; and what the banker would do was anybody's guess. For sure, Loren had five votes. If he had decided to kill the new car, he would be able to do so.

He had obviously given some thought to the arrangement of the room. The directors sat around a table. Angelo sat in a chair behind them, against the wall, where corporate counsel also sat. The stenographer who would transcribe the meeting on her Stenotype sat beside Angelo.

"You have been given copies of the minutes of the last meeting of the board," said Loren. "Without objection they will be received as written. You have copies of the treasurer's report. Without objection it will be received as submitted. This is the first meeting of the directors since the death of my grandfather, and we have major decisions to make. Unless someone wishes to bring up something else, I would like first to take up the report of our consultant and vice president, Mr. Angelo Perino, who proposes that this company build a new automobile. No objection? Mr. Perino."

Angelo stood. He spoke without notes. "As with the case of the minutes and treasurer's report, you have copies of my report and recommendations. Before his death, Mr. Hardeman the First somewhat reluctantly came to the conclusion that this company could not survive in the automobile business if it continued to build what we may call a traditional American car. Indeed, I will go so far as to say that the American automobile industry as we have known it cannot survive if it continues to build what has come to be regarded as the traditional American car.

"It is a joke in America, ladies and gentlemen, that when you drive a car out of the dealership it instantly depreciates fifty percent. That's not too far from the truth. But it's not true with a Volkswagen or a Mercedes. Ten days after you buy it, it's worth only a few dollars less than what you paid for it. The same is true of Japanese cars, only more so.

"The reason is that foreign cars are better designed and better built. Not all foreign cars. British cars . . . well, see what you can get for your two-week-old Jaguar. I walked around a 1979 Jaguar on a dealer's floor not long ago. It was rusting visibly, right there on the showroom floor. I've got a seventy-six Riviera. When it rains, the windshield leaks. Water drips in my lap. The dealer can't seem to fix it. A friend of mine drives a Mercury. The power windows stick—sometimes open, sometimes shut. If it's raining, he

THE STALLION

can be sure they're stuck open. When he approaches a tollbooth, he can be sure they're stuck shut. I don't have to go on with a list like this. What does your own car do?"

"What about a Sundancer?" asked Roberta with a subdued smile. She sat well down the table from Loren, as if to suggest she was not there just because she was his wife. She was dressed in a severe salt-and-pepper tweed suit. Her eyes met Angelo's as she asked the question, and, he thought, it was lucky for both of them that Loren didn't seem to see the innuendo in them.

Princess Alekhine noticed and glanced quizzically at Angelo. He could have warned Roberta that the princess was shrewd, that nothing much got past her. She was like Betsy in that respect. Wearing a burnt orange cashmere suit, the princess carried off her assumed aristocratic persona with total élan.

"This company doesn't pay me enough to ask me to drive a Sundancer," said Angelo. "On the other hand, GM couldn't pay me enough to ask me to drive a Chevy. Chrysler couldn't pay me enough to ask me to drive a Plymouth. They were good enough cars in their day, but technology has outrun them. When you drive a Shizoka out of the showroom, it doesn't depreciate fifty percent in ten minutes; neither does a Honda or a Toyota. Why? Because those cars don't start falling apart the first time you put them in gear and shove down the accelerator."

"Quality control," said Loren dryly. "Mr. Perino is a fanatic on the subject."

"Quality control," said Angelo. "But more than that. New ideas. GM put out the Corvair. It was a fine, innovative design; but Americans weren't ready for rear engines, air cooled, and the Nader fanatics sent up a howl that killed it. Well, rear engines? No, not yet. Air cooled? No, not yet. But you've seen the design. A transverse engine. Fuel efficient. A sturdy body built to high standards of quality control. Ladies and gentlemen, I'd like to build a car that will need service *twice a year*—fluids and filters changed and nothing more."

"Our dealers have big service departments," said Randolph.

"Which the company pays for, because most of what they do is warranty work," said Angelo.

Congressman Briley stood and uncovered a drawing that sat on an easel. "This is the car that Mr. Hardeman the First wanted to build," he said.

The drawing was of the car Angelo's team had designed, softened by Number One's French curve.

Princess Anne Alekhine sighed noisily. "There is only one good thing to say about Number One," she said. "*He is dead.* And let us thank God it is so. Let there be an end to his destructive meddling in our business and our lives."

"Anne!" cried Loren.

"Do you disagree, *nephew*?" she asked coldly.

Few in the room knew what she meant by "nephew," and the directors glanced back and forth among themselves awkwardly.

Loren stared at Roberta, tapping his fingers nervously on the table. "Uh . . . the chair will entertain a motion that the design and manufacturing plan recommended by Mr. Perino be adopted."

"So moved," said Anne.

"Seconded," said Roberta.

Loren flushed visibly. "May we have a unanimous vote?"

Myron Goldman, the banker, raised his hand. "Can the company afford this thing, Mr. Perino?"

"The financing is in place, sir," said Angelo. "Some money from New York, some from London."

"May I review the financing with you, Mr. Perino?"

"I'll be happy to review every detail of it with you, Mr. Goldman."

"Do we have, then, the unanimous vote?" asked Loren.

He had it.

Loren nodded dramatically. It was almost a bow. "So," he said, "our company is off on a new venture. I'd like to break out champagne, but I have a few more things to bring to the attention of the board."

"Before we take up anything else," said Princess Anne, "would it be inappropriate for this board to put on its minutes a resolution of thanks to Mr. Angelo Perino for having presided over the design of a new venture that may be the salvation of Bethlehem Motors?"

"It will be *more* appropriate," said Roberta, "when Mr.

Perino's car has in fact saved Bethlehem Motors. But I will, for now, move a resolution of thanks to Mr. Perino."

This time Princess Anne caught an unmistakable leer in the glance Loren's wife shot at Angelo Perino.

"I assume Mrs. Hardeman seconds," said Loren. "May we have a unanimous vote?"

They had it.

"Now," said Loren, "I would like to recommend certain changes in . . . well, in basic matters. My grandfather built his first car in his bicycle shop in Bethlehem, Pennsylvania. We all know the history. It was an odd contraption, but he brought it to Detroit and made it a success. He named his company Bethlehem Motors, after his hometown. He might have named it Hardeman Motors. Henry Ford named his company for himself, and so did Walter Chrysler. But the name Bethlehem has a religious connotation and, in my judgment, has become an albatross around the company's neck. I would like to change the name. I wish we could call the company BM, but . . ." He paused and smiled slyly. "I guess it is obvious why we can't. BM: bowel movement."

This time Roberta grinned at Angelo. BM was the name he had suggested in London—showing that he, too, was capable of a stupid mistake. He laughed.

Loren grinned at Angelo—such a genuine grin that Angelo for an instant wondered if Roberta hadn't told him Angelo had suggested the name—then he went on: "We're entering a joint venture with Shizoka, but we can't call our company BS either."

Everyone chuckled.

Loren went on. "I hired a consulting firm that specializes in product and corporate names. They've been damned successful also in creating logos. They've got an idea that X is an intriguing letter. EXXON, LEXIS, and so on. God forbid that we should get stuck with a name like UNISYS. So, ladies and gentlemen, here is what they've come up with—"

The corporate counsel removed the cover sheet from an easel.

Loren shone with pleasure. "The new corporate name, ladies and gentlemen—XB Motors, Incorporated—and the name for our new car."

The directors smiled and nodded.

"Can you imagine the chutzpah of a company that would call its car an Edsel or a Henry J? One or two suggested we call the new car a Loren." He paused and grinned. "Even my grandfather resisted that."

"A pretty radical change, isn't it?" asked Goldman. "I mean, dropping the name Bethlehem Motors that has won the respect of—"

"I beg your pardon, Mr. Goldman," said Angelo. "I think Mr. Hardeman is absolutely right, and I appreciate his contributing this idea."

2

The board drank champagne before they disbanded. Loren looked for a chance to talk to Angelo alone before he left. He found it.

"Well," he said. "We bet the store. All I can say to you, Angelo, is don't plan on my going down and your surviving. If I go down, you come with me."

"And vice versa," said Angelo. "Loren, I wouldn't have it any other way."

Roberta came up and took Loren's arm as Angelo walked away. "Easy, lover."

"How many times do I have to have my face rubbed in shit?" he asked, his voice breaking. *"That wop son of a bitch!"*

XIII

1979

1

Amanda's nudes of the teenager Greg created a stir in the art world. They bolstered her reputation as a talented new realist, and they sold for $20,000, $23,500, and $27,000. The fourth one was a gift to Cindy and hung in VKP Galleries for a long time before Cindy took it home.

The boy's parents would not let him pose again unless he was paid a much higher fee, arguing that the appearance of the paintings in magazines and gallery catalogs had caused him immense embarrassment at Greenwich High School. They suggested he should be paid a percentage of the sale price of any future paintings. Amanda shrugged and told them she would not require Gregory's services again.

Her flower paintings did not sell nearly as well. She was established as a painter of photographically accurate nudes. One critic wrote, "The greatest of photographers—Weston, Steichen, Outerbridge—never succeeded as well as Ms. Finch in portraying the infinite subtleties of the human physique. She is a worthy heiress of the oldest tradition in graphic art."

Her career took a strange new turn when Abraham and Corsica d'Alembert, two Wall Street brokers, commissioned her to paint them nude together, holding hands and staring into each other's eyes. Amanda injected a special dynamic into the painting by posing the husband on the model platform and his wife on the floor, with him reaching out with his hand to help her to mount the platform. The couple wanted a memorial of the early years of a middle-aged marriage and they were willing to pay $50,000 for it.

That painting was on an easel in the studio when Dietz von Keyserling posed for Amanda. Her picture of Dietz showed him in a reclining pose, lying on a dark blue blanket laid over a mattress pad on the platform, reading a book while the artist painted. He planned to display it prominently at VKP Galleries and not to sell it.

Dietz and Amanda became lovers. She could not see him naked hour after hour without developing an interest in him. The paintings she had done of herself had aroused in him a similar interest in her. It was understood between them that the affair was simply a physical attraction to each other and included no commitment. In fact, if he was committed to anyone, it was to Cindy. But he could not be with her often, and he was not a man who could make love only infrequently.

Amanda was a young woman with little experience who was content simply to lie underneath a man, spread and receive him, and get what enjoyment she could out of something that did not entirely satisfy her.

Cindy satisfied her more. The tongue was more supple and better controlled than the lingam. What Amanda really yearned for was to have them both, both at once.

And one afternoon in July, that was what she got.

2

She suggested it diffidently to Cindy, in the kitchen. Dietz lay naked on the platform. He really was reading the book he was being depicted as reading; otherwise, he had said, the hours of posing that her realism required would have daunted him.

Cindy shook her head. "I never thought I'd hear a proposition to do that," she said.

"I hope I don't offend you."

"No . . ."

She glanced through the door at Dietz. Amanda was painting his small, uncircumcised penis exactly as it was; Cindy had wondered if he really wanted to put that on display in public. She knew it grew when it stiffened, but still . . . Amanda saw her glance at Dietz, then focused her own slightly myopic eyes on Cindy. It was a warm afternoon in the greenhouse studio, and Amanda wore only a pair of cut-off jeans and a halter, the jeans smeared with old paint. Cindy leaned forward and kissed Amanda. They'd been kissing often lately, with their tongues.

Dietz happened to look up at that moment. "Girls, really," he said with a grin. "I had no idea."

"You are observant as an art *dealer*," said Cindy. "Not as an artist."

"If what I failed to observe can be observed by any artist," he said, "I think you two have created a serious problem for yourselves. Who knows who's an artist?"

"I see the thought of it is giving you an erection, Dietz," Cindy teased. "Congratulations. You can always use one. Amanda ought to run porno tapes for you while you pose, so you—"

"Don't be a bitch, Cindy," he said. "If you want to complain I'm not adequate, now is hardly the time."

"I suggested to Cindy we try a threesome," Amanda interjected.

"Like—"

"Use your imagination, Dietz," said Cindy.

Following the suggestions of her imagination, not his, Cindy lay naked on her back on the blanket-covered pad on the model platform. Amanda squatted over her face and received her tongue into her furrow. Dietz mounted Cindy and drove himself into her with all the vigor he had. After a while they changed positions. Amanda offered her tongue to Cindy, and Cindy took Dietz in her mouth.

Oddly, it was not satisfying for Cindy. She found the pleasure thin, and for the first time in her life she was ashamed of something she had done. She decided to focus all of her sexual energy on Angelo. She did, and three months later she was pregnant with her fourth child.

3

When Keijo Shigeto nodded, he sometimes nodded from the waist, and Angelo was not sure if he meant it as a bow. Try though he might, he had not yet mastered the subtleties of Japanese etiquette.

"I have not yet told you," Keijo said to Angelo, "that my grandfather was a brigadier in the Japanese army. He served in the campaign to take Singapore, later in Burma. He survived the war and was accused of no crimes. He said little to me, a lowly grandson. But he did say something I remember. 'Be discreet always,' he told me. 'To be discreet is of the utmost importance.'"

"I understand you fully," said Angelo dryly.

He understood that Keijo was telling him, in his oblique way, not to worry about the momentary encounter between them last night in a fine restaurant, where Keijo had walked past his table and seen him sitting with Betsy. Keijo had shown not even a flicker of recognition. Even so, Angelo had no doubt that Keijo had recognized him and had in all likelihood guessed the identity of the young woman with him.

Betsy had an uncanny knack for knowing where he was going and when. He wondered if she hadn't paid off a clerk in his travel agency, or several clerks at several airlines. He could never be sure when she would appear, when she would knock on the door of a hotel suite—especially in Tokyo.

"I wish to show you a questionnaire—I believe you would call it—from a firm of accountants representing XB Motors, Incorporated." Keijo pushed across his desk a forty-page set of questions, inquiring into every aspect of the financial status of Shizoka Motors. "It would require a great deal of time to assemble all of that information, some of which is confidential."

Angelo quickly glanced through the questionnaire. He smiled, shook his head, and pushed it back to Keijo. "Tell them that all the information you are willing to provide is available in public documents, to which they have ready access."

"I could assemble some reports and—"

"Let them find it themselves," said Angelo. "Why do their work for them? Bean counters. They make me sick."

"I have received a call from a Mr. Beacon. He wants a detailed report on the engineering aspects of our power-train modifications."

Angelo stabbed the desktop with a finger. *"No,"* he said. "When I see Peter Beacon I'll tell him that any information he wants about the Stallion will have to come from me. I'll tell him not to make demands on our Japanese partner. Ignore him. If he calls again, just tell him to talk to me. Better yet, don't take his call. I'll see him next week and tell him to mind his own business."

"He said he spoke for Mr. Hardeman."

"I don't care if he speaks for Jesus H. Christ. Tell him to go fuck himself. You know what that American expression means?"

For the first time the smooth and mentally agile Japanese was flustered. He giggled. "I do," he said.

"Okay. You won't use that expression. I imagine you have one equally good and equally applicable. Use that."

Keijo's office was much like Angelo's in New York, though not as large. It was in an office building that adjoined a large manufacturing plant of Shizoka Motors. Keijo's office was sparely furnished and obsessively neat. Any paper not immediately needed was filed somewhere. Obsequious young women ran in and out fetching files as needed. The only personal items in the office were a photograph of Keijo's family and a vase of flowers—at this time of year, chrysanthemums.

"If I had reported anything to Mr. Beacon," said Keijo, "it would have been that the necessary adaptations are being made as planned and on schedule except for one thing. The unit is going to cost approximately one hundred and twenty-five dollars more than projected."

Angelo shook his head. "That could destroy us in the market," he said. "It's going to be highly competitive.

You've got to cut that. An extra fifty dollars I can accept. An extra hundred and twenty-five dollars can make the difference between success and failure."

Again Keijo made that deep nod that may have been a bow. "May I ask this question? Will your company be able to meet its own projected costs?"

"A good question," said Angelo. "I'm beating heads against the walls. One thing I have to fight is this incessant demand for personnel time for reports and projections. It's a curse of the American way of doing business. The bean counters insist they need to know how much this, that, and the other thing is going to cost in nineteen eighty-two, when I can't even figure out what it's going to cost in nineteen eighty."

"This is the result of insecurity," said Keijo. "Timid men want to know how things will be next year and the year after, when instead they should be focusing on this year."

"My battle," said Angelo. "I'll fight it. Meanwhile, do try to cut back that hundred and twenty-five dollars."

"We will do our best."

"A prototype body and chassis will be shipped to Japan next month. Handmade. I'm having it loaded on a 747 freighter and flown to Tokyo from Detroit. I'll be here to see you install the power unit. You'll have one ready?"

"One will be ready."

"We'll drive it on a test track, you and I—if it fits."

"It will fit," said Keijo with a broad smile.

"I know it will. Now . . . You saw me last night. And you saw the young woman. You know who she is, don't you?"

"I have no need to know."

"I suppose you don't, but you do know. If I saw you in a hotel with a woman in the States, I'd know who she was— or I'd find out. It's business. You could trust me not to talk about it, and I trust you. We are friends."

Keijo nodded. "We are friends," he said firmly.

4

"He mentioned it?" Betsy asked.

"Yes, he mentioned it. Only to assure me that I need not worry about his discretion."

"For as smart a fucker as you are, you can sometimes be damned naive," she said.

"I trust the man," said Angelo simply.

"I'm not talking about that. I'm talking about the fact that you seem to think my father has rolled over and is playing dead. He's watching everything you do and still hopes you step on your cock."

"He's got a record for doing that; I don't."

"No? Seven years ago you did it. Number One lied to you and made you believe him. You sacrificed everything you could to achieve something he told you he wanted, and he cut your arm off at the elbow. My father's not nearly as good at it as his grandfather, but he's a Hardeman."

"I'm going to take the fuckin' company away from him, Betsy," said Angelo simply.

"I'll help you," she said. "But you must never trust my father. More importantly, you mustn't trust Roberta. My father would rather destroy the company than let you take it from him. What he really wants is to destroy *you*."

They'd had dinner brought up by room service, the most expensive kind of food the Japanese served: steaks. It was no wonder beef was so expensive in Japan, Angelo reflected; the cattle must have been raised on milk because the beef was especially tender and juicy. The butter on the mashed potatoes tasted like English butter because it had a far higher fat content than American butter and was far more flavorful. The wine had been Australian, but it was good. They also had brandy, and coffee stayed hot in a huge electric pot.

Betsy was as she liked to be when she was with him: naked except for a pair of tiny sheer white crotchless panties. He wore a blue slingshot, nothing more.

Tomorrow night they were going out to the country to stay at an inn Keijo had recommended, where they would live Japanese style, bathing in a communal bath, eating such delicacies as snakes, and sleeping in a room separated from their fellow guests only by bamboo screens.

But tonight—

"Will you give me an honest answer to an honest question?" Betsy asked.

"Sure."

"Have you ever fucked Roberta?"

He frowned and shook his head. "Are you kidding?" he asked.

She reached for his hand. "Number One kept concealed video cameras in some of the bedrooms in his house in Palm Beach. He had tapes made of the shenanigans that took place in those rooms. The night he died I gathered up all those tapes, took them out on the beach, and put the cartridges on the glowing remains of a picnic fire, after which I threw the melted remains in the ocean. One of those tapes was of you and me."

"How do you know?"

"How do you think? Didn't you ever get it through your head how *evil* that old man was? He showed me the tape of you and me."

"And?"

"Maybe looking at it again, with the live me sitting there, is what caused his coronary—that is if God didn't cause it, to do justice at long last."

"Are you sure you got all the tapes?"

"All that were in his room. I doubt there were any others."

"What's all this got to do with Roberta? That's the subject you—"

"Angelo, I didn't have time to look at his collection, but if there was a tape of you and Roberta it's very likely he showed it to my father. That would have been like him, to sow a deeper hatred. Angelo, the old man was *wicked*."

"There was no tape of me and Roberta," said Angelo.

"All right. She's got the same mentality as my great-grandfather. If you ever did it with her anywhere, you better wonder if she taped you. The woman is capable of—"

"I don't know much about Roberta," said Angelo. "I don't want to know anything more than I know already."

"Another question," said Betsy. "Number One couldn't have made those tapes. So who did? And when will we hear from them? We've got blackmail in our future, my love."

"There are only two ways to deal with blackmailers. One, you pay them. Two, you kill them."

"Angelo—"

"If anyone contacts you with blackmail in mind, let me know."

5

"I bought you something," said Betsy a little while later. "While you were doing business, I went out exploring."

He had noticed a small wrapped package lying on the coffee table and expected that sooner or later she would open it. She handed it to him to open. He took off the paper and found a small wooden box with a lid that slid back. Inside the box, on a pink silk lining, lay three leather straps with buckles and a dozen rubber rings, plus printed instructions in Japanese, English, French, and German.

> THE WORLD'S FAMOUS "ARABIAN STRAP"
> FOR THE MORE HANDSOME MANLY PARTS
> FOR THE MORE PLEASING FUCK

Betsy helped him follow the instructions. The straps were made of soft black leather, about half an inch wide, and were fitted with steel buckles. Betsy read the instructions and laughed, but she watched intently as he did what the instructions said. He slipped out of his slingshot. First he passed the longest strap through loops on the ends of the two shorter ones. Then he looped the long strap under his scrotum and over the root of his hard-on, pulled it tight, and buckled it.

"I like the way it squeezes up your balls," said Betsy. "This is good already."

The rubber rings came in three sizes. Angelo rolled one of the middle-sized ones down his shaft. He stretched the ring to roll it over the two short straps, one on each side. Finally, as the instructions said, he tightened and buckled the two short straps. His cock, already erect, stiffened even more and grew even larger. It stood high and turned a little red.

"Does it hurt?" asked Betsy.

Angelo laughed. "Hell, no . . ."

"The instructions say that if you don't pull it too tight

you can walk around all day with it on, giving you a very showy bulge."

"Like a woman in a pointy bra," he said.

"Pull your underpants on. I want to see what you'll look like."

"I'm not sure I can *get* 'em on."

He tried and succeeded, stretching the slingshot out in a great pointed bulge. He walked to a mirror and looked at himself. He pulled the underpants off and stared at the mirror.

Betsy pointed at his freakish engorgement. "I *want* that," she said, pulling off her panties.

She shrieked as he entered her. But two minutes later she moaned and grimaced. The strap caused premature ejaculation. But it kept him hugely erect, and he did not even pull out. He continued until he had come three times and she had come two or three times.

Betsy hurried to the bathroom to wash herself. When she came back out she poured two Scotches. "You like your present?" she purred.

Angelo grinned. "That was the best I ever had."

"Let me help you take it off. I don't want it to damage you." She worked the buckles and loosened the straps. "It's *your* present," she said. "But it stays with me. I don't want you using it with any other woman."

He kissed her. "I don't want you letting any other man put it on."

"I don't know another man who'd be willing to try it," she said. "Maybe you don't know another woman who'd be willing to have you with it on. We're a pair, Angelo, like I've always told you."

XIV

1979

1

 Having answered the telephone in the kitchen, Cindy returned to the dining room, where she and Angelo were eating a Chinese dinner brought by a caterer on the Post Road. The meal was tasty, even if the service was inelegant—they were serving themselves from the paper cartons in which the meal had been delivered.

"It's Roberta," she said. "She apologized for calling so late."

Angelo shook his head. "God, has she become a Hardeman! She's learned Number One's bad habit of calling any time of day or night."

"I told her we are having dinner. She said she wouldn't take a minute."

He left the table and went to the kitchen. He stood looking out at the snow that had begun to fall an hour ago and was now accumulating.

"What's up?" he asked Roberta.

"Loren has called a board meeting for Thursday," she said. "You'll be summoned."

"What? Two days after Christmas? What the hell's the matter with him?"

"Nothing's the matter with him. He's just being Loren. He figures calling you back to Detroit from Connecticut two days after Christmas will piss you off and make you an angry man at the board meeting. Angry means less effective."

"What's he trying to do?"

"Knock you off balance. He's mad as hell, Angelo. When you told Beacon he couldn't talk to the Japanese and had to ask all questions through you, Loren was furious. Also, he figures you're the reason why Shizoka is stonewalling his accountants. His ego is injured. He says he's still CEO, and you're his subordinate—which he intends to make clear."

"You called to warn me?"

"I called to warn you. You'll get official notification of the meeting by certified mail tomorrow."

"Thanks, Roberta. I'll sharpen my knives and wear my bulletproof vest."

Cindy was picking unenthusiastically at her food when Angelo returned. She was pregnant, and it had been her idea to order Chinese. Now her fancy for it seemed to have subsided.

"What was that all about?" she asked.

"Loren has called a board meeting for next Thursday."

"In the week between Christmas and New Year's? Angelo, your folks will be here!"

"My parents will be here for ten days, if we don't get so much snow the airports are closed tomorrow."

"How can you leave when they're here?"

Angelo smiled. "Since they called me to Detroit this particular week, I'm going to let the company pay for a chartered jet. I can leave here at eight, fly from Westchester Airport to Detroit City Airport in time for their ten o'clock meeting, and leave right after it and be back here by the middle of the afternoon. That'll be a finger in Loren's face."

2

Angelo's parents had visited the house in Greenwich once before, shortly after Angelo and Cindy had bought it; but they hadn't seen it since Cindy had finished her redecorating.

The house sat on six acres of partly wooded land, off North Street in the posh backcountry area of Greenwich. It was a fieldstone house with a slate roof and copper spouting, built in the early 1920s and substantially remodeled at least twice. It was not as grand as some of the neighboring houses, but it was a solid, handsome home and roomy enough for a family that would soon have four children.

As she had done in the apartment, Cindy had had all the walls painted white, the better to display art. She had installed some track lighting, but not in the main rooms, since it would have been incongruous with the carved woodwork and leaded windows. Almost all of the furniture from the apartment had been banished to the bedrooms and sitting rooms upstairs. English-country-house style was more suitable to the downstairs rooms, and that was what Cindy had bought—overstuffed, comfortable couches and chairs, upholstered in flower prints, and Oriental rugs for the oak floors.

Similarly, most of the art she had displayed in the apartment did not suit the downstairs decor. The long hall upstairs was her gallery, seen only by her family and closest friends, and there hung the Amanda Finch nude of the heavily pregnant Cindy. The elder Perinos had stopped and stared at it for a long time when they first saw it, but neither of them said a word. They said nothing either about the nude of the teenaged boy. The only works of Amanda's that hung downstairs were some of her flowers, which the Perinos did not recognize as the work of the same artist until Cindy pointed out to them the identical style used on a different subject.

Saturday's mail did in fact bring notice of the meeting of the board of directors and a summons to Angelo to be present. He had to explain to his parents why he would be absent part of a day during their visit, so he showed the letter to his father.

They were sitting in the living room. His father was glancing through a catalog of offerings from VKP Galleries, and he laid it aside to read the letter.

"I have never been able to understand your fatal fascination with the Hardemans," he said. "I would have thought you would have put aside all thoughts of having anything to do with them, after what they did to you in nineteen seventy-two."

"I'll tell you why," said Angelo. "I'm going to take their goddamned company away from them. That son of a bitch thinks he's gonna kill me. I'm gonna kill *him*."

3

Sunday morning, the day before Christmas, the children's nanny answered the phone and informed Cindy that Mrs. Hardeman would like to speak with her.

Roberta. What could Roberta want now? And why did she want to speak to her, instead of Angelo? Cindy went into the library, sat down at the small leather-topped desk there, and took the call.

"Hello. This is Cindy."

"I'm afraid we haven't met," said the voice on the line. "If we have, I apologize for not remembering. I'm Alicia Hardeman. Does the name mean anything to you?"

"I, uh . . . well, yes. You're—"

"Loren's first wife. Betsy's mother. Alicia Grinwold Hardeman."

"Of course."

"I'm having a few friends in for oyster stew on New Year's Day. Not New Year's Eve. All of the television sets will be tuned to various bowl games, so people will have their choice of football. Anyway, I don't send written invitations. I call people. I'd be very pleased if you and Angelo could come. I live in Greenwich, you know, and I'm sorry we haven't gotten together before."

"Well, I appreciate the invitation," said Cindy. "I do have a little problem. Angelo's parents are visiting—Dr. and Mrs. Perino, from Detroit. They'll only be here a short time, and Angelo has been called to Detroit for a corporate board meeting on Thursday. We—"

"Dr. and Mrs. Perino are invited too, of course. It will be very informal. No neckties. No particular hour to arrive or leave—just sometime between one in the afternoon and, say, seven. My daughter will be here. Betsy. No party can be rigid or formal with Betsy present. Please do try to come."

"It's very kind of you. I accept the invitation. If it turns out we can't come, I'll call and let you know."

"If you can't, we'll get together some other time soon. But do try to make this party. It will also be a good chance for you to meet a few people. We associate only with the laid-back kind, so I know you'll find my little circle of friends easy to like."

Back in the living room, where Angelo sat chatting with his mother and father, Cindy grinned and said, "Honey, we've all been invited to a party. All of us. And you'll never guess by who."

4

"You're late," said Loren curtly as Angelo entered the board room.

"Bad flying weather," Angelo replied.

His chartered Learjet had in fact landed half an hour ago, but he had taken time to have a leisurely drink in the airport bar before he went out to the limousine he had rented. If Loren wanted to play games, he could play them too. He had chosen to wear a navy blue blazer with gold buttons over a pink cashmere sweater and a white shirt open at the collar. It was, after all, a holiday week.

"You might have taken an earlier flight," said Loren.

"This one was early enough," said Angelo.

Not all the directors had accommodated Loren's wish to have a meeting on December 27. Princess Anne was not there. Neither was the banker, Myron Goldman. Peter Beacon, XB vice president for engineering, sat in one of the chairs behind the directors' chairs.

Roberta, wearing a heavy cable-knit white sweater and smoking a Chesterfield, sat with her chair pushed back from the table. She kept her eyes away from Angelo.

Loren stared for a moment at Angelo, as if tempted to comment on his informal attire, then apparently decided not to. "When are we going to see this car of yours on the test track?" he asked bluntly.

"It's been on the test track, in Japan."

"Are you suggesting we fly over there to see it?"

"If you *want* to see it before, say, March. We'll have half a dozen of them running on the test track here, in March."

"Flown over from Japan," said Beacon. "Not cars assembled here."

Angelo shrugged. "When you get your new quality control in place, we can start assembling them here. Not until then. At the present rate of progress, I'd estimate Shizoka will have a thousand cars in showrooms and on the road in Japan before one goes to dealers here."

"You're a loose cannon, Angelo," Loren complained. "You seem to trust the Japanese more than you trust our people. You've got a car running on a test track over there that none of us have even seen. Hell, we haven't even seen film of it."

"Let's get New Year's out of the way, Loren, then you and I can fly over and you can see the car and drive it yourself. It's available to you. No one's hiding it from you. You just can't sit on your butt in Detroit and see it."

"You can't even assemble a prototype in our plant?"

"It costs money to assemble a prototype. We're trying to keep costs down," Angelo explained. "Besides, if we assemble one here and it goes out on the test track and a door falls off, every television station in town will be running pictures of that on the evening news. Not only is XB quality control substandard, so is XB security. I'm going to fly six or seven cars over here from Japan, and we can put on a show with them. Their doors won't fall off."

"How are we to know that?" asked Beacon. "Shizoka won't talk to us."

"Shizoka *will* talk to you. Through me. The Japanese are different from us, you know. I've established a rapport with them. It would take just one bumbling conversation between one of them and somebody here to sour the whole relationship." He turned to Loren. "When you and I go, I'll tell you what to say and how to say it—and what not to say."

Loren flushed. "*You're* going to tell *me*? Who's the CEO of this company?"

"This company has one chance to survive," said Angelo. "The XB Stallion—and I thank you for the great name,

Loren. That chance depends on close cooperation between us and Shizoka. If anybody queers the deal . . . well, if the deal gets queered, Loren, you won't be CEO of anything."

"I won't be CEO of anything if the car can't go on the market for less than six thousand dollars," said Loren. "But your Jap friends won't respond to our accountants' questions about costs. How close are they going to be to their cost projections?"

"I'm looking at forty dollars over the original figure," said Angelo. "It may be fifty dollars, but it won't be more."

"How can we know if they won't let our accountants examine—"

"You'll know," said Angelo, "when they start selling us drive trains at a price. How close are we going to come on our chassis and bodies?"

"We don't know yet," said Loren. "Everybody's working on the numbers."

"*I* know," Angelo asserted. "You're looking at more than five hundred dollars over projections. If the car goes out of here with that hanging around its neck, the base model, stripped down, with no accessories to speak of, will have to be priced at sixty-five hundred dollars. That'll be about two hundred and fifty dollars more than GM's X car and five hundred dollars more than Chrysler's K car. Which shoots us out of the saddle."

"It costs money to do business in the States," said Beacon.

"More than it costs GM and Chrysler?" Angelo asked.

"Well, the Big Three have economies of volume that we can't meet," said Roberta.

"We can if we do what we have to do," said Angelo. He stood. "Gentlemen . . . lady, you've got to cut this company's payroll by fifteen percent."

"The first thing that would produce is a strike," said Beacon.

"No, it won't. Because it's not unionized production-line people you've got to cut. This company is top-heavy. There are too many clerks and bean-counters. You've got to cut them. Period."

Professor Mueller, the administrative director of the

Hardeman Foundation, shook his head. "The ratio of white-collar to blue-collar employees with Bethlehem Motors—excuse me, with XB—is roughly the same as the ratio with the other automakers."

"Exactly," said Angelo. "And theirs is bad. They're top-heavy, too. The difference is, they have those 'economies of volume' that we don't have."

"Well, just where would you start?" Loren asked.

"To start with, I'd get rid of that screwball little local accounting firm Number One hired to cover his shenanigans. They sent Shizoka a forty-page, single-spaced questionnaire. I nixed it. Apart from the fact that the Japanese considered it insulting, it would have required thousands of man-hours to assemble the data your bean counters wanted—and didn't need. I don't have the statistics for this, but I bet more than twenty percent of your white-collar man-hours are spent on what are called projections and plans. There was a questionnaire on my desk the other day. Among the things somebody wanted to know was how much I would be spending on travel, office supplies, and a half dozen other things in the third quarter of 1982. Hell, I don't even know if there'll *be* an XB corporation in 1982, much less what it will spend on paper clips. MBAs, my friends. How many have you got? How many Harvard ones? Fire all the Harvard ones and seventy-five percent of the other ones. Then let go of all the people that waste time generating reports and statistics for MBAs. What we need around here is somebody who knows how to build cars— and appliances, too, since we're staying in that business. Show me a man with a desk who doesn't know a socket wrench from a ball-peen hammer, and he goes out the door."

"Radical restructuring," said Professor Mueller.

" 'Radical restructuring' my achin' ass," said Angelo. "I'm talking about slicing off fat. I'm talking about cutting the cost of doing business. I'm talking about cutting the cost of the chassis and bodies we put in the XB Stallion. I'm talking about survival."

Angelo sat down. To everyone's surprise, Roberta stood. "I'm not sure if Mr. Perino's right or wrong," she said. "I have observed one thing—and I have some experience in business, you know. For a number of years, Number One pretended to be running this company and interfered in every effort my husband made to achieve some of these changes—I mean, adopting modern management methods and cutting fat. Well, Number One is gone. His successor—some call him Number Three—is now at liberty to make changes. I know he has already been looking closely into some of the things Mr. Perino mentioned. I imagine he will find Mr. Perino is right about some things and wrong about others. In any case, it's what he knows how to do." She paused and smiled warmly at Loren. "I'm not sure if my husband does know the difference between a socket wrench and a ball-peen hammer. I know he doesn't understand how robotic welders work. But that's what Mr. Perino is with us for. And Mr. Beacon. For the good of the company I suggest administration let engineering do its work and engineering let administration do its work."

She sat down. For a long moment Loren sat silent, as if stricken. Then he smiled and said, "You see why I married her. Well, one of the reasons." He turned to Angelo. "I *want* to go to Japan with you. I want to see this car and drive it, as you suggest." He turned and spoke to Beacon. "Work on that quality control, Pete. Angelo is right when he says we can't have doors falling off. Or windshields leaking."

Loren expanded to his role as arbiter executive. "I'm sorry to have had to call you here today, but you can all see we face problems that won't wait."

5

Roberta managed to find a moment to speak with Angelo alone. "Find something he can change on the car," she said urgently. "Feed it to me, and I'll feed it to him. He's got to think he's making a contribution."

Angelo nodded.

"Where you staying tonight?" she asked.

"North Street, Greenwich, Connecticut," he said. "My kids were asleep when I left, but they won't be when daddy gets back. Besides, my parents are there."

"How you going to get back so fast?"

Angelo grinned. "I cut costs. I chartered a bizjet and a limo."

She laughed. "You son of a bitch! Make time for *us* sometime, lover. Make time for *us*."

6

If there was a group called accepted Greenwich society, Alicia Grinwold Hardeman was a member. Her home on Round Hill Road was a white clapboard house built in the 1870s and had once been the manor house overlooking hundreds of acres of farmland. The house's original owner, a man named Mead, had made his fortune in shipping. His portrait still hung over the mantel, and the town swarmed with his descendants.

Alicia, Loren Hardeman the Third's first wife and the mother of his only child, Betsy, lent a dignity to the house it probably had never known before. At forty-seven she was taller than most women, thinner, and confidently in control of a life that resulted from her marriage into the Hardeman family and then a comfortable settlement from her ex-husband. She owned 5 percent of what was now called XB Motors, Incorporated; but if the company went under, her trust fund, which had been established when Number One and Number Three were more secure than Number Three and XB were now, would continue her lifestyle as long as she lived. In fact, shrewd investments had improved her financial security and her lifestyle. She was a woman with nothing to worry about—in terms of money.

For her New Year's party, she wore a formfitting brocade dress, gold and green and red over beige. She smoked unfiltered Camels and drank straight gin with only a cube or so of ice.

"Angelo! And you must be Cindy! I'm glad you could come. And this must be Dr. and Mrs. Perino. Welcome! Please— My daughter, Betsy. Hardeman . . . van Ludwige, whatever you want to call her."

"Thank you, Mother," said Betsy. "How nice of you to set me off so well. I've met Angelo and Cindy. Dr. and Mrs.

Perino, it's nice to meet you. Whatever you've heard about me, it is probably true."

"We have heard nothing but complimentary things about you," said Dr. Perino.

Betsy was wearing a red-orange knit dress, with narrow green-and-dark-blue stripes. It was short, and it clung to her. "I'd offer you a drink, Cindy," she said, "and will if you're not swearing off until—"

"Until April," said Cindy.

"Congratulations," said Betsy, both to her and to Angelo.

"We take great pride in our grandchildren," said Jenny Perino.

"I take great pride in my son," said Betsy. She glanced at Alicia and Angelo. "I count on my mother and Angelo to be sure he inherits what he is entitled to."

"I'm not sure I have any influence over that," said Angelo.

"Yes, you do," said Betsy. The expression in her eyes turned hard. "I count on you to see to it that my father dies soon."

"Betsy has always been a difficult child," Alicia said with cold, condescending fury.

Betsy retreated. "Uh, figuratively speaking, of course."

Dr. Perino smiled. "We understand that everyone is speaking figuratively and in riddles. But why? I was able to go to medical school because during Prohibition the first Mr. Hardeman was one of those who bought their liquor from my father. Who broke the law more, the seller or the buyer? We don't talk about these old things anymore. We don't talk about who blew up Joe Warren, do we? Joe Warren was Bethlehem Motors' Harry Bennett, but he suddenly died very conveniently. Henry Ford the Second had big trouble getting rid of his grandfather's thug. For Number One it was easier. Joe Warren was killed in an explosion that was never explained. There is a long alliance between the Hardeman and Perino families. I don't think my son needs to defer to any Hardeman. Without the Perinos, there would be no Hardemans."

The cluster of people—Angelo, Cindy, Betsy, Alicia, and Jenny Perino—gaped.

Dr. Perino went on. "Loren the Third had my son beaten, nearly killed. I could have had Loren killed within twenty-four hours. And it would not have been a pretty death, either. But problems are not solved that way. My son could have demanded that kind of revenge, and it would have been done. He didn't demand it. My son is a worthy man."

Angelo spoke. "My father speaks a bit simplistically. We are going to build the new car and make it a success—whether anyone named Hardeman likes it or not."

7

"Your father said some very interesting things," said Betsy to Angelo a little later, when they were apart and looking at Alicia's elaborate buffet spread out over the dining table and three side tables in the candlelit dining room. "He doesn't pull his punches, does he?"

"Neither did your father's thugs," said Angelo. "And while we're on the subject, you were pretty blunt."

"I meant I want him destroyed, not killed."

"At least we know what our goals are. Don't forget that mine is to build a car."

"You're like Number One in that respect, aren't you? Is the XB Stallion something you want to devote the rest of your life to?"

"The Stallion is only the beginning," he said. "I've got other plans. Once the Stallion is a success and reestablishes the company as a player in the automotive industry, we'll go on from there."

"Angelo . . ." She smiled at him playfully. "Are you going to build the Betsy for me? At last."

He grinned. "Why not? When our family car is a success, we'll build a sporty car."

"I'll take that as a promise," she said. She glanced into the living room. "There's someone you ought to meet. My mother's boyfriend. C'mon."

The man she led him toward was what every backcountry Greenwicher aspired to be: cleft-chin handsome, conspicuously at ease, physically fit, wearing a double-breasted blue blazer with a blue-and-white striped shirt and a rep tie, gray flannel slacks, Gucci loafers.

"Let me fill you in a bit," said Betsy. "I heard what you said about firing all the MBAs, especially the Harvard ones. The man you are about to meet is a Harvard MBA. He's an investment banker. He was a Marine captain in Vietnam. Tennis player. He owns a beautiful sailboat. He's five years younger than my mother. She must give him a hell of a fuck. His name is William Adams."

Betsy introduced Angelo to Adams, who invited him to call him Bill even before they finished their handshake.

"I've been interested in your automotive analyses," he said to Angelo. "To tell the truth, I was sorry you went back with the corporation. I was beginning to rely on your reports."

"When a man has it in his blood to build automobiles, it's difficult to stay away from it," said Angelo.

"I'd like to talk with you about that sometime," said Adams. "There's a takeover artist in New Jersey named Froelich who might try to buy XB."

"It's family owned. That might be a little difficult."

"Difficult but not impossible. But's let not talk about it now. I met your charming wife a few minutes ago and suggested that after she has her baby you might like to come out on the Sound with Alicia and me. We love to sail. Do you sail?"

"Afraid not."

"You used to do something else that fascinates me. You raced cars. I was in Europe in nineteen sixty-four and saw you drive in the Targa Florio. I'm sorry I can't remember what car you were driving."

"That was a Porsche 904," said Angelo.

"Well, driving and sailing are two very different sports. I don't race. Not anymore. Alicia has become a very competent first mate. She handles a boat very well. I imagine you and Cindy will be first-rate sailors, too."

"I'll be happy to try."

"Cindy says she's due in April. By July or August she should be game for sailing. Let's hope we see each other before that, though."

"Yes, let's do," said Angelo.

This was the first time anyone in backcountry Greenwich had made an offer of a friendship to him.

XV

1980

1

Roberta sat comfortably in an overstuffed chair in her living room. It was a windy winter evening and she was wearing a quilted green robe and smoking a Chesterfield. Loren entered the room. He was naked, and he carried Scotch and soda and a bucket of ice on a tray. He mixed her a drink.

"You took your damned good time about it," she said.

"I had to open a new bottle," he said humbly.

"Then start moving and get the goddamned hors d'oeuvres," she said.

He hurried back to the kitchen and quickly returned with a tray of small open-face sandwiches that had been prepared by the maid earlier that day. He knelt by the coffee table and began to lift sandwiches onto a plate, using a silver spatula. Gray Poupon mustard and mayonnaise filled two tiny glass bowls. Using small knives, he spread mustard on two sandwiches, mayonnaise on two others.

Roberta crushed her cigarette in an ashtray. Without rising from his knees, Loren seized the ashtray and dumped the butt and ashes into a silent butler. He wiped out the ashtray with a Kleenex and tossed the Kleenex into the fireplace.

Roberta smoked, but she did not like the stench of dead butts near her food.

"Serve the cucumbers and carrot sticks," she said.

He lifted those with little silver tongs and added them to her plate.

"Now listen carefully," she said, "and Mama will tell you what we're going to do when we get to Japan."

As she spoke, he bent down and licked her feet.

"Chances are, Angelo and the Japanese have put together a pretty good car," she said. "But not a perfect car. So, we're going to find fault with it, you and I. It can't be anything that requires a big retooling. But we'll find something. We'll find something that he and the Shizoka people have to change. It'll be a good idea for Shizoka to see how you can order Angelo to change things. You got it, Daddy?"

Loren sighed. "I'm not sure I'll be able to recognize anything that needs to be changed. I wish we could take Beacon along."

"And have the Japs think Beacon, instead of you, gives orders? Don't worry about it. We'll find something. On the flight you can read those two books I gave you. I've read them. There are ideas in them. You were a very effective CEO on December twenty-seventh. You'll be that again."

Loren rose, but only to his knees.

"Take some food," she said. "Fix yourself a drink."

He took sandwiches and vegetables on his plate. He poured himself a stout drink. "I'm glad you're going with me," he said.

"Be a *man,* lover."

Loren looked up and smiled. "You think I'm not being one right now? Well . . . there are ways and ways of being a man. When I've got my face in your crotch, I'm being a man. And—"

"Be a man about Angelo Perino," she said sternly. "Which doesn't mean—"

"Let him have his Stallion. Maybe it will save the company. But I'm going to have that wop's ass. You watch me, Roberta. It's not going to be pretty for Mr. Angelo

Perino. I'm going to have his car, then his ass. You watch."

2

Loren and Roberta planned to fly to Japan on Tuesday, January 22. Angelo was going over a week earlier, on January 15. Four times during the week before his flight Angelo had to take telephone calls from Roberta. During her call on Thursday, January 10, she told him for the first time that she was going, too. She insisted she had to see him before the trip, for business reasons as well as personal reasons.

"We haven't got things set up," she said, and he heard a note of urgency, even of panic, in her voice.

"Okay, I'll fly to Tokyo from Detroit, on Northwest Orient, if I can arrange it. I'll spend Tuesday night in, say, Ann Arbor and fly over on Wednesday. That puts me in Tokyo a day late, but I guess Keijo and I are close enough friends now that he won't take offense."

Tuesday he flew to Detroit, rented a Ford at Metro Airport, drove out to Ann Arbor, and checked into a Holiday Inn. He had a couple of drinks and a club sandwich in the restaurant and was lying on his bed reading when Roberta arrived at about two o'clock.

She slipped out of her coat, sat down on the couch facing his bed, and tugged off her knee-high boots. Her midcalf-length skirt was of gray wool, and her bulky sweater was cream white.

Angelo poured them two Scotches.

"Business first," she said. "You haven't told me what fault Loren will find in the Stallion."

"I'm going over a week early to install them," he said. "It's a silly goddamned charade, Roberta. I'm going along with it, but—"

"What would you do if he sold his stock in XB? And if the Hardeman Foundation did?"

"Who'd buy it?"

"There's a corporate raider in New Jersey who's talked twice to Loren."

"Number One would kill him!"

"Number One is dead. Think of it from Loren's point of view. The company is a lot of goddamned trouble. It dominates his life. It always has. And you are a source of repeated humiliations. So he sells his stock. With ten or twelve million dollars in the bank, he moves away from Detroit and takes up residence in, say, Paris."

"Would you go with him, Roberta?"

She hesitated. "I haven't decided. He won't go if I won't. But listen. He's going to be fifty-one years old shortly. He's been defeated too many times. So he gets a big charge of cash. I've got resources. So we move to Paris and forget all about Detroit and automobiles."

"Throw away everything the family ever stood for," said Angelo.

"Throw away something else. You. This time you'll lose, Angelo. The new guys will liquidate the company's assets— loot it is a better word—and they won't build the Stallion."

"I've heard of these guys," said Angelo. "They may have a hard time coming up with the money."

"Loren won't sell if he thinks he's about to be the new Hank Ford. Lee Iacocca built a car for him and saved his ass. Hank never forgave him for it. Loren will forgive you if we can make it look like he contributed important things to the Stallion. And make the world believe it."

"I said I'd go along with the charade." Angelo opened his briefcase and handed her drawings of the dashboard of the Stallion. "Notice that the top of the dash is flat and has ridges on the sides and at the rear. You see, it forms a little tray where you can put maps or pencils or tollbooth change—or a cup of coffee. Keijo is tearing that out of the prototype right now and installing a sloped-back dash. Anything you put on that is going to roll off on the floor. What's more, this is dark gray. The sloping dash will be beige. It will reflect sunlight up on the windshield and reduce visibility."

Roberta nodded. "Okay, but that's basically cosmetic. Isn't there anything more fundamental?"

"If you want it. We can build a serious oversteer into the suspension. Suppose Loren drives the test car into a shrieking skid. It might even roll over."

"And kill him," she said dully.

"He's going to be in test-driver harness and helmet. Besides, the test car is equipped with roll bars. We can give him a chance to do something dramatic and get madder'n hell about it."

Roberta smiled and shook her head. "Angelo, you're a prince," she purred. "Roberta's gonna show you she can be very grateful."

She undressed quickly. "Enough talking business," she said. "Now let's *do* business. I've been thinking about something for two weeks."

"What's that?" he asked.

"Something you're going to like. But first I want to take one of those showers together, like we did in London. God! You know that's been more than a year ago? Only four times since then. You don't take good care of me, Angelo."

"I'm trying to save a company."

"I'd say a man that doesn't get it regularly couldn't save anything, but I'm sure you get it more than regularly."

"So do you," he said.

"But it's very different," she said. "You're very different, Angelo. You're . . . you're *competent*."

"Italians know how to make great art and great love," he said.

"Tell me how great it was after we do it," she said.

When they came out of the shower, she led him by the hand to the bed. "Now, lover," she said, "Roberta is going to bring you with her lips and tongue *exclusivement*. No touch with hands. In fact . . . you can tie my hands behind my back with your belt if you want to."

Angelo shook his head.

"It'll take a while," she said, "but when you come, you'll know you've come." She grinned. "Then there'll be no premature ejaculation when you give it to me."

She was right when she said it would take time. Usually a woman used her hands toward the end, to add more friction and vigor and bring him to a climax faster. Roberta kept her hands away, as she said she would. She licked him. She sucked him between her lips. She held his cock between her lips and massaged its head with her tongue. She licked his length. She licked his scrotum. She dipped her tongue in her glass, held it against the ice for a moment, then licked him with a cold tongue. His sensations were at first shallow but slowly his arousal became more complete and more profound, until he felt that something inside him was going to wrench loose. He began to gasp.

From time to time Roberta looked up, raised an eyebrow, and smiled. Her face was flushed and perspiration gleamed on her forehead, on her cheeks, and on her breasts. Doing what she was doing this way was hard work: bobbing her head up and down, burying her face in his crotch to reach his scrotum with her tongue without lifting it in her hands, then coming up again and sucking him as deep into her mouth as she could.

"Coming, no?" she gasped.

He moaned and nodded. His body stiffened, and his legs extended tautly, as his violent spasms began. She closed her lips around him and sucked as he throbbed and squirted. She swallowed. Only after his last spasm, when he began to soften, did she lift her head. Even then she came down again and licked him a little more, to gather the last drops.

She grabbed for her glass and gulped the last of her Scotch.

Angelo bent forward. He felt incipient cramps in his legs. He was still hard and big, though he couldn't believe he could be.

"Tell me you've had it better," said Roberta.

He could honestly say, and did, that he'd never had it better.

"It's an acquired taste and a learned skill," she said.

"I thought I sensed that you liked it, too, that you were having a good time."

"Sure," she said. "Some."

" 'Acquired taste and learned skill,' " he repeated. "How'd you come to acquire the taste and learn the skill?"

"You know something? Girls do it today when they're twelve or thirteen. They know they can't get pregnant that way. But when I was a teenager . . ." She shook her head.

"Me, too. We're the same age, about. When we were kids, nice girls didn't takes boys' dicks in their mouths. If they did, they weren't nice girls anymore, acquired nasty reputations, and were called nasty names."

"There's an old cliché," said Roberta, "to the effect that it was a brave man who first ate an oyster. Well, it was a brave Roberta who first took a cock in her mouth."

"It was a brave Angelo who first put his tongue in a girl's cunt."

"Why did you do it?" she asked.

"To seduce her. I wasn't getting anywhere with her, so—"

"How old were you?"

"Twenty-six or -seven."

"Do you like to do it?"

"I can handle it," he said. "I'm not wildly enthusiastic about it."

"Don't worry, I'm not going to ask you to do it. I've got something else in mind. I was thirty-four the first time I gave head. My husband wanted me to do it. He'd begged me to do it. I was sure I'd gag, maybe vomit. But I didn't, and gradually I got used to it and even got to like it. He got so he liked it too much. We'd leave the office winter evenings when it was dark, and he'd ask me to go down on him while he drove. Can you imagine? I bet I sucked Harold off a hundred and fifty times on Jefferson Avenue. If we got stuck in traffic, I'd have to sit up, then get down and start all over when we were moving again. Sometimes he drove past our turnoff because he wanted me to finish before we got home. That's when I learned to swallow it. It made too much of a mess if you lost any trying to spit it in a Kleenex."

Angelo kissed her. Her lips were a little swollen and a little tender. "You're one hell of a woman, Roberta. I hope Loren appreciates you."

"You wouldn't *believe* how much he appreciates me," she said. She sighed loudly. "Let's have another drink. Then I want you to give it to me doggy style. Twice. Then I gotta go home. And I'll see you in Tokyo."

3

When Angelo arrived at the Shizoka R&D lab, he found a bemused Keijo Shigeto, who had already installed the deficient dashboard top in the prototype Stallion. Angelo had explained to him on the telephone why they were modifying the car to introduce defects. It was almost impossible to make him understand the vagaries of American corporate politics.

Or maybe not. It occurred to Angelo that maybe Keijo understood entirely but was inhibited by Japanese standards of courtesy from acknowledging that he did.

On the flight from Detroit to Tokyo, Angelo had reviewed the best means of introducing a profound oversteer. Keijo reviewed his proposed modifications and agreed they could easily do it—and easily return the car to its stable configuration.

On this occasion and on this occasion only, Angelo heard a sharp exchange between two Japanese. He could not understand what they said, but it was obvious that one of Keijo's assistants did not want to make the change. His voice rose as he protested. Suddenly Keijo spoke brusquely. Obviously he gave a blunt order. He bowed shallowly and curtly and strode off.

Two days later Angelo tested the modified Stallion, which had been transported by train to the test track.

The oversteer was subtle. It didn't show up in the gentle curves of the test track, even at high speeds. In a quick ninety-degree turn, as at an intersection, the car forcefully tightened its turn and resisted straightening out. A driver who didn't anticipate it, or who lacked experience with oversteer, could find himself ramming the curb.

Angelo assured himself the car would not endanger Loren. He'd make no tight turns until he pulled off the track. When he did that, he'd have to turn sharply to come through a gate. If he wasn't a damned good driver, the car would get away from him. But he would have slowed down by then, and he couldn't hurt himself.

Then he could raise all kinds of hell, and Angelo would promise to fix the problem.

What a way to run a business!

4

Loren needed to be briefed on how to deal with the Japanese. But he wasn't to have that luxury. His flight from

Detroit would arrive in midmorning, he would have some
time to sleep, and that same evening he was to be honored
at a dinner given by Mr. Tadashi Komatsu, chief executive
officer of Shizoka Motors.

Angelo's invitation, brushed in Japanese characters but
accompanied by a typewritten English translation, arrived
at his room with his breakfast tray. He telephoned Keijo a
little later and learned that Mr. Tadashi was pleased to
invite his American guests to a Western-style dinner. A
limousine would call for Angelo and the Hardemans and
take them to a country club a short distance out of town.
The dinner would not be black tie.

Loren called Angelo as soon as he arrived. Angelo told
him to get as much sleep as he could; he might be facing a
demanding evening.

Roberta came to Angelo's suite at about two o'clock. She
wanted assurance that Loren would not be killed if he
crashed the XB Stallion. She also wanted a quickie. She got
both.

5

Membership in a country club was a conspicuous
luxury in Japan. Devoting valuable land to playing games
was widely considered an arrogant waste of a natural
resource. Nonetheless, a few wealthy businessmen had
bought land, laid out golf courses, and built luxurious
accommodations. The initiation fee for membership in the
club Angelo and the Hardemans visited that night was
exactly $1,000,000.

Golfers did not change from street clothes to golf clothes
in a locker room. Each member had a ground-level suite for
that purpose. Members played tennis on indoor and out-
door courts, handball on indoor courts. There were game
rooms, exercise rooms with trainers, steam baths, and
massage rooms.

Many members had additional suites on upper levels,
arranged so they could move in and out discreetly, accompanied by whomever they wished. A dozen or so young
prostitutes lived in cottages in a grove separated from the

clubhouse. They could reach the clubhouse through a tunnel and then ascend to the upper floors in a private elevator.

The club was self-consciously Western. It made only two concessions to its few traditional members: a communal bath in which members and their friends could soak in scalding water, and one small restaurant that served Japanese food.

Guest suites had been prepared for Angelo and the Hardemans, where they could—as their driver-escort told them—refresh themselves until it was time for the reception and dinner. A petite maid in a short skirt, little white apron, and white cap attended them there, to serve them drinks and offer tiny hors d'oeuvres.

Keijo Shigeto came to Angelo's suite, accompanied by his wife, the exquisite little Toshiko. The last time Angelo had seen her she'd been in traditional Japanese dress, and now he sensed she felt uncomfortable in a short black tight cocktail dress and high-heel shoes.

"Mr. Tadashi suggested that because Mrs. Hardeman will be present for dinner, my wife should be present too. She will sit beside her, with an interpreter at the next place, so they can converse together."

"That's very thoughtful," said Angelo.

It was also going to be an ordeal for the petite Japanese woman—maybe also for Roberta, who would be obliged to keep up some kind of conversation, while really wanting to take part in the men's business talk.

At seven they left the suite and went to Mr. Tadashi's suite, where he was waiting with an array of his executives.

Tadashi Komatsu bowed deeply to Loren, a little less deeply to Roberta and Angelo, less deeply still to Keijo, who had already bowed very deeply to him. The strict Japanese sense of hierarchy governed their courtesies. It also governed their speech. Though Angelo could not hear the distinctions, he knew that Tadashi would express a thought to Keijo in slightly different terms than Keijo would use to express the same thought to Tadashi, his superior.

Angelo had warned Loren and Roberta not to try to understand and certainly not to try to mimic their hosts.

The best they could do was be courteous in the American way. The Japanese preferred that to flawed attempts to be like them.

Tadashi was the archetypal Japanese CEO: perhaps sixty years old, turning gray, his eyes behind thick-lensed glasses, his clothes flawlessly tailored. He was about five feet seven. Behind his ready smile he did not conceal an intensity that clearly implied that he was very, very serious about who he was and where he was and what he was doing.

Angelo had met Tadashi several times before and knew his English was idiosyncratic. "Encountering you is the fun I have hoped to have," he said gravely to Loren and Roberta.

Most of the evening he spoke through an interpreter, either Keijo or a young man who hovered at his side and sat behind him at dinner. Another young man interpreted for Roberta and Toshiko.

Over dinner Tadashi conversed mostly with Loren, through his interpreter. Angelo tried to listen to what they were saying, hoping Loren would commit no faux pas, but Keijo kept him in conversation most of the time. Tadashi asked Loren many questions—each preceded by the ritual "Mr. Tadashi would like to know . . ." He asked nothing about XB Motors, nothing about the Stallion. He wanted to know who Loren thought would be elected president of the United States in 1980. He asked who would win the National and American League pennants, the World Series, and the Super Bowl. He wanted to know what had been Loren's favorite American film of the past year and which American authors he would recommend.

Angelo overheard some of this and was amused. He knew Loren was in torment. Loren did not follow sports, did not attend movies, and read but little. His idea of recreation was drinking and watching television, maybe playing a little golf.

"Mr. Hardeman plays golf," Angelo said to Tadashi.

"Ahh! I too dribble on the links," said Tadashi; and this launched him, speaking through his interpreter, on a series of questions about golfers, clubs, and American golf courses.

Loren shot Angelo a dark glance and struggled with the questions.

Angelo sat back and enjoyed one of the finest meals he'd ever eaten. The prime ribs of beef were the most tender and flavorful he had ever tasted. The wine was Château Lafite Rothschild.

Keijo spoke earnestly to Angelo. "I have persuaded Mr. Tadashi not to come to Nagoya tomorrow. He must not see—"

"Exactly," Angelo agreed.

"I will go to Nagoya with the Hardemans, by train. A helicopter will pick you up here at nine."

"Why here? I'm going back to Tokyo—"

Keijo shook his head. "That would offend Mr. Tadashi, who has arranged for you to stay here."

Angelo frowned. "Uh . . .?"

Keijo frowned. "Yes."

No explanation about travel arrangements was given to Loren or Roberta. If they wanted to object, they had no chance. Everything was organized. Before they realized that he was not coming with them, Angelo had been ushered away by Keijo and two smiling Shizoka executives.

Tadashi accompanied Loren and Roberta to their limousine and said, "Before you fly, we must have fun again."

6

Keijo accompanied Angelo only to the foyer for the private elevator. There he gave Angelo a key, which was for the elevator and suite 3B. Breakfast, he said, would be brought up at eight. The helicopter pilot would be waiting in the elevator foyer at nine.

Without much enthusiasm for what Tadashi had arranged for him, yet with curiosity, Angelo took the elevator to the third floor and used the key to let himself into suite 3B. Inside the door, he found himself in another foyer, probably where breakfast would be left by a waiter who would not see the occupants of the suite. He unlocked a second door.

"Hello, Angelo . . ."

"*Betsy!* What in the name of— How did you arrange *this*?"

She didn't tell him until after they had kissed. And not until after she had tossed aside a silk wrapper and stood naked in his arms.

"I decided it was in my best interest, and probably in yours, to get to know Mr. Tadashi. Now I know him better than you do. Angelo, we have things to talk about as well as things to do."

XVI

1980

1

The Japanese helicopter pilot was waiting in the elevator foyer at nine. He spoke no English, but he recognized Angelo Perino. He led Angelo to an electric golf cart, and they rode to a helicopter pad set to one side of the dew-drenched first fairway. The helicopter was small, a two-place machine, and Angelo sat beside the pilot inside a plastic bubble, not entirely at ease.

The little chopper was noisy, but that made no difference, since they could not converse and the pilot never removed his earphones anyway. He spoke into a throat mike, apparently to air traffic control, then lifted off and flew south over the outskirts of Tokyo and Yokohama.

Mist hung over the landscape, and there were broken clouds at six or eight thousand feet.

Angelo knew there were mountains between Tokyo and Nagoya. Indeed, Fuji itself was not far off the direct course between the two cities. The pilot knew all this too. He did not fly direct. He flew out over the ocean so far that the mist all but obscured the shore, then turned west and flew over the narrow neck of a peninsula. After that he crossed a little more water, then climbed to an altitude well above the mist yet well below the clouds, and flew west over hilly country, rivers, towns, and cities, until he reached Nagoya.

An hour and a half after takeoff he settled the helicopter onto the pad at the Nagoya test track of Shizoka Motors.

All had been timed precisely. Loren and Roberta and Keijo had just arrived and were drinking tea as they walked around the prototype Stallion and stared at it.

"I trust you had a pleasant night," said Roberta sarcastically.

"You wouldn't believe it," said Angelo.

2

"I don't need all this," Loren protested as a technician buckled the harness that would hold him in his seat. He wore a helmet and a pair of fire-retardant silver coveralls. "Why do we have to overdramatize everything?"

"This is a prototype car," said Angelo. "I'm going to put it through its paces. This is a test drive, so we are outfitted as test drivers."

Roberta leaned down and spoke in the window at Loren. "Remember how we said we'd let engineering do engineering's thing? If Angelo says you need to be dressed and harnessed like a test driver, you need to be dressed and harnessed like a test driver. *He* is."

"It's supposed to be a *family* car," Loren grumbled.

"We're gonna stretch it," said Angelo.

Loren frowned. "Nothing fancy," he said.

"Right. I'll take you around the track a couple of times, then we'll switch and you can take me around a couple of times. Or you can have it to yourself."

The Stallion was smaller than a 1980 Sundancer, smaller than a Chevy or a Ford, yet bigger than a Mustang. Nothing about it suggested that it was far lighter than any of those cars. Its squarish lines gave it a look of solid stability. This one was painted silver gray. The backseat had been removed to make room for boxes of instruments and the radios that transmitted their readings.

"The upholstery will be spiffier than this," Angelo explained. "And of course the instrument panel will look like the drawings you've seen. It will be fully instrumented, including a tach. This one's equipped with a four-speed manual transmission. The gear placement is normal."

Angelo drove out onto the track and accelerated rapidly. The Stallion shifted and accelerated smoothly with a minimum of noise—because the engine was not pulling a lot of weight. Angelo brought it up to eighty miles an hour.

The track was not an oval but a curving track with turns in both directions, some shallow and some deep. The Stallion was surefooted in the turns, never threatening to skid and not leaning.

Loren looked at the speedometer. "Is this its max?" he asked.

"It's got more in it, and I can handle it. I'm not sure you can, in the turns. We assume our family driver will not go into turns at more than eighty miles an hour."

"What if he does?"

"He can lose it. It will warn him, though. I can show you."

"I'll take your word for it. I'd like to drive it myself."

"Sure. We don't stop on the track. We'll go back in and switch drivers behind the fence."

Angelo brought the car down to twenty miles an hour before he made the ninety-degree turn through the gate. Even at that speed he felt the oversteer.

They got out.

"You want me to go with you, or you want to take it alone?" Angelo asked.

"I'll take it alone," said Loren. He turned to Roberta. "You want to squeeze into one of these silly suits and get strapped in?"

"I'll wait till we're ready to go without silly suits and harnesses," she said.

As Loren was strapped into the driver's seat, Angelo leaned over and told him, "It's perfectly sure in regular curves. Be a little careful with sharp turns. There's a tendency to oversteer."

"Gotcha," said Loren.

He drove out onto the track and accelerated in the long straightaway that faced the garage where the instruments

141

were housed. When the Stallion was out of sight, Angelo and Roberta watched the readings on the speedometer. Loren did not drive as fast as Angelo had. He entered the curves at about sixty and accelerated as he came out. He became a little more daring as he got the feel of the car.

"You're sure he's not going to kill himself?" Roberta murmured to Angelo.

"Not unless he tries damned hard."

They stepped outside to watch him as he came along the straight and passed the garage. They waved but couldn't see if he waved back.

On his second circuit of the track, Loren increased his speed a little but not much. The instruments indicated that he was entering the curves more sharply. Angelo did not want him to encounter the oversteer out on the track and considered getting on the radio and warning him. But Loren was not approaching a problem.

"How's he handling it?" Roberta asked as Loren approached the straightaway past the garage.

"So far, so good," said Angelo. "Let's go outside. I suppose he'll come in this lap."

"When's he gonna lose it?" she asked quietly.

"Now or never," said Angelo.

The entry to the garage area—what might have been called a pit at an American raceway—was a simple gate. The driver had to cut ninety degrees and come through. For Loren it would be like making a right turn at a street intersection. The gate was flanked by two white wooden posts about six feet tall. The entire pit area was enclosed inside white picket fence.

Loren braked and brought the Stallion down to maybe forty miles an hour, braked again and brought it down to thirty-five or less, then spun the wheel and turned sharply into the gate.

The Stallion made the turn, but it kept on turning. The rear end skidded to the left, and the nose rammed the fence. Wood flew as the car plowed through the picket fence. Skidding sideways and left, the car shredded its left rear tire and skidded then on its wheel. The wheel broke off the axle, and the car dropped and tore off its left rear fender.

"Jesus Christ!" shrieked Loren.

"Spectacular," muttered Angelo.

3

"Your fuckin' car's not only a fuckin' failure, it's a fuckin' MENACE!*"*

Loren did not wait until he was where the Japanese could not hear him. He screamed at Angelo as he scrambled out of the harness and out of the wrecked Stallion.

"Easy, Loren, easy. I warned you about the oversteer. It's a small problem. We knew about it and know how to fix it. I warned you."

"*Fix it*? Don't bother to fix it! The project's *dead*! I don't want another fuckin' dollar spent on it!"

Loren threw his helmet down on the ground.

"Loren," said Roberta. "You've got too much riding on this—"

"To put a fuckin' *murder car* on the highway?"

"I believe," said Angelo, "you've seen test cars have problems before. *Induced* test problems, filmed by snakes. Remember?"

Loren blanched. "You have to bring that up, don't you? I thought we said bygones—"

Angelo pointed at the wreck. "I told you not to put it into too tight a turn. I told you we had an oversteer problem to solve."

"Oversteer? A. J. Foyt couldn't drive that car safely!"

"Give us two days," said Angelo, "and you can run it through that gate at forty miles an hour. You can snap it into the turn and—"

"I'll never drive that son of a bitch again! And neither will anybody else. Not another dollar, Angelo! Not one more fuckin' dollar!"

"Fine," said Angelo coldly. "What will be your price for the machine tools and jigs to build the body and chassis? Or will you sell them?"

"What are you talkin' about?"

Angelo glanced at Roberta. "Mr. Tadashi and I are going to build the car," he said. "With XB or without it. With you or without you."

"With whose money?"

"Does Mr. Tadashi impress you as a man without resources?" Angelo asked. "Do I? I'll sell my XB shares, for one thing. Shortly after we announce we are going ahead without XB, the shares will be worthless. There's a difference between you and me, Loren. You want money and power and prestige. I want to build an automobile. Like Number One always did."

Loren sighed heavily. He stared at Roberta, looking for a suggestion. It was a suggestion she couldn't give him. "You can fix this thing in two days?" he asked. "Seriously?"

"Seriously."

"Well, let's not get overexcited. Jesus! You can understand a man getting excited when he—"

"I'm sorry about that, Loren, but we're going to build the car."

"I'll come back and see it come through that gate at forty," said Loren. "And if you can shoot that son of a bitch through there at forty, so by God can I!"

Loren went inside the garage to change out of his test-driver outfit.

Roberta seized Angelo by the elbow. "This is not exactly the way this was supposed to turn out."

"Better," said Angelo. "When he drives through at forty, he'll—"

"You were bluffing," she interrupted. "You and Tadashi—"

"Mr. Tadashi and I will build the car," said Angelo. "One way or the other."

4

Betsy sat astride him. He had just come and was still very deep in her, feeling her work him with her inside muscles.

"What would you have done if he'd called your bluff?" she asked.

"I never had to think about it," Angelo replied.

XVII

1980

1

    Cindy gave birth to her fourth child in April. She and Angelo named the little girl Valerie.

    John, named for his grandfather, was now seven; Anna was five; and Morris was three.

    Previous owners had allowed the swimming pool behind the house to fall into disrepair, then converted it into a fish and lily pond. That spring Angelo hired a local pool company to dig it out and replace it with a landscaped pool. He had a heater installed, so the water was warm enough by May, when the air was still too cold for swimming; and he had a motion detector installed, which set off a loud alarm if child or dog entered the water when no adult was at poolside watching.

    The dog was more of a problem than the children. Cindy had bought a black Labrador—Greenwich's most fashionable dog—and named him Number One. ("Because he'll piss on anything that stands still.") The dog loved the pool more than anyone else in the family did, and he set off at least one alarm every day. Most of them were answered by the au pair, who begged Angelo to install a fence around the pool. In July the fence was installed.

    For months the Perinos had been ignored by Greenwich,

145

but once they had been seen in the company of Alicia Hardeman and Bill Adams, they were welcome almost everywhere. They held an open house and invited all their neighbors. They received more invitations than they could honor.

Angelo settled into a routine. He flew out to Detroit on Monday morning, stayed in a furnished efficiency apartment near the plant through Thursday night, worked in his Detroit office through Friday morning, and flew back to New York on Friday afternoon.

He varied this routine with two more trips to Japan and with three long summer weekends when he and Cindy went sailing with Alicia and Bill.

In April Shizoka shipped two thousand Stallion power trains to Detroit. In May, XB Motors shipped one thousand bodies and chassis to Japan. It was settled that the XB Stallion would be introduced in the United States on Tuesday, October 7. By that date, every dealer would have a minimum of ten Stallions to show. That was an ambitious goal, and Angelo worked hard to meet it.

2

"We've never done it this way," Peter Beacon objected.

"Pete, I don't give a damn how you've done it or have never done it."

Someday, Angelo swore, he would write an article listing the world's weakest excuses.

Among those he had heard over the past few weeks, "We've never done it this way" was the most frequently used. Others were "Number One would never have approved," "There is nothing in the plan for this," "It can't be done until the idea has been run past—," "The committee hasn't looked at it yet."

He had come to the conclusion that Peter Beacon did not want to see the Stallion built. What he did want was a future without Angelo Perino. Beacon was vice president for engineering. Angelo was vice president for research and development. Hierarchically, Beacon was entitled to refuse to initiate a manufacturing technique from research and development until it had been run past Loren and maybe even the board of directors. Politically, though, Angelo was riding high. What he wanted, he got.

For the moment, Loren was happy. He had been in a good mood since his second test-track drive in the Stallion prototype—with its suspension system restored and fender replaced. He had watched Angelo ram it through the gate at forty, then had brought it through himself at thirty. The Stallion was surefooted. And handsome. For the moment Loren was dedicated to manufacturing an automobile.

"It's going to cost eighteen dollars a unit," Beacon said, shaking his head.

"No, it's not. If you can't put it on the car for seven dollars and fifty cents, I'll buy it and have it installed by Merckel."

"Bethlehem Motors cars have never been bastardized with odds and ends of parts from other manufacturers."

"That's one of the reasons why the Sundancer costs too much and is on the verge of bankrupting the company," said Angelo "If you can't handle it, give me your resignation."

"Give *you* my resignation?"

"I don't give a damn who you give it to. Either perform or get your ass out. And don't you ever tell me again what Number One would have done. *Number One is dead!*"

3

Amanda's reputation grew. Her paintings sold for higher prices. She experimented with a new style: still determinedly realistic, yet a little bolder, with broader strokes. Standing a few feet away from one of her paintings, the viewer saw an all-but-photographically realistic right index finger laid alongside a subject's eye. Moving in closer, the viewer learned that the realistic finger was just four deft brushstrokes.

Angelo at last found time for her to paint his portrait. She complained that her paint dried between the sessions when he came to her studio to sit for her, but she completed the painting and gave it to Cindy. The picture reproduced his appearance faithfully. Actually, it did more than that. As Angelo said of it, it did not stop at the surface but captured what was beneath his skin.

He was clothed. He had gently but firmly declined to pose nude.

Alicia Grinwold Hardeman did and paid Amanda $20,000 for the painting.

Since Alicia was a stockholder of XB and she and Angelo had developed a personal friendship, he had made a habit of keeping her informed about what was going on in Detroit.

On a Saturday afternoon in August, on his way home from a visit to a barber shop, Angelo stopped by the house on Round Hill Road to show her a set of the photographs that would be used in the print advertising campaign for the Stallion.

He was surprised that Bill Adams was not there. Usually he was, on Saturday afternoons. Alicia welcomed him into the house. She had been sitting beside her pool and was wearing a short white terry beach coat. He surmised there was a bikini under the coat.

"It seems to me," she said to him as they walked through the house, "that you used to be an aficionado of dry martinis. When did you switch to Scotch?"

"I didn't. Decent Scotch is easier to come by than well-mixed martinis."

"Try me?" she asked as she turned into the kitchen.

"Sure."

She had Beefeater gin. She cracked ice cubes in the palm of her hand, under the impact of an odd little hammer with a flat spring for a handle. Into a tall thin glass pitcher she put ice, gin, and a touch of vermouth. She stirred with a glass rod. Expertly, she cut a curl of lemon peel, then twisted it into a long-stemmed glass. She poured.

He sipped.

"A dry martini well mixed," said Alicia.

"Well mixed," he agreed, saluting her with the glass.

She cut and twisted another bit of lemon peel and poured for herself. "When you can't make automobiles or launch great stock issues or run for Congress, you cultivate the small, civilized skills, like making a good martini."

Once again, Angelo lifted his glass in salute. "The roads are crowded with cars," he said. "Most of them junk. But good martinis are rare."

"Altogether too many Americans," she said, "content themselves with Bud Lite and think it's beer, with instant decaf and think it's coffee."

"What can you expect of generations brought up on burgers and fries from McDonald's or Burger King?"

"Angelo . . . Have you seen the painting Amanda Finch did of me?"

"No. I understand it's—"

"Yes, of course. I'm starkers. And it's *beautiful*. Someday, after I'm gone, it will hang in a gallery. I don't mean a sales gallery; I mean a museum. Come. I'll show you. I keep it upstairs. I don't show it to everyone. But I swear to God, if the Bruce Museum wanted to hang it, I'd let them."

He followed her up the stairs and along the hall to her bedroom, where the painting dominated one wall and in fact the whole room. He had guessed what Alicia Grinwold Hardeman looked like nude, but facing the painting he realized the naked woman looking lazily out of the painting was more realistically Alicia than Alicia was herself.

She was sitting on a graceful Victorian chair upholstered with black horsehair—a chair taken from her living room to Amanda's studio. Like Manet's *Olympia,* she wore a cameo on a black ribbon around her neck. Her dark brown hair was tied back. She wore a faint smile, perhaps defiant.

She sat with her legs crossed at the ankles and relaxed at an angle to the left. The pose did not display her crotch, only her belly down to the edge of her pubic hair, where Amanda had painted a few curly strands.

Alicia was forty-eight years old, and Amanda had made no attempt to portray her as younger than that. Her breasts were pendulous and soft. She was slender, but she had a full little belly. Amanda had not failed to depict the stretch marks from the birth of her one child, Betsy.

"Not bad for an old girl, huh?"

"You're beautiful, Alicia," said Angelo.

She sighed. "I wanted that picture done before I have to kid myself," she said. "I've had Bill take Polaroids of me. When I'm a really old woman, I want to have evidence that I wasn't always an old woman. *Capisce?*"

Angelo nodded. *"Capisco."*

She crossed the room to the window and parted the sheer curtains and looked out. "As the years go by, you know more and more vividly that you haven't lived all you could have lived. You think about chances you didn't take."

"I know."

"Not *you*," she said. "Racing driver . . . all the rest of it. You're still at it. You don't miss anything, do you? Do you have any idea how many people envy you?"

"Alicia . . ."

"Bill, for example. Bill Adams. God, man! You *go after* what you want!"

"Alicia . . ."

"If only—Can you guess what *I* want right now?"

"Alicia . . ."

"I want you to put me down on that bed and make love to me, Angelo. It may be the last chance I'll ever have, to—"

"It could be a big mistake," he said.

She smiled and shook her head. "Don't spoil the romantic, dashing image of Angelo Perino. Don't turn into Mr. Caution. Right now it's perfect. No one can possibly know. Maybe another time will come. Maybe not. I'm not an hysterical woman, Angelo. I know there's no future for us. But by God there's *now*! This one time, and maybe never again. Angelo . . ."

She *was* wearing a bikini under the beach coat. A skimpy yellow one. She jerked it off and stood for a moment with her hands on her hips, to let him look at her naked body. Then she offered herself in the missionary position and murmured and groaned the whole time he was inside her.

It was an odd experience for Angelo. Alicia was not a sexpot like her daughter, not a woman of uncommon appetites like Roberta; she was just a woman who enjoyed straightforward copulation, who was happy just feeling a big hard driving deep into her. Only when he came did she throw her legs around him to pin him inside her and prevent him from withdrawing.

She held him inside her for a long time as she came down slowly.

"Sometime again, Angelo," she whispered. "When it's absolutely safe. Don't worry. I won't embarrass you. No risks. Just . . . when we can."

Driving home, he had an unworthy thought—unworthy, that is, of the fine woman he had just been with. He had now fucked all of Loren's wives and his daughter.

4

On Monday evening, October 6, Cindy's Porsche was put in the garage and the door was closed. Two XB Stallions, one white and one metallic blue, were brought to the house and parked in the driveway. The men who delivered them drove away with Angelo's Sundancer.

The family went out to look at them. Of the children, only seven-year-old John understood what they were, and he gravely pronounced them beautiful. Shortly a third Stallion arrived, driven by Alicia, to whom a red one had been delivered a few minutes ago. Bill Adams was with her.

"Looks to me like you've got a winner here," he said to Angelo.

"I've only got one question," Cindy muttered under her breath to Angelo. "How long do I have to drive this goddamned thing before I can take out my Porsche again?"

"A week," he said. "Me, I'm in heaven. Now I won't have to drive that clunky Sundancer anymore."

Two couples from the neighborhood arrived. They admired the Stallions and pronounced them handsome cars that would surely be a big success.

Shortly everyone went in the house, where a buffet and bar had been set up. The Stallion would be introduced to America on *Monday Night Football*.

The telephone began to ring. Loren called to say the car looked good, and Roberta added a word of congratulations. Dr. John Perino called. Mr. Tadashi called from Japan to say he wished "excellence" to Angelo Perino and Loren Hardeman.

Dietz von Keyserling arrived, bringing Amanda Finch.

Alicia followed Angelo into the library, where he

switched on another television set and tuned it to WABC. They were alone for the moment.

"I'd like to talk with you for a moment," she said.

"Sure."

"I don't know what to do about Betsy," said Alicia somberly.

"What's the problem?" Angelo asked.

"Oh God, she's pregnant again!"

"Well, it can happen. Who's the lucky guy?"

"Her psychiatrist. Or so she says. She's been seeing this shrink in London, and apparently he administered his favorite therapy."

"He's married, I suppose."

"With three children. He wants her to come to the States and have an abortion. She wants to have the child. She says she can take care of another one. She has a home and a nanny. Little Loren is old enough to be placed in an English public school, so the nanny can give all her attention to the new one. The odd thing about her, Angelo, is that in spite of all her wildness and all her traveling around the world, she has been a good mother. She says mothering gives her a purpose."

Angelo took Alicia's hand between his. "You opened this conversation by saying you didn't know what to do about Betsy. I think you're going to have to let her do what she wants to do. Aside from giving her advice, I don't see how you can influence her."

"I suppose I can't. It's for damned sure her father can't influence her. I think that shrink took advantage of her."

"Oh, there you are," said Bill Adams. "They're about to kick off. When's the commercial, Angelo?"

"It runs twice in the first half, twice in the second. Four different commercials, not a repeat."

At halftime they walked out to the buffet and picked up some food, then went to the bar for drinks.

"The commercials are *great*!" Amanda exclaimed.

Angelo thought so. He had hired a New York advertising agency to do them, taking the account away from the firm that had handled Sundancer advertising since 1966. The Stallion had to be introduced by a glamorous star, he said—

not only that, but by a glamorous star who had done few or no commercials before. The agency had managed to convince Natalie Wood to introduce the new automobile. Her fee was exorbitant, but half of it went to charities of her choosing—a fact that had been publicized by all three major network news broadcasts in the past two weeks.

At least *some* viewers would stay in front of their sets to see Natalie Wood.

She was superb. Angelo had authorized the line, "It's not a car for *me*, I suppose. I live in Europe, where the roads are narrower and there are no speed limits, and I drive a Lamborghini. But when I come home and rent a car, I hope it will be an XB Stallion. For the American way of driving, it has to be the best car you can find—safe, reliable, economical."

5

Angelo's secretary in his New York office knocked on his door and stepped in. "You've got an odd telephone call," she said. "The man insists on talking to you and says you'll want to talk to him for sure, but he won't give his name."

"I'll fix his ass," said Angelo as he grabbed the phone. "Hello!"

"We've met, Mr. Perino."

"I wouldn't know, since you haven't identified yourself."

"Who I am is immaterial. I have something you want. I can arrange to deliver it to you, in return for . . . a consideration."

"Really? And what's that?"

"It's a videotape, Mr. Perino. It was shot in the Hardeman house in Palm Beach in 1974. You may remember my mother. She was Mr. Hardeman's secretary."

"Mrs. Craddock," said Angelo.

"You remember. Well, I worked for Mr. Hardeman, too. You may recall I handled the guard dogs. Also, I kept the alarm system working. Anyway, Mr. Hardeman ordered me to install hidden cameras and microphones in the house and record certain events in certain rooms. Which I did.

This particular tape was one of his favorites. It stars you and Miss Elizabeth Hardeman. Do I need to describe it to you?"

For a moment Angelo wondered if the man had copied Number One's tapes. But only for a moment. Number One had been too smart to let that happen. Anyway, why would this idiot have waited two years before attempting blackmail? No. Betsy had destroyed them, as she had said. The man on the other end of the line had seen them, though.

"What do you have in mind?" Angelo asked coldly.

"The years haven't been kind to my mother and me since Mr. Hardeman died. He wasn't at all generous to us in his will. I thought maybe a few thousand for people struggling to make a living—"

"Let me tell you something, Craddock. In the first place, there are no tapes. They were destroyed."

"Do you think so? Do you know how easy it is to copy a tape, Mr. Perino?"

"Well, I know just two ways to deal with a blackmailer: one, you pay him, two, you kill him. Which way do you think I'm going to handle you?"

6

The XB Stallion did not take off like a rocket. As a Wall Street analyst reminded his readers, it came after all from a company that had almost failed in the past five years, that had clung too long to its outmoded Sundancer, and that might yet fail. Even so, the dealers sold out their minimum stocks of ten before Christmas and ordered a few more. By February they were selling an average of four Stallions a week, by March an average of six.

Word of mouth sold the Stallion. People who bought one liked it. In June 1981, XB Motors announced that it would not offer a 1982 model. The original Stallion needed no major modification, and people who bought one would still have the latest model, through 1982. Small changes had been made and would continue to be made. None would be merely cosmetic.

The car was solid, surefooted, comfortable, and economical to drive.

THE STALLION

At the board meeting when Angelo recommended there be no 1982 model, he also recommended the Sundancer be discontinued. Loren joined him in the recommendation, and the venerable family car initiated by Number One died a quiet death. Dealers had stopped ordering it. They wanted their showroom space for Stallions.

XVIII

1981

1

In March 1981, Betsy gave birth to a baby girl she named Sally, for her grandmother. She was to be Sally Hardeman because she could not carry the name of her father, the psychiatrist.

Max von Ludwige had a pronounced sense of honor. He flew to London and broke the psychiatrist's jaw. The psychiatrist told everyone he had fallen down a flight of stairs.

Loren van Ludwige left home that spring for St. George's School. His father had arranged for his enrollment there and agreed to pay his tuition, though Betsy said she could afford to pay it herself. She agreed with Max that the boy should receive part of his education in a French secondary school, then take his university degree in the States. He was to be a cosmopolitan man.

2

In June Angelo flew to London to meet with British backers of the idea of importing the XB Stallion. They agreed that the car would be assembled in a plant in Manchester. The power trains would come directly from

Japan, and XB would export to Britain the right-hand-drive version of the bodies and chassis.

He stayed at Dukes Hotel and found in his room, after he'd checked in, a vase of flowers with a note from Betsy. Worse, he had a telephone message from Roberta, who was staying at the Hilton.

Pleading a heavy schedule of appointments, including dinner with his British associates, he put off Betsy the first night and met with Roberta.

"We have to think carefully about something," he said, when they met in Harry's Bar. "Loren's daughter lives in London. I'm not exactly an anonymous character. If someone recognizes me, sees me with you, tells her, and . . . Well, you understand."

"*I'm* anonymous," said Roberta. "Nobody knows me."

"That's not the point."

"I don't have to see you in public, lover. Only in private."

"Okay. Not tomorrow night. I'm being taken to a show, then to dinner."

"You can call on me at three A.M."

"And do business the next day? Hey—"

"We need to talk and fuck, Angelo," she said grimly. "Both."

He nodded. "I'm looking forward to the one but am a little apprehensive about the other."

"What do you want to bet nobody of Betsy's acquaintance knows about our little Lebanese restaurant? I want some more lambs' balls!"

They walked the short distance through narrow streets to the restaurant, and over the lambs' testicles and gorgeous Middle Eastern olives and a Lebanese wine, Roberta talked about Loren.

"Hank Ford had to get rid of Lee Iacocca," she said. "He *had* to. As he often reminds people, the name on the building is Ford. If he had to get work suited to his abilities, he'd be lucky to be a produce manager in a supermarket. Loren knows something like that about himself."

"I don't put him down quite that far," said Angelo. "I think he could manage a Woolworth store."

Roberta smiled bitterly. "Every big news story about the Stallion—in the *Wall Street Journal, Time, Newsweek,*

Forbes, Business Week, you name it—calls you the man who built the Stallion and saved the company. How could Loren not hate you?"

"It would never occur to him to be grateful, I imagine."

"You've made a fool of him. Again. He's the president of a company, and everybody calls it *your* company. I can emasculate him, but that's in private. You do it to him publicly."

Angelo shrugged. "So what am I supposed to do, lie down and play dead for the sake of Loren's balls? To be frank with you, Roberta, I don't give a damn about Loren's balls. I tolerate him. And I'm gettting sick of tolerating him."

"You don't have to be so fuckin' obvious about tolerating him."

"I suppose he wants to get rid of me."

She nodded. "Any goddamned way he has to."

"I don't know why I don't take my father's advice," said Angelo. "He's said to me a hundred times, 'Quit bailing out the Hardemans. They're not worth it. Do your own thing.' Why don't I?"

"Why don't you?"

"Because my 'thing' is automobiles. It used to be driving them. Now, it's building them. The Stallion is my automobile, and it's only the first. I've put up with the Hardemans because they've got the only company I can take over and use to build cars."

"You can *take over?*"

"Haven't I? Didn't I once before?"

"Loren would rather see the company die than have it taken away from him."

"I'm willing for him to play the Henry Ford role," said Angelo. "We can put his name on the building. So long as I have a free hand to build cars. My peers, the people I respect and who respect me, will know who's building the cars."

Roberta stirred the food on her plate. "Ironic, isn't it?" she murmured. "We're talking about putting Loren's balls on a plate in gravy, just like these."

Angelo glanced around the restaurant. He could not rid himself of the thought that Betsy might walk in.

"Angelo—"

"If it comes down to it, Roberta, whose side are you on?"

She drew a breath and hesitated for a long moment. "I don't know," she said quietly.

"Let's hope you don't have to decide."

The lambs' testicles were an appetizer, and she lifted the menu and began to study the entrees. "Lover," she said, "what are you going to do for me when we get to the hotel?"

"What do you want?"

"I want you to pepper my butt. I *want* you to, Angelo. I asked you before. I won't be back in Detroit for another eight days. The welts will be gone by then."

He lowered his eyes and shook his head. "I don't go for that, Roberta."

"When I *beg* you for it? 'Cause that's what I'm doing. I'll tell you a secret. I do it to Loren. But I wouldn't let him do it to me. That's another big difference between you and Loren."

Angelo shook his head again.

"You think I'm strange, don't you? Well, don't knock it if you haven't tried it."

"*De gustibus non est disputandum,*" said Angelo.

"*Chacun à son goût,*" said Roberta. "Hey, I'm the one who'll be taking it. Anyway, think about what a confession I'm making to you, begging you to beat me. Angelo, I want you to."

He smiled and shrugged. "Well, Daddy always said, 'Please the ladies if you can.' "

3

Betsy's splendid flat on Chester Terrace overlooked Regent's Park. Angelo hoped it was a neighborhood into which Roberta would have no occasion to venture. He could hope also that Betsy would accept dinner in a neighborhood restaurant and would not want to go—God forbid—to Mayfair, where the Hilton was located.

Fortunately, she wanted to introduce him to a tiny Czech restaurant just off Marylebone Road. She was known there, and they were given a table beside a streetside window, where they could see the people walking past.

Betsy was exquisitely beautiful, as always. Tonight she wore a simple Grecian dress: white, trimmed with gold, with a knee-length skirt but spectacular décolletage. At twenty-eight, she was still young, still fresh. Her adventures had not spoiled her. Angelo knew he shouldn't see her, shouldn't be intimate with her; but he couldn't resist her. Besides, he rationalized, if he tried to break away from her completely, she might very well tell all.

"So what's the story of the psychiatrist?" he asked her.

"He seduced me," she said with such innocence that he might almost have believed her. "Max is an old-fashioned man. He came over from Amsterdam and beat up on him."

"So I heard."

"Do you know Roberta's in London?" Betsy asked.

"I know."

"I'm having lunch with her tomorrow. She's coming by to see little Sally, and then we're going somewhere—somewhere elegant and expensive. It's on her."

"How do you like her?" he asked.

Betsy paused for a moment, then said, "I'm going to tell you something about her and my father. I suppose you ought to know. My grandfather, the one they called Number Two, was sexually dysfunctional. You know all about that. Well, so's my father, in his own way."

"You mean he's gay?"

Betsy sneered. "We should be so lucky. No, he's a masochist. She's a sadist. She beats him."

For an instant Angelo felt a stab of apprehension. What did Betsy know? He calmed himself and asked, "How do you know? What makes you think so?"

Betsy stared at Angelo through narrowed eyes. She opened her mouth and ran her tongue across her upper teeth. "Number One told me. Not long before he died."

"How would *he* know?"

"Angelo, he knew too fuckin' *much*. I told you about the videotape he had of us. Well, he had one of my father and Roberta, too. He didn't show it to me, but he told me about it. That was one of the tapes I burned on the beach the night he died."

Angelo put his hand on hers. "We carry a hell of a lot of heavy baggage, don't we, Betsy?"

"Anytime I think of those tapes I feel uneasy," she said. "Number One didn't make those tapes himself. Someone else did it for him. I wonder why the person who did it has never come forward and tried to blackmail any of us. Three years—"

Angelo decided to say nothing about the call from Craddock. He'd heard nothing more from the man. "He couldn't. When he went to look for the tapes, he couldn't find them. He didn't dare ask about them."

"But he *knows*! God, what he knows!"

"And doesn't dare mention. Our word against his. If there had been others, or any other evidence, we'd have heard about it by now. Number One had servants. He pretended to trust them, but he didn't. So far as he was concerned, they were always servants."

"And you were always an employee," said Betsy.

"Well, I was never a Hardeman."

"Neither am I. Am I, Angelo?"

"Miss Elizabeth, you may be the most Hardeman of them all."

"Shit, Angelo!"

"You're the only true heir Number One left. You've got his guts and his smarts."

"And he hated me."

"Of course he would."

"He was an evil man," said Betsy. "Ruthless. Sadistic. Have I got that in me, too, Angelo?"

"That remains to be seen," he said smoothly. But he knew the answer was yes; she did have those traits, too. She was the true heir and would be a far more formidable foe than her father. "You haven't shown the dark side of the Hardemans yet," Angelo lied.

They were sharing a bottle of dark red Hungarian wine with an appetizer of tiny pastries stuffed with meat and mysterious spices. Betsy lifted the bottle and refilled their glasses. As she leaned across the table to pour into his glass, she showed him her breasts in the deep V of her dress. Tomorrow she was meeting with Roberta. That would be a real confrontation, Angelo thought. Loren was insignificant compared to either one of them.

"I want you to do something for me," she said.

"Okay. I say okay without even knowing what you want."

"You haven't built *my car* yet. The Stallion is successful, but I wouldn't be caught dead driving one. Whatever happened to the Betsy?"

"I've been busy staving off bankruptcy," he said. "And protecting my back against your father's knives."

"I want my car, Angelo. You can't call it the Betsy. But I want you to build a car *you* can be proud of and *I* can be proud of. That's what the Stallion is good for: to generate the revenues that will make it possible for you to build *my* car."

"I'm proud of the Stallion, Betsy."

"Sure. And with good reason. But you grit your teeth every time you drive it. There was a story in *Financial Times* to the effect that Cindy drove hers for two weeks and will not drive it anymore. She drives a Porsche. Where's *our* Porsche, Herr Doktor Engineer Perino?"

"I couldn't shove a sports car past the XB board of directors with a bulldozer."

"What Angelo wants, Angelo gets," she said. "And so does Betsy. I want to be able to drive a car from our company on European roads and be able to say, 'Here, you fuckers, look what *my* company can do! *My* company and *my* lover, Angelo Perino, built this!' Like they wrote on late-medieval works of art: *AP fecit*. It means, 'Angelo Perino made this.' Huh?"

"Tempting," he said. "Shizoka is working with a new material: epoxy resin. You can build extremely strong but extremely light bodies with it. A muscle car doesn't need a muscle engine if it doesn't have to lug around tons of steel."

"I want to be able to pass a Porsche or Ferrari on the Corniche. Can you do it?"

Angelo nodded. "I can do it."

"Then *do* it."

He sighed. "Jesus Christ, Betsy! Just when I have a success under my belt and—"

"That's your life, my wonderful, loving man. You don't sit around congratulating yourself. You *do*! That's the point. You *do*. And Betsy will be behind you every step of the way. Angelo, if I had to *kill* my father to get him out of your way—"

"Betsy, Jesus Christ!"

"Well . . . you know what I mean and what I don't mean."

"Betsy—"

"*My son* will be Number Four," she declared. "He'll be good enough. Among the things he'll be good enough to do is to appreciate you and let you build cars the way you want to build cars, without interference. All we have to do is brush Number Three out of the way. That shouldn't take much more than a flyswatter for people like you and me. I may never be married to you, my love. But you and I are going to take the company and run it. And whatever scruples discourage you from doing, *I'll* do. I did something already. I can do it again."

"What are you talking about, Betsy, for Christ's sake?"

"Christ has nothing to do with it. Forget I said it."

"Betsy . . ."

Her eyes turned glittering hard, like two chips of ice. "Forget it," she muttered.

Angelo sighed and shook his head. He guessed she had come close to a highly significant confession.

She grinned. "Remember our Arab strap? It's waiting for us in my bedroom. Let's eat and get on with things."

XIX

1982

1

    The annual meeting of XB dealers was held in Detroit in April.

Betsy came. She opened a hospitality suite in the Renaissance Center and invited the dealers. There she presided as a princess, a vivacious, stylishly dressed personality who could trade jokes with small-town automobile dealers as easily as she discussed incunabula with London booksellers. Her hospitality suite was far more popular than Loren's.

Hanging on the wall behind the bar in her suite was a framed designer's drawing of a sleek, low-slung yellow sports car. The drawing featured a logo—

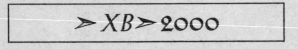

"Hey, Tom. You think you could sell that?"

She asked every dealer the same question. A few expressed doubts. Most of them said they were sure they could sell the 2000.

"I could sure sell it if I had *you* working my sales floor, Miss Hardeman," said Tom Mason.

She grinned. "How would the car do without me?"

"There'd be a limited market for it, quite frankly. But I think we could sell a few. The problem of course is—"

"Wait a minute," she interrupted him. "Here's Angelo. I want him to hear what the problem will be."

She gestured to Angelo. He walked across the room to join her and the dealer.

"Tom Mason, Angelo Perino. Tom was about to tell me about a problem he might have selling the 2000. I thought you ought to hear what he has to say."

Angelo had met most of the dealers, including this one. Mason was a heavy-set, flush-faced, jolly man. In his agency in Louisville, Kentucky, he also sold Chiisais and BMWs. He was a straightforward, practical man who had sold Sundancers and had been glad when the Stallions replaced them. Angelo understood that, like most of the dealers, Mason felt no loyalty whatsoever to XB Motors and would dump the line and sell another make if he saw any good reason to. Angelo's job was to make cars; Mason's job was to sell them. He was good at it. He had continued to sell Sundancers even when they were losing market share precipitously. He said that people who came to his agency came to buy cars from Mason and didn't much care what line he sold.

"So what problem do you see, Tom?" Angelo asked.

"All your dealers will have to stock a whole new line of parts," said Mason. "And we probably won't sell great numbers of that car."

"I'll tell you a little secret," said Angelo. "Under the 2000 shell there'll be a Stallion power train and chassis. We'll bore out the cylinders to get two hundred more c.c.'s. The engine will be fuel injected, so no carbs. You'll have to stock kits of parts for the fuel system. Also for the instrument panel. Finally, there's the body. It's going to be made of epoxy resin. You'll have no bodywork to do in the old sense. The stuff is extremely resilient. Little dings and creases will simply spring back out. If it's punctured, you can patch it. If a part is really torn up, you just detach it and replace it. There's no painting; the color goes all the way through the material."

"Meaning we have to carry body parts in all the colors?" asked Mason.

"There will only be one color, at least at first. Yellow. If we're a big success, maybe we'll add a red one."

"What price?"

"We're not sure. Think in terms of a hundred and fifty percent of the price of a Stallion."

"Look at the picture," said Betsy. "Isn't it *beautiful*!"

The car in the drawing had a wedge-shaped front sloping up between the fenders. The headlights were set into the fronts of the fenders. The windshield sloped sharply back to a low roof. The car was so low that the diameter of the wheels was half its height. It looked sleek and fast.

"When will we see these cars?" asked Mason.

Angelo shrugged. "It's a drawing, Tom. We've done a little of the engineering work, but the company has not committed itself to building it."

"Is Mr. Hardeman committed to it?" Mason asked Betsy.

She smiled. "My father is going to build it whether he likes it or not."

2

It was past midnight when Angelo said good night to the last dealer and returned to Betsy's suite. She had closed her bar and locked the door. When he knocked she was emptying ashtrays and flushing the ashes and butts down a toilet. The hotel staff would clean up the suite in the morning, but she couldn't suffer another minute of the wretched stench from the ashtrays.

She asked who was there before she opened the door. "Pour us something," she said to him as she closed and chained the door again. "I'll be finished with what I'm doing in a minute."

He decided to take the time to mix martinis. While he was pouring and stirring, Betsy went in her bedroom and stripped naked. He was behind the bar, and she stood and stared at the drawing of the XB 2000. She lifted and massaged her breasts, newly freed from the bra that had confined them all day.

"That's gonna be a *car*," she said.

"If we ever get it built," said Angelo.

"We'll get it built," she said confidently. She accepted the martini he handed her, sipped, and said, "You and I are unbeatable."

"I hope—"

She was interrupted by a firm knock on the door.

"Betsy! I need to talk to you!"

"Just what I need," she muttered to Angelo. "My father."

Angelo realized there was no way out of the suite except through the door on which Loren was knocking. Betsy pushed him toward the door to her bedroom.

"Daddy, I'm not dressed."

"Well, *get* dressed and let me in."

"All right. It'll take a minute."

She had a black silk kimono in her bedroom closet. She pulled it on. "It may be good for you to hear this," she said to Angelo as she left the bedroom and closed the door.

"Daddy, what do you want in the middle of the night?"

Loren lurched into the suite. He was drunk. He pointed at the drawing of the 2000. "Where the hell did you get that? Where the hell do you get off telling our dealers we are going to build a piece of junk like that?"

"We are going to build it, Daddy. That's the Betsy that Number One promised me."

"Number One is dead! That's a car Angelo Perino promised you! You think I'm a fool?"

"Great-grandfather promised me a car I could be proud of."

"How many millions of dollars do you want us to throw into that . . . *plaything*?"

"Whatever it takes," she said.

Loren glanced around. "Who's in your bedroom?" he asked.

"Whoever it is, he'll punch your lights out if you open that door."

Loren staggered, then sat down abruptly on a couch. "Your great-grandfather called you a slut. To my face he told me my daughter is a slut."

"Do you know what he called *you*?"

"I don't want to know. He was a rotten old bastard."

Betsy walked to the bar and picked up the martini Angelo

had mixed her. "You have no idea how rotten. He called you a masochist. He said you let Roberta beat you with a belt. Wherever could he have gotten an idea like that?"

Loren blanched. "He was . . . crazy!"

"Was he? He had videotapes of you. And of me. Casa Hardeman was wired."

"Where are those tapes now?"

"I took them. He showed them to me in his room that night—I mean, the night he died. I was there when it happened, you know. You remember, he ordered me to come to his room that night. He'd watched the tape of me and decided I could do the same for him. I mean, I *was* doing something unusual. He—"

"Are you telling me that Number One wanted you to—"

"Why do you think he ordered me to his room? He showed me my tape, he showed me your tape, and ordered me to do for him what I was doing on my tape."

"With who?"

"Never mind with who. Let me show you what killed him, Daddy." She pulled her kimono open. "When he saw, he began to choke."

"You didn't call for help?"

"He didn't need help. He died quite handily, all by himself. But lucky for us, I'd seen the tapes. I gathered them all up."

"Where are they now?"

She closed the kimono. "Never mind where they are. They're where you can't get your hands on them."

Loren struggled to his feet. "Why should I believe any of this?"

Betsy shrugged. "You want to tell me Roberta doesn't put angry red welts across your ass with your belt? Don't you tell her how great it is and beg to her to do more? Didn't you let her do it to you in a guest room in the house in Palm Beach? Think, Daddy! How else would I know?"

Loren struggled to reach the door. He stopped and looked at the bedroom door. "I bet anything the wop's in there," he mumbled.

"Actually, it's the boy who's gonna clean up the room," she sneered. "As soon as we have a quickie."

Loren lurched for the bedroom door and threw it open. He lunged through just in time to meet Angelo's fist, which caught him full on the jaw and knocked him off his feet. He lay on his back, dazed, shaking his head.

"Get up and get your ass out of here, Loren. And quit calling me wop. Some other people can, but you can't."

Loren had to struggle to get back on his feet. "I'll call Cindy," he muttered. "Just as soon as I get back to my room."

Betsy stopped him. "How would you like a full public airing of your love life with Roberta, *Daddy*? I mean, I can show your tape to anybody, not just to Angelo."

Loren snapped his head back and forth, glaring at Betsy, then at Angelo. "This isn't the end," he said darkly. "Between us. You'll both live to regret this night."

3

While the hotel staff cleaned up the living room of the suite, Betsy and Angelo showered together and enjoyed each other one more time before she began receiving dealers and he went to Cobol Hall to walk around the display of Stallions and talk with more dealers.

Loren would be the only speaker at the dinner for the dealers, which was to be given that evening. Loren and Roberta would be at the head table, as would Betsy and the members of the board of directors. The vice presidents and dealers being recognized for setting sales records would be at a lower table. Angelo would be among them. He would be among the dozen or so people Loren would mention as having contributed significantly to the development of the Stallion.

"Next year in Jerusalem," Betsy said to him as they spent their last few minutes in bed that morning. "Next year *you'll* be the star, and he won't even be here."

Angelo shook his head. "Let Loren have his moments of glory. I don't make speeches, just cars."

She turned her head on the pillow and smiled warmly at him. "You may have made something else last night," she whispered.

"Hmm?"

"I'm off the pill. I have to be, for a while. You're the only man who's been in me since—"

"Betsy!"

She raised her shoulders and turned her head. "*Ours*, my true love. Our car. Our baby. I hope."

4

In Greenwich, Cindy and Amanda lay together on the couch in the Perino living room, casually inspiriting each other with caressing fingers and tongues. They did not satisfy each other. In fact, all they had succeeded in doing was making each other itch more.

"You want to do it, or not?" Amanda asked.

Cindy glanced at her watch. "The kids'll be home soon," she said.

"We've got enough time."

Cindy nodded and pulled down her panties. She stiffened as Amanda found her clit with her tongue and began to caress it.

She was determined not to give herself to any man other than her husband. Angelo was man enough for any woman. But he was away from home so much! She couldn't help wanting what a woman wanted. She knew she wanted it more than most women did. So did Amanda. But that wasn't *their* fault.

Anyway, she knew Angelo very well. Who was he sleeping with on those long and frequent business trips? Betsy, she guessed. And who else?

They had chosen this style of life. Angelo, she told herself, could have remained a consultant and writer, commuted from Greenwich to his New York office, and made reputation and money. But no cars. And if he couldn't build cars, he'd be miserable. That was his life; it was all he wanted, and he would tolerate anything for it: constant separation from a family and home he loved, living in hotels, boneweariness, risk, frustration, and the Hardemans.

And she wasn't part of it.

Amanda looked up for a moment. "Dietz is back," she

said. "He spent some money in Europe. The things he bought haven't come yet, but he told me about them."

"I had to make him another loan," said Cindy.

"It's none of my business," said Amanda, "but you own the gallery now, don't you? He just works for you."

"I own it," said Cindy. "He's a consultant. On contract."

Amanda lowered her face into Cindy's crotch again, but she said, "He'll be at my place tonight for dinner. Would you like to join us?"

"Seven?"

"Seven."

By the time Amanda was finished satisfying Cindy it really was too late to go on and risk the children or the au pair coming in and seeing them. "Put it on account," said Amanda as she reached for her clothes. She left the house before the school bus stopped at the end of the street.

John was nine. He put his books away in his room and said he would come down to the kitchen for milk and cookies. Cindy came out of the bedroom and found him standing in the hall, staring thoughtfully at the painting Amanda had done of her when she'd been pregnant with Anna. She had noticed him staring at it before.

They went down to the kitchen.

"Do you like the painting?" she asked him.

"Which painting?" he asked.

"The one of me—naked and pregnant."

He flushed. "Oh . . . ," he said. "Yes. It's pretty."

"Does it bother you in some way?"

His flush deepened. His lower lip trembled. "Mother . . . I can't take my friends up to my room!"

Cindy frowned. Her lips parted. "I hadn't thought of that," she said.

"They wouldn't understand," said the boy.

"All right. The painting goes in the bedroom."

He blinked and squeezed out tears. "I'm sorry," he whispered.

She reached over and patted his cheek. "It's all right, John," she said. "Some of your friends *wouldn't* understand. It's okay as long as *you* do. Miss Finch—Amanda—is a wonderfully talented artist. She sells her paintings to

171

collectors and galleries all over the world, and she makes more money than some of your friends' fathers do in their businesses. When I posed for that painting, I was carrying your sister Anna. You saw me. You were too young to remember. Your father thinks it may be the most beautiful work of art he's ever seen. But we don't keep it downstairs, and we only show it to people who can understand. Your little friends ought not to see it. Not at their age. I'll move it."

"I'm sorry. I know it's beautiful. It's just that . . . the kids would think about what you did to get that way."

Cindy smiled and patted his cheek again. "Your father and I did exactly the same thing their fathers and mothers did, or you wouldn't have those friends."

"I guess . . ."

"No guess, John. That's how children come to be born. There's no other way. Every man, woman, and child on the face of the earth is the result of what your father and I did to have you and to have Anna and Morris and Valerie. And you may have another brother or sister someday."

"You mean you *still* do it?"

She couldn't help but laugh. "Of course. What did you suppose?"

"Oh . . ."

Cindy repeated the conversation to Amanda and Dietz over dinner in Amanda's studio.

"That reminds me of something," said Amanda. "I've been meaning to say to you, we ought to do another picture of you. How old were you when we did that one?"

"Twenty-six."

"Time for another," said Amanda.

"I'm not unwilling. It could be a Christmas present for Angelo."

"As soon as you're finished eating, strip down and climb on the platform. We'll set a pose, and I'll do a sketch this evening."

When Cindy was set on the platform and Amanda was at work with her huge sketch pad and charcoal, Dietz lounged with a brandy and studied her critically. He knew the days when she would tumble with him were over. He would stay the night with Amanda, but he could not have Cindy.

"You are like good wine," he said. "You improve with age."

"You are like the Bible," Cindy retorted. "You are a treasury of clichés."

"Beautiful woman," said Dietz, "I have a business proposition for you. Have you ever heard of a dealer called Marcus Lincicombe?"

"The name is . . . I guess I've heard of him."

"He thinks he might like to join us. He's one hell of a dealer, Cindy. He has an eye I can envy. Among other things, he is one of the world's most eminent collectors of netsuke. You know netsuke?"

"Little Japanese ivory carvings," said Cindy.

"In the West, Lincicombe is the foremost authority on them. Anyway, he's looking for an association. Would you like to talk with him?"

Cindy shrugged. "Why not?"

XX

1982

1

"He's gone overboard," said Loren to Peter Beacon. "The XB 2000 is a piece of shit."

"Worse than that," said Beacon. "He wants to close the Sundancer plant and open a new automated plant, filled with robotics. Robotic spot welders. All that kind of stuff. And not only that. To work with this epoxy resin material he's got in mind, we'll have to develop a whole new technology. Nobody in the industry is planning to use that stuff. The cars are going to cost twenty thousand dollars apiece unless we sink tens of millions into the new equipment it will take to manufacture huge quantities of his epoxy resin."

"Is *anybody* doing anything with it?" Loren asked.

"Bill Lear. Before his death he was planning a new business airplane called the Lear Fan. Big propeller on the rear, driven by twin turbines. The claim is that it will fly almost as fast as a bizjet, for half the cost. The secret is supposed to be that the fuselage is made of this epoxy resin material, which is as strong as aluminum but so light a man can pick up an automobile fender made of it with no strain at all."

"And it costs a fortune," said Loren.

"Unless you build the new technology to mass-produce it," said Beacon.

"We're talking about tens of millions of dollars," said Loren.

"Scores of millions," Beacon corrected.

"I'm under heavy pressure to build this car," said Loren. "My daughter wants it done. My . . . Anne wants it. Jesus Christ, I think even my wife wants it!"

Beacon raised his eyebrows. "Well, there's one possibility we shouldn't overlook."

"Which is?"

"If the XB 2000 fails, that's the end of Angelo Perino."

"It might be worth what it costs," Loren mused. "Suppose we invest in the technology to make this epoxy stuff. Can we sell it?"

"Maybe so," said Beacon. "It could be used to manufacture a lot of things. Aircraft . . ."

"Or automobiles," said Loren.

"Or automobiles. Let's face it. It could revolutionize the industry. But let's not forget that Perino tends to go off the deep end. He was going to build a turbine-powered car, you remember."

"The Betsy."

"He makes mistakes. Maybe you should put his name out front on this one. If he makes the damned thing work, we've got a profit center. If he fails—"

"Pete— He's dickin' my daughter. I want his ass! I don't know which I want more: a billion-dollar success in this 2000 or Perino's ass. I'll take either one."

2

Betsy insisted on being with Angelo when he met with Marco Varallo, the Italian coach designer who had made the drawing she had displayed in April to the dealers in Detroit.

He had to fly to London so she could join him on a flight to Turin. They took two rooms in their Turin hotel, to give the appearance that they did not sleep together. Now that

Loren knew they did, they had to be a little more careful. A Xerox of a room registration card—*Sig./Sig.ra Angelo Perino*—could be mailed "anonymously" to Cindy. Neither of them wanted that to happen.

Varallo received them in his studio, a large sunny room dominated by a huge drafting table and by clay models of cars, one full-size.

"It's going to sit on a Volkswagen platform," said Varallo, pointing at the full-size model.

He was a short, square, florid man with white hair. He was filled with enthusiasm for everything he did, and he spoke in a thin, high voice and gestured wildly with both arms. His English was idiosyncratic. Angelo could have conversed with him in Italian, but then Betsy would not have understood.

Varallo flipped through engineering drawings on a table, pulled one out of the stack, and carried it to his drafting table. "This is the XB Stallion platform, no?"

"Yes," said Angelo. "That's the Stallion, absent its body. That's what we're going to use, with very few modifications."

"I have worked on that assumption. You liked—yes?— the drawing I sent?"

"We did. Very much."

"I do wonder, though," said Betsy, "if you have any alternative ideas."

Varallo smiled. "The ladies like to shop," he said. "Is it not so? They never wish to buy the first item they see. As a matter of fact, I do have some other sketches."

Looking them over, Angelo and Betsy could see he favored low-slung cars with wedge-shaped fronts. Their air scoops were beneath their front bumpers.

That troubled Angelo. "I've driven race cars with radiators down near the pavement," he said. "The air scoops pick up water and mud. And dust. Why not open a narrow scoop in the slope of the hood?"

"And spoil the line?" asked Varallo.

"It won't spoil *your* line, Signor. I'm confident you can design it so it will look as though you put it there to make the car more beautiful."

"Anyway," said Betsy, "there'll be high pressure on the slope of the hood."

Varallo seized a pencil and sketched in a narrow slit from fender to fender. "The width depends on the tests," he said. "Then the air for the passenger compartment comes in through—?"

"Side scoops," said Angelo. "Just behind the doors."

"I'd like disappearing headlights," said Betsy.

"Too expensive," said Angelo.

"Then put them inside Plexiglas nacelles that follow the curve of the fenders," she said. "As they are, they break the lines."

"This is a good idea," said Varallo.

"I like this sketch," she said, pointing to a drawing of a car even lower than the one she had shown in Detroit.

"Give me three days, I make you a little clay model."

"Take two weeks, Signor," said Angelo. "I have to fly to Japan."

3

In Angelo's room Betsy took off her clothes and stretched out on the bed.

Angelo poured two Scotches. He handed her one, but she shook her head.

"What's the problem? Want something else?"

"Can't drink for a while, lover," she said quietly.

"Why not?"

Betsy smiled. "I'm pregnant," she said. "Our baby. Which do you want, a girl or a boy?"

It would have been pointless to ask her if she was sure it was his. He sat down on the bed beside her and took her hand. "I'm glad, Betsy," he whispered. It would have been cruel to say anything else.

4

Loren lay naked on his belly on his and Roberta's bed. His wrists and ankles were securely tied to the posts at the head and the foot. He had recently bought a carriage whip for Roberta to use on him, and he had six angry red welts across his bottom.

She sat comfortably in an overstuffed chair, smoking a cigarette and sipping Scotch. She wore a sheer black bra, nothing more.

"The little slut is pregnant again," he said. "She called from London this morning."

"So? That's Betsy. Who planted this one in her?"

"That's the worst part. She wouldn't say, but I'm just about certain I know."

"So. Who?"

"Angelo Perino," he muttered.

Roberta's face stiffened and turned red. She stood, grabbed the whip, and it came down viciously on Loren's backside. The blow cut him, and blood oozed from his welt.

"*Oww!* Jesus, Roberta! Take it easy!"

She did it again, then a third time. Loren screamed.

They had to wonder if the person who rang the doorbell heard that scream. Roberta released Loren's left wrist and left him to finish untying himself while she went to the door.

"Who the shit?" she muttered as she pulled on a robe.

She recognized the man who stood on the doorstep in the light from the lamp above the door. Burt Craddock. Number One's factotum. Son of the nasty, officious secretary who had listened to the old man's telephone calls.

Dressed in white tennis shoes, a blue turtleneck sweater, and khaki slacks, Burt carried himself like a dancer: lightly, on the tips of his toes. He was gray now, prematurely, and his flushed face suggested he had fortified himself with more than one drink before coming to the Hardeman residence.

"Do you remember me, Mrs. Hardeman?"

She nodded coolly. "What can I do for you?"

"I've come to talk to you about something. I know you'll be interested."

She hesitated for a moment, then stepped back and let him enter the house. She led him to the family room at the back of the house.

"Oh," he said. "I'd *die* for a Steinway like that. Do you mind?" Without waiting to hear if she minded, he sat down at the baby grand piano and struck a chord, then played a phrase of music.

"What is it you want to talk about?" she asked.

"Well . . . Mr. Hardeman should hear, too."

Roberta lit a Chesterfield. "Want a drink?" she asked as she went to the bar and picked up a bottle of Black Label.

"Scotch? Yes. Thank you."

Loren came into the room, wearing a robe and pajama pants and walking a little stiffly. "Craddock," he said. "To what do we owe the pleasure?"

Craddock remained seated on the piano bench. He sipped from the Scotch that Roberta had given him. "Well . . . your grandfather was a singular man, don't you agree? Among the things he did, he had the house in Palm Beach wired—microphones hidden in many rooms, video cameras hidden in a few. That was part of my job: to install and maintain that equipment. To state the matter very, very succinctly, Mr. and Mrs. Hardeman, the late Mr. Hardeman asked me to tape *you*—in the intimacy of your bedroom. Which I did. The tape is very interesting."

"Bullshit," snapped Roberta.

Craddock raised his eyebrows, tipped his head, and smiled. "The late Mr. Hardeman was amused that he had a grandson who is a masochist married to a sadist. I can quote lines to you from your performance the night you were taped. Shall I?"

"Never mind," said Loren rigidly. His face had reddened. "Are you saying you *have* this tape?"

Craddock nodded. "A copy. Mr. Hardeman owned three taping machines. It was simple to wire two of them together and dupe the tapes."

"Tapes . . .," said Roberta. "Other people besides us?"

Craddock grinned. "Mr. Hardeman, you have a daughter who is a sexual athlete."

"With—?"

"Mr. Perino."

Loren sighed. "I suppose you want money." He poured himself half a glass of straight Scotch and gulped down half of it.

Craddock grimaced and shrugged. "Only what is fair, Mr. Hardeman. Your grandfather was miserly in his will. He left a pittance to my mother, nothing to me, for years of faithful and confidential service."

"For a fee you will deliver the tapes to me?"

"Yes."

"How much?"

"Would two hundred thousand be unreasonable?"

"Totally unreasonable. But let's suppose I pay it. Where are the tapes and when do I get them?"

"The tapes are in Florida, of course."

"Are you going to bring them here?"

"If you wish"

"All right."

"Please understand that we were left poor people. Flying up here and renting a car . . ." He shrugged and held up his empty hands Could you advance a bit of cash?"

"I suppose so. I'm not sure how much I have in the house. I'll have to open a safe. I'll be a minute or two."

Roberta shook her head at Craddock. "Let me hear something my husband said on that tape."

"He said, 'Oh, honey, that's great! Do it again.' Another time he said, 'Hey, not quite so hard! Jesus, that hurts!' Then you said, 'Hurts good, though, huh?' Shall I go on?"

"And Betsy? What did she and Perino do?"

"Well . . . maybe I shouldn't say."

Roberta crushed out her cigarette. "How do we know you won't dupe the tapes again and come around for more money?"

Craddock smiled. "You'll have to trust me."

"Like shit," said Loren. He stood in the doorway. In his right hand he held a .38 Smith & Wesson revolver.

Craddock jumped to his feet. *"Hey!"* he shrieked.

Loren fired. Craddock had turned to run for the back door, and Loren's slug tore through his left buttock. Craddock screamed and jumped, struggling still to reach the door. Loren fired again. He missed the man entirely. This slug punched into the wall.

Loren trembled as he aimed the pistol again. His hands shook, and his jaw trembled.

Craddock screamed and screamed.

Roberta grabbed the pistol from Loren, took aim, and

fired. Her shot struck Craddock in the chest. He didn't scream any more.

Loren stumbled to the bar.

"No!" Roberta yelled. "We've got a mess to clean up. We've got a body to dump. And a car. Not another goddamned drop!"

"I had to do it," Loren mumbled.

"You had to do it," she agreed. "What you didn't have to do was fuck it up."

5

They didn't fuck up the rest of it. When the body was discovered and identified, the police questioned them, since Burt Craddock had been employed by Number One. But the connection between Craddock and Mr. and Mrs. Loren Hardeman the third was so tenuous that the detectives did not pursue it.

They drew the same conclusion about the connection between Craddock and Angelo Perino. Over the phone Angelo confirmed that he had known Craddock but hadn't seen the man since the last time he'd visited the Hardeman home in Palm Beach.

Mrs. Craddock wept loudly but insisted she had no idea why her son had gone to Detroit.

6

Tadashi Komatsu would not manufacture a Japanese XB 2000.

"You can sell this kind of car in the United States and in Europe," he said; "nowhere else, I think. You make him, we make him, then we compete. Not enough market for that."

"I was hoping we could be partners in it," said Angelo.

Mr. Tadashi bowed but shook his head.

"Other companies besides yours are developing epoxy resin materials and the technology to manufacture it at reasonable cost. I am impressed with yours, though. Will you license us to use your technology?"

HAROLD ROBBINS

"Oh, yes. Oh, yes."

"Will you lend me Keijo Shigeto? He and his family could live in the States for a year or two. I have much respect for his abilities as an engineer."

"Oh, yes. If he is willing."

7

Cindy was pregnant again, and she wanted to enjoy sailing on the Sound before she became awkwardly heavy. Bill Adams had taught her and Angelo the elements of sailing his thirty-five-foot yawl, *Eve,* and with Alicia they made a crew of four who did not have to struggle to manage the boat.

Bill liked to avoid weekend sailing, so it was on a Tuesday in August that they sailed west on Long Island Sound and anchored for lunch in Little Neck Bay. While Cindy and Alicia unpacked the lunch in the galley, Angelo and Bill sat in the stern and talked.

"I don't usually talk business when I'm sailing," said Bill, "but the word on the Street is that you're committing XB to making a sports car."

"I am. I want to expand the line. The Stallion is successful—"

"It saved the company," Bill interrupted.

"I'll accept that," said Angelo, saluting with a martini.

"The word is that you're going to build the body with an epoxy resin material."

Angelo nodded. "It's as strong as steel, with less than half the weight. We can get muscle-car performance from an engine that won't guzzle gas."

"I'm going to make you a suggestion. Do you mind if I make you a suggestion?"

"Not at all."

"I told you a long time ago that a corporate raider in New Jersey has his eyes on XB. His name is Herbert Froelich, the president of Froelich & Green, Incorporated. They've masterminded half a dozen takeovers of medium-sized industrial corporations over the past eight or nine years. Not one of those companies still exists. They sell off their assets for a profit, then dissolve them. Now that XB looks far more

182

sound than it used to, they're looking for the money to buy the stock."

"A lot of it is family held," said Angelo. "A lot of it is held by the Hardeman Foundation. I don't think any of them will sell."

"You never know," said Bill. "Cash looks awfully good sometimes. Loren the Third is married to a woman who might want to get out of Detroit. They could go wherever they like and live like the Duke and Duchess of Windsor."

Angelo shook his head. "I don't know what I can do about it."

"That's what I want to suggest—what you can do about it. You want to license Shizoka's epoxy resin technology. Buy the license yourself, manufacture it yourself, and sell it to XB."

"I can see two problems," said Angelo. "First is financing the license—"

"We can find the money. The Perinos and Morrises are not poor. You've got a record. So does Shizoka. If Tadashi Komatsu will license the technology, he'd probably give you better terms than he'd give the company."

"The second problem is that there's a conflict of interests," said Angelo. "As an officer of XB, how can I—"

"Essentially, you be sure the company is completely informed of what you're doing. Conflict of interests usually implies secrecy. Anyway, it might be arranged that Mr. Tadashi won't license to XB."

"Arranged . . .?"

"Let *me* arrange it. You don't know about it."

8

The board of directors assembled around the big table in the boardroom. As usual, Angelo Perino, vice president for research and development, sat in a chair set back against the wall, not at the table. Peter Beacon, vice president for engineering, sat in a chair that was similarly positioned.

Loren presided. Roberta sat to his right. James Randolph, Professor Mueller, and Alexander Briley sat along the two sides of the table. As usual, Princess Anne Alekhine had not chosen to fly in from Europe for the meeting. If she had, she would have been the only vote Loren could not count on.

Angelo sensed renewed hostility from Loren. Well, why not? He'd lost his temper that night in Betsy's suite and decked the man. That would cost him something, sooner or later. But Roberta? Why was she cold?

"The purpose of the meeting," said Loren, "is to decide whether the company should continue with the XB 2000 project, in light of a serious recent setback. It seems that an essential element of Mr. Perino's sports-racing car will not be available to us. Shizoka, the Japanese company that was to have supplied the technology for manufacturing the epoxy resin material that was to have formed the body of the car, will not license that technology to us. Without it, the car will weigh far too much to perform as promised. I can't see any option but to drop the project."

Everyone was staring at Angelo to see what he would say. "That's a somewhat facile conclusion, Mr. President. There are other ways to acquire the technology."

"What I'd like to know," said Professor Mueller, "is why Shizoka won't sell the technology to us."

"Mr. Tadashi," said Loren, "has some idea that our company is in danger of being acquired by a corporate raider. The raider has an unsavory reputation, in the view of Mr. Tadashi, and he does not want the technology to fall into the hands of people he doesn't trust. In view of the fact that a majority of the shares is represented right here at this table, in my shares and those owned by the Hardeman Foundation, that's obviously a fanciful notion."

"He offered XB a license," Angelo clarified, "on the condition that the company not fall under the control of new management."

"Our lawyers say we can't buy that," said Loren. "It's contrary to American corporation law to make it impossible for a corporation to change management."

"And the new car can't be built without this stuff?" asked Briley, the retired congressman.

"The whole cockamamie project depends on that and a few other things that are entirely uncertain," said Loren sullenly.

184

"I can get us the material," said Angelo.

"Oh? How?"

"Mr. Tadashi will not license the technology to the company. But he will license it to *me*. I can form a corporation that will manufacture it and sell it to XB Motors."

"And how much money do we have to put up?" Loren asked.

"None, till I deliver the product," said Angelo. "My company will manufacture the epoxy resin, form it into bodies for the XB 2000, and deliver it for a price that will probably be less than the cost of manufacturing it in an XB plant."

"I fail to see," said James Randolph, the director of the foundation, "how a corporate officer can lawfully and ethically sell to his own corporation."

Angelo stood and handed a paper to Loren. "That's my resignation as a vice president of XB Motors," he said. "If XB is not going to build the 2000, I have other things to do. If it is, I will sell you bodies. I will also continue to offer my services as a consultant, if you want them. My lawyers say there is nothing illegal about this arrangement. There is nothing unethical about it, either, because I have just put it all out on the table."

"May I inquire as to how you are going to raise the money to do all of this?" Loren asked.

Angelo grinned. "I have some money of my own, as you know. So does Cindy. She's a major stockholder in Morris Mining. And, well, maybe I'll pledge my stock in XB Motors."

"This board has already committed the company to building the 2000," said Roberta. "Mr. Perino already got us to stick our necks way out. The only reason for reviewing that decision was the problem in securing the body material. If we can get it—"

"Then we've got nothing to think about," Loren interrupted her. He turned and faced Roberta. "You think we should go ahead?"

"Nothing has changed," she said. "Our newly resigned vice president has committed us."

"Very well. I'd like the approval of the board to negotiate a contract with Mr. Perino. I accept his resignation."

9

Roberta took Angelo aside in the hall outside the board room.

"Someday you're going to outsmart *yourself*," she said. "From what I gather, this epoxy resin stuff may be the only part of this project that's worth anything. How'd you work it with the Japs?"

"Roberta, I swear before God that I didn't. Mr. Tadashi didn't hear about the takeover rumor from me. You told me about the New Jersey raider and the possibility of your and Loren's moving to Paris, but I swear I didn't mention it to anyone, much less to anyone in Japan."

She sighed. "Okay. So you say. You're going to own the best part of the deal."

"Maybe."

"Swear to me something else," she said grimly.

"What?"

"Swear to me the child Betsy is carrying is not yours."

Angelo nodded. "I swear."

She settled a cold, steady gaze on him for a long moment. "I don't believe you," she muttered.

"You want to ask tough questions and be skeptical about the answers? I have a question for you and Loren. Do you want to swear to me you had nothing to do with the death of Burt Craddock?"

"Who's Burt Craddock?"

"Thank you. You've just answered the question."

XXI

1983

1

On January 28, Betsy gave birth to a baby boy. Angelo could not fly to London to be with her. That would have said too much to too many people.

She was not alone, though. Max van Ludwige came over from Amsterdam, and Princess Anne Alekhine came up from the south of France.

When Angelo did arrive on February 3, for a meeting with the six British dealers who were selling Stallions, Princess Anne was still there. Betsy had confided to her who the child's father was. The three of them sat in Betsy's living room overlooking Regent's Park, and she talked frankly in the presence of Anne.

"Even though I wanted to, I couldn't name him Angelo, could I? So he is John, named for your father, Angelo. John Hardeman. I don't know if you want to tell your father he has another grandson."

"I've already told him. And you know what he did? He put in a call to Jacob Weinstein in Arizona, the man we call Uncle Jake, who manages the Perino family money. He told Uncle Jake to put half a million dollars in a trust fund for this grandson. He told him to invest it so the boy will have a nice nest egg when he's old enough to need it. Uncle Jake also manages a trust fund for me, and I had him put half a million of that into the new trust. Little John is a millionaire already, and he'll be that many times over by the time he's a young man. Uncle Jake is an investment genius."

The baby was asleep in a bassinet. The nanny had taken little Sally, who was two years old, for a stroll in the park.

"I'm nursing him," said Betsy. "I didn't with the two others, but the doctor convinced me to do it for little John. It's a little confining. You'll have to come here for dinner. I can't go out. Both of you, of course. Say, seven?"

"Yes. I'm meeting my dealers for lunch and some bankers in the afternoon, but seven will be fine."

Betsy stared fondly at little John. "I told you I'd have your baby someday," she said.

2

When Angelo and Princess Anne left Betsy that night after dining with her, they shared a cab. She was staying at the Savoy. When they reached the hotel, Anne suggested he come in for a nightcap.

"I didn't want to suggest one before, when poor Betsy can't drink."

She led him into a small dark bar where they could talk rather than be entertained, and they ordered brandies. Even in the Savoy, where extraordinary people were ordinary, Princess Anne Alekhine drew glances and some stares. She was tall, and at the age of fifty-three still kept a tight and flawless figure. She wore a long mink coat, open and showing her pink cashmere dress and a double strand of pearls around her neck. She was conspicuously an aristocrat. She hadn't been born one, but she had studied carefully and learned the trade. She successfully cultivated an air of elegance and sophistication.

"I don't mean to imply anything unkind about your wife, but it really is too bad you and Betsy couldn't have married. You are a perfectly matched couple."

Angelo smiled. "In what sense?" he asked.

"You're both smart. You know what you want and go after it. You're not afraid to take risks."

"I shouldn't have gotten her pregnant," he said. "Actually, from my standpoint it was an accident. She wanted it and—"

"She told me."

"I'm glad there's someone she confides in. I think she's lonely. I can't be with her except on occasion."

"She has no family," said Anne, "except the one she's making for herself. My nephew is a cipher. And that woman he married is beneath contempt."

"I'm going to be a father again in a couple of months," said Angelo. "Our fifth. And final. Cindy is thirty-five. It's time to stop. Though . . . she gave me a beautiful painting of herself for Christmas. Have you heard of Amanda Finch?"

"She painted Alicia, nude," said Anne. "I understand she's a fine artist."

"She did a painting of Cindy when she was pregnant with our second child," said Angelo. "Yes, nude. She was twenty-six and heavy with our little Anna. Last year, Amanda painted her again. Amanda is unrelenting in her realism. Cindy looks a year or two older than she was before. Not more. Having children hasn't hurt her."

"You love her."

"Of course."

"You come from a loving family, which was a model for you. I often wonder what Betsy and I would be if we hadn't been Hardemans. Number One was a monster. Number Two was a weakling. Number Three is a wretch. Except for me, there was only one child born to each generation. Until now. Betsy has three—only one legitimate, of course. Loren hates her for it."

"The problem with Loren is, he hates himself."

Anne raised her snifter and swirled her brandy. She smiled playfully. "Tell me something, Angelo. How many of the Hardeman women have you had?"

"I really can't talk about that."

She tipped her head. "Well, obviously you had Betsy. And you had Bobbie, Lady Ayres."

"Not when she was a Hardeman."

"Alicia speaks of you with a fondness that is highly suggestive. Also, is it just a coincidence that when you come to London, Roberta comes, too? I'm surprised she's not here now."

Angelo tipped his snifter and finished his brandy. "The conversation is getting a little—"

"Too personal? Well, Angelo, I am curious to know what the special attraction is. For Betsy, not being married to you is the tragedy of her life. She tricked you into getting her pregnant because she thought you couldn't abandon her if she were the mother of your child." Anne paused and raised her eyebrows. "A lot of wives have thought that way, too."

"'Abandon her' is hardly the right expression," said Angelo.

"Separate yourself from her. Refuse to see her. Withhold your love. There's more between the two of you than just sex, isn't there?"

He nodded. "Yes, of course."

"You're—what?—twenty years older than she is?"

"Twenty-one."

Anne gestured to the waiter for two more brandies. "Loren is convinced you're this baby's father."

"I gave my word to Roberta that I'm not."

"Good for you! The meddling bitch. I bet she asked you."

"She asked me."

Anne reached across the little round table and put her index finger lightly on Angelo's hand. "I know you didn't have sex with my mother," she said. "You did with one of Loren's wives, and my money says you have with all three. And you have with his daughter. Would you like to complete the set, Angelo?"

"Why?"

"I confronted Number One and had it out with him. Maybe someday I'll confront Number Three. It would be fun to be able to say, 'Angelo Perino has slept with every living woman in the Hardeman family.'"

"Not a very worthy motive, Princess. I don't want to play games."

"All right. A better motive. Besides the Hardeman women, you've had quite a track record. There must be something awfully good about you. Why can't *I* experience it, if all the others have?"

"It would be a betrayal of Betsy, wouldn't it?"

Anne smiled with real amusement. "Do you think you're the only man she sleeps with—apart from the psychiatrist?

You're with her a few times a year. Do you suppose she's chaste between those times? Angelo . . . following out *your* logic, either you betray your wife every time you make love to Betsy, or you betray Betsy every time you make love to your wife."

"Supposing we do this, do you plan to tell her?"

"Of course not."

"Won't both of us be thinking about her all the time?"

"Will that make you incapable of doing it?"

3

In the foyer of her suite, they kissed. She parted her lips, and he pushed his tongue into her mouth. They stood there for half a minute, their tongues working together, before she turned and led him into the living room.

She unclasped her pearls and put them aside on an escritoire, then unzipped her dress and pulled it over her head.

Under her cashmere dress, she wore just one item: a sheer black bodysuit that combined stockings and a basque. Undressing did not diminish the elegant dignity of Princess Anne Alekhine. She picked up a bottle and two snifters from a table by the window and poured two tiny splashes of brandy. When she handed him a snifter, he drew her into his arms and kissed her again.

Though it covered her from her armpits to the tips of her toes, the bodysuit was so sheer he could see all of her. Her legs were long. Her breasts were small. The lines of the bikini she wore when she sunbathed were clearly shown by the boundary between tanned skin and white.

She opened the bedroom door and used a graceful gesture to invite him in.

He undressed, as she watched. She helped him push down his underpants, then took his penis in her hand and gently squeezed it. She knelt and kissed it, just brushing her lips on it and quickly rising to her feet again.

She slipped out of the bodysuit and then, surprisingly, pushed her feet back into her shoes. Through the sheer fabric he'd thought he'd seen that her crotch was shaved, or had perhaps been waxed, and now he saw he had been right.

He ran his fingers over her outer lips. The skin was so smooth that he guessed she had had herself waxed.

"Angelo, I don't much care for the missionary position. Do you? And I don't want to hurry, either. You probably know the way I want to do it. Can we?"

He let her lead him. He had never made love exactly this way before. They sat facing each other on the bed, each with legs spread wide apart. She scooted up until their crotches were together, then inserted him. She leaned back and asked him to do the same. When her knees were in his armpits and his were in hers, she reached for his hands. They pulled on each other's arms, which pressed him more deeply into her. For half an hour they remained that way, slowly moving, twisting their hips. Sometimes they let go of each other's hands and leaned back, afterwards grabbing hands and pulling again.

The sensations were enduring and exquisite. Their movements were slow and careful and varied. They did not exhaust themselves or sweat. They experimented with movements, slowly and carefully, savoring the strong and varied feelings they could generate. Neither came to an orgasm. Each time he was near, Angelo paused so as not to end the experience.

Her scent was part of the experience. He had smelled her perfume. To that was now added a subtle, musky odor from her body, faint but provocative.

Eventually, Anne slowly raised her legs over his shoulders and brought her feet together behind his head. "Now . . .," she whispered calmly. He rammed himself deeper into her and began the thrusts that quickly brought both of them to explosive climaxes.

In the shower a little later, she kissed him and remarked in a throaty voice, "Okay, I understand the fatal attraction. Now, admit it. Every living Hardeman woman . . ."

Angelo sensed that he could trust her. He nodded.

4

In March Cindy gave birth to a baby girl they named Mary.

Keijo Shigeto and his wife, Toshiko, arrived in Greenwich

the following week. Their children would come later, when their school year was completed. In the meantime they would live with their grandparents in Tokyo.

Angelo had decided to establish Keijo in Greenwich, where he could help him and where he would be handy for consultation as often as possible. He provided him an office in the Angelo Perino, Incorporated, suite of offices on Third Avenue and accompanied him on the train on his first few commutes.

Cindy had hoped to be able to help Toshiko establish herself in Greenwich, but the move had been planned during the final stages of her pregnancy and had been accomplished within a week of the birth of Mary. Fortunately, she was not needed to help the family find a house. Shizoka took care of that. There was a Japanese real estate agency in Greenwich. Japanese companies bought houses and leased them to their own employees or the employees of other companies during their time in the States. Keijo leased a house on a hillside street in the Cos Cob area of Greenwich, furnished and entirely ready for the family to move in.

It was not where Cindy would have suggested they live. Keijo had a three-mile drive to the railroad station. Toshiko would have to drive two miles or so to the grocery store and the post office. Within two weeks of arriving, the family had acquired two cars: a Buick and a Chrysler. Keijo drove the Buick to the station. Toshiko drove the Chrysler everywhere. They were fascinated with the big American cars. Neither of them drove well, but they drove.

Angelo had identified a vacant industrial plant in Danbury as a possible site for installing the machinery and personnel to manufacture the epoxy resin material that would become the bodies for the XB 2000. The manufacturing process was not heavy industry. The liquid material was rolled out into large, thin sheets, which could be stretched over fiberglass forms to shape it into fenders, doors, hoods, and so on. As many as twenty layers would be laid on, fastened together with epoxy cement, forming laminated body parts that would be extraordinarily strong and resilient, as well as light in weight.

Single sheets of the material could easily be trimmed with scissors, though they would in fact be trimmed with specialized electric shears that cut by vibration rather than mechanical movement. The plant would use no dangerous machine tools, and there would be no heavy lifting. Care had to be taken with the chemicals, but workers could be trained to protect themselves. Once a sheet hardened, as someone put it, it could safely be used in place of a rubber sheet in a baby crib.

Manufacture of epoxy resin sheets would employ a hundred workers or so at first, and most of them could be women. The little city of Danbury enthusiastically welcomed Angelo Perino and Keijo Shigeto. They were invited to speak at a dinner held by the Chamber of Commerce and at luncheons of the local Rotary, Kiwanis, and Lions clubs.

Angelo planned to make prototype bodies in Danbury. After the prototype XB 2000s were tested, he would ship epoxy resin sheets to Detroit to be formed into bodies in an XB Motors plant.

He formed a corporation to license the process and manufacture the material. He called it CINDY Corporation.

5

Toshiko made herself into an American woman as quickly and thoroughly as she could. For dinner at the Perinos', she appeared wearing a pleated tartan skirt and a dark blue cardigan sweater over a white blouse.

"Greenwich Academy," Cindy murmured to Angelo when they were in the kitchen pouring drinks.

Speaking English remained a challenge for her, but the little Japanese woman had plunged into it and somehow managed to make her wishes known in the local stores.

"Are gin," she said, tasting her martini. "Rike this. Not so much rike Shots."

"*Scotch,*" Keijo corrected her curtly.

"Shotch . . ."

"*Scotch.*"

"Scotch. Yes. Is good. Gin more good."

At midnight, Angelo and Cindy lay in bed together. They had been benignly amused with Toshiko's attempts to speak English and at the same time sincerely respectful of the way she was facing the challenge of life in a country that was vastly different from her homeland. They chuckled as they repeated some of the things she had said.

Times like this, nights together in bed, when they were not exhausted from the demands of the day, had become too infrequent for Cindy and Angelo; and they had learned to cherish them. They lay in each other's arms, comfortable with flesh against flesh, since neither of them ever wore anything to bed.

"Darling . . .," she said.

"Hmm?"

"Are you comfortable?"

Angelo nodded.

"So am I. And maybe we shouldn't be. Maybe we're too *damned* comfortable. Did you ever think of that? We're not the kind to be comfortable. Still here we are, domesticated and cozy. I never thought we would get to be that way. In 1963 you were the second-ranked racing driver in the world—and would have been ranked first if that crash hadn't sidelined you so long. When I met you, you were still great. I loved racing. They wouldn't let a woman compete, but you let me be a test driver. We used to live on the edge, man!"

"I'm not sure what you're getting at," he said.

"Maybe I'm not sure either, but I have a sense that we've lapsed into middle-age boredom—in our *personal* lives, I mean; your professional life is adventurous enough. We go sailing, but Bill doesn't race the yawl. There's no challenge in sailing with him. I'd like to take flying lessons, but I suppose as a mother of five—"

Angelo grinned. "If you flew, you'd want to go into aerobatics. And so would I—if I flew. Are you telling me you're bored, Cindy?"

She shrugged. "It's such a damned cliché," she said.

"The gallery—"

"I ought to spend more time in there. I've let Dietz run things too much. And Marcus Lincicombe. Marcus is a fine dealer—too good to be a junior partner."

"No reason why you shouldn't spend more time in the gallery. You do trust the au pair, don't you?"

"Yes. She's all right."

"Well, then . . ."

Cindy ran her hands down her cheeks, then down over

her breasts and lifted them. "Do you remember the line in *The Godfather* when Mike tells Kay he'll let her ask him one question about his business but never another?"

Angelo nodded. "She asked him if he'd killed his brother-in-law, and he lied and said no."

"Right. Will you let me ask you one question about your personal life?"

"Yes."

"Are you the father of Betsy's latest child?"

Angelo did not hesitate for more than a moment. He drew a deep breath and said, "Yes."

"I thought so," she said calmly. "I'm not going to forgive you, because I don't think it's something you need be forgiven for. I can understand. She's drop-dead beautiful. She's smart. She's vital. She was *there* a lot of times when I couldn't be. Besides, she's a Hardeman. Fucking her, you fucked the whole clan."

"I'm sorry, Cindy."

"I'm going to show you how much I love you, Angelo. I could hold this over you, but instead I'm going to tell you that I've strayed on you a time or two. If you were a commuter who came home on the train every night, I don't think either one of us would have found an occasion to do anything outside our marriage. But that's not the way it is. Do you love her?"

"Well—"

"You damned well better. You'd better love the mother of your son. It's okay, too—as long as you love me more."

"I love you more, Cindy. A whole lot more."

She smiled and reached out with both hands. "Show me," she said.

XXII

1984

1

Two prototypes of the XB 2000 were cobbled together—Angelo's term—by the end of February 1984. He had leased the space in Danbury, had installed the necessary equipment to mix the epoxy resin material and roll it out into sheets, had ordered forms built according to the Varallo design, and had produced two bodies. They were flown to Detroit and installed on Stallion frames and chassis with modified engines. They carried Stallion gear boxes, instrument panels, and other interior components, and so were not really 2000s. Even so, they *looked* like the new car; and on the test track the modified engine drove the light vehicle with a performance that felt like the new car.

Betsy came to Detroit and demanded one of the prototypes. She drove it on a test track, then on the streets, then on the Michigan highways, picking up one speeding ticket and outdistancing the second police car that chased her.

Princess Anne was interested, and she and Igor came to Detroit and drove one of the prototypes. Pulled over by a Grosse Pointe patrol car, she indignantly showed the visa stamp in her passport that proved she had not been the woman driving the yellow sports car on the night when it had outraced the same police car.

197

It was not possible to have two XB 2000s available to every dealer by the time of the April dealers meeting. Two cars were ready for display in Cobol Hall—this pair complete with 2000 gear boxes, instrumentation, and all interior appointments.

Betsy was to unveil the car at the annual dinner for dealers. She was popular with the dealers, especially those who remembered her hospitality suite from the meeting two years before. When she was introduced by her father, the dealers rose and gave her a standing ovation—as they had done for Angelo Perino a few minutes before.

2

Loren and Roberta sat side by side at the head table, she all but obscured from the dealers by a large basket of white carnations.

"I shouldn't have let you talk me into this," muttered Loren as Betsy, looking splendid in a white silk dress, took the microphone and beamed at the clapping, shouting dealers.

"Keep cool, lover," Roberta whispered to him. "The 2000 is gonna fail. And when it does, whose car was it? Let Betsy and Perino have their hour of glory. Their honey will turn to vinegar very shortly. And it damned well better, too. Perino knows too fuckin' much."

Betsy gave a short speech. She spread credit around. It was Angelo Perino's project, she said. Applause. Based on something she had been urging him to do. Applause. Because her great-grandfather had promised her the company would do it. Applause. Possible because of the support of her father. Applause. Assisted by his vice president for engineering, Peter Beacon. Applause.

"XB Motors, formerly Bethlehem Motors, has maintained a secure niche in an industry increasingly dominated by the Big Three, because our company has always given the American consumer what he and she wanted. The Sundancer was a *great* car. The XB Stallion is a great car—as the sales figures you are returning every month clearly show. And now, for those Americans who want something different . . .

"I've driven it, ladies and gentleman—as a wonderful officer from the Grosse Pointe Police Department, who couldn't catch up with me, can testify. I—"

Betsy laughed. She took a portable microphone from a technician who was ready with it. "Will Officer Bill McIntosh please come forward?" She walked down from the podium and waited for the policeman to wind his way down among the tables. He had been eating and drinking with a table of dealers and was not entirely steady on his feet.

"Bill has something for me," said Betsy. The officer, in civilian clothes, stepped up to her, reached into his jacket pocket, and handed her a slip of paper. Betsy put her face up to his and kissed him. She waved the paper in the air. "This is my speeding ticket. Well deserved. Thank you, Bill, and . . . you wanta cuff me and take me in?"

The officer, blushing, shook his head.

"Well, stay here beside me and have a closer look at the car you were chasing that night."

The lights went down. A 2000, in the light of a powerful spotlight, crossed the floor and stopped in front of Betsy.

The audience stood and cheered the car they saw. It was even lower and sleeker than the car they had seen in the drawing in her suite in 1982. It was yellow. It looked like a crouched cat ready to spring. Betsy and the policeman, standing behind it, towered above it and were clearly visible to all the dealers.

"Okay!" Betsy yelled. "The S Stallion—Super Stallion! You'll have them in October. How many are you going to sell?"

3

"Six," said Tom Mason, the dealer from Louisville. He spoke quietly to his wife and the other dealers at his table. "I can move BMWs faster than I can sell that." He shook his head. "A two-seater. Radical technology in that epoxy resin body. It's a racing car. Oh, we'll sell it, but we won't be able to move many."

"You know what that car's gonna do?" said one of the other dealers, a man named Greene, from Albany. "That's gonna bring guys in to look at it. They won't buy it, but they'll buy something else you got on the floor. We can afford to put one or two of them on the floor to attract trade. But XB's not a big enough company to sustain a loss leader."

"I'll tell you one thing," said Mason. "I'm gonna drive my demonstrator. That's gonna be *my* car."

"No way, José," said his wife.

"Why not?"

"In the first place, every time you get in it, you'll have to twist and squeeze to get your fat butt through the door. In the second place, if you had *me* with you, you wouldn't be able to get a bag of groceries in there with us. The car's a *plaything,* Tom, and there aren't many families in Louisville who can afford to have a plaything car."

"Particularly when they realize that all that's underneath that slick body is a bored-out Stallion engine and a Stallion platform."

"With a racing transmission," Mason pointed out.

"Priced," said the other dealer, "like a . . . well, like a Porsche?"

"You can't get a Porsche for the price," said Mason.

"But when you have one, you have a *Porsche.*"

"Hey!" said another agent across the table, a younger man. "Being a single, unmarried fellow, I'd *die* for a Super Stallion. Wherever I go, people are going to notice."

"Girls," said Mason's wife, grinning.

"Speaking of which . . .," said Mason, nodding at Betsy.

"There's a story around," said Greene. "The story is that Betsy Hardeman's most recent baby was fathered by Angelo Perino."

"Good for Angelo," said Mason. "There's the guy *I* trust. The Stallion was his idea, and it bailed the company out. It bailed out all the Bethlehem dealers. I'd have dropped the Sundancer line sooner or later. It was a great car in its day, but its day had passed."

"He's not a vice president anymore," said Greene. "I don't understand the whole deal."

"No Perino, no company. That's the deal," said Mason. "You know why? He's got fire in his guts about building

THE STALLION

cars. Number One had that. I guess Betsy's got it. Loren the Third does not. No Perino, no XB cars. If they really get rid of him, I'm out."

4

Angelo and Cindy sat at a table below the dais. With them were Keijo and Toshiko, Alicia Hardeman and Bill Adams.

Cindy watched Betsy accept her speeding ticket from the Grosse Pointe officer. She nudged Angelo. "It's easier to understand," she whispered. "She's something special."

He squeezed her hand beneath the table. "Thank you for understanding," he murmured. "Do you see what she's doing?"

"She's rubbing Loren's face in shit," Cindy whispered.

"You got it."

Bill Adams leaned across the table toward Angelo. "The car is absolutely beautiful," he said. "Can you really sell enough units to make it a viable product?"

"No."

"Really?"

"It's Betsy's car," said Angelo. "It's an ego trip for her. She and Princess Anne Alekhine are going to make personal appearances all over the country. But they'll never make that car sell. People who buy it are going to love it. I love it. But the country's not ready for it. There's no market niche for it. The original Thunderbird was a beautiful little two-seater, and everybody loved it, but it didn't sell. They turned it into a bathtub on wheels, and *then* it sold."

"Then why'd you do it, Angelo?"

Angelo glanced at Cindy. "Betsy can be persuasive," he said. "Anyway, we've learned some important lessons from it. The epoxy resin material is a complete success."

"And you've got that to yourself," said Bill, grinning.

"*We've* got that to *our*selves," said Angelo. "CINDY, Incorporated, has many parents."

Alicia spoke. "Who was it that said success always has many parents but failure is an orphan?"

201

5

Cindy drove her S Stallion, for the time being leaving her Porsche in the garage. She quickly discovered its shortcomings. Vision to the rear was limited by the narrow, sloping window. The driver had to rely on the outside mirrors. It was so low slung that it was invisible to drivers in other lanes, particularly to truck drivers. She learned to accelerate rapidly when parallel to a truck on its right side—after two truck drivers innocently tried to change lanes to the right and nearly ran over her.

In fact, that's what happened to an S Stallion driver in Boston. The fatal accident was featured by all the news media.

Even so, Marcus Lincicombe was determined to have a Super Stallion, and after she had driven hers for three months, Cindy got Angelo's permission to sell hers to Marcus. When he was sideswiped by a taxi on Lexington Avenue and the epoxy resin body yielded and then sprung out again, leaving the cab with a collapsed fender and the Super Stallion with no visible damage, that story also received nationwide attention.

Marcus Lincicombe was a small, precise, intense man of thirty-three. He was bald, having only a fringe of black hair around the sides of his head. He wore gold-rimmed round spectacles and smoked a pipe, which, when it was not lighted, he carried in a pocket of his tweed jacket. He was fussy about the pipe, constantly cleaning it. He was fussy in the way he loaded it with an aromatic tobacco. In fact, some people thought he was fussy about everything.

He had been an asset to the gallery. As Dietz had suggested, he had a fine eye for art; and because of him they displayed and sold a wider variety of pieces than they had sold before. He had bought into VKP Galleries, but even so, he didn't demand that the name be changed to reflect his interest. Dietz was now an employee. Marcus was a minority owner.

He was one of the world's foremost collectors of and authorities on netsuke, the tiny ivory carvings once used in the manner of buttons on the sashes of Japanese gentlemen.

Small personal possessions were once hung from sashes by using netsuke as fasteners. Genuine antique netsuke were valuable collector's items. They were also the basis of a cottage industry in twentieth-century Japan, and some of the modern ones were worth collecting, too. Netsuke were carved in the images of men and women, animals and birds. Some of the most prized ones were images of men and women having sex.

Marcus displayed parts of his own collection in the gallery, and the gallery offered netsuke for sale—its provenance precisely labeled. Cindy had wondered if selling netsuke would not turn VKP Galleries into a Fifth Avenue–style purveyor of pseudo-Oriental, pseudoantique junk, but she quickly learned to appreciate the artistic value of what Marcus collected and sold.

He was what she was: the heir to some family money, which made it possible for him to be an art collector and dealer. He lived beyond the earnings he achieved in the gallery.

His favorite place for lunch was the Bull & Bear, in the Waldorf. He invited Cindy to join him there.

He introduced her to the maître d'. "Remember her. This is Mrs. Angelo Perino—Cindy Perino. If she comes without me, give her a table you'd give me."

Oversized martinis were a specialty of the house; and free at last of pregnancy and nursing, Cindy called for a Beefeater martini on the rocks with a twist.

With their drinks before them, they talked for a few minutes about a show they were assembling. Marcus used his apartment the way Cindy had used hers: as an intimate gallery for showing small collections to little groups of likely buyers. He was not an admirer of Amanda Finch, certainly not in the way that Cindy and Dietz were, and he mentioned that he did not want to offer any of her work at a dinner they were planning.

"We don't have to show her every time we invite people in for something special," said Cindy. "But you have to admit, she makes money for us."

"A not inconsiderable consideration," said Marcus gravely.

It was difficult for Cindy to know whether he was being

sincere or facetious when he made a pronouncement like that. She smiled and did not respond.

He was not an easy man to know. He was mysterious, probably intentionally so. His precise little smiles were meaningful, but what meaning was behind them was all but impossible to guess.

He smiled now. "I should like to make you a small present," he said. "Would you accept it?"

"Marcus, I don't know. What is it?"

He took from his jacket pocket—the one opposite the pocket that bulged with his pipe—a little red velvet bag, closed with a drawstring. He handed it to her.

She opened the bag and pulled out an exquisite netsuke. Not more than an inch and a half in any dimension, it was so finely carved that it portrayed what it portrayed not only accurately but in detail. Two tiny ivory figures were having sex. The woman's tongue was out, and she was licking the man's lingam. The middle finger of his right hand was in her furrow. So carefully were they portrayed that the tension in their bodies was apparent.

Cindy understood that the carving was worth thousands of dollars. To accept it from him—and to accept so erotic a piece—would alter the nature of their relationship.

"I don't know what to say, Marcus."

"Say you think it's beautiful."

She nodded. "I think it's beautiful."

"It's about a hundred years old. It was done by one of the finer carvers. He seems to have specialized in this sort of thing."

"I'm hesitant to accept a gift like this from you," she said.

"The subject?"

"The value."

"I'd like for you to have it."

"What does it suggest, Marcus? That this couple could be you and me?"

He blushed. "Oh, no! Though . . . though nothing would be more wonderful. But no. I just thought of it as one of the better of the pieces in my collection, and I wanted you to have it—as a mark of my respect."

She smiled at him. "You are being disingenuous," she said.

He picked up the netsuke and turned it over and over in his hand. "I don't deny I would like for us to become closer friends," he said. He placed the netsuke again in her hand, letting his fingers linger on hers.

Cindy put the netsuke in its velvet bag and the bag in her purse. "This is more than just kind of you, Marcus," she said.

She had let him become a closer friend.

XXIII

1984

1

"He can't decide whether he's happy or sad,"
Roberta told Angelo.

They sat over a room-service dinner. Since the waiter
would not return until he was called for, Roberta had
stripped to her garter belt and stockings. She exulted in
displaying herself to him and had complained that he did
not provide her with enough opportunities to do it. She had
no sense at all that he no longer wanted to do it. She had
no idea that he regarded her as gross—and suspected she may
have acted with Loren to kill Burt Craddock. For his part,
he was not really certain anymore what motivated her to
come to him.

Loren was in Florida, meeting with the Southern dealers,
which left her free to spend the evening, though not the
night, with Angelo in his suite in the hotel in the Renaissance Center. In a very small sense, she reminded him of
the way Betsy had once been if he refused to see her
anymore, he could not be sure how she would react and
what she would do.

He could not tell Roberta to put her clothes back on, but
he took no pleasure in looking at her. He knew she meant to

use him anyway she could. Okay. He could play that game at least as well as she could. What could he get from her?

"I know what he's happy about," said Angelo. "The S Stallion."

She shrugged. "I had to talk him out of having a champagne party to celebrate the termination of production."

"A lovely fellow, Loren. He made his own little contribution to the death of the S."

"Meaning?"

"Meaning he planted stories in every newspaper and magazine he could, reporting what a failure the car was, how dangerous it was. All behind the scenes, trying to keep his name out of it, he did a job on the Super Stallion like Nader did on the Corvair."

"You've got that one wrong, Angelo."

"The hell I do. Did he really think I wouldn't find out?"

"He *does* have reason to hate you."

"I don't give a damn."

"I don't give a damn about him," said Roberta. "But I give a damn about *me*. The survival of XB Motors is more important to me than it is to him."

"I don't give a damn about that either," said Angelo. "I've *ceased* to give a damn about it."

"Kid me not," said Roberta. "You've admitted to me more than once that the only real thing in your life is building cars. Hell, man, you like building cars more than you like having your cock sucked. I hate that old cliché 'fire in the gut,' but, man, building cars is what lights the fire in your gut."

Angelo drew a deep breath and sighed. "And XB is the only company I can get control of to build cars the way I want to."

"The Big Three would take you on and be overjoyed to have you. But you'd have to work—"

"Within committees," he finished the sentence. "Inside management."

"And Angelo Perino won't work that way," she said. "Angelo Perino doesn't like organizations, will not abide hierarchy, won't call anyone his boss. I like that about you. I don't call anyone boss either. Never did and never will."

"I put my cock on the anvil for the S Stallion. I can see why Loren is happy it failed."

"It didn't fail, lover," Roberta corrected. "America failed. The country failed the car."

"Same thing," said Angelo. "Rationalizations don't help."

She stood up and walked to the window, carrying with her a glass of red wine. She stood there for a moment. She had to be visible to hundreds of people looking out of hundreds of windows in the great Ren Center complex. Angelo rushed over and pulled the cord to close the drapes.

Roberta smiled lazily at him, letting him see she had liked the idea that people might have seen her. She returned to the table and sat down over their dinner.

"The Stallion is in trouble," she said quietly.

"It's four years old," said Angelo. "It was *my* idea to continue a model several years, so buyers wouldn't have it shoved in their faces that come October they were driving what was conspicuously last year's car. We've made a few cosmetic changes, but essentially we're still offering the eighty-one car. The time has come for a completely new model. Loren and his board don't want to do it."

"Money," she said.

"No business makes money without spending money," said Angelo.

"They're determined they won't make a car with an epoxy resin body. They say that's what you want because you own the American rights to the Shizoka epoxy resin process."

Angelo shrugged. "Loren and his board of directors think in terms of their own morality. Because they cheat, they assume everyone else does."

"Apart from that," she asked, "what would you do with the Stallion?"

"Restyle it," said Angelo. "Downsize it a little. There's very little market anymore for what used to be called an American family car, a car big enough to haul six people. Families who want to cram six in a vehicle buy vans. Look at the cars on the roads. Ninety percent of them are carrying just one person."

"A whole new model," she said.

"Which we can't make and sell for an acceptable price, using the obsolete old Sundancer plant. I've talked about robotic welders and all kinds of other technology. *Essential*, Roberta. You say you want the company to survive? The twenty-first century is coming. XB has got to be a twenty-first-century company."

"Would you come back as a vice president if you could make the changes you want?"

"No. Keijo and I are doing all right with the epoxy resin. A new airplane is going up with it next month. I'm still a well paid consultant to XB. I make my recommendations, even if they don't follow them. Roberta, at XB I'm up to my ass in midgets. It's nothing but frustration. And that's apart from the fact that Loren, and others, would like to . . . well, maybe not kill me literally, but destroy me. I'd have to protect my back every minute. I don't want it. I don't need it."

"And you're not building cars," she said. "Where's the fire in the gut?"

"I may go to Japan. Maybe I can do better with Shizoka."

"Don't kid yourself. No Japanese company is going to give you autonomy."

"And Loren would?"

"Loren faces two possibilities," she said. "The company's in trouble again. He changes things or he sells out."

"The raiders are still out there?"

"They figure they can get it cheap and make something out of it." She grinned. "Hey, the first thing they'll do if they get the company is offer you the presidency."

Angelo shook his head. "And let me build cars? I doubt it."

"Tuck your goddamned pride in a little bit, Angelo," said Roberta. "Using a little bit of smarts, you can be a vice president again, with more power than you ever had."

He shook his head again. "Fuck it, Roberta. Why would I want to buy grief? Besides, what makes you think Loren and his lackeys would—"

"Let me tell you what makes me think so—makes me *know* so—if you're not smart enough to figure it out. *The dealers,* lover. The goddamned dealers are in your corner, and Betsy's. If they bail out—"

"There's nothing."

"You got it," she said. "No dealers, no company. Dead."

She began flexing her shoulders, twisting her neck, and rubbing her breasts—fixing on Angelo a smile that let him know exactly what she had in mind.

"Autonomy," he said firmly. "Absolute autonomy."

"I can *get* it for you," she said, showing a little impatience. "Let me handle Loren, as usual. Now you handle me. I'm going to give it to you good tonight. I'm still the best you ever had."

"You've got the biggest ego about it anybody ever had."

That didn't discourage her. She set to work on him. He was not yet ready to make her an unalloyed enemy, so he accepted as much of her as he could take.

2

"You let me handle Mr. Angelo Perino," Roberta said to Loren. "Let's get on with what I told you I want. You don't need to undress. I want it right now."

She pulled her black skirt up around her hips, shoved her panties down around her ankles, and spread her legs. Loren put his jacket aside but otherwise fully dressed got down on his knees in front of her. He pushed his face up into her crotch and began giving her cunnilingual sex.

Roberta lit a Chesterfield and leaned back comfortably on the couch.

Loren used his hands to spread her a little more. He licked her petals, found her clit and flicked it with his tongue, then bobbed his head to run his tongue up and down her whole furrow.

"You've gotten a whole lot better at that than you were when I introduced you to the idea," she said in a throaty voice.

"Practice makes perfect," he said, and then paused. "Perino, huh? We really have to?"

"Or see the company go under," she said. "We're going to have to borrow money. Perino is essential. Without him the banks won't go along. There'll be time later to dump his ass."

"Dump isn't enough. I *want* his ass."

"You're going to get it."

Loren nodded, then pushed his face into her crotch again. He worked vigorously, and Roberta gently tousled his hair.

"You know," she said, "at first you didn't like this and did it only because I wanted it. Now I'm damned if I don't think you like it."

"Umm-hmm," he murmured. *"Mmmmm!"*

"Damned good thing you like what I like. 'Cause you and I are committed to each other *for life*. We got a *murder* between us, lover. The idea of sitting in a cell in the Michigan reformatory for women for the rest of my life doesn't appeal to me."

3

"There's another advantage to putting XB Motors heavily in debt," said Bill Adams. "It will make the company a whole lot less attractive to raiders. Froelich & Green will back off fast when they find out the company has borrowed four hundred and seventy-five million dollars."

"I can't thank you enough," said Angelo.

Bill laughed. "I'll get some fees."

They were at the Indian Harbor Yacht Club for dinner. Angelo and Bill were in the bar. Cindy and Alicia were coming separately and had not yet arrived.

"I took the option on the land," said Angelo. "I'd have liked to build the plant somewhere besides Detroit, but the mayor was very persuasive about how much it would hurt the city if we moved the company somewhere else. Anyway, our suppliers are all set up to deliver to Detroit. We'd have had to make too many changes."

"Are you aware," asked Bill, "that a group of people here in Greenwich have formed an S Stallion owners' club?"

"Yes. They've asked me to make a speech. I don't know how I'll handle the question about why Cindy and I don't drive ours anymore."

"Do you want to say anything about what kind of car the new Stallion will be?"

"It will be smaller," said Angelo. "The concept of the six-passenger sedan is all but dead, and it's absolutely dead for XB. I've encountered strong resistance to the epoxy resin body for a standard-size passenger car, so it will be steel again. I can use the basic engine; there's nothing wrong with that. It will be a front-wheel-drive car. Restyled. Sleek. I'm flying to Turin to meet with Marco Varallo. I think he can design what I want: an American two-door, suitable for four people, not a sports car by any means but not a boxy family car either."

4

Cindy urged him to stop in London on his way to Turin, to see his son—and Betsy.

The toddler looked like a Perino. Pointing at Angelo, Betsy told him that this man was his daddy. The child seemed to understand and let Angelo hold him on his lap.

Betsy insisted that little John know who his father was, from the beginning. The twelve-year-old Loren van Ludwige had been told, as had been little Sally, who was three.

After the nanny took charge of the child, Betsy poured brandies, and she and Angelo stood together by the window that overlooked Regent's Park. Betsy wore soft, well-faded blue jeans and a white T-shirt with no bra underneath.

Cindy had written a letter to Betsy, telling her she knew that Angelo had fathered a child by her, telling her that she hoped they could be friends and that Betsy would bring little John to the States to see his grandparents while they were still alive. She assured Betsy they would be welcome in the house in Greenwich, where the little boy would be known to the Perino children as their half brother.

"I'm grateful to Cindy," said Betsy, "but it's all a little to damned civilized to be believed."

"Cindy's had an affair, too, at least one," said Angelo.

"Well, I have news for you," said Betsy. "If you were planning to sleep with me tonight . . . I'm sorry."

"I am, too. I was looking forward to it."

"I have news," she said. "I'm going to be married again. Within a month or two."

"Forgive me, but—"

"Am I pregnant?" she interrupted. "No."

"Who's the lucky man?"

Betsy sighed. "Well, he's not Angelo Perino. That's the

tragedy of my life, you know: that I couldn't marry the man I loved—still love, will always love. I'm thirty-two years old, and I'll never be able to marry that man. I'm a single woman with three children. I'm alone too much. I know my father is not alone in thinking I'm a hellion. But I'm not; I'm here with my kids most of the time."

"Who is the man, Betsy?"

"A very decent man," she said. "That condemns him, doesn't it? He knows everything, including that I would leave him in an instant and come running to you if something happened to Cindy and you called me. Despite all that, he's willing to help me raise my children."

"What's his name? What does he do?"

"His name is George Neville. Angelo, don't laugh. He is George, Viscount Neville, and when I'm married to him I'll be Viscountess Neville. His family is scandalized that he is marrying a divorced woman with two illegitimate children. They are less scandalized that he has an illegitimate child of his own. He's a barrister, specializing in patent and copyright litigation. He's four years older than I am. Angelo, he took me fishing in a stream in Scotland—just the kind of thing I love, as you can imagine—and during the afternoon, while I was clomping around in big rubber waders and trying to get the hang of casting, he came upon a friend of his and introduced me. I suspect it was arranged, but that doesn't make any difference. His friend was Charles, Prince of Wales!"

Angelo finished his brandy. "I hope he'll make you happy."

"I can't sit around waiting for you to show up once a month or once every two months. You'll have to meet him. You have to come here and visit John as often as you can, and George will be here."

Angelo nodded.

"I still love you, understand."

He kissed her. "I still love *you,* Betsy," he said quietly.

5

He ate dinner with Betsy so he could stay in the flat and spend as much time as possible with his son. The little boy became fussy after he had eaten his own dinner, and the nanny took him away for his bath and bed.

Conversation lagged over dinner. They had said all there was to say about loving each other. Angelo told her about the new plant and the new Stallion. She said she still drove her S Stallion and that everyone who saw it admired it. He didn't tell her that Cindy found it unsafe and that he was worried about product-liability suits.

He left her not long after eight, promising to stop in London on his way home from Turin.

When he stopped for his key at Dukes Hotel, the clerk handed him a small, pale blue envelope with an embossed crest. "It was brought by messenger, sir. From the Savoy."

He didn't open it until he was in his room. He guessed who had sent it, even though he did not recognize the crest. The note read—

Quite by chance, I find myself in London on the occasion of your current visit. I know you will not be staying the night with Betsy. If you would like to share a drink and ... whatever, telephone me at the Savoy. I will be in my suite after nine.

Anne

She waited for him in her suite at the Savoy. When he embraced and kissed her in the foyer, she was wearing a black jacquard chemise combining lace and sheer nylon. As before, she aroused him with her perfume: a subtle, clean scent that was in no way cloying. They sipped brandies, then went into the bedroom.

He had never known a woman like her. Nothing disturbed her poise.

First, she took out of her handbag a small vial of an essence, which she rubbed into herself before he put his tongue to her. It was a subtle flavoring, tasting something like brandy, though it contained little or no alcohol. It was a pleasant variation. Somewhere he had read—was it in Philip Roth?—that licking a woman's cunt was like licking raw liver; you could do it, but it was difficult to say the taste was a pleasure. He was glad she had bought the brandy essence.

She came twice. He knew only because she stiffened and closed her eyes. She did not moan.

With consummate grace, she blotted her lipstick on a tissue, then lowered her face over him and began to stroke his penis with the tip of her tongue. She nibbled. She sucked. Watching her was like watching her eat a meal: with restraint and elegance. She manipulated him as she manipulated a knife and fork: coolly adroit, without a single awkward movement. He had never been sucked with such calm skill, and it was hugely erotic. When he came, the spasms were deep and violent. She received all he ejaculated into her mouth, then spit it into a wad of tissues—after which she used her tongue and lips to collect his last drops and wiped those off her lips, too.

They sat before a fireplace that was cold but filled with two huge baskets of yellow flowers—both of them still naked, sipping brandy.

"Once a year, Angelo?" she asked. "For me, it was worth the wait. You?"

"More than worth it."

"Once a year is not enough."

"We'll improve on that," he said. "The necessity of being discreet is—"

"A burden. But, as you say, a necessity. We have good marriages, I suppose. Still, these times with you are . . . memorable. Between them, I relive them in memory."

"So do I."

This was the first time he saw her light a cigarette. It was a Gauloise, a harsh unfiltered French cigarette, too strong for American tastes.

"Igor says that putting XB Motors four hundred and seventy-five million dollars in debt is the most brilliant move you've ever made," she said.

"If we're going to compete, we've got to modernize," he said.

"Of course. But that's not what Igor has in mind. I received an offer for my stock. The offer was eight hundred and fifty dollars per share, which is a good deal more than the market price. I have no doubt the same offer was made to Betsy and Alicia, though neither of them has said so."

"It was made to Alicia," he said. "I doubt it was made to

Betsy. I think she would have told me. Of course, they didn't make it to me."

"They've made it to Loren, obviously—and to the Hardeman Foundation. That's the hazard. But two weeks ago they withdrew the offer."

"It's what is known as the poison pill," said Angelo. "When XB acquired a load of debt, it wasn't worth nearly as much to the raiders."

Anne dropped the cigarette into a silent butler, closed the lid, and let it go out—having taken only three or four puffs. "For the moment, you've outfoxed them," she said.

"No. For the moment, I'm making the company do what it has to do if it is to go on competing in the automobile market. That the huge sum we're borrowing is a poison pill is just an additional benefit."

"Angelo . . . Loren will sell. The foundation will sell. As much as I hated Number One, it troubles me deeply to see his company fall into the hands of people who want only to dismantle it and sell off the pieces for as much as they can get."

"He was a rotten old bastard," said Angelo. "But I want his company to survive. For you and me and Cindy and Betsy and Alicia . . . and for Loren the Fourth. I've got more surprises waiting for the raiders." His smile was deadly.

XXIV

1985

1

Angelo's constant presence was required at the construction site where the new XB Motors plant was going up. Even though he was again a vice president with almost complete autonomy, he knew his explicit orders might not be carried out if he was not on the site personally supervising.

On the days when he could not be there, Keijo Shigeto was on the site; but all he could do was report to Angelo if he saw anything wrong; no one would take orders from him.

Angelo had leased a small Learjet to shuttle him and Keijo back and forth between Detroit City Airport and Westchester Airport, so he could always be on the construction site within a few hours of receiving a call from Keijo. Even so, the circumstances compelled Angelo to be away from home a great deal more than he wished or had intended. He'd arranged for the company to lease two suites in a Ramada Inn near the job, one for himself and one for Keijo. He spent more nights there than he wanted to.

2

The Perino children had become accustomed to the idea that their father was not an ordinary man who kept ordinary hours. For that matter, most of their friends' fathers were out of the ordinary, too. Backcountry Greenwich was not a neighborhood of men and women who worked nine to five.

John, who was almost thirteen, attended a private day school for boys. Anna was in a day school for girls. Morris, who was eight, was doing well and was happy in the nearby elementary school, where his sister Valerie was also enrolled. In the middle of a weekday, only two-year-old Mary was apt to be at home; and many afternoons she was playing at parks or walking on the beach with the au pair.

As she'd said she should, Cindy began to spend more time in VKP Galleries.

Marcus Lincicombe had come to exert a powerful new influence on the business. He had convinced Cindy that they should rent the second floor of the building that housed the gallery, install spiral steel staircases, and expand the scope of the gallery by acquiring new lines of art. Glass cases in one of the upstairs rooms displayed netsuke. Two other rooms displayed eighteenth- and nineteenth-century English genre paintings: horses especially but also barnyard and cottage scenes and scenes of squires hunting.

"You don't much like them, and I don't much like them," Marcus said to Cindy and Dietz, "but a significant segment of the public likes them—significant in the sense that they have the money to buy them. You see them in Greenwich homes, don't you? You see them in Park Avenue apartments. The well-to-do feel comfortable with nice, sleek horses and the like. They are *art,* and everyone can recognize what they are. Besides, they're more than a hundred years old."

"They're boring," said Cindy.

"Now, now. Your tastes in art, Cindy, are so eclectic that I am sure you confuse most of the guests who come to your home. Most people don't want to be confused, and they don't want to be challenged."

He was right. The traditional paintings of hounds and horses sold well.

An exhibit of works of the American Leica school—that is, more paintings as photographically realistic as Amanda Finch's—didn't sell as well.

Amanda's work continued to sell. It became apparent as the years passed that her appeal was in the straightforward eroticism of her realistic nudes. She hired more teenage models, always with their parents' consent and almost always with a parent present when she painted. She hired a boy of sixteen and his sister who was twelve and painted them together in wholly innocent scenes of nude brother and sister playing innocent games like checkers and Monopoly. With no explanation as to why a preadolescent girl and an adolescent boy were playing board games naked, the paintings inspired speculation and sold quickly and for high prices. Cindy understood that Amanda had developed a sense of what sold. She painted what sold, and if that was abandoning artistic freedom for money, Amanda did not mind. She was mildly sensational, and she accepted that.

Occasionally Marcus came out to Greenwich. He visited the house only rarely, more often walking up from the railroad station to Amanda's apartment and studio, where Cindy came and joined the two of them. They went to lunch. Three times Cindy and Marcus returned from lunch to spend an hour or so in Amanda's bedroom. Much more often, Cindy took the train to the city, spent time at VKP Galleries, routinely had lunch with Marcus, often with Dietz or an artist joining them, then sometimes spent a midafternoon hour in Marcus's apartment.

It was all but inconceivable, Cindy told herself, that a woman married to Angelo Perino could give herself to Marcus Lincicombe. Angelo was everything that Marcus was not. Except that Angelo was absent too often. Marcus was *there*. He had time. He *took* time.

He rarely saw her children, but he asked about them, and he was patient with her stories of their sayings and doings. He convinced her he was interested—and maybe he was. He was poised in the presence of Angelo and tried to ask him cogent but nonprying questions about XB.

Cindy's only objection to him was his ever-present pipe. When they were in a place where he could light up, she asked him to brush his teeth before they drew close together. The stink of his tobacco clung to his clothes and even to his skin. Only after they had showered was he free of it.

He was an ingratiating lover. He seemed to wonder if he were capable of satisfying, and labored to prove he could— prove to himself perhaps as much as to her. Though he was a small man, he was well hung. He was knowledgeable. He mounted her like a stallion, but he made small adjustments in his posture and hers, to penetrate as deeply as possible and vary the sensations as much as he could.

Because she had stopped taking the pill, they used condoms.

3

In the fall of 1985 the restyled Stallion was delivered to the dealers. It was lower. It was sleeker. Cindy did not protest having to drive one for a few weeks. It was a little more powerful than the earlier model. Virtually every one sold was air-conditioned, and it needed more power to run the compressor without needing downshifting on hills. It was an immediate success.

Trade publications and even general-interest magazines ran articles on the plant in which the Stallion was built. Dealers reported that some buyers at least were attracted to the car because they had heard it was built to high quality standards in the most modern of automated factories.

The new Stallion was also called another major success for Angelo Perino.

1986

4

Everyone who knew thirteen-year-old John Perino called him a handsome boy because he was tall and muscular, with dark hair and dark eyes. He played lacrosse and tennis and had already won ribbons and a trophy for swimming. Girls took an interest in him, and he was beginning to receive telephone calls, some of which would drag out for an hour as a girl or several girls giggled on the other end of the line. He received invitations to parties. Some of the parties turned out to be kissing parties.

Sondra Mead was fifteen in the spring, and her parents promised her a grown-up birthday party—a party where parents would not be present to supervise. They exacted a promise that the kids would not drink, but apart from that they were free to party as they wished.

The Meads lived on an estate. They had converted a fieldstone building that had once been a carriage house into a party house. Sondra's parents used it for that purpose themselves. It had a pool table and a Ping-Pong table, as well as a table with a roulette wheel and a bar that could be locked.

Sondra, who was usually called Buffy, invited John Perino to her party. He was not her date; she invited several other boys; but when he accepted her invitation, she announced her triumph to her classmates at Greenwich Academy—

"Guess who's coming! *John Perino*!"

"Oooh!"

The party began at seven. Cindy intended to stop by at ten to drive John home, but Sondra's mother said she was driving another teenager home who lived near the Perinos, so she'd be glad to drop John off.

He wore a maroon cashmere sweater over an open-collar white shirt, with charcoal gray slacks. He carried the present Cindy had bought for the girl: a silk neck scarf.

John was not shy. He had poise. When he handed Buffy her present and she kissed him, he was not flustered.

None of these teenagers were shy or felt uncomfortable about being with members of the opposite sex. The girls and boys did not retreat to opposite sides of the room and titter. They chatted together, and shortly they began to dance. Buffy sought out John and waited for him to ask her to dance. He did.

She was a newly matured girl: blond and softly, strikingly beautiful. She was taller than some of the boys at the party, though not taller than John. Her figure was filled out, perhaps as much as it ever would be, which set her apart from most of the girls. She wore a little pink lipstick. Her blond hair hung smoothly around her shoulders.

"Hey, Perino," said one of the boys as he and a girl danced close to John and Buffy. "You sticked me at practice Tuesday."

"Sorry, Ken. I didn't mean to. I apologized at the time."

"You're sure it was an accident?"

"If I ever do it intentionally, you won't stay on your feet," said John.

Buffy squeezed John. "You!" she laughed.

In spite of Buffy's promise that no liquor would be drunk at her birthday party, it was available. One of the boys generated a huge laugh among the other boys when they went in the bathroom and gingerly untied a condom bound to his leg. Poured into two glasses, it contained more than half a pint of vodka.

Vodka was the liquor of choice, because it would not be on the young people's breath when they went home. Besides the half pint delivered in the stretched condom, other half pints arrived in flasks and other concealable bottles. The liquor went into Cokes and ginger ale. A little of it was tossed back straight.

John had never tried it before but, of course, was not going to refuse. Ken made sure his Coke got an especially heavy shot of vodka.

None of them refused it. None got drunk—they had not smuggled in enough to do that—but an hour after the party began every one was gently happy.

Some of the boys began a chant—"Tit-ies, tit-ies, tit-ies!"

It was a game. The boys went down to the cellar of the

carriage house, where lawn tools were now stored. The girls took off their sweaters, blouses, and bras. Each boy in turn was blindfolded and allowed to fumble his way up the stairs and into the game room. There one of the girls took his hand and led him to each of the others. He was allowed to feel the bare breasts of each girl and say who he thought she was.

All the boys identified Buffy. She was the most fully developed. John identified her, and she kissed him on the cheek. She was the only girl he identified. Some of the other boys had played this game before and had a sense of what some of the girls were like. Others went steady and knew very well the feel of their own girl's breasts. Everyone laughed as each boy guessed.

Then another chant, this one from the girls. "Peck-er, peck-er, peck-er!"

The girls trooped to the cellar. The boys took off their pants and undershorts and stood around the pool table. Each blindfolded girl circled the table, giggling as she handled shafts and scrotums, blushing as she spoke a name.

Buffy lifted John's erect shaft in her left hand and ran the fingers of her right hand over it. "This is John," she whispered. All the boys applauded. She kissed him on the mouth before she returned to the cellar.

In the kitchen a little later, where they poured tiny amounts of vodka into their Cokes, she took his hand in hers and said, "I knew it was you. Okay. I've touched it. Now I want to see it."

5

Buffy could not contain her excitement. On the telephone the next morning, she told all to her friend Linda Falstaff.

"Oh, God! You won't *believe*!"

"Are you telling me you . . .?"

"Jesus! Yes! And, hey! It was perfect! It was, like, more than I ever imagined! Oh, God, Lin! *Jesus*!"

"How *could* you? I mean . . . the necessary privacy?"

"Luck is how. Goddamned luck! Hey! You 'n' me went to see *Prizzi's Honor* last week. I touted it to my father and mother—hey, never dreaming that would get to be important. But I knew when it let out. I knew they wouldn't be home before a quarter after eleven. And the moms and dads picked the kids up about ten. Your mom—"

"Old prompt-and-conscientious picked me up on the dot of ten."

"Right. By a quarter after, nobody was left but John and me and Muffy. Mom had said she'd drive Muffy home, 'cause her folks were in New York for a play last night. She was gonna drive John home, too. So we had an hour to—"

"But what'd Muffy do, sit and watch?"

"We poured her all the vodka that was left. She had a pack of smokes. She sat on the bench outside and drank and smoked. Besides giving us our privacy, she was our watchdog, just in case. Talk about a friend."

"So what'd you guys do?"

"Well . . . you know. What we wanted to do."

"Buffy Mead, if you don't tell me every detail, we're not friends anymore. We've had a deal for a long time. Right? The first one would tell the other one every last detail, so the other one would have the benefit of the experience. So it turns out—"

"*Okay!* You couldn't *keep* me from telling you."

"So. So how'd it go?"

"I'm gonna admit something. I mean . . . faced with it, I mean really, I kinda chickened. And, hey! So did he. We both said, we don't really *have* to. He said I didn't have to. I asked him if he really wanted to, and he said yes. Well . . . that'd have made me a cockteaser, if I'd backed down. So I said, hey—and we did it."

"Stop there and I'll kill you!"

"Well . . . okay, we had to take off our clothes, of course. And we did that. And then we kissed. And he played a little bit with my boobies. But . . . you won't believe this . . . he was kind of soft. I mean, it wasn't the way it was when I grabbed it during the game. I was glad. He was a little afraid, the way I was. So I took it in my hands and rubbed it against my belly, and it got big and hard again, right off."

"I've touched them in the game. Would you believe I've never *seen* one?"

"Lin, the thing is *beautiful*! I mean, it's the total symbol of male power! We tried it on the couch. Not enough room. So I climbed up on the pool table, and he climbed up on the pool table, and . . .well . . . you know."

"Yes, I know. But tell me!"

"Well . . . Lin . . . it's not as easy as you might think. I spread my legs, and he got on top of me and started to shove himself in, and . . . well, it wasn't easy. I was too tight for him. And then he went limp again. I used my hands to get him up, and he tried again. It . . . okay, I got up and bent down on him and spit on him, to make him slipperier. Then it worked. Then he got in. And then . . . God, Lin, it was heaven! I mean, he shoved it in *so hard* and *so deep*!"

"Didn't it hurt?"

"Yes, it hurt, but it hurt *good*! I tell you, Lin, if my father and mother had walked in right then, we'd have gone on till we were finished and talked about it afterward."

"Jesus! Didn't you guys use a *rubber*?"

"We'll have to think about that next time."

"Buffy! You lucky bitch! *John Perino*!"

"I love him, Lin. And he loves me, too. We talked about how we'd get married after we get out of school."

6

Loren van Ludwige was fourteen years old. His father was proud of him. So was his mother. As had been agreed, he had finished his elementary schooling in an English public school and was now a student at l'École St. François Xavier in Paris.

If the choice had been his, Loren would not have been there. Nor would he have attended St. George's, where his bare buns had been flogged, first by masters, then by upperclassmen performing their duty of hazing. He had not wanted to play rugby, or to run cross country, or to row a scull. But he'd done it—and showered afterward under cold water. Knowing he would be sent to school in Paris later, he had studied French diligently and had won honors in the subject. He had won honors in math as well. His masters marked him deficient, though, in moral philosophy and economics.

At l'École St. François Xavier he was no longer beaten. His worst punishment there was boredom. He knew all the French he'd ever need to know, and the subtleties of seventeenth- and eighteenth-century grammar, as found in the plays of Racine and the essays of Montesquieu, did not interest him. Educated at St. George's to regard Napoleon as a monster, he was intrigued to discover that the emperor was a great national hero to the French. His instructors admired Loren's mastery of numbers, but engineering courses were not offered at l'École. The curriculum emphasized the arts. He was expected to draw and paint, to compose a work of music, and to write a play—all in the manner of some French artist of another century, precisely identifying the influence and elucidating it in notes accompanying his work.

None of the students were allowed outside the walls of the school's grounds, except when they went together in the company of an instructor to visit the Louvre, Les Invalides, or some other museum or monument.

Loren was intelligent enough to know he was receiving a superb education. But he looked forward to the day when he would move to an American university and taste the freedom he had heard American students enjoyed.

The boarding schools his parents had chosen for him had given him one more thing he appreciated. At St. George's his schoolmates had not liked the name Loren any better than he liked it himself. They had called him Ren. The French pronounced Loren *Loh-rawn* and would have called him Ron if he had not objected. He asked his classmates to call him Van, for van Ludwige. They liked that. To the French, "Van" was *vin*—wine. So he became Van. Some of his instructors innocently called him Van van Ludwige. To his father's annoyance, he began to write his name Van

Ludwige. Betsy was amused that he had dropped his first name, but she still thought of him as Loren the Fourth and didn't tell her father he had renounced the name.

Van had inherited the best of the Hardeman genes, plus some very good ones from Max van Ludwige. He was an exceptionally handsome, tall, well-built young man.

At fourteen he had the same problem many fourteen-year-old boys confronted—he was sexually mature and sexually deprived. So was his roommate, Charles Bizien. They looked to each other to solve the problem—promising, however, that they were not "that kind of fellow" and would turn to females as soon as an opportunity arose.

Their sexual encounters were dangerous. Monitors patrolled the halls of the dormitories and could walk in on them at any moment. The first one who woke, probably to go to the bathroom, at, say, three or four in the morning, woke the other.

They did something that was a tradition at l'École St. François Xavier: rather than go down the hall to the toilet at three or four in the morning, they pissed out the window. It was so common that windows in the dormitory were called *pissoirs*. Whoever woke first would stir his roommate before he went to the window. The one who had not wakened first paid a penalty: to have to take into his mouth the final drops of urine that could never be gotten rid of and remained for the roommate to taste. They sucked each other off in the hour before dawn. They rarely missed a night. Nearly every pair of roommates did it.

As Van and Charles were both Europeans, neither boy was circumcised. Neither one could imagine how a man could enjoy sex if his most sensitive nerves had been cut off and thrown away. They pinched each other's foreskins between their fingers and used their tongues and lips on them to further animate their pulsing penises.

They did not attempt anal penetration. It didn't appeal to them, though it did to some of the boys at l'École St. François Xavier. For variation, they masturbated, sometimes rubbing their cocks together, sometimes each boy manipulating his own, sometimes each doing the other.

They proclaimed themselves undying friends who would love each other all their lives. Each one, though, declared he wanted a girl and would love her even more.

7

      On the night when John Perino took Buffy Mead's virginity—and gave her his—Van Ludwige and Charles Bizien sucked each other for the hundredth or hundredfiftieth time. Because of the time difference, it may have occurred at the same hour.

At that hour, too, Cindy was in bed with Marcus in Amanda's studio apartment. Betsy, who had by now given birth to a daughter by Viscount Neville and had just learned she was pregnant again, awoke and roused Angelo. Her husband was trying a case at the Winchester assizes, and she had been unable to resist the opportunity to be with Angelo at least one more time.

XXV

1987

1

Loren and Roberta sat over lunch with Betsy in the Neville town house facing Grosvenor Square. It was a Regency house, not entirely as elegant as the flat Betsy had given up on Regent's Park, but roomier, with lots of space for the three children living at home: John Hardeman and Charlotte and George Neville. The viscount's mother had moved out reluctantly, consenting to do so only when she learned that three young children were about to move in. She had taken most of her furniture, which had suited Betsy perfectly. At Angelo's suggestion—though the origin of the suggestion was known to almost no one—she had engaged Marcus Lincicombe as a consultant to help her explore the shops of London for the furniture and art that turned the house into a showplace.

Most of the money spent on the refurnishing of Neville House had been Betsy's.

Betsy was thirty-five years old. Another secret, known to Angelo and her husband and to no one else, was that Betsy, now the mother of five, had submitted to surgery that made it impossible for her to become pregnant again. She was no longer the playgirl she had been for many years, nor was she yet the incipient matron; she was an impressively handsome

229

woman, ageless in the beauty that promised to remain with her all her life.

Her elegance did not approach that of Princess Anne Alekhine—she remained too earthy for that—but the Viscountess Neville had been presented to the queen, in spite of the fact that she had an illegitimate son and daughter, and had carried herself off so well that the London tabloids pounced on her and declared her a new celebrity.

The first course of their lunch was cold borscht. Loren's third Scotch sat beside his soup plate. He was in a Hardeman mood.

"Can you really promise your husband that his children are his and not Angelo Perino's?" he asked.

"Fuck off, old boy," Betsy replied. "Can you really promise anyone I'm your daughter? Anne wasn't your father's daughter. Am I yours? Or did Number One do it again?"

Loren flushed deep red. "Damn it, you go too far."

Roberta fluttered her hands. "Stop it, you two! Loren . . . Betsy. Please."

Betsy sighed. "In the Hardeman family, nobody knows who is what. How can any of us be sure of anything? I'm sure of one goddamned thing. You've got two children, Father, who are really Angelo's."

"Betsy! What the hell?"

"Two XB Stallions. What's kept the company alive. Without them—"

"No one's going to argue about that," Roberta interjected. "The man's an automobile genius."

"The man's a genius *thief*," said Loren. "He means to steal everything that's ours. Everything! Will you ever be able to get it through your heads that Perino's a mafioso?"

"Without him, there wouldn't be anything to steal," said Betsy calmly. "He bailed out Number One's ass, and he's bailed out yours."

"You give him too much credit," said Roberta. "And your father deserves more credit than you give him."

"For what?" Betsy sneered.

"You say there'd be no company without the Stallions. Well, there'd be no Stallions if it hadn't been for your father. Angelo Perino is an engineer. Without very capable management, there would have been no money to build the cars."

"It was Angelo's name that moved the New York banks to let loose the four hundred and seventy-five million dollars," said Betsy.

"Because he meddled," said Loren. "I could have gotten the money."

"Where?"

"My friend Herbert Froelich could have come up with it."

Betsy smiled and nodded. "You'd have had to pledge every share you own and every share the Hardeman Foundation owns. Froelich would have pressed for payment before the Stallion began to make money, and he'd have taken over the company."

"What do you suppose Perino plans to do?"

"He'll be the next CEO of XB Motors," said Betsy bluntly.

"Over my dead body."

"That way or any other way."

"I've got a big surprise for you, slut. When I cash out—"

Betsy nodded. "I know. There won't be any XB Motors for Angelo to take away from you. But don't count on cashing out. It may not work."

"I can do it," said Loren stubbornly. "You just watch me."

2

Angelo and Betsy lay in each other's arms on a king-size bed in his hotel suite in Tokyo. Angelo was there to talk to Tadashi Komatsu. With her usual perspicacity, Betsy had learned he was going to Japan and where he would be staying. She had somehow managed to convince her husband that she needed to fly to Detroit, which is where he thought she was. In fact, that is where she had changed planes.

"I had to see you as soon as possible," she said. "He's gonna do it. He's going to sell out."

"Well . . . he has control," said Angelo quietly.

"Right. Look, it's like this . . . Number One gave my father and Anne each ten percent of the stock in Bethlehem Motors many years ago. My father lost half of his when my mother divorced him, so she owns five percent. Then, under Number One's will, my father got another twenty-five percent, which made him thirty percent, but he gave five percent to Roberta. I got fifteen percent. Number One handed out three percent to employees he thought were loyal to him. He funded the Hardeman Foundation with thirty-five percent. The foundation will vote its stock whatever way my father says, so that gives him control."

"You and Anne are trustees," said Angelo, "but you are outnumbered."

"Randolph and Mueller are my father's creatures—not to mention that he's made Roberta a trustee. Number One was stupid when he let my father appoint Randolph and Mueller trustees. In those years he wasn't paying enough attention."

"So you have fifteen percent, Anne has ten percent, Alicia has five, and I have two."

"A few short of a majority," she said wryly.

"That thirty-some percent may be more significant than you think. I've been talking to Paul Burger. Minority shareholders have rights. I'd talk to Paul if I were you. We might be able to elect a director. Maybe even two."

"What difference would it make?"

"Well, I'm going to confront Loren with a big new proposition. That's why I'm here in Japan. A new car. A totally new car. For the twenty-first century."

Betsy nuzzled his neck. "How often do I get to be with you, my one love?" she whispered. "Fuck cars. We can talk about cars and directors in a London restaurant, with George listening. Goddamnit! I want to make love with you! Why else did I fly all the way to Japan? Two nights . . . three nights at best. Then I have to go home. Tell me you love me, Angelo Perino! Tell me that, and I'll reward you. Tell me that and the Viscountess Neville, a chum of the queen, is gonna suck your cock till you can't come any-more!"

232

3

"When we repay all the loans, Froelich will move again," said Angelo to Bill Adams. They sat together in the Four Seasons, over a lunch of crab cakes.

"He wants that state-of-the-art plant you built to manufacture the new Stallion," said Bill. "He could sell that to— he could sell it to any number of companies. It's a beautiful piece of engineering. Any one of the Big Three car companies would like to have it. The Japanese would buy it. The Germans. The Russians would buy it if they could find the money. Anyway, he—"

"All Froelich has to do is quit manufacturing automobiles," said Angelo. "Kill the Stallion."

Bill Adams nodded. "He can sell the plant for what he proposes to pay for the stock. Then he unloads everything else the company owns, as profit."

"Betsy says Loren will sell his stock. On top of that, he'll tell the trustees of the Hardeman Foundation to sell its stock—and since they were Number One's creatures and are now his, they'll do what he says. A foundation is better off with a hundred million in cash than—"

"There's the key," said Bill.

"Key?"

" 'In cash.' Suppose Froelich & Green can't come up with enough cash to buy the Hardeman Foundation's stock plus Loren's? Then they'll offer something besides cash: stock in their own company, warrants, notes, whatever. Loren Hardeman might be fool enough to accept what they offer. But the foundation is subject to Michigan laws that limit the kinds of securities a charitable trust can buy and hold. Blue-sky securities offered by Froelich & Green won't qualify."

"What if they come up with cash?" asked Angelo. "I mean, I suppose they have *some* financial clout. They've raided successfully before. Maybe they can raise enough cash."

Bill Adams smiled. "I very much doubt they'll be able to do that," he said. "They're not well thought of on the Street."

4

Angelo relieved Keijo Shigeto of all responsibilities relating to the Stallion. Satisfied that his Japanese partner was an engineering genius, he wanted his undivided attention for a new project.

They sat in the Perino living room: Angelo and Cindy, Keijo and Toshiko. By now everyone had abandoned the pretense that Keijo was on loan to Angelo. The family had been in the States five years now, and none of them expressed any desire to return to Japan, except of course for filial visits.

Three aircraft companies were using their epoxy resin material for wings and fuselages, and their license had just been renewed by Shizoka. CINDY, Incorporated, was earning revenue and a profit. In fact, Tadashi Komatsu had acknowledged the value of manufacturing improvements made by CINDY, and the new license was more a partnership agreement than just a license. Shizoka remained committed to the idea that epoxy resin would be used in automobile bodies. Its success in the S Stallion was ample evidence of its practicality.

The four had been discussing this over martinis before dinner when Angelo grinned and said, "Of course, that's not the big change that has to come. The real change is something far more fundamental."

Keijo nodded. "The electric car," he said.

"I've read two business-page stories in the last week saying it can't be done—worse, that it can *never* be done," said Angelo. "Well, by God, I'm convinced it *can*. More than that, it *has* to be done. We can't go on burning fossil fuels. Even if we don't run out of them, which we will sooner or later, they are expensive, inefficient, and polluting."

"Did you see the cartoon?" Cindy asked. "I mean the one showing the car going along pulling a trailer with tons of batteries?"

"Chemical batteries," said Angelo. "Lead cells, with acid. Chemical batteries are to the new technology as mechanical typewriters are to computer word processors."

"Or worse," said Keijo. "Like sailing ships to intercontinental jet aircraft."

"Fuel cell," said Toshiko with a bright smile.

"One possibility," said Angelo.

"How are you going to fuel a car with hydrogen?" Cindy asked. "The stuff is dangerous. You could have an explosion like the one that destroyed the *Hindenburg*. Anyway, how would a filling station handle it?"

"The most successful experiment right now," said Angelo, "cooks methanol, which breaks down into carbon dioxide and hydrogen. The hydrogen goes into the fuel cell. The CO_2 is discharged into the air. A fuel cell small enough to fit under the hood of a conventional automobile can produce as much power as an eighty-horsepower engine. Of course, there are disadvantages—cost being one."

"There are other approaches," said Keijo. "The flywheel battery is one."

"Do you really expect XB Motors to build an electric car?" asked Cindy. "Loren—"

"To hell with Loren," said Angelo. "We're going to build the car, with him or without him."

"The difference in with him or without him," said Cindy, "is that with him you have big manufacturing capacity and a chain of dealers, and without him you'll have a little company building experimental cars in a garage."

"Something like that is how Apple Computers and Microsoft got started," said Keijo somberly, yet with a measured smile.

5

"He's a handsome kid," said Amanda quietly to Cindy, nodding toward John, who stood nude on her model platform.

"I don't think he's a virgin anymore," said Cindy, equally quietly.

"At *fourteen*?"

"If you two are going to stand over there talking about me, I don't know if I'll be able to do this," said John.

"Sorry, John," said Cindy. She walked away from Amanda and her easel and sat down on the studio couch.

"Are you absolutely sure you want to do this?" Amanda asked. She was sketching with charcoal on a stretched canvas. "I don't want a model who's posing when he doesn't really want to."

"It's a family tradition," said John with a faint smile.

"We discussed it," said Cindy. "I didn't want him to think I was pressing him about it."

"I'll be the only guy in my class who was ever painted this way," said John. "I wouldn't even think of doing it if you weren't a genuine and well-known artist. I like the paintings you did of my mother. I like my father's portrait."

"I have to warn you," said Amanda. "A boy who posed for me several years ago later said he regretted it. It embarrassed him with his classmates to have them see his picture in galleries."

"I'm not bashful," said John simply.

Cindy and Amanda exchanged amused glances. They were not sure why, but as he stood there holding his pose, his member was not flaccid but stood at a slight angle from his scrotum, in a nascent erection.

At fourteen he had the musculature and organ of a man. He was angular, no longer soft. His father was a hairy man, and apparently John was going to be too; already he had dark hair on his chest, not just in his armpits and crotch. His self-assurance was impressive.

Cindy was glad she had chosen to bring the family out from the city to Greenwich and enroll the children in private schools. John's friends were intelligent, poised, and well mannered, just as he was. So were Anna's friends. Her only concern was how soon they would be exposed to drugs and alcohol and how early they would become sexually active. Amanda would pay John well for modeling, and Cindy wondered what he intended to do with the money. It would be his own; he would not have to account to her or his father for it. She wondered if that—and not his admiration of Amanda's artistic talent—were not his chief motive for agreeing to pose.

Anyway, the picture he was posing for now would be hers. She had already bought it. He would pose for five. The other four would go on sale at VKP Galleries.

1988

6

John and Buffy went into New York on an afternoon train, on a frigid Saturday in February. He took her to VKP.

"*John!* Oh, my *God!*"

She had not seen the painting his mother had bought. It hung in the master bedroom, and he had not taken her there again.

A woman browsing in the gallery recognized John as the model for two of the paintings hanging there in the main room on the first floor and she smiled at him.

"How about you?" he asked Buffy. "Amanda pays a good fee."

"My parents would go ballistic."

He shrugged. "Well, my mother owns the gallery. I guess that makes a difference. I mean, our whole family is into art."

"I wish I could get my parents to buy one of those," said Buffy.

"Uh, I'd just as soon you didn't," said John.

XXVI

1988

1

At 10 A.M. Loren Hardeman the Third rapped on the table with a ballpoint pen and called to order the 1988 meeting of the stockholders of XB Motors, Incorporated. Present were himself, Betsy, Roberta, Angelo, and James Randolph, director of the Hardeman Foundation.

"The chair takes note," said Loren with a note of grim sarcasm in his voice, "that Elizabeth, Viscountess Neville, holds proxies for her mother, Alicia Hardeman, and her aunt, Anne, Princess Alekhine. This means that my daughter Betsy will be voting three hundred thousand shares."

Betsy glowered at him. "Not exactly," she said. "During his lifetime my great-grandfather made some small gifts of stock to six employees he considered loyal to him and deserving of his gratitude. Five of those six, or their heirs, have also given me their proxies. The heirs to the sixth will not be voting. In addition, Mr. Perino has given me his proxy. I will be voting three hundred and forty-six thousand, five hundred shares. I hand you those proxies."

Loren turned to the corporate attorney, Ned Hogan, who sat uncomfortably behind him. "Can she come in here with additional proxies on the very day of the meeting?"

The lawyer nodded.

"Fine," said Loren, dismissing Betsy with a contemptuous gesture. "So you're going to vote three hundred thousand whatever. Why would the six employees or their heirs give *you* their proxies?"

Betsy smiled. "It could be because I asked them and you ignored them. It could be because they consider me a more worthy heir to Number One than you are."

"Fine, fine. So you're going to vote a little more than a third of the shares," said Loren impatiently.

Betsy nodded and now grinned. "The chair has also taken note, I trust, of the written notice filed ten days ago."

"It has been reviewed by counsel," said Loren. "This . . . 'notice of intention to vote cumulatively' means, the lawyers advise me, that a stockholder voting thirty percent of the stock is entitled to elect a member of the board of directors."

"Basic corporation law," said Betsy. "Protection of the rights of minority stockholders. With more than thirty-four percent of the stock, nearly thirty-five percent, the minority is entitled to elect two of the five directors."

Loren glared at the attorney, who raised his eyebrows and nodded. He leaned forward and spoke in Loren's ear. "Maybe not with thirty percent even," he said. "But with almost thirty-five—"

Loren turned and faced Betsy, his face flushed with anger. "Well, just which of our directors do you propose to discard? And who do you propose to replace them?"

"Dump your deadwood," she said, chuckling. "I'll leave it to you to decide who *they* are. My nominees are myself and Angelo Perino."

Roberta spoke. "I move," she said, "that the stockholders meeting be adjourned for one hour."

2

After lunch the newly elected directors gathered around the same table. They were Loren, Roberta, James Randolph, Betsy, and Angelo. Missing were Professor Mueller and Congressman Briley.

"Isn't this cozy?" said Loren.

Roberta touched his hand under the table. After the conclusion of the stockholders meeting and during the lunch break, she had worked to calm him in his office. She had given him sex rather than take it from him, and when that had not calmed him she had poured him a heavy drink of Scotch.

"I move," said Betsy brusquely, "that Mr. Loren Hardeman the Third be reelected chairman of the board of directors and president of XB Motors, Incorporated."

"I second the motion," said Angelo.

"Those in favor?" Loren asked weakly.

All raised their hands.

"I move," said Betsy, "that Mr. Angelo Perino be elected vice chairman of the board of directors and executive vice president of the corporation."

Loren's face reddened more darkly, but Roberta spoke up quickly and said, "I second the motion."

Loren sighed and said, "Those in favor?" When his wife's hand went up, he raised his own.

Seeing that, Randolph raised his.

3

Betsy grinned at Angelo over the dinner table in the hotel in the Renaissance Center. "It only takes one vote," she said. "Frankly, I was surprised at Roberta. I never imagined she'd do it. So my father's unquestioned control is broken."

Angelo shook his head. "Don't count on it. Roberta's no dummy, and she doesn't surrender. I figure she decided this was not the ground on which to fight. Also, I figure she wants to give us a chance to shoot ourselves in the foot. It was too easy. The real battle is not going to be that easy."

"When are you going to present the idea of the electric car?"

"Not yet. That's when the fight comes."

"Maybe sooner than that, when he tries to sell his stock to Froelich."

Angelo shook his head. "Froelich won't buy it unless he

can buy the foundation stock also and take control. And to do that, he's going to have to come up with cash."

Betsy grinned. "I hope you don't ever outsmart yourself," she said.

She reached for his hand, but Angelo pulled it back. "Betsy, aren't you aware that we're being followed and watched?"

"What are you talking about?"

"Don't look now at the man and woman about two thirds of the way around the fountain. The big guy with the bullet head. The frowsy blond."

"Are you sure?"

He shrugged. "I'm going to find out."

"Jesus, that's *creepy*!"

"I'm going out to make a phone call. Don't look at them. Just glance around casually and pretend you don't notice them. I'll be back in a few minutes."

4

An hour and a half later Angelo and Betsy left their table. Instead of going up to their rooms, they walked out into the parking lot behind the hotel. They walked through several rows of parked cars before they returned to the hotel.

The man who was following them took a blackjack shot to the back of the head, slumped quietly against a Volvo, and dropped to his knees, then to his face, on the pavement. The woman took the second shot, squarely across her face, smashing her nose and breaking a cheekbone. She fell.

Ten minutes later Angelo heard a discreet knock on his door on the eighteenth floor. He did not go immediately to the door. He knew enough to wait a minute. Then he went over and picked up a card he spotted lying on the floor, halfway under the door. One corner was brown with drying blood.

DIXON & BRAGG
Investigators
All Work Strictly Confidential
Leonard Bragg   (333) 867-0500

He went to the telephone and called Betsy's room. "The coast is clear," he said. "My place or yours?"

5

Cindy lay beside Marcus in Amanda's bedroom. Amanda had gone out, and her answering machine was taking her calls. The machine was in the bedroom, and they could hear her messages.

One was from Dietz, who said he'd be coming in on the 4:07 train from Grand Central, which would arrive at 4:45. He suggested she make a dinner reservation.

One was from Mrs. Marna Mead, Buffy's mother, who wanted Amanda to call her as soon as possible. She was familiar with the paintings of Greg Hammersmith, admired them very much, she said, and had taken an interest in Buffy's suggestion that she buy one of the paintings of John.

This call had come just as Cindy was rolling a condom onto Marcus. The voice coming through the recorder was brisk and businesslike; Mrs. Mead wanted to buy a painting of John Perino, and if all of them had been sold she'd commission the painting of another one. While they listened, Cindy leaned over and licked Marcus's dark, wrinkled bag. She smiled when she looked up and finished rolling the rubber down his shaft.

"Are there any left for sale?" he asked.

"No."

"Will he pose for another one?"

"No."

"Is he sorry he posed?"

"No."

Sex between Cindy and Marcus did not vary much. Both of them were imaginative, but neither had exhausted the possibilities of straightforward plunging—not with each other. For her, one of the satisfying elements of it was the warmth that accompanied the heat. Marcus was affectionate, not just ardent.

He had said he was sorry she was married and the mother of five children. Obviously he could not ask her to abandon her husband and her children. He said he would wait. If when all her children were adults she—

No, she had told him. It could never be. She confided in him that Angelo was the father of Betsy's son John. She loved Angelo. She loved Marcus. Betsy loved Angelo. Angelo loved Betsy. It was a tangle.

She did not tell him, and he did not guess, that she loved Amanda, too—not as fervidly, and without a commitment, yet with enough intensity that she did not want to give it up. She and Amanda made love almost casually and not more often than once every other week, but they knew when they wanted each other; the feeling mysteriously came on them at the same time; and they found time and occasion to satisfy it.

Cindy was forty years old. She needed assurance that she had matured handsomely, and the best assurance would be another painting by Amanda. It was on the easel. She would pose for a while when Amanda came home. She knew she could depend on Amanda not to amend, not to flatter, but to portray her with the bleak honesty of a mug shot.

The unfinished painting showed her exactly as she was: a woman with a few shiny stretch marks on her full and rounded belly, with breasts a little softer and not quite as firm as they had been fifteen years ago, with a tush a little slacker than it had once been, but still a woman with much to be proud of, who had lost nothing that couldn't be lost without regret. She had seen Buffy beside the pool and could not help but envy the girl's sleek, taut flesh. Still, the only way to stay that way was to do nothing else, care for nothing else, and still lose the battle in the end.

Amanda would keep this painting. It would hang in her bedroom.

Usually, Marcus made love deliberately, not allowing himself to race ahead of her and finish too soon. In this as in much else about him, he governed himself rationally. Sometimes she wished he would break loose and pound away, heedless for once of whether or not she was going to be fully satisfied. No. Instead he slipped in and out at a measured pace. The sensations were delicious but never tumultuous.

Maybe he was trying to avoid rupturing the condom. This time he did rupture one. When he pulled out and sat back on his heels, there it was, like a collar around his diminish-

HAROLD ROBBINS

ing organ. His gray-pink glans gleamed with the ejaculate he had squirted into her.

She didn't have a douche. They ran water in the bathtub, and she sat in it and rinsed herself out as thoroughly as she could, without confidence.

6

The bullet-headed Leonard Bragg sat at a table in the Red Fox Inn, with his female partner, Patricia Warner.

Len Bragg was a bulky man, broad shouldered, carrying a bit of paunch. He was bald. His brows loomed over his eyes, almost obscuring them. His gray suit fit him poorly; he had gained weight since he bought it.

Trish Warner was a tough-looking woman. Maybe there was nothing she could do about it, but she seemed to have made no attempt to soften her image. Her hair was blond and cut short. Her face was square, with a more prominent jaw than most women had. Her nose was a little less than straight, and she had a small white scar on her right cheek.

Loren came in and sat down at their table.

"I've got another doctor's bill," said Trish. "For eighteen hundred and seventy-five dollars."

"I haven't got it on me in cash," said Loren. "I'll get it to you."

"He says he can take off the scar." She touched the line on her cheek. "But the nose will never be right."

"I still have headaches," Len grunted.

"The worst part is, I'm scared," said Trish. "They took a card off Len. They know who we are."

"You didn't warn us," said Len grimly.

"Well, I said I'd pay for the plastic surgery to put your face back together," Loren said to Trish. "And I have. I'm not sure I owed you, but I'm paying it."

"What do you mean you don't owe it?" asked Len darkly.

"You're in a dangerous business. Are you going to tell me this is the first time you've been slugged?"

"All we were supposed to do was follow Perino and the broad. And get some pictures if we could. You didn't tell me who Perino was."

"Who'd you think he was?"

244

"You didn't tell me who his grandfather was. That's the point."

Loren looked up at the waiter who was approaching the table. He ordered a double Scotch with a splash of soda. When the waiter was gone he said, "So you took some lumps. Who you mad at, me? You were doing a perfectly legal job: tailing somebody and trying to get some pictures. Perino had you beaten up. *Perino,* not me. All you've done about it for six months is groan about your hurts and whine about the injustice of it all. You want to *do* something about it?"

"Like what?" asked Trish. She ran her fingers down her nose. That had become a nervous tic with her. "What'd you like us to do, kill him?"

Loren raised his eyebrows. "For, say, half a million bucks?"

Len shook his head. "We'd never live to enjoy it."

"You will if you're smart. In the first place, you don't do it in Detroit."

"Smart . . ."

"Smart. Figure it out. Tell you what I'll do. I'll give you ten thousand for expenses. Figure it out. I can fill you in on where he lives, where he stays when he travels, and all that. You come up with a plan."

"And then?"

"You make your plan. But you don't do a damn thing more until I tell you. I want it done sooner or later, but it's got to be timed right. You've got almost as much reason to hate Angelo Perino as I've got. But don't let that get in your way. You be cool and work out a plan. I'll get some cash to you in a day or two—the eighteen hundred and seventy-five dollars for the doctor bill, too."

7

Dr. John Perino died on August 6, 1988. He was eighty-two years old.

The telephone call came at two in the morning. Angelo was not at home, and Cindy answered. She spent the next four hours trying to reach Angelo and finally succeeded only with Keijo's assistance. Angelo was with Tadashi Komatsu at the country club outside Tokyo, where they were discussing the development of the electric automobile.

Angelo caught a Northwest flight to Detroit and arrived there after his shock had settled down to numbness. Cindy had brought John and Anna with her. The other three children remained at home with the au pair.

Angelo's brother and his wife brought three of their children and five grandchildren from Florida. His elder sister came without a husband but with four children and four grandchildren. His younger sister came with her second husband and children from each marriage.

The widow, Jenny, received all these people and many others with reserved dignity, wiping her eyes occasionally with the handkerchief she clutched in her left hand, otherwise bearing up and listening intently to each condolence. She greeted most people in English, some in Italian.

The funeral, held at St. Jude's, attracted more than five hundred mourners. Betsy flew in from London. Alicia Hardeman came from Greenwich. Loren and Roberta were there. The aged and fragile Jacob Weinstein arrived from Arizona on a private jet. A contingent of four Sicilians came all the way from Palermo: two old men and two middle-aged men dressed uniformly in black suits and shiny black silk neckties. They were greeted with respectful *abbracci* by a score of swarthy Italian-speaking men. The Governor of Michigan came, as did the mayor of Detroit. As many as fifty physicians and surgeons attended the funeral.

"You see," Cindy whispered to John and Anna, "your grandfather was a great man."

John nodded solemnly. Anna, brought to tears by the occasion, covered her face and wept.

A dozen television cameras stared at the church steps as the bell tolled and the casket was carried out by pallbearers. Four open vehicles carried the flowers. Sixty cars followed the hearse to the cemetery.

The house was not large enough for the reception following the burial service, so it was held in the garden of the Italian-American Club, the scene of many such sad receptions and also of many joyful wedding receptions.

Of the sons and daughters of Dr. John Perino, only Angelo remained fluent in Italian. He greeted the visitors from Sicily on behalf of the family and thanked them for coming.

"*Buongiorno, Signore Calabrese. Molte grazie, molte grazie. Questa è mia moglie, Cindy. Anche mio figlio e mia figlia, Giovanni ed Anna.*"

Jenny was invited to go home with each of her sons and daughters. She insisted she would remain in the house where she and her beloved husband had lived for so many years. She had many friends in the old neighborhood and would not be alone.

Cindy and Betsy stood together, sipping red wine. Since Betsy knew that Cindy understood who was the father of her son John and had not made any great fuss about it, she felt drawn to Cindy.

"I've always wondered what it would be like to be a member of a big, loving, supportive family," said Betsy.

"It could be smothering," said Cindy. "Of course, they never smothered Angelo, but—"

"Who could smother Angelo?" asked Betsy.

"I guess I've started a big family," said Cindy. "I hope they won't smother each other."

"Number One had two children," said Betsy. "Number Two died thinking he'd had two, but Anne wasn't his. My father only had one. He's said some disparaging things about my having five. He's said some disparaging things about your having five."

Cindy smiled and shook her head. She hadn't told Angelo and didn't tell Betsy that she was carrying a sixth.

XXVII

1988

1

Cindy confided in Amanda.

"I'm not afraid of what Angelo will say," she told her. "After all, he has a son who is not mine. Anyway, he can very well believe it's his."

"Until the child grows up and is prematurely bald," said Amanda. "I'm not sure you could keep the secret. You won't want to live with that. Anyway, how could you ever let it happen?"

"As soon as I was married, I wanted children. We had one the first year. Then I took the pill for a while, to put two years between John and Anna. I did the same thing with Morris and Valerie and then separated Mary from Valerie by four years. After Mary, I went on the pill again and took it for five years. Then my gynecologist told me it was time to quit taking it, at least for a while. So . . ."

Amanda was still working on her third painting of Cindy. Cindy stood on the platform. Amanda left her easel, came over and stepped up beside Cindy, and kissed her, first on the mouth, then on each nipple. She caressed her, then hugged her, before she returned to her work.

"Marcus wants to tell Angelo. He wants the baby."

"He doesn't have to raise it," said Amanda.

"I don't have much time. I have to make a decision."

"Is it difficult for you?" Amanda asked. "I mean, if you decide to have an abortion, is that difficult for you?"

Cindy nodded. "When we were in Detroit for the funeral, Angelo's mother asked me if the children had been baptized. I had to tell her no. She asked me to promise her they would be baptized. Of course, she wants them baptized Catholics. I can't have that done. A priest won't do it unless you commit yourself to raising the children as Catholics. I haven't done anything about it yet. I was baptized in a Presbyterian church. Angelo was brought up as a Catholic. The point is, if I have an abortion, I'm not sure I can tell him. I think I know Angelo, but—"

"Let me ask you something, hon," said Amanda. "He confided in you about the child he gave Betsy. Has he confided anything else? I mean, has he been with other women besides Betsy?"

Cindy shrugged. "Well, I never told *him* about Dietz, either, and certainly not about you and me. Or Marcus. I don't know what he thinks. He's realistic . . ."

"What do you guys call what you've got? An open marriage?"

Cindy smiled. "I'm a child of the sixties. I never became a yuppie. When I took Mary into preschool, I was the oldest mother there. Over tea and cookies one of the young mothers remarked that I probably wasn't as serious as she was, since people of my generation didn't share the same values as people of hers."

manda laughed. "Values," she said. "That word makes me nauseous."

"Anyway, I have to decide."

Amanda came to the model platform again and this time did not step up but leaned forward and kissed Cindy's cleft.

"I can't," Cindy whispered. Suddenly she sobbed. "I just can't have another child!"

Amanda stood with her arms around Cindy's hips, nuzzling her belly. "I'll help you, hon. I've had two abortions. There's a clinic in New Haven. My doctor is a woman. She'll take good care of you. I'll drive you there and back."

The following week, in a clinic in New Haven, the fetus
was removed. The doctor advised Cindy not to take the
pill anymore. She suggested a tubal ligation. The following week, when Angelo was in Detroit and on his way to
Japan, Cindy returned to New Haven and had the operation.

She had not told Marcus. He visited a surgeon in an
office on Park Avenue South and submitted to a vasectomy.
He told her about the vasectomy before she could tell
him about the ligation. She decided not to tell him what
he had done had not been necessary—not for them,
anyway.

2

Trish Warner did not check into a hotel or motel in
Greenwich. She had rented a car at LaGuardia and driven
to Stouffer's Inn on the Cross-Westchester Expressway. She
and Len had agreed that it would be better for her to explore
Greenwich alone. She could change her appearance to some
extent. He could not.

She had run a shaver over her head, reducing her hair to
about a quarter of an inch. That way, her handsome,
expensive dark brown wig fit her perfectly and was much
less likely to be observed as a hairpiece. Perino had of
course never seen what his thug's blackjack had done to her
face, so her disguise was probably perfect.

Her rental car was an inconspicuous Ford. She carried
with her a Nikon camera with a compact mirror telephoto
lens. She mailed her film cartridges to Len in Detroit, from
a post office in Rye, New York.

In the course of four days she had photographed the
Perino house from several angles and had good shots
of people going in and out. She had identified the wife.
And the children. She had an excellent idea of the lay of the
land.

The job could be done with a rifle. Whenever Hardeman
said go.

3

Herbert Froelich was sixty-seven years old. His hair was white, as was his bushy mustache. The flesh of his face sagged and was furrowed with deep wrinkles. He wore little round horn-rimmed glasses and carried himself with the air of a man who was right and honest but had to guard at all times against slanders and attacks.

"I have often dealt," he said in sober, pontifical tones, "with the heirs of men who built empires. Their work was so challenging, so sustaining, so satisfying that they wanted nothing more in their lives. But for their heirs . . . well, the task of maintaining what their ancestors built is not so challenging, is not something they are willing to dedicate their lives to at the cost of all else. They are entitled to some security and comfort."

Loren, Roberta, and Froelich sat over dinner at the Hardeman home in Detroit. Loren had revisited the bar and poured from the Scotch bottle after Roberta had ceased to pour for him, and he was a little fuzzy.

"My husband inherited control of a company that was in deep trouble," said Roberta. "The Sundancer was losing market share. The first Mr. Hardeman had lost touch with reality in his later years."

Froelich nodded and lifted a glass of wine in salute to Loren. "And Mr. Hardeman had the perspicacity to employ Angelo Perino as his automotive engineer and form a partnership with Shizoka to build the XB Stallion, thus snatching the company back from the brink."

"That's exactly right," Loren mumbled.

Froelich nodded and lifted his glass higher. He wore a gray three-piece suit marred by a pack of Marlboros conspicuously bulging his vest pocket. "My associates and I have meticulously analyzed your company," he said. "Since the stock is only privately traded, it is difficult to fix a value. At one time we were prepared to offer eight hundred and fifty dollars a share for it. We contacted you about that. I need hardly tell you, though, that the market collapse of nineteen eighty-seven radically altered all stock values. At this time I am thinking more in terms of six hundred dollars a share. I might be able to convince my associates to offer six hundred and fifty dollars."

"That's quite a comedown, Mr. Froelich," said Roberta gravely.

Froelich nodded. "Money is tight, Mrs. Hardeman," he said. "I doubt you could find another buyer who would pay more than five hundred and fifty dollars. Although the company is paying it off, it is heavily laden with debt."

"What that damned Perino had us borrow to build the fancy new plant," grumbled Loren.

"Which is today your best asset," said Froelich.

Roberta shook her head. "The new figure is a disappointment," she said.

"Look at it from my point of view," said Froelich. "In a situation where money is difficult to come by. If I offer six hundred and fifty dollars a share, I have to offer it to all the shareholders. If all of them accept, I have to raise six hundred and fifty million dollars. And then look at it from your point of view. At six hundred and fifty dollars a share you will be worth a hundred and sixty-two million, five hundred thousand dollars. Granted that at eight hundred and fifty dollars a share you would have been worth fifty million dollars more, you will still be very wealthy people. And freed of the cares of managing the corporation."

Loren nodded. "I guess after all the taxes I'll still be able to buy a first class place in Paris and keep a yacht at St. Tropez."

"Are you going to give us a written offer?" asked Roberta.

"Exactly," said Froelich. "I have to impose some terms. I have to buy control—which means I must have the Hardeman Foundation stock as well as your own. Then, of course, you can't expect me to come up with six hundred and fifty million dollars in cash—a hundred and sixty-two million, five hundred thousand dollars to you. My associates and I will offer a deal, paying part cash, part notes, and part warrants in our own corporate stock. The latter will be priced so as to afford you a substantial profit when you sell the warrants or exercise them. As I said, you can't help but come out of the deal as exceptionally wealthy people. The Paris flat and the St. Tropez yacht will come out of small change for you."

Loren smiled lazily. "I have to see the documents and let my lawyers and accountants review them," he said. "But I think you've got a deal."

4

"I think you don't have any deal at all," said Roberta when Froelich had left the house.

She sat in the kitchen, drinking coffee. Loren, stark naked, rinsed dishes and loaded the dishwasher. Lately, he begged her not to beat him, saying he couldn't take the pain anymore. Sometimes, even so, she flicked him with the whip. It lay on the table now, and twice since he had begun clearing the table and loading the dishwasher, she had snapped him on his buns and made him jump and shriek.

"Come here." He approached her and knelt before her. "First it was eight hundred and fifty dollars a share," she said. "Now it's six hundred and fifty dollars—and not in cash, in funny money. It'll go lower."

"I'm going to be sixty years old this year," he said. "If all we get is *twenty* million, we can retire and live— It doesn't have to be in Paris."

"Is that what you want?"

"I want to have some kind of *life,* Roberta. I want to go where I don't ever again have to hear the name Angelo Perino. He'll take the ultimate screwing on this deal. Number One didn't screw him any better."

"It's your decision," she said.

He lifted his face and looked into her eyes. He nodded. "I'm cashing out," he said.

5

Roberta sat on the couch in Angelo's suite in the Hyatt Regency in Houston. The hour was 10 A.M. She had spotted him in the lobby bar when she checked in last night.

He had been with a woman, and she had not called his room until she could feel confident that the woman, whoever she was, was gone. She mentioned her, and Angelo had laughed and told her the redhead was a computer guru who might be able to contribute something to the design of the electric car. Then they had begun to talk about the car and the company.

"Why kid around?" she asked. "I don't know where my loyalties ought to lie. I'm past that. I can't figure it out."

"Where does Loren think you are?"

"He thinks I'm right here. He thinks I'm down here exploring Houston as a possible place to retire."

"What happened to Paris?"

"They speak French in Paris. I suspect he thinks he'll never learn it."

"He'll never learn to speak Texas either," said Angelo.

She shook her head. "He's not as bad a guy as you think." She sipped from the cup of coffee Angelo had poured for her from the pot on his room-service breakfast tray. "In some ways he's even worse," she added.

"In some ways, I'm more nearly the heir of Number One than he is," said Angelo. "I won't let him destroy the company."

"Can you stop him, really?" she asked.

"Ask me no questions, I'll tell you no lies. Since you don't know where your loyalties should be, it's better not to talk about it."

Roberta shook her head. "I saved one company, and who gives a shit? My first husband died and—"

"People do give a shit," Angelo interrupted. "There are families in Detroit who've worked for Bethlehem Motors, now XB Motors, for more than fifty years. There are people who've been driving Sundancers and now Stallions for as many years—and wouldn't have any other kind of car."

Roberta reached for his hand. "We gonna fuck?" she asked.

He smiled wryly. "You do know where your loyalties lie."

"Don't make fun of me, Angelo," she said quietly. She bent over and kissed him on the neck just below the ear.

"Betsy and I share a tragedy. She couldn't marry you, and neither could I."

"I didn't know you'd thought about it."

"I haven't thought about it. Not really. And my tragedy, really, is not that I couldn't marry you but that I couldn't marry a man *like* you. I've dominated two husbands. I had to. If I hadn't—"

"Don't tell me too much," Angelo interrupted.

She put the coffee cup aside. "What'd I'd really like is a Scotch," she said. "That says something about me, doesn't it? A Scotch before noon."

"How 'bout a martini? Ice cold. A clean taste that doesn't linger. I'll join you in one."

She nodded, and he went to the little bar. "Shall I undress?" she asked.

"We can't fuck if you don't."

"What I plan to do first, lover, we can do without taking off a stitch. Bring it here. Let's see what it feels like when a woman has ice-cold martini on her lips."

6

The Viscountess Neville had ways of getting what she wanted. She wanted her first child, Loren van Ludwige—by now universally known as Van—to be educated at Harvard. He was admitted, to begin in the fall of 1989.

She called Cindy and asked for a favor. Could Van come to the States in June and live with the Perinos until he moved to Cambridge? He had never been in the States, and it was important for him to acclimate himself before he settled into a dormitory in Harvard Yard.

Cindy made a suggestion. Betsy should *bring* Van to the States, not send him, and she should bring John, who could meet his half brothers and sisters.

So it was arranged. They would arrive on June 3: Betsy with her two sons, Van, seventeen, and John, six. Three guests would overflow the house, so Betsy and John would stay with Alicia. Only Van would move into the Perino house, where he would live all summer and, it was hoped, be at least halfway Americanized before he went to Cambridge.

7

Len Bragg wore his best suit, dark blue with a pinstripe. He wore a white shirt with button-down collar and a dark blue tie with tiny white dots. It was a warm spring evening, and he did not need a topcoat or raincoat. Trish wore a burgundy linen suit.

She would drive. She knew the area. Besides, he was a little nervous and did not want to risk making a driving mistake that might attract the attention of the police.

They were sharing a room in a Courtyard Inn in Westchester County: Mr. and Mrs. David Englehardt of Boston. Paying with cash would make a desk clerk remember him, so Len had applied for and received a Visa card in the name Englehardt. He would use it only this once and would pay it off and never use it again. Trish had rented a Chevrolet with the credit card of their agency in Detroit. But that was at LaGuardia, where thousands of cars were rented every day.

Len had bought the rifle in Indiana a year ago. For cash. It was a bolt-action Remington, mounted with a fine telescopic sight. He could drop his man from a hundred yards away. He wouldn't have to come closer. What was more, he could get two or three shots into him within ten or twelve seconds. Once the man fell, he would be an easier target than he'd been when he was standing and probably moving. From a hundred yards away. It would not be necessary to approach closer.

Trish had surveyed the land well. In this part of Greenwich, Connecticut, people tended to build stone walls in front of their houses. That meant that Perino's neighbors were unlikely to spot this car pulled over to the edge of the road.

The way they were going to handle the job was simple. From the parking lot at Westchester Airport they would be able to identify the XB corporate jet as it landed. It had the logo on the tail. They would watch for Perino to come out of the general-aviation building—the facility for nonairline flights—and go to his car. Shooting him was an alternative Trish had suggested they consider. But there would be too many people around. And police, as they discovered when they parked. No, the better way was to shoot him when he got out of the car at home.

Trish had observed that Cindy Perino parked her Porsche inside the garage. The Perino daughter drove a Stallion, which was usually in there, too. Perino parked his own Stallion on the driveway.

All Trish had to do was get ahead of Perino on the road—which she could do by leaving the airport parking lot before he did—and stay far enough ahead of him that he didn't catch up and pass. She didn't want to reach the road in front of the house too soon, either. If they sat on the edge of the road more than two or three minutes, they might attract attention. What was more, Greenwich was a town with a heavy police presence. They patrolled the roads constantly.

This was Thursday evening. If Perino followed his usual schedule, he would arrive at Westchester just about sunset. If he didn't, they would have to watch for him again tomorrow night. He was at home most weekends.

Luck wasn't with them. The XB jet did not land. They waited until ten o'clock.

Len and Trish were not lovers. Placed in the same room, in the same king-size bed, they gratified each other, without much thought or enthusiasm. Any partner would have suited either of them as well.

In the morning they returned to Westchester Airport to see if the jet had come in during the night and was sitting on the ramp. It had not.

They did not drive past the house during the day on Friday. The road on which the Perino house sat was a residential street, and a strange car with New York plates might be noticed if it drove by too often.

They sat in their motel room, nervously watching television. Every five minutes Len went to the window to look out at the car—obsessed with the idea that someone might somehow discover the rifle hidden in the trunk. They ate nervously, too, and drank very little.

At six they went back to the airport.

As the light faded, it was more and more difficult to identify the landing bizjets. But then it came: the XB corporate Lear. It was easy enough to identify, by the prominent logo on the fin—

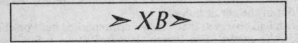

Shortly Perino came out of the general-aviation building. They recognized him—they had watched him for hours that night in the Renaissance Center. He was a bigger man than they had remembered. Knowing his age, which was almost sixty, they had visualized him as smaller. He carried a small suitcase and had a raincoat folded over his arm.

Trish started the rented Chevy, drove to the gate and paid for her parking, then drove up the road toward Greenwich. They were well ahead of Perino, but they could be certain he was back there, no more than two or three minutes behind.

Neither of them spoke a word. In the course of their careers as private investigators, both of them had done despicable things. They had committed burglaries. They had committed assaults. They had tapped telephones illegally. Either one of them could have been in prison. Trish had, in fact, spent thirty days in jail for criminal trespass. But neither of them had ever killed anyone. They had never even contemplated such a thing.

But this . . . They hated Perino. He'd had them slugged. Trish carried on her face the marks left by the heavy blow of a blackjack. She remembered the terror and the pain. Besides, Hardeman was paying them half a million dollars for this hit. They had half of it in hand already. They had laughed over what was so far their worst problem: what to do with money they obviously could not report on their income tax returns.

They had planned their hit carefully, almost lightheartedly. Now, suddenly, the enormity of it was bearing down on them. They were going to *kill a man*! They were silent and thoughtful.

They reached the street. Trish pulled the car over at the

spot she had identified weeks ago as the best place. She turned out the lights.

Len reached to the floor of the backseat and lifted the rifle. It was rolled in a blanket, and he unrolled it. The Remington was a hunting rifle, and the clip was loaded with long, slender cartridges. The bullets had flat tips, so they would expand as they tore through flesh, giving a deer a fatal wound. They would do the same to a man. Len had fired at trees and had marveled at the damage the slugs did, even to wood.

He rolled down the window. He worked the bolt to bring up a cartridge from the clip to the chamber. For the moment he set the safety.

Perino passed them and turned into his driveway.

Len flipped off the safety and put his eye to the telescopic sight. Perino would be getting out of the car under the glare of bright lights mounted on the overhang of the garage roof. That was one place where he could be shot: right there in front of the garage as he got out of the car. The other place was on his doorstep, when he stood with his back to the road and put his key in the lock. The latter would be the better chance, when he was standing still; and that was where Len had decided he would make the shot.

He saw that his judgment had been right. Perino was a man of abrupt movements. He ducked out of the car, grabbed his suitcase and raincoat, and strode toward the house: a bad target. But at the door—

Suddenly that door flew open. Two little girls ran toward Perino. They threw their arms around him, jumping up and down, and pulled him toward the house. Then another one came out, this one a pretty teenage girl who grabbed Perino by the hand. He was surrounded by his children.

"Jesus Christ . . .," Len muttered.

"You can't," Trish whispered shrilly.

"No."

"There'll be another time."

"There *has* to be another time. We've got a quarter of a million dollars of Hardeman's money."

8

"Let it go for now," said Loren. "Things are developing. It may be to my advantage to keep him alive for a while. But don't bank my money and forget about it. I'll call on you again, sooner or later."

9

Another opportunity would not come quickly. Angelo stayed home for a week, to be with the son he rarely saw and to spend time with the rest of the family. They went into New York City to see sights his Connecticut children had never seen: the Statue of Liberty, the view from the top of the Empire State Building, and Manhattan as viewed from a Circle Line cruise ship.

Cindy gave Angelo and Betsy an opportunity to be alone. They did not take advantage of it.

In bed the third night of Betsy's visit to Greenwich, Angelo murmured to Cindy, "I don't deserve a wife as perfect as you. To accept my son by Betsy—"

"Angelo. I'm no saint either."

"I know. I guessed, anyway. Dietz? Marcus?"

"Please. I haven't asked *you* many questions."

"God . . . I'm not going to say I don't care. But I love you more, not less."

Cindy reached for his jock, held it, and squeezed it gently. "I guess . . . probably every woman in the Hardeman family. Including Alicia. Christ! Mother and daughter. And . . . Oh, my God! Even Roberta, huh? Is that why she's so helpful sometimes?"

Angelo smiled and kissed her. "Business is business," he said.

"But you still love me more than all the rest of them put together, don't you? I love you more than anyone else I've ever been with, put together."

"I love you more than all the other women in the world put together," said Angelo.

In this moment of mutual frankness, so beautifully free of recrimination, she was tempted to tell him about the abortion. She had told him about the ligation, saying she'd had it done because her doctor told her she could not take the pill anymore. But the abortion—no. She *couldn't* tell him.

10

For Van, adjustment to American ways was fascinating, welcome—and difficult. He couldn't believe he was supposed to call Mr. Perino and Mrs. Perino Angelo and Cindy. John and Anna Perino introduced him to young Americans. He was astonished to hear them say words like "cock" and "cunt" and, most unbelievable of all, "fuck." They seemed to have no sense of propriety or modesty.

When John took him to his parents' bedroom and showed him the paintings of Mrs. Perino nude and of himself nude, Van blushed.

As he said good-bye to his mother and his little half brother John Hardeman, who were returning to London, Van wondered if he were not being left in a barbaric land with a barbaric family.

But there was one member of the Perino family whom he found truly congenial—fourteen-year-old Anna Perino. She was the most beautiful girl he had ever seen. Not only beautiful, she was gentle and tender; she seemed to understand his confusion and sympathized with him. He hadn't known Anna a week before he decided he loved her. But he hadn't the remotest notion what to do about it.

Van was perplexed by the freedom Americans enjoyed. He and Charles had lived in terror that someone might find out what they were doing at night. He wasn't sure Americans would care.

John took him to parties where young Americans drank, took drugs, fondled one another, and exposed themselves to one another. God knew what else they did. Oh, it was the freedom he had always dreamed of—he and Charles, who would never know it because he would remain all his life in France. The difference between himself and Charles and his new American friends was that he and Charles had done what they did and were ashamed of it—but the Americans felt no shame. Like young animals, they followed their desires wherever they led them and seemed not to think twice about it.

John Perino was intimate with a girl named Buffy. Their best friends were a couple named Jeff and Kara. Buffy was eighteen and would attend Wellesley in the fall. She was two years older than John, who would not graduate from high school for another year. Jeff and Kara were seventeen and also had to complete their senior years of high school.

Kara's father, who was a surgeon at Greenwich Hospital, owned a thirty-foot sports cruiser, which he berthed in Cos Cob Harbor. Jeff had demonstrated enough skill and responsibility with the boat that he allowed Jeff to take it out on weekday afternoons. On a Thursday afternoon in August, the three couples—John and Buffy, Jeff and Kara, Van and Anna—carried picnic baskets aboard and set out eastward on Long Island Sound, going nowhere in particular and planning to anchor in some cove where they would eat their lunch and maybe slip over the side to swim.

The girls wore colorful bikinis. Kara in particular filled hers to overflowing. The boys wore White Stag Speedos, tight, showing proud bulges.

The boat, named *Finisterre,* could be controlled from a flying bridge atop the main cabin or from a control center inside the cabin. As he eased the boat away from the dock and out into the harbor, Jeff worked from the flying bridge, where he had the best visibility. He used minimal engine power, causing no wake. Only when he was well beyond the harbor did he shove in the throttles and send the boat charging forward into a light swell.

The other five sat in the cockpit, feeling in their feet the vibrations from the engines. John opened an ice chest and passed around bottles of beer.

When they were two miles offshore and abreast of Shippan Point, in Stamford, Buffy pulled off her bikini top and cast it aside. Kara immediately followed suit. Anna was conspicuously reluctant to do the same but was also unwilling to be different. She took off her top, showing a fourteen-year-old girl's small, pointed breasts.

Kara climbed to the flying bridge, taking Jeff a beer.

Van noted that no one seemed embarrassed. Apparently, his new friends were doing what they always did. He wondered if next the boys would pull off their Speedos and expose themselves naked. He wasn't sure if he could do that.

As they cruised east on the Sound, the sky behind them darkened, the wind freshened and turned cooler, and the water became choppy. Jeff switched on the radio on the bridge and listened to the Coast Guard frequency.

"No problem," he told the others. "A squall passing through. I'm going to run inside the islands just ahead and find a cove where we can anchor."

The three girls retreated into the cabin. The boys stayed on deck, and John and Van went out on the bow to be ready to drop the anchor when Jeff called for it. By the time they reached sheltered water in a cove, hissing rain had reduced visibility to almost nothing. When the boys came into the cabin, they were wet. Kara had taken towels from the locker, and the three boys rubbed themselves dry. Their Speedos were wet. Jeff and John pulled theirs off. Van hesitated but decided he would look silly to the others if he didn't do the same. Jeff knelt at the rear of the cabin, opened a hatch in the bulkhead, and hung the trunks on hooks in the engine compartment, where the heat would dry them.

The girls broke out their sandwiches and chips, and the boys opened more beer. The boat rocked on growing swells but was in no way threatened.

"Cozy," said Kara, snuggling against Jeff. He put his left arm around her and cupped her breast in his hand. "Mmm-hmm," she murmured. "Very cozy."

John bent over and kissed each of Buffy's nipples, leaving them glistening with the saliva from his tongue.

Van looked at Anna and saw apprehension in her eyes. He put his arm around her shoulders, and she smiled shyly and kissed him quickly on the cheek.

As they ate, the Greenwichers talked about their schools and the upcoming football season, and they laughed as they tried to explain to Van the fundamentals of American football.

As soon as Jeff and Kara had finished eating their sandwiches and drinking their beer, they went down a short

ladder and opened a door that admitted them to a narrow
cabin.

John and Buffy stretched out on the settee on the right
side of the main cabin and began to kiss and fondle each
other.

Van kissed Anna. It was the first time he had kissed her on
the mouth. He was thrilled. Her dark, solemn eyes fastened
on his, and she lifted her soft, moist lips to invite him to
kiss her again. He wanted to touch her small bare breasts.

But—her brother was just across the cabin!

John had pushed Buffy's bikini bottom down. He
kneaded her taut little rear.

Van put his right hand gently on Anna's left breast. She
gasped but did not move away from him or try to move his
hand away. She only stared into his eyes with increasing
solemnity. He kissed her again. They relaxed, settled back
on the settee, and continued kissing.

The rain slackened, and visibility around the boat improved. Van and Anna could see the islands around them
and the mainland shore. Other boats were at anchor not far
from them, and Van wondered if people on those boats were
doing what they were doing on this one.

The door opened. Jeff and Kara came up the ladder,
grinning.

"Next!"

John and Buffy descended into the front cabin. Jeff and
Kara sat down and opened two more beers. Van and Anna
said they wouldn't have any more for now.

Jeff grinned impishly and said, "They don't circumcise
everybody in Europe, do they?"

"No. Only if parents specifically ask for it to be done."

"You have to in this country. It's the law."

"No it isn't," said Kara.

"I always heard it was," said Jeff.

"Well, my father's a doctor. He ought to know."

"Come to think of it, not all the guys at school are.
Anyway . . . they didn't do it to you, huh, Van?"

"No," said Van very quietly. The other three were all
staring at his penis, and he knew he was blushing. This was
really too much, but he had no escape from it. "In Amster-

THE STALLION

dam, where I was born, it is regarded as a religious rite only."

"Did you go out for any sports in your schools?"

" 'Go out'?"

"Did you play any sports?"

"Oh, yes. Rugby especially."

"That's a rough game, isn't it?"

"It can be very rough. Have you ever heard the joke about it? They say rugby is a game for hoodlums, played by gentlemen. Football is a game for gentlemen, played by hoodlums. And ice hockey is a game for hoodlums, played by hoodlums."

The others laughed. Van was glad they had turned their attention away from his crotch.

Jeff resumed his explanation of American football.

John and Buffy came up. John nodded at Van.

"Uh, well, perhaps . . .," Van murmured.

"Don't be bashful," said John. "Anna's not."

One small brass lamp on the bulkhead lighted the cabin. It was tiny and warm and cozy. It was equipped with two narrow bunks, with hardly enough room to stand between them. Van and Anna lay down facing each other. He was embarrassed to find his fully engorged organ pressing between her legs. She showed no sign of dismay but only looked at him with those appealing dark eyes of hers and offered her mouth to be kissed.

He kissed her warmly, more warmly than passionately. "Anna," he whispered to her, "we will not take off the rest of your swimsuit."

"No," she said. "We mustn't."

"You can touch me, though, if you want to."

She closed her hand around his shaft and instinctively knew what to do. Only a minute passed before he ejaculated into her hand and onto her legs.

"Anna," he said. "I want you to understand that I love you. I will see no other girls until we are old enough to marry."

265

XXVIII

1989

1

Alicia invited the Perino family to Thanksgiving dinner. Her grandson Van Ludwige had come down from Harvard and was staying with her. Everyone gathered in her living room around a crackling fire in the formal marble-bordered fireplace. They nibbled hors d'oeuvres and sipped drinks.

Bill Adams and Angelo stood apart from the group for a few minutes of private talk.

Froelich & Green had at last made their offer. It was $625 per share, on the condition that F & G acquire a minimum of 51 percent of the stock in XB Motors. The price would be paid $150 per share in cash, $400 per share in warrants for stock in Froelich & Green, $75 per share in notes.

"I was beginning to wonder if they hadn't backed off," said Angelo, sipping from a martini.

"They had a difficult time raising the money," said Bill. "I put the word around, which didn't help them."

"But they raised it," said Angelo.

"Some very sharp guys are working with them," said Bill. "They've got the hundred and fifty million dollars they'd need if all the XB stockholders accepted their offer. They can secure the notes. They've sold enough junk bonds to cover those. It's the warrants that are doubtful. They value their stock at four hundred and fifty dollars and offer warrants for it at four hundred dollars. But the warrants may turn out to be worthless."

"If their stock isn't worth four hundred dollars a share."

"Precisely."

Angelo shook his head. "I don't understand how these guys can raise money. Hell, Boesky's in jail. Milken is going there. The world has to be full of suckers."

"Including one named Loren Hardeman the Third," said Bill Adams.

2

Neither Van nor Anna could conceal what their eyes told anyone acute enough to see. The way she looked at him and the way he hovered over her attentively and lovingly was only a little short of conspicuous.

"What's going on between those two?" Angelo asked Cindy when they were alone in their bedroom.

"They're in love."

"Christ! She's fourteen!"

"He promised her he will not date any other woman and will wait for her until she's old enough to marry him," said Cindy. "She gave him the same promise."

"Gimme a *break*! Don't tell me they—"

"No. She swears not, and I believe her. She said they had chances last summer and agreed not to. I wish I could say the same for John and Buffy. He doesn't confide in me, but I've got a pretty good idea."

"I did it when I was sixteen," said Angelo.

"Well, you never asked me for my intimate autobiography, but I lost my virginity—lost it? Not the way to say it. I gave it away gladly when I was fourteen."

Cindy stood before a long mirror, critically examining the red marks around her waist that had been left by the panty hose she had worn all afternoon and evening. Those things would take hours to disappear. Garter belts didn't leave marks like that. She resolved to quit wearing panty hose. She avoided bras as much as she could, too, and when she did wear one, it was sheer and flimsy and not too tight so that it wouldn't mark her.

"Maybe we're lucky in a way," she said. "Our kids seem to be monogamous. In the age of AIDS, you have to think about that."

"They don't do drugs, either—do they?"

"Anna has beer now and then. She told me. I imagine John goes further. But I've seen no problem."

Angelo lay on the bed, waiting for Cindy. He shook his head. "I've done a lot of things," he said, "but I've never had a snort of coke. Did a little grass one time, but that's all."

"So did I," said Cindy. "Back when I was hanging around the tracks, I used to share roaches. You could hardly live and not do it. But I've never tried anything harder."

"You know something? We're a couple of *old* farts. In a couple of years I'm going to be sixty years old!"

Cindy looked at him and grinned. He lay on his back, and his cock, standing just behind his balls, looked vaguely like the stake behind the last two arches on a croquet court. "You're still young and handsome, my husband," she said. "Will you do me a favor?"

"What?"

"Let Amanda paint you. I'll put John somewhere else and put you beside me."

Angelo ran his hands down his face. "If I can find time," he said with a mock groan.

1990

3

"Thirty-seven fuckin' million!" Roberta yelled. "What the hell became of *two hundred and twelve million*?"

"We've been through it," Loren protested impatiently. "Nineteen million more from the notes. That makes fifty-six. And the Froelich & Green stock is worth four hundred and twenty-five dollars a share. When I exercise my warrants, I'll get a hundred and six million more."

"You believe that, you believe in the tooth fairy," she snorted.

"If all I get out of it is the thirty-seven, that'll come without capital gains tax, and I'll wind up a wealthy man who can retire in comfort with a wife he loves, someplace where we can look at the ocean."

"Ocean, my achin' ass! What ocean? We were gonna live in *Paris*!"

Roberta was drunk. He had found her drunk when he came home. For some odd reason she was dressed in a pair of blue jeans—something she almost never wore—and a plain white bra. She was not just drunk; she was slobbering drunk. He himself had overdone the Scotch on the way home, but she was out of control, weepy and profane and unsteady on her feet.

There was no reasoning with her, not when she was in this condition. He had seen her drunk before but never as drunk as this.

Nothing she said could make any difference. This afternoon he had signed the papers, selling his 250,000 shares of XB Motors to Froelich & Green. Their check for $37,500,000 was in his bank—in escrow only until March 1. Their notes and warrants were held by the bank, also in escrow.

What was more, the trustees of the Hardeman Foundation had been polled by telephone, and he had secured authority to sell the foundation's stock, too. He had deposited $52,500,000 to an escrow account for the foundation.

The deal was done. The terms of the escrows had already been met. He had sold 60 percent of XB Motors to Froelich & Green: a clear controlling interest. That was why Roberta was so upset. She had become accustomed to dominating him. Well, it was one thing to tie him to the bed and beat his ass with a belt; it was quite another to browbeat him about his business.

"It's done, Roberta," he said. "You say I have good business judgment. You've said it repeatedly. Well, I've exercised my judgment."

"You did it because you hate Angelo Perino more than you love the business your grandfather built!"

Loren smiled. "That son of a bitch and his electric car are kaput. Now, if I could just kaput him . . ."

4

Betsy took a cab from Kennedy Airport to the Perino house in Greenwich. She accepted a martini and sat down in the living room, almost tearful.

"It's done! He sold out. He had enough flunkies on the board of trustees of the Hardeman Foundation to—"

"It's not done," said Angelo. "Here's yesterday's *Wall Street Journal*. Front page. Read it."

The story read—

XB Motors Acquisition Challenged in Suit
by Michigan Attorney General
Special to *The Wall Street Journal*

By Jane Loughlin

The sale of XB Motors stock by the Hardeman Foundation was challenged in a suit filed yesterday by Michigan attorney general Frank Fairfield. A temporary injunction, granted immediately by Judge Homer Wilkinson of Detroit Circuit Court, blocks for the moment the attempt by Froelich & Green, Incorporated, to take over the nation's fourth-largest automobile manufacturer.

The Hardeman Foundation, established by the first Loren Hardeman, the founder of Bethlehem Motors, the corporate predecessor of XB Motors, holds 35 percent of the stock in XB. That stock is the foundation's sole asset. The closely held stock is almost never traded, and its value has been estimated from as high as $800 to as low as $550 a share. Froelich & Green offered $625, of which only $150 is to be in cash, the rest being in notes and warrants.

The attorney general's complaint describes the notes and warrants offered by Froelich & Green as "of highly questionable value." In any event, the complaint goes on, charitable trusts in Michigan are limited by statute law to investment in specific kinds of securities. The notes and warrants, he alleges, do not meet the requirements of the Michigan statutes.

"The Hardeman Foundation is the chief support of maternity clinics, vocational schools and worker retraining programs in several Michigan cities," said Attorney General Fairfield. "We cannot stand by and allow its assets to be dissipated."

Loren Hardeman III, the grandson of the founder, commented that from time to time over the years the big automotive company has failed to pay dividends or has paid only minimal dividends. "This sale gives the foundation more than fifty-two million dollars in cash," he said. "It can invest that money in the very soundest of blue-chip securities and government bonds and actually have a better basis for its charitable gifts than it has now."

Attorney Paul Burger, formerly a judge of the Michigan Supreme Court, representing several minority stockholders, including XB's executive vice president, Angelo Perino, and Loren Hardeman III's daughter, Elizabeth, Viscountess Neville, disagreed and said the sale "put the Hardeman Foundation in grave jeopardy."

"But are we going to win this suit?" asked Betsy. "Surely Froelich & Green must have looked into the law before they raised the money and made the offer."

"I'd guess they thought it would be all over before anyone could stop them," said Angelo. "I'd guess that Loren didn't believe you and I would go so far as to invoke the power of the Michigan attorney general."

Betsy smiled slyly. "How'd you work that one, Angelo?" she asked. "Family friends?"

"No. The attorney general was a law clerk for two years to Paul Burger when he was a judge. Something else your father and his friends didn't know."

Betsy tapped the newspaper with one finger. "But is this suit based on sound law?"

"If Paul Burger thinks it is, it must be," Angelo said firmly.

5

Loren sat behind his desk in the XB office building. He had been drinking and had a glass of Scotch on his desk. With him was Herbert Froelich, James Randolph, director of the Hardeman Foundation, and Ned Hogan, corporate counsel. Each of them had politely declined his offer of a drink.

"Whatever the outcome, this lawsuit will be pending for *years*," said Loren. "In the meantime, Mr. Froelich will vote my twenty-five percent of the stock, and Jim Randolph will vote the foundation's thirty-five percent. With that sixty percent and three of the five directors, we can rid this company once and for all of an executive vice president who had the balls to precipitate a lawsuit against us—that and his cockamamie electric car project."

"I'm afraid not," said Randolph. "Here is an order that was served on me at the gate just now." He handed the papers to Hogan. "The Superior Court has appointed a conservator to manage the assets of the foundation until the issues raised in the suit have been resolved. The conservator is Benjamin Marple, assistant vice president of Detroit City Bank. Until the suit is resolved, *he'll* vote the foundation's stock."

Struggling to focus his eyes, Loren turned to the lawyer. "Is that goddamned paper valid?" he demanded.

"It's a court order," said Hogan. "Marple is to conserve the assets of the foundation, et cetera, et cetera, and file monthly reports with the court. He cannot sell assets without specific written approval of the court. He will vote the foundation's shares in XB Motors."

Loren flushed deeply. "Are you telling me we've lost control of XB Motors?" he shouted.

Hogan nodded. "Until further order of the court."

Loren stared at Froelich. "What do you want to do?" he asked apprehensively.

Froelich shook his head. "I'm afraid I have no choice but

to invoke the provision in our contract that voids the whole deal if corporate control cannot be passed."

"Well, that remains an open question until the lawsuit is settled," said Loren.

"No. Our offer is open until March first, nineteen ninety. If by that time a controlling interest has not been sold to Froelich & Green, Incorporated, the offer expires. Although I delivered to you a check for thirty-seven million, five hundred thousand dollars, you deposited it as we required: in an escrow account. If by March first—"

"Screwed!" yelled Loren.

6

Which was what he yelled at Roberta as soon as he walked through the front door of their house. *"Screwed!"*

She shook her head. Roberta was sober, though she had a Scotch in one hand, a Chesterfield in the other. She wore tight white stirrup pants and a bulky white sweater. "Not screwed. Calm down."

"As of today I am thirty-seven million, five hundred thousand dollars poorer than I was yesterday, and you tell me I'm not screwed? Angelo Perino again," he growled. "Perino screwed me!"

"You're not screwed," she said. "You got your stock back. It's worth four times the thirty-seven goddamned mill. Instead of a quarter of what the stock's worth and a lot of shabby paper issued by a pack of hustlers, you own twenty-five percent of XB Motors. Personally, I'm grateful to Angelo Perino, and you should be, too."

Loren shrugged out of his black cashmere overcoat and let it fall to the floor of the foyer. "The man screwed my daughter, and he screws me every chance he gets. I need a fuckin' drink," he said as he strode from the foyer through the living room and into the big family room.

"What you need is to fuckin' relax," she said. "Get your clothes off, lover. You're going to make me feel good, and then I'm going to make you feel good."

For a moment he stood in the center of the floor, staring hard at her. "I really need a drink," he said quietly as he began to strip. "It's not over between me and Perino. I'm gonna have his ass. Sooner or later I'll have his ass. One way or another."

"Use your brains, Loren," Roberta said sternly as she poured Scotch for him. "Just one time, think with your brains instead of your ass. *Help* Angelo build a revolutionary new car that could make your stock worth a thousand dollars a share, worth two thousand dollars a share! You could be so rich no Ford could come close to you. Fight him and you could kill the goose that lays golden eggs."

Loren was naked when he took his drink from her hands. "Promise me something," he said quietly.

"What?"

"That he hasn't screwed you, too."

"Loren . . . Jesus! Angelo *Perino*? No, baby. What would I want with Angelo Perino when I have you?"

"I'd rather die than lose you, Roberta," he whispered as he dropped to his knees before her. "I'd rather lose the company. Perino can have it. I want *you*. I need you."

She reached down and caressed his face, then let him kiss her hands. "You listen to Mama," she told him. "And what I want you to do right now is relax. Relax, lover. You want me to warm your bottom a little?"

Tears streaked Loren's cheeks as he looked up and nodded.

XXIX

1990

1

"The whole family is flawed," said Alicia to Angelo. "Every damned one of them, including my daughter. Betsy's a loose cannon. I warn you."

"What Betsy wants, Betsy gets."

"Except the one thing she wanted more than anything else—to be married to you. She is capable of hating you, Angelo. There's a fine line, you know, between love and hate."

He had made a point for more than ten years now of calling on Alicia from time to time and filling her in on what XB Motors was doing. She owned 5 percent of it, after all, and in most corporations that made a person an important stockholder.

Once or twice a year, they found time to slip up to her bedroom and lie together on her bed, sometimes only kissing and caressing but usually undressing and doing it all. She was not casual about it, but she did not live for the occasions when she could make love with Angelo Perino.

Just a little while ago he had rolled off her and she had lit a cigarette and started talking about the Hardemans.

Of Loren's three wives, Angelo thought, Alicia was the

most satisfying in bed. Lady Ayres had been an athlete, sometimes violent. Roberta was mercurial and demanding. Alicia was just a good, quiet, intimate companion. She did not stint. She gave herself freely and completely and obviously found enjoyment in it. What was more, he could tell that she cared whether or not he enjoyed it. Loren had made another of his many mistakes when he gave up Betsy's mother.

"I think it would have been better if Elizabeth—I mean Number One's wife—had lived longer. I never knew her, of course. She died before Loren was born. People who knew her said she was a stabilizing influence."

"That's what my father said."

"The family has gone to hell, Angelo. That may have started when Number One's Elizabeth died."

Angelo nodded. "It may have," he said.

Alicia put her cigarette aside in an ashtray on her night table. She caressed his cheek—not his crotch; she never touched that after they had made love. "My grandson," she said. "Van. He's in love with Anna."

"So I'm told. They're very young."

"They're the key to everything, Angelo. What if they married and had children? That would lock everything together. Betsy's child. Your child. You must save the company for *them*. That's the point."

"We're being a little premature, Alicia. They're still just kids."

"Van is Loren's grandson, too. When he finds out his grandson is in love with Angelo Perino's daughter and may marry her someday . . ."

Angelo nodded and smiled wryly. "I take your point."

2

The 1990 stockholders meeting of XB Motors convened on Monday, February 13, 1990. Since that was two weeks and one day before the Froelich & Green offer would expire and the Michigan attorney general's lawsuit would become moot, the conservatorship remained in effect. Benjamin Marple, not James Randolph, would vote the stock of the Hardeman Foundation. Loren had wanted to postpone the meeting, but the bylaws of the corporation would not allow it.

Betsy was present with the same proxies she'd had last year. Angelo was in attendance, and, of course, so were Loren and Roberta.

The first order of business was the election of directors.

Betsy spoke. "The present directors are my father, Loren Hardeman the Third, his wife, Roberta Ford Ross Hardeman, James Randolph, Angelo Perino, and myself. Mr. Perino and I are directors because the minority stockholders exercised their right to vote cumulatively—which we will do again this year. I move that my father, his wife, Mr. Perino, and I be reelected. I move further that Mr. Randolph be replaced by Mr. Marple."

Marple, who was a compact man with prematurely white hair, shook his head. "My lady," he said, addressing Betsy formally, according to her title, "I am flattered, but I am afraid I cannot serve as a director of XB Motors. Since my conservatorship will expire in two weeks, I will no longer be involved in the affairs of the company, and I can't give the directorship the time it would require."

"What I want, Mr. Marple," said Betsy, "is a director who is not my father's flunky. The very fact that Mr. Randolph went along with the deal offered by Froelich & Green calls his integrity as well as his competency into question."

"You go too far!" Loren barked.

"The director representing the foundation," Betsy continued, "should be someone of good judgment. I do not ask that my father's lackey be replaced by someone beholden to me. We need a neutral director."

Paul Burger had suggested to her and Angelo that they take this approach. Marple would not vote the foundation's stock so as to give control of XB Motors to its minority stockholders, he said; but he probably would agree to the election of a neutral director.

"Do you have anyone in mind?" asked Marple. "That is, besides me."

"I thought you were the perfect man, Mr. Marple," said Betsy, bestowing on him an engaging smile. "I hadn't really given much thought to an alternative. Angelo . . . ?"

"I have one idea," said Angelo. "One of the most success-ful of our dealerships is the one in Louisville, Kentucky—owned by Thomas Mason. Tom was a Sundancer dealer. Number One knew him and respected him. We could do worse than have someone from the sales side of the business on the board of directors. Thomas Mason has been with us for decades and knows the business from the sales angle. We are amply represented in design, manufacturing, finance, and so on. We could use a salesman, a dealer."

"I guess I've met him," said Loren tentatively.

"I remember him," said Betsy. "I talked with him when I was here during the dealers meeting in—what year was it? Anyway, I nominate Mr. Mason."

"Now, wait a minute!" Loren yelled. "This comes in out of left field, out of a clear blue sky. What do we know about this guy? How do we know he'll serve if we do elect him?"

"I imagine he'll be flattered," said Betsy.

She *knew* he'd be flattered. She and Angelo had spoken to him on the telephone yesterday. He had FedExed his curriculum vitae to them, which they had reviewed this morning. Tom Mason was a graduate of the University of Kentucky, with a master's degree in marketing. He had served four terms in the Kentucky legislature. He was a member of the board of directors of several local companies in Louisville. He had qualifications that would impress Benjamin Marple.

"Well, I think we had better adjourn the meeting for two or three weeks until we have had a chance to check him out and interview him."

Betsy grinned and shook her head. "Nice try," she said. "Unsubtle but nice. I move we adjourn until two o'clock this afternoon. During that time we can telephone Mr. Mason and ask him if he's interested. If he is, he can fly up here tomorrow, we can interview him, look over his qualifi-cations, and meet on Thursday or Friday to decide."

Loren glowered.

"I see no reason not to talk to the man," said Marple. He voted for Betsy's motion.

Tom Mason flew to Detroit, bringing with him the résumé Angelo and Betsy had already seen. The conservator was impressed. On Thursday he voted to elect Mason to the board of directors.

On Friday the five directors met. They elected Loren chairman of the board and Angelo president and chief executive officer of XB Motors.

3

Angelo had leased a luxury apartment in Detroit. He spent so much time there that he decided it was a waste of money to live in hotels. He had warned Betsy not to come to that apartment. He had arranged to discourage one set of private eyes, but he doubted Loren had given up on the idea of getting photographs of him and Betsy together.

In the apartment, Angelo waited until eight before he went out to dinner, thinking she would call and they would meet somewhere. When she didn't, he went to the Red Fox Inn—recalling that it was the restaurant from which Jimmy Hoffa had disappeared—and had a steak and a bottle of Châteauneuf du Pape.

4

Betsy had a different agenda for that night.

When Tom Mason appeared at the door of her suite in the Renaissance Center, she was dressed in a pair of tight black pants and a loose sweater that fell casually off one shoulder or the other and suggested constantly that it would at any moment fall off both.

"Miss Betsy . . . You forgive me if I don't call you Viscountess whatever. Isn't Angelo Perino having dinner with us?"

"Believe it or not, he's the father of five and rushed back to Connecticut for some reason or other."

"Well, uh—"

"Sit down, Tom. Bourbon?"

Tom Mason grinned. "Believe it or not, I'm a strange Kentuckian. Rather have Scotch."

"How do you like martinis?"

"I've been known to imbibe them," he said with a boyish grin.

Betsy grinned back at him. "Come over here and help. On the rocks or up?"

"Well now, up, Miss Betsy. Up."

"Then crack some ice, will you please?"

Tom got to work. "What happened, Miss Betsy?" he asked. "I get the idea we took the corporation away from your father."

"Yes, unless he recovers control of the foundation stock, which he may do. And if you don't quit calling me Miss Betsy, I'm gonna kick you in the nuts."

"How's Lady Neville?"

She laughed. " 'The Right Honorable, the Viscountess Neville.' How old was I when you met me, Tom?"

"Oh, twenty, twenty-one."

"When Angelo met me I was sixteen. He called me Miss Betsy until—he's the father of my son John. Did you know that?"

"I heard that."

"So, don't call me Miss Betsy, Tom."

They sat down with their martinis. She brought a platter of cheese, fruit, and wafers from the refrigerator—supplied by room service.

"We didn't bring you up here to become a yes-man to me and Angelo," she said. "We told you that. Angelo and I nominated you because we wanted someone who could use his judgment and brains. Ben Marple was the key vote, and he accepted you on that basis. Angelo and I wanted someone who might disagree with us but would disagree for valid reasons, not just because he was my father's puppet. The company is going to be run differently from the way it was run before."

"If you'll forgive my saying so, it's damn well time."

"Number One was a *monster,* Tom. I don't think you have any idea."

"I'm old enough to remember that the original Henry Ford was a great admirer of Hitler," said Tom.

Betsy nodded. "On the other hand," she said, "a camel is a horse put together by committee."

"If I know Angelo, he'll run the corporation with an iron hand."

"While he lasts."

Tom finished his martini, as had she, and he reached for the pitcher and poured for both of them. "Tell me about the electric car," he said.

"Angelo will have to tell you. It won't be a runabout for old ladies, I'll tell you that. Everything depends on it. Initially, it may depend on you, on how you vote as a director."

"I've got a lot of respect for Angelo."

"Tom, so do I. I wanted to marry him, and I fuck with him every chance I can get. But I'd like to have *your* judgment as to whether or not this electric car is—is life or death for XB Motors."

Tom nodded and swallowed half of his second martini. "Where are we having dinner?" he asked.

"Room service," she said. "It wouldn't be wise for us to be seen together in a Detroit restaurant."

"Oh . . ."

"Tom"—she grinned again—"on the few occasions we've been together, you seem to spend half your time staring at my tits."

"Oh . . . I'm *sorry,* Miss Betsy!"

"Really want to see them?" she asked—and she shrugged, letting the sweater fall down off both her shoulders.

5

At home, Loren lay with his head in Roberta's lap and wept. "The bastards took it away from me!" he complained over and over again.

"Only temporarily," she said calmly. "Here, have a drink. It'll make you feel better."

At three in the morning, when she was asleep and snoring, he went downstairs and telephoned Len Bragg.

Bragg was sleepy and impatient. "Thought maybe you'd given up on the idea."

"I have *not* given up. I told you to stay ready. Have you got another plan?"

"Trish went back to Greenwich and watched him again.

We can get him when he comes out on a Monday morning. The kids don't follow him to the car. While he's stuffing his bag and briefcase into the car."

"Do it!"

6

Alexandria McCullough was the redheaded computer guru Roberta had seen with Angelo in the lobby bar of the Hyatt Regency Hotel in Houston. She had worked for Texas Instruments but was now an independent consultant. Forty-four years old, she was a committed jogger who got in her five miles every morning, no matter what the weather. Her body was hard. She drank and ate whatever she wanted, but she remained hard and slender, because in addition to jogging, she worked out in a gym three nights a week. Her hair was flaming red. Her eyes were pale blue. Her face was round, and she had pursed lips, and freckles dotted her cheeks and forehead.

She and Angelo had worked all afternoon in her office and now were having dinner in the restaurant overlooking the Hyatt Regency lobby. They'd eaten oysters and were now cracking crab legs.

"I'm a committed environmentalist," she told Angelo. "That's why your electric car interests me so much. It won't be filling the air with the products of the combustion of hydrocarbon fuels."

"Well, where will the power come from that we use to charge the batteries?" he asked. "Power plants still burn fossil fuels."

"In a far better controlled way," she said. "Anyway, once the antinuclear nuts fade away, we'll generate our electricity from fission and fusion—that, plus solar and water and wind power."

"Batteries are my bugaboo, of course," said Angelo. "I've looked at fuel cells, flywheel battery systems, and lithium-polymer cells."

"I can't help you with battery technology," said Alexandria. "What I can do is show you how to use computer technology to extract the utmost performance from your power source."

"An electric motor on each of the four wheels," he said, summarizing what they had discussed that afternoon.

"Each motor pulling only as much power as it absolutely needs," she said. "Anybody who drives with a straight stick knows that you roll forward a great deal of the time without using engine power—not just rolling downhill but rolling up to a traffic light with your transmission in neutral. You expend energy to get a ton or more of steel moving, then waste it braking. Your idea is to use that kinetic energy to run a generator and recharge. My contribution is to develop a computer system that analyzes energy requirement and use instantly, using every erg of energy to move the car."

"Four motors . . . ," Angelo mused.

"A car turning right," she said, "is pulled around by its left front wheel, with some assistance from the right rear. Why power the right front and left rear wheels when they are not doing any of the work? You power the wheels that are contributing something besides holding up the weight of the car—and let the others rest, so far as power is concerned. But it takes a computer to analyze what is going on fast enough and allocate power accordingly."

"We can gain—"

"Hell, Angelo. A conventional automobile uses not more than twenty percent of its energy effectively. Why not use ninety percent effectively?"

"Alex, you scare me."

"You scare me, you Italian stud. You know what reputation runs ahead of you. But I've got a surprise for you. I'm in love and one hundred percent committed—to Lucy."

He reached for her hand. "Maybe that makes it easier for us to work together," he said.

She nodded. "Maybe. I won't deny that I'm damned curious. But . . ." She shrugged. "If it was okay with Lucy . . ."

"Go ahead and discuss it with Lucy," he said. "In the meantime, let's focus on automobiles."

7

The following Monday morning, when Angelo left his house, Len Bragg and Trish Warner were waiting on the road. This time she was driving a long black Cadillac they had rented at Newark Airport. They had stayed in the Holiday Inn in Fort Lee, New Jersey, and had driven to Greenwich at four in the morning. This time they were not able to be so precise in their timing and had to drive back and forth on the road, watching for the lights to come on in the Perino house.

Finally lights did come on, and through his telescopic sight Len could see Perino and his wife moving inside the house.

"Jesus Christ!"

Len saw the reflection just in time and jammed the rifle under the seat as far as he could. The reflection was of the flashing lights of a police car that had pulled up behind them.

The officer walked up to the car. Trish put down her window.

"Are you folks lost or something?" asked the policeman.

"Exactly," said Trish. She'd had the presence of mind to unfold the Greenwich town map that lay on the seat. "Round Hill Road?"

The officer shook his head. "You're a long way from there. Let me show you on the map."

While the officer showed Trish the way to Round Hill Road, Len feigned interest but kept his heels pushing as hard as he could on the rifle.

"Well, thank you. I can find it now."

As they pulled away, Angelo Perino came out of his house and got into his car. The police car followed them for a few minutes—whether because the policeman was suspicious or so he could be sure they went the right way, they could not guess.

"Screwed," Len muttered. "What rotten luck!"

"Rotten, my achin' ass. What kind of luck was it that he didn't see the rifle? He would've if he'd looked down."

"Perino's the one with luck. That son of a bitch leads a charmed life."

8

"Expenses. We've had expenses. That was the deal, you know: half a million, but we pay expenses."

"So how much of my money have you spent?" Loren demanded.

He met with Len and Trish in his car, in the parking lot of a shopping mall. He didn't dare take them to his office or home. Roberta didn't know about them.

"Also, we have to be compensated for the time we've put in."

"So how much?"

"About fifteen thousand dollars, roughly."

"So you've still got two hundred and thirty-five thousand dollars?"

Len nodded. "Something like that."

"I don't suppose you plan on giving it back."

"Is the deal off?"

Loren drew a deep breath, frowned, and pondered. He shook his head. "You can't do it in that driveway. That cop may very well have been suspicious. Who knows? He may actually have told Perino about you, warned him."

"Where else then? We can't do it in Detroit, and we can't do it in Greenwich . . ."

"Cool it awhile. When I've got an idea I'll let you know."

XXX

1991

1

"Good afternoon. My name is Robert Carpenter. Have I the pleasure of addressing Mrs. Perino?"

Cindy looked up from a stack of eighteenth-century prints she was examining in the gallery. The man who had addressed her was tall and blond, with blue eyes fixed intently on her, and a voluptuous smile. He had a close-trimmed graying beard and was dressed nattily in a dark gray pinstripe suit with a cream-colored tattersall vest.

She nodded and let him see a cautious smile.

"One of your competitors told me you may have some DeCombe figures. I rather favor them. I have one and am thinking of acquiring another."

"As a matter of fact, we have three DeCombes," she said. "They're in the next gallery." She closed the portfolio of prints. "I'll show you."

François DeCombe was a sculptor who produced exquisite small bronzes in the realistic style favored by VKP Galleries. The three DeCombes in the gallery were a ten-inch figure of a boy reclining on his stomach and reading, a ballerina the same size standing on one point, and a larger nude of a paunchy man in late middle age lying on his side with one leg drawn up and also reading.

"Very nice," said Robert Carpenter as he walked around the sculptures, studying them with a squint.

"We have a catalog as well," she said. "We can order anything he hasn't already sold. Also, he will do work on order. You can tell him what you want, and he will do the piece. I would suggest, though, that if you do that you go to Quebec and visit him. You have to be quite specific about what you want. It would be a good idea, too, to go up and look at the clay model before he casts it."

"What are the prices of these three pieces, Mrs. Perino?"

"The reclining boy and the ballerina are fifteen thousand dollars each. The man is twenty-five thousand."

Carpenter smiled. "I bought mine four years ago. I see I made a good investment."

"Yes, he brings much higher prices now than he used to. He won a couple of prizes and was given a one-man show at the Pompidou Center. That sort of thing always raises prices."

"Better than dying," said Carpenter.

"In one aspect, anyway," said Cindy.

Carpenter chuckled. "Let me give you my card," he said. "I may be interested in buying one of these—the ballerina, I think."

He presented her an engraved card—

Robert J. Carpenter
100 Hollyridge Drive
Los Angeles, California 90068

"If I decide to purchase, I will give you a check and will not of course expect to take possession until it has cleared. The price is firm?"

"On DeCombes the prices are firm," she said.

He glanced around. "Your gallery is extremely interesting. I'll browse a bit."

"Let me show you a few things we think are especially interesting," she said.

Over a late lunch at Quilted Giraffe he wrote her a check for fifteen thousand dollars.

2

Roberta unpacked the DeCombe ballerina. Cindy had packed it lovingly in a wooden box stuffed with excelsior. Carpenter had carried it aboard the plane from New York as cabin luggage.

"Fifteen thousand dollars . . . ," Loren murmured, shaking his head.

"First installment," said Carpenter. "And a very small first installment. You're going to have quite an art collection."

"Yes. You decided to do this," Roberta reminded Loren, "so you can't skimp on it and expect it to work."

"Besides," said Carpenter, pausing to take a sip of Courvoisier, "what you've got there is worth every dime of the fifteen thousand dollars. You could sell it right now for twelve or more, easily—and maybe for the whole fifteen. In a couple of years it will be worth twenty or twenty-five. Think of it as an investment. It's my fees and expenses that you'll never see again."

"It's beautiful," said Roberta. "We certainly can't begrudge the fifteen thou."

"I suppose you didn't find out anything," said Loren.

"Of course not. I didn't even say I knew her husband is *in* the automobile business. I didn't ask any personal questions, and neither did she. We talked about art."

"When are you going to see her again?" Loren asked.

"Certainly not until after you make another deposit to my account in United California Bank. Then . . . well, it would be a mistake—wouldn't it?—to appear again too soon. Not for a month at least."

"What is she supposed to think you are?"

"A man who appreciates art and has the money to buy it. If the question arises, I'll probably say I'm a yacht broker. That's a sufficiently obscure business to discourage their checking on me."

"Do you have any problems yet?"

"One. Marcus Lincicombe. He looked at me sort of strangely. I can't imagine where he could have seen me before my visit to VKP, but the art world is small and clannish. It's not impossible that we passed each other somewhere and he remembers."

"You told me you never worked in the East or in Europe."

"I've never taught anywhere but in the Southwest and in California. But Lincicombe, I suppose, could have come West for some showing or festival and—"

"All right, Professor. Let's hope not. Where will you be until your next trip to New York?"

"At home, of course. I'm still a professor of art history. I have classes to teach. I have a show to hang." He smiled. "I also have a very competent forgery to conceal."

"Don't take any chances, Professor," said Loren. "You're working for me now, for plenty. Postpone any ventures in selling forgeries until our business is finished."

"I suppose I could take a sabbatical next year and devote myself full-time to your project."

"Do that. I don't like part-time employees or part-time commitments."

An hour later Loren lay on his stomach on the floor of the bedroom. Roberta walked around the room, a Scotch in one hand, a Chesterfield in the other, alternating her attention between the sculpture of the ballerina and her naked husband, lying with his hands handcuffed behind his back. A drum table that had held a lamp made a temporary pedestal for the bronze.

She put the cigarette aside and picked up a whip. Loren cringed, but he smiled and lifted his bottom, welcoming the sting. She flicked the whip and added another narrow red welt to the four already on his hinder cheeks. *"Ooh!"* he grunted. "Ooh, Jesus, honey. That one was a little much."

"It's too bad we have to hide the statue in the bedroom," she mused.

"Not forever," he said.

Roberta stared at him. He was disgusting. She had long since ceased to find any stimulation in binding him, cuffing him, whipping him. She did it and she would continue to do it, because she knew she could never endure life with him if she didn't dominate him.

"Betsy's flight will be coming in about now," she said.

"We really should invite her to stay here. She *is* your daughter, after all."

"She'd never accept an invitation," he said. "If she were here, instead of in a hotel, she couldn't sleep with Perino— or whoever she's sleeping with these days."

"I want to talk to you about the stockholders meeting."

Loren grinned. "Maybe we'd better do that later. I'm not exactly in the posture of a corporate executive, am I?"

Roberta raised the whip over her head and brought it down hard across his shoulders. He yelled.

"I want to talk about it now, while you are the way you are. I want to try to prevent you from destroying yourself."

Loren writhed, twisting his neck, trying to see if she'd drawn blood. She had.

"Listen to me," Roberta ordered. "With Randolph voting the foundation stock again, you can put him back on the board of directors."

"You're damn right," he muttered.

"Well, don't."

"Whatta you mean, don't?"

"Randolph was Number One's flunky," said Roberta. "Now he's yours. The court pushed him out and put in a conservator once. It can do it again. His judgment on the Froelich & Green deal was so conspicuously bad that—"

"*My* judgment, you mean."

She slashed him across the legs. "Have it your way, but listen to what I'm telling you. Tom Mason's not a bad director. He's not in Perino's pocket. The dealers like the idea of having one of their own on the board. You drop him after one year—"

"I don't have control of my own goddamned board of directors!"

"You're not *supposed* to have control. You can't run the company the way Number One did."

"I can't run it *anyway*. Little by little, it's being taken away from me."

"You hate Angelo Perino. But you've gotta fight him smart, the way you're fighting him by hiring the professor. Give that a chance to work. A confrontation tomorrow could be the gunfight at the OK Corral."

"I'm gonna beat him smart or I'm gonna beat him crude. One way or another . . ."

3

     The stockholders meeting was a surprise to Angelo and Betsy. Loren moved that the existing directors be reelected for another year. They had expected a brutal confrontation, and it did not happen.

The directors met after lunch to hear a presentation from the president of the company.

Angelo came equipped with specifics, some of them presented on charts.

"The day of the fossil-fuel car is limited," he said. "That is the basis of everything I have to say to you. The Big Three are working on electric cars. They're under heavy pressure from the federal government and from California to do just that. We are number four in the industry. We entered the eighties selling a sixties car, the Sundancer, and it nearly killed the company. The Stallion is more of a success than any of us could have hoped. But we are about to enter the twenty-first century, still selling twentieth-century cars. GM and Ford and Chrysler can survive longer than we can, doing that. If they get ahead of us in the development of an electric car, it will kill us. We've got to be first."

The other directors—Loren and Roberta, Betsy, and Tom Mason—were not readily convinced. Even Betsy expressed her uncertainty.

"You're talking about betting the store, Angelo," she said. "We have to be damned sure we're right. The Big Three can make expensive mistakes and survive. We can't."

Toward the end of the meeting, Tom Mason spoke. "I have to think about whether I can sell electric cars in Louisville, Kentucky," he said. "If I can't, then nobody else can sell them either, because I'm a pretty good auto salesman, if I do say so myself. That's the key, isn't it? Can we sell them? The question isn't, will they run? The question is, will anybody buy them?"

"Tom," said Angelo, "I can't quote this exactly right, but somebody once said that the key to selling a product is to make what you believe in and make other people think that's what they wanted all along."

"We're considering a major corporate commitment here," said Roberta. "How would you react, Angelo, if I move that we defer a decision for six months, while you explore the technology further and refine your idea even more?"

"I'll accept six months," said Angelo, "providing two things. First, that it's understood that we'll be spending money on research and development during that six months. And second, that it's understood that I'm going to build this car, with XB Motors or without it. If this board decides not to build the new car, I'll resign and build it on my own."

"This company will own the research you've done," said Loren.

Angelo shook his head. "If it rejects my conclusions, I will be free to go ahead on my own. In other words, Loren, what XB has is the right of first refusal."

4

Just before the XB corporate Learjet swung around toward the taxiway, a car pulled up beside it, and very quickly, an additional passenger hurried up the steps and entered, before anyone watching could see who it might be.

It was Betsy. The jet would land at Boston before it went on to Westchester Airport. She would fly from Boston to London. Angelo had already told the pilot and copilot that he would require absolute privacy during this flight.

Betsy did not wait until the jet swept off the runway and into the night sky over Detroit to strip naked. "Tell 'em to fly fuckin' slower," she whispered. "An hour and a half is not enough time for me to give you your birthday present."

It *was* his birthday. It was his sixtieth birthday. As she undressed, he opened the Dom Pérignon that lay on ice in the chest under the front seat. Caviar lay in the same ice. Betsy knew that a birthday party awaited him when he reached Greenwich, which he would do in a little more than two hours. This one, she had promised him, almost within earshot of her father, would be better.

"Take your clothes off," she urged him. "Goddamnit, we don't have much time."

After a quick toast with the champagne and a bite of the caviar, they stretched out on the settee that had been formed by folding down the arms on the center-facing seats.

"I can't give you what I'd like to give you on your sixtieth birthday," she said. "A car. A boat. Hell, even a watch. Cindy's a wonderful gal, but she wouldn't—well, never mind. There's something else I can give you. Relax . . ."

"Betsy . . ."

She began licking his balls, sucking each testicle gently into her mouth and licking it there before she released it. With long strokes of her tongue she licked his shaft from the base to the tip, then all around. She drew him into her mouth and, sucking, pulled away, again and again.

"You know I love you," she whispered. "It's never been any other way."

"I love you, too, Betsy. God Almighty, I—"

She sucked on him so hard she stopped his voice. Murmuring words he couldn't understand and probably wasn't meant to, she moved her head up and down and slathered him, mixing the juices he was beginning to make with those from her mouth.

"Sir . . . ," a cold, steel voice said over the intercom, "I'm sorry, sir, but we have a telephone call coming in for you. Overseas."

Betsy grabbed the telephone handset from its hook on the bulkhead. "Who . . . ?"

Her eyes flooded instantly with tears, and she handed the telephone to Angelo without a word.

He put it to his ear.

"Daddy? This is John," said a child's voice, with an English-schoolboy accent. *"Happy birthday!"*

For a second Angelo was speechless.

"How nice of you to call."

"It's very late here, you know. I called your home first. Mrs. Cindy gave Nanny this number, saying it would reach you on an airplane. Are you really in the air somewhere, Daddy?"

"Yes, son, I'm in the air between Detroit and Boston.

Mommy is with me. She's catching a plane from Boston to London and will be home with you tomorrow."

Betsy wept. Angelo struggled not to.

"I wanted to wish you a happy birthday," said John. "I know you are sixty years old. That is a good age to be. Happy birthday, Daddy!"

"Oh, thank you, John. It is *wonderful* of you to call. I know you called because you love me, and I love you, too. Very much."

"I love you, Daddy. When will I see you?"

"I'll be in London soon, John. And we'll go boating together this summer in the States."

"Yes! Well, Nanny says these calls are frightfully costly. I'll say good night. It is very late here. Nanny had to wake me. Good night, Daddy."

"Good night, John."

Tears glistened on Angelo's cheeks as he put the telephone back in its cradle.

Betsy wept. "I swear I didn't arrange that," she sobbed.

He reached for her and drew her into his arms. "I wish you had. That was a fine birthday present."

"Better than mine," she whispered. She sighed loudly. "Well, let me finish giving you mine."

He kissed her fervently. She broke away from his kisses and plunged her face into his crotch. She worked on him with renewed energy. What she did was all but painful. But it was the best kind of pain a man could imagine.

XXXI

1991

1

"I wonder," said Robert Carpenter to Cindy, "if it would be possible to meet François DeCombe. I wonder if, when I buy another sculpture, I won't have the biggest private collection of his work."

"You'll have three," she said. "A man in Paris has five. Even so, you will be one of his best collectors. If you want to fly up to Quebec and see him, I'll call him and tell him you are coming."

They sat together over lunch at La Grenouille. Carpenter, it seemed, was unknown in New York, yet was able to get reservations wherever he wanted to go.

"I should be grateful," he said. "I am immensely interested in him and am wondering if he would consider doing a portrait sculpture. Oh, not of me, you understand. Of a friend. From photographs. For a gift."

"I don't know," she said. "You'll have to ask him. I doubt he'd work from photographs. He works with live models. Maybe . . ."

Carpenter smiled. "A change of subject. I've learned I have been tremendously ignorant. I did not realize you are Mrs. *Angelo* Perino and thus the wife of an eminent

295

automotive engineer and designer and president of XB Motors. I had thought of you as just an art dealer."

"Actually," she said, "I was, some years back, a race-track groupie and later even a test driver." She grinned broadly. "Tell me you were once a navy frogman, Mr. Carpenter."

"I'll tell you I'm Bob and not Mr. Carpenter," he said.

"Well, I'm, of course, Cindy."

"I'm afraid I've never been a frogman, Cindy. The most adventurous thing I ever did was to fly for the Air Force—and all I flew was a big, lumbering radar picket plane. The most exciting thing I ever did was meet you."

She shook her head. "No, no, no, Bob," she said.

"Sorry."

"I won't deny I'm flattered. But I'm the most committed woman you will ever meet."

Carpenter drew a deep breath, paused, and blushed. "Tell me," he said. "Who's the man over there? With the woman in red. He looks so familiar."

"That's Vincent Gardenia, Bob."

"Trying to change the subject . . . Will you forgive me if I seemed to be trying to come on?"

"I've known cruder approaches," she said.

"I couldn't help it."

"Maybe you could have. Do you want me to call DeCombe for you?"

"I don't know. I think I'll explore your offerings and see if maybe there's something different I might like better."

Cindy grinned wickedly. "I know what you might like better. Let's talk about art."

2

In April, people did not have to show passes to go on the Greenwich beaches. The weather was warm but the water was not yet warm enough for swimming. Van had come down from Cambridge this weekend and was staying at his grandmother Alicia's house. He and Anna sat in the sand at Greenwich Point, watching a spring storm building to the west.

The sun still shone through gaps between gray clouds. The water was green and pitching, with small whitecaps.

Van wore a dark blue sweatsuit. Anna wore a gray hooded sweatshirt and a pair of red shorts. The sunlight warmed her legs.

They were alone except for a man walking his dog. He had passed them with a friendly nod and was now two hundred yards away. Van, whose arm was around Anna's waist, slipped his hand up under her sweatshirt and fondled her breasts. They had been small and firm and pointed when he first saw and touched them. They were fully matured now: larger and softer. She rarely wore a bra.

Van was finishing his second year at Harvard. He was getting good grades and it seemed likely that he would be accepted if he applied to Harvard Law. He hadn't decided to do that, but it was definitely an option he was considering. Anna would graduate from Greenwich Academy next year.

"We needn't necessarily wait until we graduate," said Van. "After you finish your second year at Radcliffe, we could marry."

"We have three years to think about it," said Anna.

"We are lucky," he said. "Our fathers and mothers offer no obstacles to our marrying."

"I want to meet your father."

"I don't see him very often," said Van. "There was an arrangement, you know. He and my mother married and were divorced, and then he remarried his first wife. You've been told of this?"

"Yes." She paused and looked into his eyes, smiling broadly. "Our families have their own ways of doing things. Your mother and my father, for example. And there are other . . . anomalies."

"We're lucky," Van affirmed. "Though my grandfather is going to be disagreeable. He won't approve of us."

"I don't hear very nice things about him," Anna said flatly.

"Neither do I. I have to wonder if there's another side to the story. After all, we hear about him from people who distinctly dislike him."

"You ought to go see him."

"No. I met him once. He wasn't very friendly."

"Well, he will be furious when he learns about us," said Anna.

"My grandfather's opinion is a matter of complete indifference to me," said Van. "I've learned the American way of saying it: I don't give a damn."

3

Angelo had never given up his New York office. He still had some interests independent of XB Motors—most prominently CINDY, Incorporated, which had the license to manufacture the epoxy resin material and had developed a market for it. Keijo Shigeto, who had never met anything but hostility and scorn in Detroit, was vice president of CINDY, Incorporated. Three models of corporate jets now flying had epoxy resin skins. Four cars in the 1992 Indianapolis 500 would have epoxy resin bodies. The material had replaced fiberglass in fifteen unlimited-class hydroplane racing boats. NASA was giving careful consideration to using epoxy resin for the under-tiles skin of the Ramparts-class space shuttles.

Often, Angelo spent Monday or Friday in New York. Much of XB's business involved financing and recruiting, and he could do both of those things better in New York than in Detroit. He was in his New York office on Friday when two telephone calls came, almost simultaneously.

The first was from Tom Mason in Louisville.

"You read this morning's *Wall Street Journal*?"

"You're the first to call, Tom. I expect to hear from others."

"I don't believe a word of it. But, shit, man!"

"Do I need to suggest where the story originated, Tom? Do I need to tell you who's at work?"

"You figure the man'd do that?"

"That and more."

"Gotta do somethin' about it, though, Angelo. Can't let that kind of word stand."

"I'll be doing something about it, Tom. Don't worry."

The next call was from Betsy.

"Goddamn my father!" she yelled into the phone. "God-*damn* him!"

"You feel sure he's the source?"

"Who the hell else?"

"Well, I mean to do something about it."

"Tell me something, Angelo. How much damage can he do?"

Angelo paused while he drew a deep breath. "XB Motors depends on bank financing. This kind of shit doesn't make it easier."

"Well, what the Christ can you do?"

"There are several things I can do. Loren should know by now that we are not defenseless."

"Talk to Tom Mason."

"I have. He called just before you."

A moment of silence followed. "Van called," she said. "Anna suggested he go to Detroit and confront his grandfather. I mean, with his intention to marry her. I said no, not now."

"She's seventeen, Betsy. She's not marrying anybody soon. We'll cope with whatever problems go with that when the time comes."

Betsy sighed loudly. "Kill the son of a bitch, Angelo!"

"Figuratively, maybe," he said.

The story in that morning's *Wall Street Journal* read—

Playboy Exec at XB Motors?
CORPORATE AUDITORS SUGGEST IMPROPRIETIES,
CARELESS USE OF CORPORATE FUNDS
Special to *The Wall Street Journal*

By Wilma Worth

Bennet & Pringle, a Detroit accounting firm that acts as auditors for XB Motors, Inc., have suggested that company president Angelo Perino may be guilty of gross misuse of company money, using corporate funds to promote his personal business interests. Mason Pringle, a senior partner in the firm of CPAs, offered such an opinion in an interview with this reporter last Thursday.

When Mr. Perino was elected to the board of directors and then the presidency of XB, it was understood that the onetime racing driver held extensive outside interests, including a consulting business and a controlling interest in CINDY, Incorporated, a company that holds exclusive licensing rights to an epoxy resin material Mr. Perino used in the unsuccessful XB Super Stallion and proposes to use in a new electric-powered car he has committed XB to develop.

Mr. Pringle suggests that should XB use CINDY, Inc.'s, material in the new car, that would involve a conflict of interests in violation of a corporate officer's fiduciary duty to the stockholders.

The auditors suggest also that Perino uses the XB corporate jet as personal transportation, flying him back and forth between Detroit and Westchester Airport as suits the convenience of his varying business interests. In a typical week, the auditors say, Mr. Perino arrives in Detroit late Monday afternoon or early Tuesday morning and flies back to New York Thursday evening or Friday morning. He rarely spends more than three days a week on corporate business, they say, and spends at least as much time on outside interests and personal matters.

The article went on to suggest that the board of directors was considering calling Angelo Perino on the carpet at its next meeting.

4

For almost twenty years Angelo had been a guest speaker at least twice a year at a forum for bankers, investment counselors, and corporate executives. These weekly luncheon meetings were sources of information about a variety of industries. The automotive industry was the subject at least ten times a year, and Angelo had a reputation for giving an objective overall view.

His first scheduled appearance after the publication of the article came ten days later, and he drew an unusually large crowd. Ordinarily, no recording was allowed, but this time he consented to having his talk recorded. He also consented to the presence of a television camera and live coverage of his speech on CNBC.

The chairman of the meeting tapped a spoon on a glass and easily got the audience's attention. These people had come to hear what Angelo Perino had to say.

Wearing a dark blue suit, a white shirt, and a maroon-and-white striped tie, Angelo was an imposing figure as he stood confidently behind the lectern and adjusted the microphone.

"I am, of course, here to give you my opinions on the state of the automotive industry. You will perhaps forgive me if I take a few minutes to respond to the *Journal* article calling me a playboy executive and suggesting I am guilty of all manner of wrongdoing.

"First, let me say I am pleased to have met Ms. Wilma Worth. I want to congratulate her on her accurate reporting of what Mr. Mason Pringle had to say. I have no objection to what she wrote, with the possible exception that she might have checked with me to learn my viewpoint on the subject. I am confident she will report my statement today with equal accuracy and fairness."

The audience laughed—even Wilma Worth.

"What issues should I address?" asked Angelo. "In the first place, let's talk about conflict of interest. That's a question of integrity. My wife and I do own a controlling interest in CINDY, Incorporated, and I do expect to use its epoxy resin materials in the new cars XB is going to build. Ladies and gentlemen, *every single officer and director of XB Motors* knows who owns CINDY and knows that I will make a reasonable profit selling materials to XB. What is more, at least ninety-five percent of the stockholders know it—and any who don't know just haven't taken the time to read their annual reports. Conflict of interest is a sneaky, secret thing. If everybody concerned knows every element of the deal, there is no such thing as conflict of interest. In this matter there has been full disclosure."

Wilma Worth tapped furiously—and conspicuously—on her laptop computer. She glanced around and saw and heard a spatter of applause. More than a few in the room had similar deals and had not liked to hear this one called a conflict of interest.

"Why," Angelo went on, "did I acquire the license for the Japanese process for manufacturing the epoxy resin material? The opportunity was first offered to XB Motors. But XB management at that time was flirting with a corporate raider with which the Japanese company was not willing to do business. Rather than see the opportunity lost, my wife and I invested personal funds in the license. It was maybe the best investment either of our families ever made, and XB is the beneficiary of our commitment of risk capital."

The applause was louder.

Angelo paused, smiled, and looked down at Wilma Worth. "So I'm a playboy? I commute back and forth between New York and Detroit. Ladies and gentlemen, I also spend time in Tokyo, London, Zurich, Houston, Los Angeles, and Washington. Let us face facts. Detroit is a backwater. We can manufacture cars there, but we can't finance their manufacture there, we can't design them there, and we can't acquire the new technologies manufacturing requires in a city that still thinks it's the height of modernity and progress to unload ore boats with conveyor belts.

"So I spend two or three days a week in New York or somewhere else besides Detroit. And I fly the corporate jet. Ladies and gentlemen, I get more useful work done in an hour between Detroit and New York than I do in two hours in either city. The phone rarely rings on the airplane—though it can and sometimes does.

"I guess the XB auditors would rather I spend my time sitting around in Detroit Metro Airport or LaGuardia, waiting for a flight. Well, my friends, the auditors can stick that you know where."

Wilma Worth typed furiously, but she joined the people around her in laughter. Many of them stood to applaud.

Angelo laughed. "How'd you like to be that auditing firm?" he asked. "They're history. The original Loren Hardeman—the man we called Number One—always believed the automobile company he founded was his personal fiefdom and that he could use its assets as if they were his own. He could lie, cheat, and steal if he wanted to, because the company was his. He hired people who would not disagree with him. Starting next week, the corporate auditors for XB Motors, Incorporated, will be Deloite and Touche."

5

Betsy arrived on the Concorde. She faced Angelo in his office, late that evening. He had not been able to get away from the phones and leave for Greenwich.

"Call Cindy and tell her you have to stay in town. I need to talk with you, Angelo."

She had a suite in the Waldorf. They arrived there at ten o'clock, and she ordered dinner brought up. She poured Scotch and remained dressed.

"Liar, cheat, and thief! My great-grandfather was a liar, cheat, and thief?"

"He was exactly that," said Angelo. "An examination of the old records proves it. Besides—"

"Besides, what?"

"Number One did think of the business as a personal fief. He cheated everybody he dealt with, including the government on taxes, because Bethlehem Motors was *his* and he wouldn't answer to anyone about what he did with it. He was one of the last of the old-time robber barons. Henry Ford was worse."

Still wearing the off-white linen pants suit she had worn on the flight from London, Betsy gulped her Scotch and strode around the room. "Doesn't the company's reputation depend to some degree on Great-grandfather's reputation? Or rather, *didn't* it? You destroyed his reputation today. I haven't seen the evening papers, but I can imagine what they'll say."

"Betsy, tell me the truth."

He had never seen her cry before. Not really. Now Betsy shoved her glass aside and sobbed. "What do you want of me, Angelo? What do you want?"

"Tell me the truth, that's all."

"He was going to disinherit me. And my son. I mean Van. He was going to leave everything to my father. I—he had videotapes. Of you and me making love."

"I think I know what you did, Betsy. But let's get it out in the open."

"What the hell do you think I did? You've guessed. I killed him. I smothered him with a pillow. While he was struggling, he had a heart attack."

"I thought so."

"But I left his fuckin' reputation—"

"Too long," said Angelo. "I put an end to that, and that's the end of Loren Hardeman the First."

"You wouldn't—"

"Wouldn't what?"

"Tell on me . . . ," she whispered.

"Call my son's mother a murderer? Betsy! You murdered the man. I murdered his name."

"We're partners?" she asked weakly.

"Lovers," said Angelo.

6

Wearing his underpants and a T-shirt, Loren scraped dishes and loaded them in the dishwasher. Roberta sat at the kitchen table, smoking a Chesterfield. She still had on the cocktail dress she had worn for the dinner party that had just ended.

"I can't believe you've done this thing," she said. "What in the name of God did you have in mind?"

Loren struggled to control his voice. "I'm going to have that son of a bitch, one way or another." He picked up his glass and drank Scotch. "I'm gonna kill him before he kills me!"

"He's not out to kill you. He's out to destroy you."

"There's a difference?"

"You better believe it. He destroys you, he'll still be the speaker at luncheon forums in New York. You have him killed, you'll eat your lunches in a prison cafeteria for the rest of your life. Or you'll pay heavy blackmail to those two scuzzball 'private detectives' as long as you live. We got away with Craddock. We'll never get away with Perino."

"He's stealing everything we have!"

"Subtlety, lover, subtlety. Carpenter—"

"You and your goddamned subtleties! *Direct*—"

"*Listen to me!* You're so fuckin' drunk you're about to fall down. I'd like a tongue in my crotch, but I don't think you can handle it. I don't want you throwing up on me. *Listen to me!* Turn around here and face me! Look at me! You're lookin' at the only chance you've got."

"I *love you,* Roberta!" he blubbered.

"I want the names and phone numbers of your fumbling shamuses. And don't you ever again try to keep something secret from me!"

7

Roberta met with Len Bragg and Trish Warner in the lounge of a Pontiac motel.

"It's very simple," she said. "My husband gave you ten thousand dollars as expense money, then two hundred and fifty thousand dollars against five hundred thousand dollars to do the job. You fucked up. Not only did you not do the hit, you got yourself noticed by the Greenwich police. I want a hundred and fifty thousand dollars. And I want you to disappear. No contact with my husband again. None with me. And, sure as Christ, none with Perino."

"Oh, that's the deal?" Trish asked with a wide smile.

"That's the deal. In cash, this week."

Trish grinned. "Fuck you."

"I can make it stick, sis," said Roberta grimly.

"Really?"

"Really. You took a swat in the face with a blackjack three years ago. That's some other money my stupid husband put up: the cost of putting your nose and cheek back together, sort of. Who do you think did that job on you, Miss Warner?" Now she turned to Len. "Who do you think let you have one on the back of the head? You give me any problems, I'll pass the word that you took out a contract on Angelo Perino and tried twice to carry it out. He can check with the Greenwich police, where there's an officer who may very well remember that last year he saw a strange car outside the Perino house at dawn." She shrugged. "I don't even need that confirmation. The guys involved will take my word."

"They'd ask you why we took out a contract on Perino," said Len.

"Not necessarily. But even if they found out, Perino would tell his guys to do you, not my husband. There's a certain . . . family relationship."

Len sighed and shook his head. "We've had a lot of expenses. How about an even hundred thousand dollars back, instead of a hundred and fifty thousand?"

"No one ever accused me of being unreasonable," said Roberta. "That's a deal. But if I ever see or hear from either one of you again, or my husband does, the deal is off."

XXXII

1991

1

"Where's Angelo?" Amanda asked. She and Cindy were in her studio in Greenwich. Amanda was working on a portrait of a Wall Street banker. He had been there sitting for it when Cindy arrived, but now he was gone. Amanda continued to work, and Cindy sat on a couch and sipped brandy.

"He's in Houston, meeting with a gorgeous redhead."

"Uh-oh."

"No uh-oh. She's gay."

Amanda laughed. "So are we, dear."

"Not really. We're bi. After all, I'm the mother of five children. And you've been seeing Dietz for eighteen years."

"Carpenter . . . ?"

"No," said Cindy. She smiled a little wistfully. "He's gorgeous, but . . . well, you'll see."

"I appreciate the intro," said Amanda. "I could use a little loot."

Amanda still sold her work regularly, but she was no longer the exciting novelty she had been in the late seventies. More and more she was doing portraits on commission, flattering her subjects enough to make them happy.

The banker on her easel was a little more clear eyed and square jawed than he was in reality. She hated this kind of work. She still did the youthful nudes, and they still sold, but they weren't in demand the way they had been when VKP Galleries first introduced them to the art-buying public.

Robert Carpenter had admired her paintings in the gallery and had suggested he would like to meet her. He was due at seven, and after he had met Amanda and seen some of her recent work, he would take her and Cindy to dinner.

He arrived on time, actually a little early. He wore a flawlessly tailored dark blue suit, white shirt, and regimental-stripe tie. He had been too long in the sun somewhere, and the vivid contrast between his beard and his skin made almost a chiaroscuro in red-and-white.

"As soon as I saw your work, I decided to become a collector in a small way," he said to Amanda as he accepted a brandy from her. He frowned at the portrait on the easel.

"That's a piece from my Norman Rockwell period," said Amanda.

"He'll pay you well," said Carpenter dryly.

"Yes. Unfortunately, I have to sign it."

"Your nudes are masterful," he said.

"I have only two here."

"They sell quickly," said Cindy.

"Do you have any of your adolescents? The two at the gallery are fascinating."

"I'm afraid I don't have one right now," she said. "But let me show you—he's a college football player. He modeled for me last summer."

The painting was of a burly young athlete, thick from his neck to his calves. He stood with his legs apart, his hands on his hips, offering his muscular body for approval and saying with the tilt of his head and his lazy smile that he dared anybody not to approve it.

"Striking," said Carpenter.

"And, this one—she's a waitress. The word's around that I pay well. She'd missed a payment on her car."

A measure of Amanda's talent was that her best paintings were biographies of her subjects. Anyone looking at the painting of the waitress could imagine that the young woman had posed nude with painful reluctance, driven by necessity. Her straight mousy hair, unplucked eyebrows, and exaggerated red lipstick suggested that she was without sophistication. She faced the artist and the viewer with shame but also with conspicuous determination.

"My God!" Carpenter muttered.

"One of Amanda's best, in my judgment," said Cindy.

"Over dinner we'll talk about a price for the two of them," said Carpenter.

2

"Trash!" yelled Loren.

Carpenter glanced at Roberta and then settled a heavy-lidded insouciant gaze on Loren. "Do you think so? All right, I'll tell you what I'll do. My retainer has been used up. You owe me three months' fees, and in three months more you'll owe me six. I'll take the Amanda Finch paintings in lieu of six months' fees. Deal?"

"Deal," said Loren. "I don't want the damned things in my house."

"You've just made a mistake," said Roberta blandly to Loren.

"I don't give a damn. What am I getting for these . . . paintings?"

"Some interesting things," said Carpenter. "When I was with Mrs. Perino in Greenwich, I learned that Perino is working with a computer designer in Houston named Alexandria McCullough. You'll find a flight to Houston on my expense statement. The redoubtable Alex McCullough is a notorious lesbian. But she and Perino have become very close friends."

"Not worth the cost," said Loren. "What else?"

"You'll also find a flight to London. Mrs. Perino was open enough to mention that her husband was going to London. He visited the Viscountess Neville three times while he was there."

"He visited her child, his son," said Loren.

"Perhaps. But the viscountess also visited him in his hotel. She spent a morning with him at Dukes Hotel. And that evening he did not return to his hotel. He spent the night at the Savoy, in a suite with the Princess Anne Alekhine."

"That son of a bitch!"

Roberta sighed and shook her head. "This is gossip, Mr. Carpenter," she said. "It's interesting, but hardly worth the price of a DeCombe and two Finches, plus expenses."

"All right. Have you seen Mr. Perino lately?"

"Day before yesterday," said Loren.

"Was he wearing a bandage on his left hand? If so, did he say why?"

Loren nodded. "He said he was frying eggs and grease splattered on the back of his hand."

Carpenter shook his head. "He told the Viscountess Neville, within the hearing of her nanny, that he was burned when a pellet of lithium caught fire. Lithium hydroxide is used to increase the capacity of dry batteries. The metal itself is corrosive and bursts into flame when exposed to air. It is a dangerous substance."

3

Carpenter had been asleep for two hours when he was wakened by a knock on his motel-room door. He struggled out of bed, wrapped a towel around his waist, and stumbled to the door.

"Who is it?"

"Mrs. Hardeman. Open the door."

"I'm not dressed."

"I'm standing in a motel hallway. Open the goddamned door!"

He pulled the chain out of its slot, turned the dead bolt, and opened the door. Roberta shoved past him into the room. She was wearing a wet raincoat over blue jeans.

"I must've looked like a hooker out there," she grunted. "You have any Scotch?"

"Sorry."

"Always have Scotch," she said. "When you're working with us, always have Scotch."

It was apparent she had already had Scotch. She unbuttoned the raincoat and tossed it on the bed. She was wearing a Michigan University sweatshirt.

"I'll get dressed," he said, moving toward the bathroom.

"Don't bother. I'm not going to be here very long," she said. "Sit down."

He sat down.

"You've got to change the way you're handling this business," said Roberta.

"Oh?"

"We don't care who Perino sleeps with. Understand? Get off that kick. If you can get in his wife's pants, fine. But that's only so you can find out more about what he's doing."

"I thought the fact that he was sleeping with—"

"We already know," she said. She pulled out a pack of Chesterfields and lit one.

Carpenter lifted his chin. "Is it impossible I might find him with somebody you *don't* know about? Is it possible I might see him with somebody you don't want *me* to know about?"

"You're asking a question you shouldn't ask," she said coldly. "Also, let me warn you about something. A private dick who tailed Angelo Perino and the Viscountess Neville wound up with a skull fracture. His partner, a woman, got her nose and cheekbone broken. Get us information, not scandal."

Carpenter nodded thoughtfully. "Actually," he said, "the only hard information I got came from establishing a relationship with Viscountess Neville's nanny. If you're telling me to stay away from his women, you destroy my effectiveness. I'm not an industrial spy. The art connection is what you hired me for."

"So you can get into the pants of Cindy Perino," said Roberta. "That's the whole idea. Information. She can tell you things we want to know. Besides, my husband wants to *destroy* Angelo Perino. When he finds out his loyal and dutiful wife, the mother of his children—"

"He'll kill me," said Carpenter.

"He might, if you're not careful."

"She's not an easy lay."

Roberta shook her head. "I don't imagine she is. But can she resist a knowledgeable art collector with money to spend—who's a handsome stud besides?"

He grinned. "You flatter me."

"What the hell is this? You've got a hard-on!" She grabbed his towel and pulled it away. What she'd said was true; his oversized member stood rigid. "Jesus Christ! Have you got a hard-on for *me*?"

"Mrs.—"

"I haven't got much time," she said. "Do you want something or not?"

"It's a stupid dog that—"

"—shits in his own bed. Don't talk in clichés. Yes or no?"

"Yes."

"Well for Christ sake," she said. She pulled her sweatshirt over her head. "How old are you, Bob?"

"Thirty-six."

"I'm fifty-nine. I've had it all. So has Cindy Perino. Let's see if you're good enough for her. C'mon. Climb into the saddle. We'll start that way."

She stretched out on her back on the bed and spread her legs. He climbed on her and entered her immediately, without so much as a kiss before. He slammed his hips hard against hers and drove himself deep inside her.

The rain had stopped, and the sky was gray with the coming dawn when she left the motel. Carpenter was exhausted, but Roberta was exhilarated.

4

Angelo sat on a rose-colored plush couch in Alexandria McCullough's apartment in Houston. He had taken off his jacket, shirt, and tie and sat in his T-shirt and pants, a martini on the table before him. Alex was in the kitchen, visible beyond a counter, chopping vegetables for a salad. She had taken off most of her clothes, too, and worked in a white bra and white bikini panties. Also dressed only in bra and panties, her friend Lucy sat opposite Angelo, smoking a joint as she lazily stared at and appraised Angelo Perino.

"I hope you don't take offense," she said to him. "I just can't bring myself to say okay. If Alex wants to give herself to a man, I can't stop her; but I'm not going to issue her a license."

He glanced at Alex. "If I wanted to make a point of the matter, I think she might come to bed with me, if only as an experiment," he said so quietly that Alex may or may not have heard. "But it would threaten a beautiful friendship. Why should I do that?"

Lucy was thirty-eight years old, a little younger than Alex. Though she had a generous mop of dark brown curly hair, her face might have been called mannish: square, with a strong jaw. Her figure was anything but mannish. She was an aerobics instructor at a local health club and a lifeguard at its swimming pool. If any woman he had ever seen had a perfect, sleek body, Lucy did.

The two women had as complete a friendship as any married couple had. This was not Alex's apartment but *their* apartment. It seemed to Angelo that Alex played the female role in the relationship and Lucy the male; but that was a simplistic description of their relationship. It was more accurate to say they were an affectionate—no, a passionate—couple, genuinely in love with each other.

"We've both experimented," said Lucy. "There's nothing you could do for either of us that we can't do for ourselves."

"Except get you pregnant," said Angelo dryly.

"There are plenty of people taking care of that function," said Lucy. "Culturally, we live in an era when it is not necessary for everyone to procreate. The primitive Israelites had to. The early Christians had to. In order to survive. Today, there's not a race or a nation left in the world who can't spare some people from that burden."

Angelo smiled. "You think of yourselves as an elite, spared the labor of—"

"Precisely," said Lucy.

Alex came in from the kitchen. She carried two martinis, a fresh one for Angelo and one for herself; but she picked up Lucy's roach and drew deeply on it before she sipped from her glass.

She and Angelo had just finished two days of going over in close detail the design of the electric car. The onboard computer would switch on the windshield wipers when they were needed, measure the rainfall hitting the car, and adjust wiper speed accordingly. It would switch on the lights when they were needed. It would recognize six separate voice-prints and unlock the doors when told to. But all these things were gimmicks compared to the basic function the computer would perform: the exquisitely efficient use of the car's power.

Alex had said the car could utilize 90 percent of its power. It would do better than that.

The major problem remaining was the power *source*. Angelo's designers were experimenting with several ideas. None had yet been adopted.

Alex sat beside Lucy. Reaching behind her, Lucy unhooked her friend's bra and began to lick her nipples.

"Do we embarrass you, Angelo?" asked Alex.

"There's nothing left in this world that can embarrass me," he said.

"Well," said Lucy. "I wouldn't have that cock of yours stuck in me for all the world. But we might do something else for it. Both of us, at the same time. What do you say, Alex?"

"I think all three of us would enjoy that," Alex purred.

They didn't want him in their bedroom, so he lay on his back on the floor. While Alex licked his penis, Lucy sucked on his scrotum. Then Lucy drew him into her mouth, and Alex licked all around. Finally both of them worked on his shaft together. Lucy sucked in and swallowed his ejaculate, and Alex used her tongue and lips to clean him up.

He sat on the couch and watched them lick each other. It was plain they were having multiple orgasms, while he'd had only one. They knew that and laughed about it—and then set to work on giving him another one.

5

"At least he didn't buy any art," said Roberta.

She sat at Loren's desk in the XB administration building. Loren, whose face was flushed with anger, had handed her a letter to read. It was from Robert Carpenter and it read—

On the evening of July 8, Loren van Ludwige flew to London, accompanied by a young woman—in fact a sixteen-year-old named Anna Perino, the daughter of Angelo and Cindy Perino. They arrived on the morning of July 9 and were brought immediately to the residence of the Viscount and Viscountess Neville. That same day Max van Ludwige arrived from Amsterdam. The conversation in the house during their visit, according to my informant, whose identity you know, does not just suggest but clearly indicates that the young man intends to marry the young woman. They did not share a bedroom during their stay.

"My grandson and the daughter of that wop!" Loren snarled.

"We suspected," said Roberta.

"The eldest son of my only child! Going to marry the great-granddaughter of the mafioso bootlegger who sold my grandfather booze during Prohibition! The goddamned family's still connected. I don't see how Betsy can—"

"You've made a point over the years I've known you of treating Betsy like shit," said Roberta.

"She's treated me like shit. She—she even had a bastard by the wop! She sued me! She—"

"She's your daughter, and you had better make peace with her."

XXXIII

1991

1

The six months the directors had given Angelo to solve his remaining design problems and make his final recommendations expired in midsummer.

All the directors—Angelo himself, Loren and Roberta, Betsy, and Tom Mason—were in Detroit for the crucial meeting.

"We have a car," said Angelo. "The only question is whether Tom thinks he can sell it."

"What's it gonna look like, Angelo?" Tom asked.

Angelo stood and uncovered a drawing on an easel. The car looked modern but was no radical departure from cars on the road. It was small and sleek, yet not a sports car.

"Next year's car," said Tom. "The ninety-threes will all look something like that."

"Designed in Italy?" asked Loren.

Angelo nodded. "In Turin, by Marco Varallo."

"He's batting five hundred," said Loren dryly. "His Stallion body was a success. The S Stallion—"

Betsy interrupted. "The S Stallion did not fail because of its body design."

"Well, you couldn't see out of the damned thing," said Loren.

"A moot point," said Roberta. "Looking at this car . . . obviously it's no family sedan."

"The family sedan is dead," Angelo stated. "Look at the cars on the streets. The vast majority of them are carrying one person. Others are carrying two. It's rare to see three or four people in a car. The van is today's family vehicle. And incidentally, I propose we build an electric van as well as an electric car."

"You've solved all the engineering problems?" Loren asked.

"All but one. The batteries. And—"

"Well, hell! If you haven't got the batteries, you haven't got anything."

"It's a matter of *choosing*," said Angelo. "I've found alternative ways of powering the car. We just haven't made up our minds which battery system will work best."

"You're sticking the company's neck out a long way, aren't you?" Roberta asked. "Everything I read says it's impossible to get acceptable performance and range from batteries."

"Alexandria McCullough has designed an onboard computer system that will maximize the utilization of our battery power. That's the key. The car will *use* all its battery-supplied energy. Internal-combustion cars waste up to eighty percent of the energy from their fossil fuels. Heat alone dissipates—"

"Can you sell it, Tom?" Roberta interrupted.

"Eventually," said Tom. "Eventually we'll have to, because sooner or later this old world is going to run out of fossil fuels—liquid ones, anyway. My problem is, how long will it take before people realize this is the car they're going to be driving, whether they like it or not? The DeSoto Airflow was the car of the future, but it was designed almost twenty years before the public began to buy cars like that. The Cord was a great car. So was the Tucker. But—" He shook his head.

"If we don't build this car, XB Motors is dead," said Angelo flatly.

"Because you have already committed the company to it," Loren said angrily. "Resources that could have been spent in developing a new model of the Stallion have been spent—"

"The Stallion has gone as far as it can go," said Angelo. "It's very close to being a perfect design, for what it is. All we could do now is hang a little chrome on it, reshape the headlights, give it a new instrument panel, and proclaim it a new car. But it wouldn't *be* a new car. It would be the same old thing, cosmetically redesigned. That's what each new model of every car in the world is, and the public knows it."

"The Big Three don't seem to be driven to a radical departure," said Loren.

"They can survive for a while longer without facing the future," said Angelo. "We can't. And by the way, before the end of the century it will be the Big Four."

"I doubt it," said Loren. He snapped a yellow pencil in two. "Six months ago the board of directors gave you time to develop a proposal. In that six months you've moved forward as if you had authority to develop the new car, virtually scrapping the Stallion in the process. We didn't authorize you to commit us. You did anyway."

"Faint heart ne'er won fair lady," said Angelo. "Nor success in a cutthroat business."

"I believe Angelo has foreclosed our options," Betsy observed grimly.

"Tom," said Roberta, "you are the swing vote on the board. You were elected to be just that. Can we sell the car?"

"Looks to me like we damned well have to," he replied. "It's gonna be all we *have* to sell. So . . . I have a lot of confidence in Angelo. I don't know anybody in the industry who understands design and engineering more thoroughly than he does—and when he doesn't know he hires experts who have the knowledge. Can we sell this kind of car? That's what he doesn't know. And frankly, I don't know either. But I do know one thing, which is that we've got to offer something better than the Stallion in the next few years. We kept the Sundancer alive too long, and we can't afford to do the same with the Stallion. We've got to bet on this car." He paused and looked hard at Angelo. "And on the man who bet the company on it."

"What are you going to call it?" Betsy asked Angelo.

"Zero-Zero-Zero," said Angelo. "Because it will *have* no piston displacement."

2

Betsy went to Angelo's Detroit apartment that night. It had become pointless for them to try to conceal their relationship.

She took off most of her clothes. She didn't even have to suggest they make love. She knew they would. She walked around the apartment in a pair of black bikini panties, a black bra, a black garter belt holding up dark stockings, and black shoes. From long experience with Angelo Perino, she knew he found that a provocative outfit.

He mixed martinis. "Do I detect that you are beginning to have doubts?" he asked.

"It occurs to me that we're gambling everything we have."

"Number One did. More than once."

"I wouldn't want to become dependent on my husband," she said.

Angelo grinned as he handed her a drink. "Is that the worst thing you can think of?" he asked.

"My father still wants your ass. He was furious when you fired the corporate accountants. I was surprised he didn't raise that issue at the meeting."

"This company has needed reputable, independent auditors for a long time. I may as well tell you; the state of Michigan is going to require an independent audit of the Hardeman Foundation."

"What does Michigan want?"

"The Hardeman Foundation is supposed to be an independent entity," said Angelo. "But it never has been. Number One set it up that way. That's how your father managed to use it against him in nineteen seventy-two. Number One had given a large block of stock to the foundation—and took the tax break on that charitable gift—but still voted the stock as if it were his, using puppet trustees."

"My father uses the foundation the same way," said Betsy.

Angelo nodded. "To control the corporation. He went along with making me president. He went along with electing Tom Mason a director. But he can get rid of me as president and Tom as a director anytime he wants to."

"That is, at the next stockholders meeting," she said.

"Right."

"He won't do it, Angelo. By that time XB Motors will be so heavily into the Zero-Zero-Zero project that it would bankrupt the company to try to back out. And XB can't build the car without you."

"I'd like to believe so," said Angelo. "But no one is indispensable. I've got some bright young people working on the Triple Zero. If the Lear should crash and kill me, they could go on."

"Except that they couldn't fight off the opposition."

Angelo frowned and nodded. "Like Peter Beacon. His emotional aversion to me is almost as bad as your father's."

Betsy kissed him tenderly. "Don't let anything happen to you, my lover," she said. "Too many people depend on you for their happiness."

3

Roberta met Van at Detroit Metro Airport. He had never seen her before, and she had come to the airport determined not to appear as his grandmother, or stepgrandmother. Though she had not been playing tennis, she came in tennis whites. The short skirt showed off tanned and handsome bare legs, and little pink pompoms on her shoes suggested playful youth. She meant to surprise him, and she did.

She drove an S Stallion. It was one of the few still on the road in Detroit.

"I'm glad we have a little time together before you see Loren," she said, avoiding the word "grandfather." "I may be able to give you an idea or two."

"Do I need an idea or two?" he asked. Van was here in response to a summons, almost, and he was not subtle.

Roberta glanced away from the road and looked at him for a moment. She shrugged. "Maybe not. But I'll offer a word or two anyway. You see, Van, you are a Hardeman, whether you like it or not. I'm not. I have the name only by marriage. So I can tell you, the whole damned family is weird as hell. You never met your great-great-grandfather, who was called Number One. In the years when I knew him he reminded me of the character Tiberius as portrayed in Bob Guccione's movie *Caligula*."

"I haven't seen it."

"Do. It will tell you something about the Hardemans. They can be . . . Hell, they *are* corrupt, evil people. Not all of them, I suppose. It's difficult to believe your mother is a Hardeman—except for that steely will of hers. Anyway, they built an industrial giant, out of *nothing;* and that takes certain qualities. Ruthlessness, of course, but insight, fore-sight, and courage."

"Is my grandfather corrupt and evil?" Van asked bluntly.

"Make your own judgment," she said. "I was going to give you an idea or two to help you."

"All right."

"Loren is disappointed that he hasn't seen more of you. He loves your mother. They clash, but he loves her. He wishes you called yourself Loren, not Van. He would like the chance to make a greater contribution to your life."

"In what way?"

"I'll let him speak for himself. All I have to tell you is, listen to him. Don't close your mind to him. He has absolutely no ulterior motive about getting to know you."

4

Loren led Van out onto the factory floor, where XB Stallions were moving along the line. They wore hard hats, both painted with the name Loren. Loren the Third wore a dark suit. Van wore a blue blazer and khakis.

"These are robotic spot welders," said Loren. "Computer controlled. Craftsmen though they were, human welders sometimes made mistakes, which cost us in terms of quality control. I studied this new technique and ordered it for this new plant. A weld never breaks in a Stallion."

Van was impressed. The factory was huge. It was brightly lighted, clean, and free of fumes. It was not noisy, as he had thought it would be. The men and women who worked on the floor were mostly inspectors, checking the work done by the machines that moved parts and fastened them into place. They wore white shirts with thin blue-and-red stripes, dark blue slacks, hard hats with the company logo, and clear plastic shields over their faces—which seemed unnecessary to Van, in this environment that seemed without hazards.

Subassemblies moved along the ceiling on chains and were lowered to the line at the appropriate places. Smaller parts moved over the floor in electric trucks, following marked lanes and flashing and beeping warnings. The whole operation was far more orderly than Van had imagined.

"You see, uh . . . if I've sometimes seemed remote and distant, which your mother sometimes has thought I am, this kind of thing is why. XB Motors didn't just *happen*, Loren. It takes a lot of hours, every day. It takes a *commitment*."

Van nodded.

They walked off the factory floor, and a chauffeur drove them to Loren's office. A buffet and bar was already set up and waiting.

"Keep the hard hat as a souvenir," said Loren. "It may not fit in your airline luggage, so I'll have it shipped to you. What will you have to drink?"

Van accepted a Scotch in the English way, with a splash of water, no ice.

"I'm sorry we've been so remote from each other, Loren," said Loren the Third. "I accept my share of responsibility for that . . . press of business and so on, the universal excuse. Try the mushrooms. They are done that way especially for me. Roberta's idea. She's one hell of a woman—not that your grandmother Alicia wasn't."

Van tried the mushrooms, even though he remembered that Claudius had died from eating poisoned mushrooms.

"You're an heir to what you saw," said Loren. "Maybe not the heir—though why not?—but certainly *an* heir."

Van had never supposed otherwise. He sipped his drink and nodded.

"There's a tradition," Loren the Third went on. "A family tradition. Your mother is a viscountess. Anne is a princess. I am chairman of the board of a major corporation. This family has a record of distinction and success."

Van nodded.

"Loren, you are the fourth of our name. I would be honored if you would call yourself Loren."

"I am enrolled at Harvard as Loren. I sign my checks Loren. I seem to have picked up a nickname."

Loren the Third grinned. "Nothing wrong with that. I wouldn't want to tell you what some of my school friends called me."

Van picked up a bite of cheese. "I'm sorry I never met my great-great-grandfather," he said. "I was only six when he died."

"He was not universally admired," said Loren the Third. "Men who achieve great success often are not."

"Rockefeller . . . Carnegie," said Van.

"Ford," said Loren the Third. "Number One, as we called him, could be a tyrant. But he was a great man. We should be honored to be descended from him."

Van raised his glass. "To him," he said.

Loren the Third stuffed another big mushroom in his mouth. "I am told . . . that you have formed a close relationship with the eldest daughter of Angelo Perino."

Van nodded. "Anna and I are very close."

"I am pleased to hear it. I've never met her but will accept your judgment that she is a fine girl. Angelo Perino is a brilliant man. He and I don't always agree, but I think there is a mutual respect between us that overcomes disagreements."

Van said nothing. He nodded and swallowed Scotch.

"I do ask you to remember something, though, Loren. Your great-great-grandfather Loren Hardeman the First was an industrialist who built a corporation respected around the world. Anna's great-grandfather was a criminal, deported to Sicily—and he might have been sent to a penitentiary. The Perino family is, as the term goes, connected, meaning associated with organized crime. Not very long ago I employed a private investigator to discover if Angelo Perino was taking improper advantage of your mother. That man and his female associate were beaten half to death, here in Detroit. I don't know, of course, if Angelo asked for that to be done. But it was done."

"The Mafia?" Van asked.

"I would not suggest Angelo Perino is a mafioso. Far be it from me. But I think you should be aware of the *possibility*. Putting that aside, I hope you will make a judgment as to whether or not the son of Max van Ludwige and the Viscountess Neville, heir to the Hardeman name and reputation, should be intimately associated with the name Perino. I leave it to you. I am sure she is a fine girl. Italian families produce angels for daughters."

5

Robert Carpenter shoved down his underpants and stepped up on Amanda's model platform. Posing nude was the only way he'd been able to think of to become quickly more intimate with Cindy Perino, and he had agreed to pay $18,000 for the painting. Loren Hardeman had specifically authorized it. The painting would be his fee for two more months of routine work and for this above-and-beyond-the-call-of-duty sacrifice.

He was hugely embarrassed, so much so that he was not sure he could cope with it. His breath was short as he watched the two women, Amanda and Cindy, staring at him and appraising him as if he were a bronze casting: with the same critical eye, examining, judging. In his career as a would-be artist, then teacher of art history, he had seen many studio models and had always empathized with them. He knew what *he* ogled when he first saw a male model, and he knew where Amanda and Cindy were staring. He thanked God he was not deficient and that, at thirty-six, he had not developed a belly or any sagging flesh under his chin or at his armpits.

"Bob," said Amanda, "would you feel more comfortable with a seated pose?"

"Whatever you think," he said.

"Do you want to be staring out of the painting, or have your eyes looking some other way?"

"Well, I . . ."

"You are either saying to the viewer, 'Here I am, untroubled about being naked, and happily letting you see me,' or you are saying, 'Dear viewer, you have surprised me. I would never let you see me naked otherwise.'"

"No one stands and poses hour after hour when accidentally discovered," he said. "Anyone who sees the painting knows that. The last thing I want to be is coy."

"Well, try clasping your hands behind your back. No. Put them on your hips. Tip your hips a little. That's it. Now tip your shoulders as much the other way."

Carpenter followed her directions. His acute embarrassment was tempered by his certain knowledge that Amanda Finch would create a distinguished work of art he could not have afforded to own otherwise. With the two he had bought before and accepted for his fees, he would have one of the best collections of Finches on the West Coast—maybe *the* best. He began to wonder how he was going to acquire more. He could always sell them, of course—though he doubted he would ever sell this one. Strictly speaking it would not be part of his collection, since he could not imagine hanging it where people could see it.

"Are you comfortable?" Amanda asked. "Can you hold that pose for fifteen minutes?"

"I'm comfortable enough," he said. "But isn't it a little contrived?"

"Maybe it is. Pose the way you feel natural."

He put his weight on his left foot and extended his right a little forward, enough to balance him. He closed his left thumb and first two fingers on his chin whiskers and let his right hand rest easily on his right thigh.

"Perfect," said Amanda. She began to sketch.

"I like your esthetic sense, Bob," said Cindy. "You appreciate the right art; and posing just now, you bring a sure grace to it that not many men could achieve."

6

They lay together in his room at the Hyatt Regency, satiated, sweaty, and breathless. Bob's face was in Cindy's lap. Though they were exhausted, he held her nether lips apart with his fingers, lazily studying the configuration of her parts, moistening a finger now and then and exploring further.

"I have a confession to make," he said.

"Make it."

325

"I've never done anything more difficult in my life than take off my clothes and stand naked in front of you and Amanda. You want to know why I did it?"

"You thought I wouldn't be able to resist you, once I'd seen you."

He shook his head. "I thought it created an intimacy between us that I couldn't create any other way. Once you had seen me like that, I could talk to you and you'd listen."

"I seem to have listened," said Cindy.

"I love you," he said. "You have to understand that. It's not just fooling around."

Cindy propped herself up on her elbow and frowned at his sober face. "Who are you, Bob?" she asked. "Don't lie to me. I can find out in an hour. You're no yacht broker."

"My father was—and a damned successful one, too," he said. "I'm a professor of art history because I'm a failed artist. I buy art because I inherited enough money to indulge myself. I really do appreciate Amanda's stuff. I'm a little afraid of what her painting of me will say. She'll see through me and portray me as a fraud. Cindy . . . where's your husband?"

"Why do you ask?"

"I can pose for Amanda every day for a week, and you and I can be together every night for a week."

"Angelo is in Germany. He'll be home Friday night."

"Germany? He gets around the world, doesn't he?"

"Battery technology," she said.

XXXIV

1992

1

       Efficiency tests of electric motors coupled to batteries through the McCullough computer system began in March 1992. The first 000s were just Stallion chassis without bodies and without engines, powered by four heavy-duty electric motors on the four wheels. The batteries were arrays of twenty ordinary automobile batteries, purchased in quantity from Sears Roebuck. The vehicles circled the test track at thirty miles per hour, discharging their batteries while instruments closely monitored the amount of energy that moved from the batteries to the wheels.

On its first test, the computer system managed to transfer 78 percent of battery energy to the wheels: an immense improvement over the most efficient utilization of the energy produced by internal-combustion engines.

Then S Stallion bodies were installed on the Stallion chassis: light epoxy resin bodies. The rear-seat area was filled with batteries. The sleek bodies, cutting wind resistance, improved efficiency so much that the energy transferred through the computer system ran the cars twenty-five miles on a charge, rather than the nineteen or twenty miles achieved with the bare chassis.

Acceleration was sluggish. The battery arrays surrendered

their power at a measured rate and could not deliver surges of power.

Batteries were the key. They had to deliver power fast when it was required. They had to hold more energy. And they could not fill the entire rear-seat area of the car and weigh a ton.

In spite of the tight security maintained around the test track, paparazzi managed to get photos of the bare chassis running with stacks of batteries on plywood platforms behind the driver, also of the Super Stallion–bodied cars with batteries piled inside. It was then that the 000 acquired the nickname Oh! Oh! Oh!

2

In May, Betsy flew from London to Detroit for a board meeting. Her father invited all the members of the board to his house for a cocktail party. All of them came: Angelo, Betsy, Tom Mason, Loren, and Roberta. Cindy had been invited but had declined to attend. Van had also been invited but had sent his excuses, saying his upcoming exams required him to stay at Harvard. Peter Beacon, who was still vice president for engineering for XB Motors, attended with his wife, as did James Randolph, director of the Hardeman Foundation.

The gathering was cordial, but each guest seemed determined to remain a polite distance from the others. Even Betsy seemed aloof to Angelo.

Loren had taken Roberta's advice to try to diminish the distance between himself and his daughter. He talked quietly with Betsy, mentioning nothing but her husband and children.

"How serious," he asked her, "is the infatuation between Loren and Anna Perino?"

"I suppose as serious as an infatuation can be between kids that age. He's just twenty. She's only seventeen. They haven't had sex, I'm certain."

"Her father would kill him."

"I doubt that. I haven't talked to Angelo about it."

"I have no influence on the matter, of course. My

judgment doesn't count. But do you think an alliance between our family and the Perinos would be wise?"

"They're very young," said Betsy. "Many things can happen between now and the time when they're old enough to form an alliance, to use your word."

"Well . . . how are your other children? Little Sally?"

"She wants to be a ballerina. She's devoted to the idea. Her teacher says she's good enough—provided she doesn't grow too tall."

"Don't let her starve herself in an effort to prevent it."

"I have that problem already. I'll be lucky if she doesn't turn anorexic."

"I'd like to come to London and see the children. All of them."

"Please do," Betsy said, smiling despite herself.

3

In June, Anna graduated from Greenwich Academy. Angelo flew in from Berlin to be there. Van had gone home to London at the end of May, but he flew back. Nineteen-year-old John Perino flew to Florida to help his eighty-two-year-old grandmother, Jenny, fly to New York. Anna's uncle Henry Morris came, with his wife and their eldest son.

Among the gifts sent to Anna were a heavy gold bracelet from Betsy, who signed her card "Aunt Betsy," and a strand of pearls from Loren, who signed his "Loren Hardeman III." Amanda's gift was a portrait of Anna, for which the girl had posed five hours. Dietz von Keyserling sent an ivory netsuke: a tiny Japanese girl smelling a flower. Marcus Lincicombe came to the house to deliver his gift: two Hermès silk scarfs.

Bob Carpenter spent the graduation weekend in a suite at the Hyatt Regency. Cindy found time twice to spend an hour with him.

On the lawn in her backyard, she took her brother aside for a moment of quiet conversation.

"You have ways of finding out things," she said to him. "So do I, but I don't want Angelo to know."

"What can I find out for you?" Henry asked, looking more solemn than usual. "Do you have a problem?"

"Surprise," she said. "Would it surprise you that your forty-four-year-old sister is seeing a man?"

"It would surprise me if you weren't."

"His name is Robert Carpenter. He is a professor of art history at California State University, Long Beach. He seems to have an amazing amount of money to spend buying art. Also, he doesn't seem to spend much time professoring. I can't help being curious."

"Professor Robert Carpenter," said Henry. "I'll check into him."

4

After the graduation weekend, Angelo flew back to Germany. Alexandria McCullough and Keijo Shigeto went with him. Keijo was going on to Turin to meet with the designer. Alex was going with Angelo to Berlin to meet with a battery developer.

"We're close to a decision about batteries," he told Keijo and Alex as they sat in the upstairs lounge of a 747 high above the Atlantic. He turned toward Alex. "If you can match your computer program to the device we're going to see in Berlin, I'm ready to buy the thing."

"You've been a little secretive on this subject," she said.

"I've been a little frustrated by the problem," he said. "We're going to have to merge two technologies, both of which are way out on the frontier."

Alex drew attention. She was wearing a green mini dress that showed off her red hair to advantage, and the legs she showed below the hem of her short skirt were spectacular. Men sitting in the lounge envied Angelo. They could not have guessed that her heart belonged to Lucy.

"We're going to have to go with the lithium-polymer cell," Angelo continued. "It solves most of our problems."

Keijo nodded. "All solid," he said. "No danger of battery acid spewing out in the event of an accident."

"It runs cool and makes almost no heat," Angelo said. "Works just as well on the coldest day of winter as on the hottest day of summer."

"How much will the cell weigh?" asked Alex.

"I'm looking at eight hundred pounds."

"What about acceleration?" she asked.

"That's where the second technology comes in. We'll supplement the lithium-polymer cell with a flywheel battery. The flywheel battery will take electric current from the lithium-polymer cell and use it to spin a flywheel floating on magnetic bearings. It spins at thirty thousand rpm or thereabouts. It has two great advantages. First, it can deliver a surge of power on demand, for acceleration. Second, it recaptures energy that would otherwise be lost—during braking, for example."

"Doesn't this thing begin to get a bit complex?" asked Alex. "A lot of things have to work right."

Angelo shrugged. "Isn't a gasoline engine complex? You have to pump liquid fuel from a tank, vaporize it, mix it with the right amount of air, draw it into cylinders, explode the vapor with a spark at just the right time, utilize the power from the explosion, exhaust the fumes—"

"Et cetera," Alex interrupted. "Okay. When all that was a new technology, it didn't work very well."

"This has got to be tested extensively," said Angelo. "Tested and tested and tested."

5

In the bar at the Bristol-Kempinski Hotel, in Berlin, Angelo glanced at his watch.

"I'm going to have to leave you," he said to Alex.

She smiled. "I hope you enjoy her, whoever she is."

"She's lovely, but it's a business appointment," he said. "So are you, but—"

"Am I the only woman you ever met who couldn't wait to feel your cock between her legs?" Alex asked.

"It would be embarrassing to admit how many times I've been refused."

"The others were probably like me," she said. "I understand the attraction. If I wanted a man—"

Angelo grinned. "Please!"

Alex glanced toward the door of the bar. "Is that elegant woman over there your date?" she asked.

He smiled and nodded. "I'll see you in the morning, Alex. Sign the bar tab. XB is paying it."

He walked over to the elegant woman, who was Princess Anne Alekhine. She extended her hand, and he turned it over and kissed her palm.

"Am I interrupting something?" she asked, glancing toward Alex.

"A computer guru," he said. "I have her on retainer as a consultant."

"Consultant in what?"

"Not in what you're suggesting. She might be interested in you but never in me."

Anne stared at Alex. *"She . . . ?"*

"She."

They left the Bristol-Kempinski and walked along the busy Kurfürstendamm, among bustling crowds ogling the rich merchandise in store windows. Anne took his arm and ignored everything but him. He remembered how she had an almost unique ability to focus her attention.

She was staying at an older and more traditional hotel, what the Germans called a park hotel. They went directly to her room, which was a perfect example of the nineteenth-century Teutonic idea of luxury: walls paneled in dark oak, two sets of stag's horns mounted on the walls, a dark, heavy bed squatting on splayed lion's paws, three potted palms, and a painting of Kaiser Wilhelm on horseback, wearing his spiked helmet.

Anne undressed in the midst of all this but kept on her stockings, shoes, and garter belt. The contrast between woman and room was dramatic.

Making love with her was invariably memorable. Once again, Angelo observed that her elegance and restraint did not temper her boldness. She withheld nothing, but whatever she did she did with confident urbanity.

She was the only woman he had ever made love with who rarely removed her shoes and never removed her stockings. He guessed why: because she had a deft sense of what was erotic.

She had a pronounced distaste for the missionary position. This evening she offered herself in the doggy position:

on her hands and knees with her backside raised in display and offering welcome. Angelo entered her and shoved himself in deep. Being urbane and restrained did not prevent her gasping, then moaning. The Princess Anne Alekhine never pretended she didn't love to be fucked.

6

Although the decor of the restaurant in the park hotel was dark and traditional, the menu offered a wide variety of choices, a majority of them French and some of them light.

What was more, the bartender knew how to mix a good American martini. Anne confessed to having developed a taste for them, and they sat over drinks, idly studying the menu and talking.

"My nephew has not given up," she said abruptly.

"I never supposed he would."

"It's Roberta you have to worry about," said Anne. "She's smarter than Loren, and tougher."

"He can't back out of the Triple Zero project," said Angelo. "It would bankrupt the company."

"He might choose to go that route," said Anne. "You've really got him by the balls . . . more than you realize. He's hurting."

"Specifically?"

"Loren the Fourth and your daughter Anna. The idea that his grandson might marry your daughter is absolutely painful to him."

Angelo shrugged.

"Before he died, I told Number One the Hardemans are a family of corrupt parvenus. He almost had the fatal heart attack that evening. I wish he had. He had developed certain illusions—the same ones Henry Ford had—and was obsessed with them. Loren is just as obsessed as his grandfather was. I'm a legitimate princess. Betsy is a legitimate viscountess. But we don't kid ourselves about what we come from."

"What should I do?"

"Watch out for your daughter. They won't harm her, of

course. Even Loren and Roberta lack the ruthlessness to do anything like that. But they'll try to separate her and Van. I don't know how. I just know they'll do something."

7

Anna was exuberantly happy her first year at Radcliffe. Her classes were stimulating, she had made a score of new friends, and, most important of all, Van was nearby all the time, not just during vacations. They were together almost every evening and certainly every weekend.

She was tearful when she saw him board the British Airways 747 at Boston's Logan Airport. He felt he had to spend part of his Christmas break with his father and mother. He would return the day after Christmas, and they would be together for New Year's.

She watched him until he was out of sight. She would take the Amtrak to Stamford in the morning, where her mother would meet her at the station.

Van had reached a decision. During his week in London he would cross the Channel to Amsterdam and, with his father's assistance, buy the diamond he would offer to Anna as an engagement ring. The time had come to formalize what they already knew and to announce it to their families.

His grandfather—to hell with his grandfather!

8

Two nights later Van went to see *Les Misérables*. His mother had seen it and didn't want to go again, so she had bought him a ticket and sent him on to the theater by himself. During the interval he went to the theater bar and bought a whisky.

"Oh, I say! Aren't you Loren van Ludwige?"

The young woman speaking to him was an extraordinarily beautiful blond in a pink mini dress.

He smiled. "I . . . yes, I am."

"I'm Penny—formally Lady Penelope Horrocks. I'm trying to recall where we met. Did you ever go to a curling match in Edinburgh?"

"As a matter of fact, yes."

"Do you remember Billy?" she asked. "He wasn't at the curling match, but—"

"Billy Baines?"

"Yes. Extraord'n'ry fellow, isn't he? Haven't seen him for years. But you—you've gone to the States! So I heard. Is it true?"

"Yes, as a matter of fact. My mother wanted me to be educated at Harvard University."

"Extraord'n'ry! I've not been in the States. If I come, would you show me round?"

Van grinned. "Well, that's a big order, you know. The United States is a big place. But I can show you around what I know—New York and Boston."

"It's good to see you again. We've but a few minutes before the curtain rings up again. Could we have a drink afterward?"

9

The chime rang, and Roberta went to the door of her suite at the London Hilton. "Lady Penelope" was there, dressed now in blue jeans and a sweatshirt.

"I'll take my hundred quid. Plus the car rental. Here's the receipt. He was hugely impressed with the Jaguar."

Roberta grinned. "C'mon in. You scored, huh?"

"If that's what you call it in the States. In a hotel room on Bayswater Road. Dinner at Wheeler's Sovereign in Soho, then to the hotel. He had to phone his mum and tell her he'd met some old school chums and would be late. What's more, he got up about two and went home. I swear, I think the boy was a virgin!"

"Did you arrange to see him again?"

"Yes. He's only in town a week, but I'll get him between the sheets once more, anyway."

Roberta opened her purse and counted out a hundred pounds. "That's on top of the fifty you got in advance. So, a hundred fifty each time you bed him. Rent that car again. Be sure you get the same one, or make some excuse that your family has several. And so on. But remember what

335

you're doing, Becky. You're not just helping him get his rocks off. He's got to fall in love with you. That's the whole point."

"I'm going to get a visit to the States out of this," said Becky.

"You better."

XXXV

1993

1

       "Cindy, I wish I could give it to you," Bob Carpenter said of Amanda's painting of him. It remained in Amanda's studio. He had not taken it to California. "I know—"

       "I could hardly hang a nude painting of you—"

       "No . . . but I wish."

Amanda had gone out, and they had her studio and her bedroom to themselves.

Carpenter stood before his painting, now standing on an easel near the couch. He admired it. No one who saw it could have failed to admire it. More than that, he cherished it. To have been painted by Amanda Finch so successfully had been a boost to his ego. He'd asked Cindy half a dozen times if Amanda had not flattered him; and when she had assured him Amanda hadn't, he smiled inwardly and luxuriated in pride.

Cindy had become a problem for him. He had begun to care for her.

It was impossible not to. She was seven years older than he was—though that would have been difficult to guess, from her still-youthful face and body. She was intelligent, shrewd, adventuresome, optimistic, sensual, caring. So far as he could see, she did not resent the frequent and prolonged absences of her husband. She was devoted to her family, of whom the youngest would be only ten years old this year; yet she had not allowed herself to be limited to the roles of housewife and mother. Neither was she a town booster. She ran a business in the city and had only limited time for local fund drives and the like.

As a professor of art history he had to respect her as an art dealer. If she was not as erudite as he was, at the very least she knew what was valid and had fine instincts.

But for the Hardemans, he would never have met her and would never have acquired the Finches. Even so, he knew now he had fallen in with a ruthless pair who were using him to damage Cindy and her husband. He was tempted to hand over the Finches and tell them he was backing out. He was tempted. But he was afraid of them.

He turned away from his painting. "It's lucky for us that your husband spends so much time outside the United States," he said. "I can't help but wonder, though, what it says for the future of American industry. Is a large part of the new car going to be German and Japanese? Have we Americans lost the ability to make the kinds of things—"

"The Big Three," she said, "can afford to operate big research and development departments. XB can't sink millions into developing new technologies. Angelo has to find them and buy licenses to use them."

"He must be a brilliant man, to be able to identify what's feasible and what's a technological will-o'-the-wisp."

Cindy nodded. "My husband is a great man. Being married to him is something like being married to a president of the United States. You can't help but respect what he's doing, but you have to tolerate his commitment, which keeps him away from home and keeps him on the telephone when he's here."

"I wish I had more understanding of the kind of thing he's doing. Batteries—"

"A flywheel battery," she said. "It works because it spins. The more he explains *why* it works, the less I understand it. But he's confident of it."

"Will you go to see the first test runs? I mean, you were yourself a test driver."

"I'd love to drive it," said Cindy. "Acceleration to match the best American highway cars. No brakes except as backup—"

"No brakes?"

"It will slow down and stop by reversing the polarity on the motors—something like the way a jet slows down by reversing the thrust of its engines. As the kinetic energy of the moving car is fed into the battery, it will convert kinetic energy into electric energy, so giving the battery a charge."

"My God! I—"

"I'm talking too much," she said, picking up her snifter of brandy as if that suggested a justification.

Carpenter stood behind her and caressed her cheeks and neck. "I love you, Cindy," he murmured.

It was the truth.

2

After midnight he plugged his portable fax into the hotel telephone jack and sent a message to the Hardeman home in Detroit—

The battery technology AP is investigating in Berlin involves a spinning battery called a "flywheel" battery. He is on the verge of securing a license to use it.

The 000 will have no brakes except as backup. It will decelerate and stop by reversing the polarity on the electric motors. In the process this will send energy back into the battery, giving it a recharge. Or so he says.

3

Loren and Roberta sat at breakfast. Peter Beacon was there, having been called to the house by a telephone call at dawn. With him were two other young engineers, neither employed by XB Motors.

Beacon pointed to one of the young men, whose name was Simpson. "Feasible?" he asked.

Simpson shrugged. "Not impossible. A number of companies, in the States and elsewhere, are working on this technology. None of them, to *my* knowledge, have got it to a point where it could power an automobile on the road in any satisfactory way."

"There are two possibilities," said Beacon. "Either Perino is relying on an extremely far-out new technology, which may or may not work, or he's going to compromise and put a small gasoline engine in his car to supplement the flywheel battery."

Loren turned to Simpson. "Feasible?"

"It's been done that way," said Simpson. "Twenty or thirty horsepower, plus the flywheel battery . . ."

"A *cockamamie hybrid*!" Loren snorted. "A bastardized—"

"Don't any of you underestimate Angelo Perino," said Roberta. "If he—"

"I went along again this year with the way we've got the company organized," said Loren, "because he has us so deep in this thing it would be ruin to try to bail out. I wish I had that ninety-one stockholders meeting to do over again."

Roberta looked at Simpson. "Can he really recapture some of the energy the car used to accelerate, taking it back from the wheels as the car decelerates?"

Simpson nodded. "It's an ingenious concept. How well it will work, I don't know. He can recapture some, for sure."

"Angelo Perino is a bold man," said Roberta.

"Yes, but there's a difference between bold and reckless," said Simpson.

4

The first test car with the lithium-polymer cell and the flywheel battery took to the test track in April. Angelo drove. The right front seat and the entire rear seat were filled with test instruments, so he went out on the track alone.

Cindy and Roberta watched from behind the fence. Loren and Beacon stayed inside the instrument shack and watched the needles on the gauges. Keijo Shigeto and Alex McCullough followed Angelo in a conventional Stallion carrying a few instruments that Alex monitored while Keijo drove.

On the first circuit of the track, Angelo made no great demands on the car. He accelerated slowly and circled the track at thirty miles an hour. He was in radio contact with Alex.

"Normal," she said at the end of the first lap.

"I'm going to give your computer something to think about," said Angelo.

"It's been thinking all along. Battery drain is within expected parameters."

"Okay. Let's see if it can accelerate."

Because generations of drivers were accustomed to the throttle in a car being a long thin pedal located under the driver's right foot, the 000 was configured that way. Angelo pressed down. The car surged forward. When he reached fifty miles per hour he eased up.

"It doesn't like that as well," said Alex. "Battery drain is outside acceptable parameters. Not by much, but more than we can accept."

"You're making notes, I suppose," said Angelo. "We know what we have to work on."

"Try decelerating," she said.

Again, in order to avoid building a car that would radically change the driving habits of millions, Angelo had had the Triple Zero's brake designed so that it was applied by pressing down a pedal. The test car had no backup conventional brakes. It would slow down as the polarity on the motors reversed, or it wouldn't slow down at all.

It didn't slow down at all.

"Shit!" yelled Alex. "I know why, too. The fuckin' computer isn't reading the command. Just keep your foot off the accelerator and let it run out of steam."

The test car eventually coasted to a stop, and Angelo nursed it back to the ramp at five miles an hour.

When he got out, Cindy was the only spectator who remained. Loren and Roberta and their engineers had left.

"A good first test," said Keijo.

Angelo slapped the test car's fender. "Yeah," he said. "We've got a week to make it work."

5

One week because . . .

Wilma Worth, the *Wall Street Journal* reporter who had called Angelo a playboy executive, was a plump and solemn little woman, probably about thirty-five.

"I know journalistic ethics don't allow you to ride around the country in corporate jets," Angelo said to her, "but I'm going to Detroit, and you're going to Detroit the same day, so what the hell? Anyway, why not have a look at that jet you wrote about?"

They boarded the Lear at eight in the morning. To Angelo's surprise, she accepted a Bloody Mary, then a second one.

"The conventional wisdom on you, Mr. Perino, is that the world has yet to see a woman who can resist you."

"The world may not see them, but I do," he said. "Anyway, in the Middle Ages there was something called the Truce of God, meaning that for a certain period of time all wars were called off so people could take care of other business. How about the Truce of God, today and tomorrow? After that . . ." He grinned and shrugged.

She smiled. "Truce of God," she agreed.

"Which means you can call me Angelo."

"And you can call me Wilma. So tell me, is your car going to run for this drive I'm supposed to take?"

"It had better," he said. "The Truce of God doesn't include your concealing any flaws you see."

"Deal," she said.

"So you asked me a question and now I ask you one. You've been fed a story that the car doesn't run, right?"

"Well . . . let's change the terminology," she said. "You can't feed my paper stories. On the other hand, we've had reports to the effect that the car failed miserably on its first test drive."

Angelo nodded. "That is about half right," he said. "In some respects it met expectations. In important respects it didn't. But that was the *first test*. It's been driven in second and third tests during the past week, and it's doing much better. It hasn't been perfected yet. It doesn't meet all expectations."

"I'm still surprised that you asked *me* to come out to see it."

"From my point of view, you're the perfect reporter to be given an advance look at the Zero-Zero-Zero. You wrote an article about me. I viewed it as critical, not hostile. But whatever . . . you're surely not my pet reporter. So you get the first official reporter's look. Deal?"

6

XB's Zero-Zero-Zero Really Does Run
REPORTS OF FAILURE CLEARLY PREMATURE
A Cruise Around the Test Track

By Wilma Worth

A test car is a funny-looking vehicle. You wouldn't want one for your family car. The backseat is full of steel boxes containing mysterious electronic instruments. The whole car has an air of impermanence about it—because as a test car it is constantly being changed and refined.

The XB engineers opened all the nooks and crannies for me. It's like they said; there's no gasoline engine hidden in there somewhere. The 000 is powered by four electric motors, one on each wheel. The current comes out of a combination of batteries, all quite mysterious to this reporter. The whole thing is controlled by a sophisticated computer that uses electrical energy so efficiently that supposedly the car can run for hours without recharging the batteries.

Apart from sitting in the midst of all those instrument boxes, riding in the 000 is very much like riding in any American passenger car. Mr. Angelo Perino, XB president, drove. The car accelerated smoothly to 60 mph and briskly circled the test track. We went around five or six times. The track is five miles around, so we went 25 or 30 miles without draining the batteries.

Then Mr. Perino offered to let me drive. I did. It was

like driving any American car—until I put my foot on the brakes. Only then did he tell me there weren't any brakes! The car slowed down from the drag on the electric motors, polarity reversed. The car will have conventional brakes for backup, but this test car has none. I wouldn't have known the difference. The car slowed down and stopped just as if it had brakes.

I drove five or six laps. At the end I still had lively acceleration, and Mr. Perino said the instruments indicated we could go around a dozen or more times before we'd begin to exhaust the batteries. We wouldn't need a recharge until we'd driven 150 miles, he said. The company expects to double that before the car is put on the market.

Whatever the XB 000 turns out to be, it is far too early to call it a failure—or perhaps, at this point, to call it a success.

7

Henry Morris came to New York. He and Cindy left the gallery and went to the Bull & Bear in the Waldorf.

"I had our personnel department run a check on your Professor Carpenter," Henry told her. "Essentially, he is what he told you: a professor of art history at California State University, Long Beach. He is on sabbatical leave right now. He lives in a modest apartment and drives a four-year-old Chevrolet."

"Where does he get the money to buy art?" Cindy asked, puzzled. "That's the mystery."

"He didn't inherit it, that's for sure. His father was a barber."

"Then he lied to me. He said his father was a yacht broker."

"How much money has he spent?"

"He bought a DeCombe sculpture for fifteen thousand dollars. And he's spent fifty-three thousand dollars on Amanda Finch nudes—including one of himself. Besides that, he flies back and forth to California; and when he's here he stays in expensive hotels."

"His checks are good?"

"Absolutely."

Henry Morris raised his eyebrows. "I guess we're going to have to go a little further. Let me talk to the security company we keep on retainer for Morris Mining."

"What have I gotten myself into?" she asked. "What's going on? Why has this man insinuated himself into my life?"

"Be careful. Don't let him see that you suspect him. Incidentally, what bank does he write checks on?"

"United California."

"Did you ever see him use a credit card?"

Cindy smiled. "I hope you didn't suppose your sister was without smarts." She opened her purse and pulled out a credit-card receipt. "A man should never leave his chit on the table when he goes to the men's room."

Henry Morris may have been incapable of laughing, but he smiled faintly and put the receipt in his jacket pocket.

8

George, Viscount Neville, broke his breakfast egg with the bowl of his spoon. He had been glancing through the *Times* but had put it aside when Betsy had come in a few moments ago. This was his habit. He tried to reach the breakfast room a few minutes before Betsy, so he could have a quick look at his newspaper and then be free for conversation. His wife was a fascinating conversationalist, always with something interesting to say, and he had broken the habit of a lifetime of always reading his *Times* thoroughly at breakfast.

A tall, slender, white-haired man, the Viscount Neville had heavy-lidded eyes that suggested hauteur, but he was in fact a most democratic man, whose sincere greetings to dustmen and cabbies sometimes amazed his neighbors and friends. He was nobody's fool, either. He knew perfectly well that his beautiful American wife had a long-standing relationship with Angelo Perino and temporary affairs with others. He cared, but he did not want to make such a fuss as to damage their marriage. He was distinctly proud of their marriage for a number of reasons, not the least of which was that it had endured far longer than his once-scandalized family and chums had predicted. Betsy did her conjugal duty for him, and he did his for her. Neither of them had any complaint on that score.

"I have something I want to discuss with you this morning," Betsy said.

"Nothing ominous in that opening, I hope."

"*Something* ominous. Van will be here tomorrow. This is the second time he's flown back here since his Christmas break, and I know why. It's a girl."

"Is that ominous, really?"

"He's an innocent, George. He went from a public school in England to a boarding school in France, then to the States, where he immediately fell in love with Anna Perino. He met this new young woman during an interval at a theater. He's absolutely *crazy* about her! She wants to go to the States. If she does, she'll break up his relationship with Anna. And *that* would be a tragedy."

"There is rarely anything one can do about such a matter," said George.

"You can do one thing for me. She says her name is Lady Penelope Horrocks. Find out for me who Lady Penelope is. Get me her history, her background."

"Hardly my speciality, you know."

"Someone in chambers will have access to an investigator who can do a rundown on her. I need to know, George. I need to know *right now!*"

XXXVI

1993

1

Van graduated from Harvard in June. He had not applied for admission to law school and said he wanted to spend the summer in London.

Alicia had a party for him. Betsy came. So did Max van Ludwige. Loren and Roberta flew in from Detroit. All the Perinos attended, as did Amanda, Dietz, and Marcus.

For once, Angelo and Loren agreed about something. Both of them took Van aside and asked why he had not applied to Harvard Law. And so did his father.

The young man became annoyed and was more than a little curt in dismissing the questions.

Betsy didn't ask him. She knew why.

The day after the party he packed his bags in his room in Alicia's house. Anna was with him.

She wept. "I won't see you until—until when? When *will* I see you, Van?"

"I . . . well, I'll be back, of course. It's just that I've been away from my mother and father so long, I feel I have to spend some time with them, something more than just a few days now and then. I do have some obligations."

"But law school. You didn't—"

347

"Other people decided I should be a lawyer. I'm not certain. I need some time to think about it."

Anna sat on the bed, wiping her tears with the back of her hand. "You've turned cold to me, Van," she said. "Is it because we haven't had sex? 'Cause, if it is, I'll give it to you right now. *Right now*!"

"No, Anna. That's not the problem."

"Then what is the problem?" she pleaded.

"It's just that . . . we're not very grown up. Neither one of us. We must take some time to think everything through."

Anna fled the house crying.

2

Betsy did not see Anna. She came up the stairs and reached Van's door five minutes later. She knocked once, then opened the door and walked in.

"Mother?"

Betsy sat down on the bed, where Anna had been. She was casually dressed, in blue jeans and a white golf shirt. For a long moment she stared at him.

"Mother . . . ?"

"I have something to tell you," she said coldly. "I spared you until after your graduation and yesterday's gala. I don't intend to spare you any longer."

"Mother?"

She had a small photograph in her right hand. It was a police mug shot of a young woman, facing the camera with a flat expression. She passed it to him and waited for him to examine it. "Recognize her?" she asked.

"Of course. It's Penny!"

"Lady Penelope Horrocks?"

"Yes! What in the world is—this?" He blanched.

"Lady Penelope Horrocks is seventy-two years old and lives in Kensington. The young woman in the photograph is twenty-five years old. Her name is Rebecca Mugrage, and she lives in Camden Town. The photograph was supplied to my husband by the Metropolitan Police. It was taken at Holloway Prison on the day she entered to serve a one-year term for credit-card fraud. She has also appeared in Bow

Street Magistrate Court three times on charges of being a common prostitute."

Van tossed the picture on the bed. "I don't believe it," he muttered.

"You had better believe it. Have you been checked for HIV? She's a damned good candidate for giving it to you."

"Why?" he sobbed. "Why would she . . . ?"

"I intend to find out," said Betsy grimly.

"She knew a friend of mine. She remembered where we met, at a curling match."

"Information she couldn't have gotten by herself," said Betsy. "Someone helped her. And I, by God, will find out who. You, you damned fool, betrayed the girl you love and who loves you, for a professional piece of tail."

"Mother!"

"That's all she is, your Penny. And worse. And for her you didn't apply to law school. I guess I haven't been a good enough mother. Max or I should have taught you some facts of life."

Van wept. "What should I do about Anna?"

"Tell her the truth. And don't touch her until you've had a medical exam. Then call Harvard Law and see if they'll accept a late application. You had an excellent academic record, and they might have an opening in the fall class. Stay here. I'll ask Angelo to find you some kind of job. And learn to know who your friends are."

3

Finding out who was behind Rebecca Mugrage was not difficult. She had presented herself as Lady Penelope Horrocks, not just to Van, but to the service from whom she'd rented the Jaguar. To rent the car without trouble, she had used a forged driving license in the name of Lady Penelope. Back in jail and facing a sentence for fraud, she gave a full statement.

Angelo stopped in London on his way to Berlin. He was dining at Neville House with Viscount George and Viscountess Elizabeth. For this candlelight dinner, Betsy had brought out the Neville antique silver: heavy ornate pieces that had survived wars and estate taxes. Although the viscount knew of the relationship between his guest and his wife, he could not have been more gracious.

Not until after dinner, when they remained at table over coffee and brandy, did Betsy tell Angelo why she had so urgently demanded he stop here on his way to Germany.

"This is a copy of the written statement she gave," said Betsy. "On the second page you see what she said about who hired her and funded her. Roberta."

Angelo looked at the viscount. "Do people do things like this in England?" he asked.

Viscount Neville nodded. "I'm afraid so," he said. "We should like it to be supposed that we are more . . . civilized than Americans. But we are not."

Angelo handed the paper back. "Betsy," he said, "this means I am going to make war on your father. I am going to *destroy* him. Do you want to bail out, or are you with me?"

Betsy hesitated for a moment. "It depends on how you're going to do it," she said quietly.

"Not that way," said Angelo.

4

Loren threw a file folder across his office. Papers flew.

"Goddamn!" he yelled. "The sons of bitches have declared *war*! Do you know what this *means*?"

For once, Roberta was flushed and flustered. Ned Hogan, XB corporate counsel, stared at the papers on the floor and made no move to pick them up—as once he might have done.

"All right," said Loren hoarsely. "In the woodpile. We know who they are. Perino. Burger. Fairfield. So Mr. Attorney General Fairfield files a lawsuit . . ."

"I have to tell you, it might work," said Hogan.

"Let me get this straight. Number One transferred thirty-five percent of the stock in what we then called Bethlehem Motors to the Hardeman Foundation. Now the attorney general of Michigan is saying the foundation has to sell a lot of that stock because—"

"Because the foundation is too heavily committed to one stock," said Hogan. "A charitable trust—"

"I *know* a charitable trust! Didn't I have Number One's ass in nineteen seventy-two because he'd retained control of Bethlehem Motors by appointing dummies as trustees of—"

"So what have you done differently?" Hogan asked. "The foundation is a quasipublic entity. Its investments are subject to state supervision. That's how Number One got the huge tax break. But he never *really* gave up control of that stock, and neither have you."

Loren slumped in his chair and looked at Roberta. "Your girl in London is in jail," he said. "That's all that comes of your goddamned *subtlety*."

"Don't lay it on me," she said curtly. "You knew what I was doing and approved everything."

Loren slumped further, as if he would disappear down inside his clothes. "If the attorney general wins this suit, what happens exactly?"

"Some part of the XB stock held by the foundation will have to be sold, so the foundation can diversify its investments."

"Sold?"

"At public sale. On the market. You have to figure that lots of investors will be interested. XB, which has always been a Hardeman family business, will become a publicly held corporation. Instead of ten or so stockholders, you're going to have a thousand."

Loren sighed noisily. "Perino will get up in a stockholders meeting—that personable wop asshole—and charm those idiots into—"

"Changing management," said Roberta.

Loren nodded. His eyes narrowed. "Only if his fuckin' car's a success."

5

Henry Morris telephoned Cindy, saying he'd like to send her a fax. She said it was okay; no one was home but her. In a few minutes the fax came through on the machine in Angelo's study. It was a report to Henry from Blakoff Security Agency—

We have been able to obtain the following information concerning Professor Robert Carpenter.

His salary as an assistant professor of art history is $56,000 per annum. Over the past two years, however, he has deposited several large checks, aggregating as much as a year's salary.

We were able to obtain the balance due on his Visa card. At present he owes Visa $6,325.87. We could not of course ascertain what he had charged.

We were able also to obtain some information about his telephone calls. One number frequently called by him, both from home and from his hotels, is in the 313 area code. That seemed significant, since that is for the Detroit area. A simple check in a reverse directory turned up the information that the number is the residence number of one Loren Hardeman.

6

Robert Carpenter heard the knock on his door in the Hyatt Regency. Cindy! He needn't dress. Wearing only his white briefs, he unlocked the door.

It was pushed in hard, knocking him back.

The man who stood before him was bigger than he was but much older—not a threat, Carpenter decided, as he guessed who the man was.

He had decided wrong. The man kneed him in the crotch; and as he bent over in agony, the man grabbed him by the hair and drove his face down against an upraised knee. Carpenter felt his nose break. Released, he staggered back and dropped to the floor.

"I guess you know who I am, Professor."

Carpenter nodded. He had guessed. Perino.

He caught the blood from his nose in his hands. It escaped and dropped on his chest and belly. Perino went to the bathroom and came out, tossing him a towel. Carpenter caught his blood in the towel.

"I have friends who'd be glad to give you a major headache," said Perino. "You know the term?"

Carpenter nodded.

"Fuckin' my wife. No, more than that—playing games

with her affections. I don't know . . . What's the right thing to do with a guy like you?"

"Mr. Perino. *I love her!*"

"Sure. For how much money? How much has Loren paid you?"

Carpenter covered his whole face with the towel.

"I don't care how much," said Angelo.

Carpenter looked up into the apparently calm face of Cindy's husband. "How'd you find out?" he mumbled.

"I didn't. *She* did. Like every cockhound in the world, you overestimate yourself and underestimate the women you play around with."

"I swear I love her. I really do."

"Tell *her* about that. Explain the calls to Loren Hardeman."

Carpenter stared at the towel. His blood soaked it, but the bleeding was stopping. He coughed. "What can I say? What can I do?"

Angelo saw the bottle of Scotch on the telephone table. Sure. For Cindy. He walked over and picked it up. He poured two stiff drinks and handed one to Carpenter.

"I could arrange a major migraine for you, Professor," he said. "Not here. Not now. Sometime, as a big surprise. But I think you're just a cheap little piece of shit that got into something you couldn't understand. Even Loren Hardeman"—Angelo nodded—"is a bigger man than you."

"A richer man than me," said Carpenter.

"So, a wanna-be," said Angelo scornfully. "What do you want to be, Professor? The word on you is that you know your business. You just don't know the business you've got yourself into."

Carpenter hung his head for a moment. "Can I get up?" he asked.

"Sure. Go in the bathroom and wash your face. You behave yourself, and I'll give you the name of a doctor who can put your nose back the way it was. He's in Switzerland, and he'll give you a new face entirely, if you want it."

Carpenter returned. He'd slapped cold water over his face. His nose was flattened. It was turning purple. "Oh, shit," he muttered and sank down on the couch.

"How'd you like a nice pill that will take away the hurt and guarantee long life?" asked Angelo.

"What?"

"Listen and repeat after me," said Angelo.

7

Carpenter sat on the edge of his bed, still in nothing but his white shorts, his chest and belly still brown with his blood. He looked up at Angelo Perino and waited as the telephone rang.

"H'lo."

"Roberta? Bob Carpenter."

"What's the word, Carpenter?"

"They're having trouble with the batteries. The damned things *explode*."

"*Solid* batteries explode? The story was, they're using solid batteries."

"Well, there's some kind of problem. They're still going to use the flywheel batteries, but with liquid batteries in the combination."

"And they explode?"

"On impact. Not safe if the car hits something or gets hit. They ran a test car into a wall. The batteries exploded and shot battery acid fifty feet in the air. They're trying to design some kind of armored container, but the thing will add too much weight to the car. They're stymied."

"Doesn't sound like anything we've heard."

"Okay. Who's lying to who? Perino to Cindy? Or Cindy to me?"

"Loren's asleep. I'll wake him up and tell him."

Carpenter hung up the telephone. Angelo handed him his Scotch.

8

Van's cheeks were wet with tears as he clutched Anna to himself and kissed her on the forehead, the eyes, the cheeks, her mouth, her throat.

"Is a man allowed to be a fool once in his life?" he asked her.

"More than once," she whispered.

"We will fly to Amsterdam," he said. "I have the tickets. I have your mother's consent for you to go with me."

Anna ran her moist lips over his face. "Why Amsterdam?" she asked softly.

"To see the diamonds," he said. "With my father's assistance, we will buy the diamonds for your engagement ring."

Anna smiled. "Van, you haven't really proposed."

"I *am*!" he protested. "Anna, my beautiful, adorable girl, will you marry me?"

She nodded. "Of course," she said.

"And forgive me for being a complete idiot?"

"A complete victim," she said. "Your grandfather Hardeman is an ogre, married to a witch. My father is going to destroy them both. Do you accept that, Van? That my father is going to *destroy* your grandfather?"

"I cannot believe my mother came from the loins of that man," said Van. "She is so kind, so gentle, so incapable of—" He stopped. "Well, Rebecca Mugrage is in Holloway Prison because—"

"Because your mother is an effective woman, who gets what she wants," said Anna. "My father is an effective man, who gets what he wants."

Van grinned. "God save us all, then, from little John Hardeman—the son of them both."

"Let's let them have it, Van."

"What?"

"The inheritance. You're Loren the Fourth. But you don't have to be. It's been a curse. Let it pass to little John, the son of my father and your mother. You go on to Harvard Law. Let's be independent of the inheritance from Number One."

Van shook his head. "I've never assumed I was going to inherit."

Anna kissed him. "Our secret," she said. "Let them fight it out. It's not *our* fight."

"It is not," said Van solemnly. "Every one of them will—"

"Not hate us," said Anna. "Respect us, in the end."

"But there is going to be a war between our families," said Van. "It's gone on, generation after generation, and it is going to be resolved in somebody's victory and somebody else's defeat."

Anna drew up her shoulders and shrugged comfortably. "Nobody defeats my father."

XXXVII

1993

1

In August, Angelo doubled the security force around the XB test track. He infuriated Loren and Beacon by denying them access to the track except in his presence. He took them in to see tests of the 000, but he kept all his personnel away from them. His team of young engineers was intensely loyal to Angelo Perino. None of them cared much for XB Motors. They understood that if the 000 failed they would be out of jobs, but they knew also that other jobs would be waiting for any man or woman who had worked on Angelo Perino's electric car.

The test cars still ran on Stallion chassis, to which it was simple to attach epoxy resin S Stallion bodies. This made the test cars roughly the same weight as the prototype 000 would be. Cindy came to Michigan and drove one of these cars. When Betsy flew in for a board meeting, Angelo took her out to drive one.

"It's exciting!" Betsy laughed. "Damn, it's an exciting car!"

Cindy was more analytical. "I'm not comfortable with the braking," she told Angelo. "It's like pushing a switch. It does what it's supposed to do, but you don't feel any back pressure from it."

357

"We're working on that," said Angelo. "Actually, when you press hard on the brake pedal you compress a spring that causes a series of switches to close. You do control the amount of braking power you apply, but you don't feel comfortable when you don't get the back pressure. We're going to let the computer generate an artificial back pressure. Future drivers won't expect back pressure from the brake pedal, but this generation does and won't feel comfortable without it. One of ten thousand little problems we have to solve."

"The big question is, how far can you go on a charge?"

"You could drive from New York to Washington without needing a charge, as it stands right now," said Angelo.

Cindy grinned. "By then you'd have to stop to pee anyway."

2

The Amanda Finch nude of Professor Robert Carpenter was put on prominent display in VKP Galleries. Who it belonged to was immaterial; it was not for sale. Before long someone recognized him. Word spread in the art world that the professor was to be seen in the altogether, painted with Finch realism; and shortly visitors began to appear at the gallery, just to see the Finch of Carpenter. None of those visitors had the money to buy, even if the painting had been for sale; they only came to gawk; and academics, somewhat to Cindy's surprise, turned out to be more than a little narrow minded. Some were scandalized.

Carpenter disappeared for a few weeks. He was in fact at Yale New Haven Hospital, where he had his nose repaired. Angelo Perino paid for the surgery, on the condition that Carpenter continue to telephone Loren and Roberta, reciting disinformation supplied by Angelo.

3

For two full weeks in September a Michigan circuit court heard evidence and argument on the question of whether the Hardeman Foundation should diversify its investment portfolio. The attorney general argued that the foundation exposed itself and its charitable works to an unnecessary risk by investing its entire capital in the stock of one corporation—and that one a family corporation with almost no stockholders outside the family. Sixty percent of the stock was held by just five members of the Hardeman family: Mr. and Mrs. Loren Hardeman; Elizabeth Hardeman, Viscountess Neville; Anne Elizabeth Hardeman, Princess Alekhine; and Alicia Hardeman. Family ownership of XB Motors made the stock an even more risky investment. Added to that was the fact that XB Motors had committed itself heavily to the development of an experimental automobile, which might fail.

Angelo Perino, president of XB Motors, was a witness on Wednesday morning of the second week.

"Are you yourself an investor in XB stock, Mr. Perino?"

"I am."

"What percentage of the stock do you own?"

"I own two percent."

"What percentage of your personal net worth does that represent, Mr. Perino?"

"I am not certain. I'd guess roughly ten percent."

"So, if the company fails, it will not bankrupt *you*?"

"That is correct."

"During the years you have been associated with the company in one way or another, how many radically new cars has it tried to produce?"

"Depending on how you define the term 'radically new,' I'd say four."

"And they are . . . ?"

"The car we called the Betsy, one that we called the Stallion, the one that we called the S Stallion, or Super Stallion, and the car currently in development, called the Zero-Zero-Zero or the E Stallion, meaning Electric Stallion."

"Of those four cars, how many can you call successes?"

"Just one. The Stallion has been a complete success. The Betsy and the S Stallion, no. How the Zero-Zero-Zero will do remains to be seen."

"If the new car fails, how will that impact the value of the stock in XB Motors, Incorporated?"

"It will have a very serious negative impact."

On Friday, October 1, the court issued an order requiring the Hardeman Foundation to reduce its holdings in XB Motors stock by 75 percent and to invest the proceeds in diversified securities lawful for fiduciary investment under Michigan law.

There was no market in XB Motors stock. It had always traded privately, among the very few people who owned any. A Detroit bank and a New York bank agreed to make a market for it. Before the court ordered a forced sale, the few shares that were sold by the estates of deceased employees were going for $775 to $800 a share. By the time the banks were ready to offer it, the bids varied from $550 to $600. To bolster the stock and to express confidence in it, Angelo bid $600 and bought $1,200,000 worth of it, so doubling his holdings. In two weeks the price rose to $675, and the stock began to sell, in dribs and drabs. By the end of the year the stock sold for $750 a share. The holdings of the Hardeman Foundation were down to 14 percent. Six percent more had to be sold to meet the requirement of the court order.

There were 518 stockholders. One of them, with one hundred shares, was Tom Mason. Twenty-eight other stockholders were XB dealers.

4

Two families and their guests gathered for Christmas Eve, in two homes in Greenwich, overspilling into the nearby Hyatt Regency Hotel. The Christmas Eve dinner was at the Perino house, cooked and served by a catering team that set up six extra tables.

Angelo and Cindy were host and hostess—he in black tie, she in a glittering white cocktail dress—receiving their guests before a twelve-foot Christmas tree.

All of their children were there. John, who was twenty, had long since broken up with Buffy Mead but had invited Deirdre Logan, who was eighteen and conspicuously infatuated with him. Anna and Van were never apart. Morris was sixteen and anxious to show that he could drink champagne and not get giddy. Valerie was fourteen and as beautiful as Anna. Mary was just ten and a little overwhelmed by the party.

The Viscount and Viscountess Neville flew in from London with all their children. Sally, from Betsy's psychiatrist, was twelve and a shy little girl who wore eyeglasses. She remained slight and moved with the grace of the ballerina she was determined to become. John, the son Betsy shared with Angelo, was ten and knew he was handsome. Charlotte and George, Betsy's Neville children, were seven and eight years old and determined not to go to bed before the party ended.

Alicia was there with Bill Adams. Van was staying with her, as were Betsy's children Sally and John.

Max van Ludwige had flown over from Amsterdam with his wife, Gretchen.

Amanda was there, as was Marcus Lincicombe and Dietz von Keyserling.

Keijo Shigeto and Toshiko and their children were also taking part in the festivities.

Jenny Perino was not able to travel up from Florida that Christmas.

Alicia had invited Loren and Roberta, but they had sent their regrets. She had also invited Princess Anne and Prince Igor Alekhine, who had sent gifts but were not able to attend.

The party was immensely confusing to the children, as it was to most of the adults.

"I will be at your stockholders meeting," Bill Adams said to Angelo. "I bought a few XB shares myself, recommended it to others, and will have their proxies. I have no doubt you will take over XB, lock, stock, and barrel. All you need is a successful car, and I have no doubt you'll be able to deliver that."

"I have two months to get the last kinks out," said Angelo.

Not all the tables could be set up in one room. Just before everyone went scurrying around looking at place cards and trying to find his or her seat, Angelo and Cindy invited their guests to assemble in the living room. The caterers made sure everyone had champagne, even the youngest child.

Angelo did not rap on a glass to ask for everyone's attention. He had a small gong, which he pounded. "I am going to ask Anna and Van to join Cindy and me here by the tree," he said. "Also Betsy and George and Max and Gretchen. Before we go to our places for dinner, I want to make a happy announcement."

The crowd fell silent. "Friends, Cindy and I are happy, very happy, to be able to announce the engagement of Cindy's and my daughter Anna and Betsy and Max's son, Loren. They make a handsome couple, don't they?"

Everyone applauded.

"Now Loren—we all know him as Van—will place the engagement ring on Anna's finger. I've seen that diamond. It's big enough to anchor a boat."

Van's hand shook as he slipped the ring on Anna's finger. Her cheeks gleamed with tears.

"A toast," said Angelo, "to their happiness. And to this union of our families—Perino, Hardeman, van Ludwige. I could not be prouder."

5

That night Van and Anna shared a room—and a bed—at the Hyatt. The families had agreed they were mature enough for it and deserved it, with the blessing of their parents. They would still defer their marriage, while he studied law at Harvard and she continued her studies at Radcliffe.

He kissed her warmly and said, "We don't have to do it tonight. If you're not ready, we—"

Anna shook her head. "I'm ready, Van. I've been ready a long time."

"Then—"

"I take the pill. I'm ready."

He blinked tears from his eyes. "Can you even *imagine* how much I love you?" he asked.

"The hook behind my dress," she whispered. "Unhook it, then pull the zipper down."

He had seen her undress before, but never in the anticipation of their immediately coupling. Everything was new, an adventure. He had taken off her bra before and had kissed her nipples, but never like this. He knelt before her to pull down her panties and to take off her garter belt and stockings.

When she was naked, he was still entirely dressed. She pulled down his zipper, took out his penis, and held it gently in her hand, caressing it, as he undid his tie and unbuttoned his shirt.

They lay down together. Anna was inexperienced but had a sure instinct. She knew what he was going to do, and she welcomed it. She had thought of it. She had dreamed of it. She had not talked about it to other girls. She'd not read sex manuals. She just knew. She turned on her back and spread herself for him. He entered her, and it was just what she'd expected.

1994

6

Loren was drunk. Roberta was drunk. They had left home and flown to West Palm Beach that morning. In a suite in a Marriott motel where no one could find them, they laughed as they thought how the telephones would ring and ring in the house, and no one would answer. Then reporters would come to the door, and no one would answer.

In the privacy of this suite, which they had rented under the name Smith, Roberta had costumed herself for her role as sadist to his masochist. She wore black patent-leather shoes with spike heels, mesh stockings held up by a black garter belt, sheer and crotchless black panties, and a sheer black bra with holes cut out to bare her nipples. Last week, she'd had her hair cut even shorter than usual: almost a butch haircut.

She knew that after twenty-one years of marriage she was not the same woman who had first whipped Loren. Even five years ago she would have worn no bra, but her breasts sagged now. Her nipples were no longer well defined and shiny but somehow seemed smeared on. The flesh was loose under her arms and under her chin. Her belly stood out over the top of her panties. She knew—oh, God, how painfully she knew it—that she was a grotesque caricature of the dominatrix, a role that no longer suited her.

He—well, what the hell role could he play? she wondered. He crouched naked on the floor. She had wrapped the chain between his leg irons twice around the link between his handcuffs. He could scoot around on the floor but could not stand or even crawl. She had poured his Scotch into a bowl left over from their room-service dinner, so he could lap it up. He could not lift a glass. He was helpless, which was what he wanted to be.

Even so, he had not aged as much as she had. A little thicker maybe, he was still very much the man she had married; and she had to wonder if he had not noticed the difference between them.

The thought incited her to grab up her crop and give him a shock across the backside. *The son of a bitch!*

"Oh my God, baby!" he cried.

"We can always quit this," she said. "I don't *have* to beat your ass."

Loren gasped. "Just take it a little easy," he whispered hoarsely. "An' hey! Time to turn on the tube."

She got up from the couch, went to the television set, and switched it on.

Commercials. Endless commercials. Annoyed, she flicked him between the shoulders. He gasped but did not complain.

And finally—

"*America!* Wake up, America, and join us . . . *Behind the scenes!* This is the program that takes you where they don't want you to go! That shows you what they don't want you to see! That tells you what the spin doctors don't want you to know! This . . . *is* . . . *Behind the Scenes!*

"Tonight! A supposed cure for baldness that actually kills your remaining hair follicles! A cereal that contains every vitamin and mineral the human body needs *but only a cow can digest*! And, an electric automobile that—well, you'll see. If you drive one of these you'll want an umbrella, because you may find yourself drenched by a shower of battery acid!"

During twenty minutes of breathless talk about hair follicles and nutrients trapped in cellulose—plus commercials for laxatives and denture adhesives—Roberta flicked Loren impatiently, hard enough that he grunted. The one big welt on his backside swelled and turned purple. The others were just pink.

Then—

"We don't say what the following videotape really shows. We don't know. You watch. You judge. XB Motors is in the process of developing an electric car, supposed to run on batteries. It is being developed inside some of the tightest security ever used at a Detroit test track. *Behind the Scenes* has been able to obtain the tape we are now going to show you. You will recognize the car as an XB Stallion. They are using the Stallion chassis and body as a platform for the new electric drive train. We don't know exactly what it is that you are about to see. But watch, in slow motion . . ."

The TV image switched to a somewhat ill-focused black-and-white tape. A Stallion entered the picture from the left and moved slowly toward a thick wall. It hit. In slow motion the body crumpled. Then the body of the car suddenly filled with an explosion of fluid. The fluid erupted through the shattered windshield and windows and obscured the car. For a quarter of a slow-motion minute the car had the aspect of a waterfall, until the eruption subsided and left the crushed Stallion broken and streaming.

"What does that mean, ladies and gentlemen? *Behind the Scenes* leaves it to you to decide. Tomorrow night—perhaps—a word of explanation from XB Motors."

Loren rolled over on his back and grinned at Roberta. "How y' figure, kid?" he asked. "We got Perino? We not got him?"

7

Within two days of its national debut on *Behind the Scenes*, the tape of the exploding Stallion had been shown on all the major networks. In each instance the network anchor piously described the snippet of tape as something from tabloid TV—still, they ran it.

XB Motors stock fell to $450 a share.

Wilma Worth called Angelo. "Am I still your favorite reporter, or am I not?"

"The stockholders meeting is in ten days," he told her. "Be sure you're there."

Betsy called from London. "How can those batteries explode? I thought you said—"

"Miss Betsy," said Angelo, "your father put his cock on the anvil—and brought the hammer down hard. Notice, he did it to himself. I didn't do it to him."

XXXVIII

1994

1

For the first time in the history of XB Motors, Incorporated (formerly Bethlehem Motors), the annual stockholders meeting could not be held in the conference room adjacent to the president's office. Angelo, as president, had arranged for the meeting to be held in Cobol Hall. More than four hundred seats were reserved for stockholders, who now numbered 631. Few shares would not be represented, either in person or by proxy. In addition, two hundred seats had to be available to the news media and another hundred for curious spectators.

When the meeting convened at 10:00 A.M. on Wednesday, February 16, all the Hardemans were present at the head table—Loren and Roberta, Betsy, Anne, and Alicia. In a special box set aside for them at one side, Cindy, Van and Anna, John Perino and John Hardeman, George, Viscount Neville, and Igor, Prince Alekhine, watched the proceedings.

Tom Mason sat among the stockholders, as did Bill Adams.

Angelo presided, with Loren at his right hand. The first order of business was identification of the stockholders and proxies, to determine who had the right to vote. The tellers took half an hour to do their business and certify their results.

Angelo read their report. No one objected. "Ladies and gentlemen," he said, "you all have before you the minutes of the last meeting and the report of the treasurer. Without objection, neither will be read but will be received as submitted. Do I hear an objection? Hearing none, the minutes and report will be received as submitted."

He went on. "Before proceeding to other items of business, I ask consent to show a short piece of videotape."

The audio-visual people had been cued. As a huge screen descended behind the head table, the lights dimmed. An image appeared on the screen. It was the tape from *Behind the Scenes*. The Stallion ran across the screen, hit the wall, and exploded.

The lights came up.

"Ladies and gentlemen," said Angelo, "here is the XB Zero-Zero-Zero—the E Stallion—in two models: the first is the car as it will be offered for sale, the second is the same car with the body removed."

The two cars, driven by two attractive models in short skirts, entered the hall in the glare of floodlights and stopped before the head table.

"With the consent of all concerned," said Angelo, "I adjourn this meeting for thirty minutes, so that everyone here can examine these cars and look for any liquid batteries that might explode in a collision. The E Stallion, as you will see, is powered by a lithium-polymer cell and a flywheel battery. It has no liquid battery that could explode and send out a shower of battery acid. See for yourself."

2

When the half hour was over, Angelo rapped the gavel and waited some minutes for stockholders and reporters to return to their seats.

"The chair will entertain a motion, if anyone wants to make it, that the meeting adjourn until tomorrow, to afford all stockholders and the media people a chance to go to the test track and see the cars run—and drive them themselves. I will invite everyone to take note that there is no place on the track where the videotape of the crashing test car could have been made."

In the moment of confusion that followed, Bill Adams rose. "Mr. President," he said, "I move that the number of directors of XB Motors be increased from five to nine."

Tom Mason shouted a second.

The motion passed without discussion.

"Mr. President," Adams said then, "I would like to nominate a slate of directors."

Angelo nodded.

"Mr. President, I nominate you. Then I nominate Mr. Loren Hardeman and Elizabeth Hardeman, Viscountess Neville. I nominate Mr. Thomas Mason, the company's most successful dealer. I nominate Mr. Keijo Shigeto, an engineer who has contributed much to the development of the Stallion. I nominate Miss Alexandria McCullough, whose computer design runs the new car. I nominate Mr. Henry Morris, president of Morris Mining. I nominate Judge Paul Burger. And finally, Mr. President, I nominate myself, as owner of shares and proxy for many others."

Betsy stood. "Mr. President," she said, "I second all Mr. Adams's nominations and call for a vote."

Angelo rapped the gavel. "Every stockholder is entitled to nominate other candidates," he said. He waited a full minute, and no one spoke. "Those in favor of the election of the directors nominated by Mr. Adams will signify by saying 'aye.' Those opposed by saying 'no.' The ayes have it, and the directors are duly elected."

3

Buses were provided to transport all stockholders who wanted to go to the test track. They would be served box lunches, and ten E Stallions were ready for them to drive.

The nine directors met in the conference room at the XB Motors administration building. In a meeting that lasted less than an hour they elected Angelo Perino chairman of the board, president, and chief executive officer; Elizabeth, Viscountess Neville, executive vice president; Keijo Shigeto vice president for engineering; Alicia Hardeman secretary; and William Adams treasurer.

The directors authorized the president to move the company's administrative offices to New York and to sell the old plant where the Sundancers had been manufactured. The new, automated factory where the E Stallions were made would become XB Motors' only remaining manufacturing facility.

Loren objected to nothing. All the votes were unanimous.

4

At the track, Roberta sat glumly in a lawn chair and watched E Stallions speeding past. Some of the stockholders were testing the limits of the cars.

"C'mon, Roberta," said Cindy. "I'll take you for a ride."

Roberta frowned, but she nodded and rose to walk with Cindy to one of the cars. Cindy waited until Roberta had fastened her belt, then pulled the car out onto the track and smoothly accelerated to seventy miles an hour.

"I was once a test driver, you know," Cindy said. "I've circled this track thousands of times."

"I want one of these cars," said Roberta quietly.

"Now that you're sure the batteries won't explode," said Cindy. "How was that Stallion on the tape rigged?"

"A huge rubber bladder full of water, with a small explosive charge," said Roberta. "It was done in Canada."

"We guessed it was something like that."

"Loren was trying to defend his inheritance," Roberta explained.

"By destroying the company? What did he inherit besides his stock? He's a wealthy man, and my husband is making him wealthier. Accept that, Roberta. No more games."

"What else can I do?"

"You can take Loren to the Riviera or someplace else far away and keep him placid. We expect your cooperation."

Roberta smiled bitterly. "What more can you do to us?" she asked.

Cindy drove the E skillfully through an S curve. "Betsy looked through the inventory of Number One's estate. There was an item, three million dollars, listed as 'recovery of trust fund.' Do you know what that was, Roberta?"

"I have no idea."

"Betsy's lawyers found out. Before he died, Number One told Betsy he'd put a lot of money in a trust fund for you, which would be yours when you met certain conditions. When he died, you hadn't had time to meet the conditions of the trust, and the money was returned to his estate. You remember this?"

Roberta's jaw twitched, and she said nothing.

"You were to receive three million dollars when you divorced Loren—so he could remarry and produce a Hardeman heir. You were to find him a girl and facilitate his giving you grounds for divorce. Does this refresh your memory?"

"You couldn't prove it."

"Why not? The trust indenture was in the estate file."

"If Loren found out—"

"He's not going to find out, Roberta," said Cindy. "He's going for a ride with Angelo and Betsy so they can talk privately, the same way you and I are talking. They're going to cover a lot of ground. The proposition Number One offered you to end your marriage with Loren—which you accepted—will not be mentioned."

"Why not?" Roberta asked in a small voice.

"Because we have a job for you. Keep him happy. Keep his thoughts off destructive conspiracies. If he tries to pull any more tricks, the trust indenture will be only *one* of the secrets that will be disclosed. You have your ways of handling him. We know you can do it."

Roberta nodded. "I can do it. Don't humiliate Loren any more."

"We haven't humiliated him. He's still a director. His daughter's a vice president. The Hardeman name is still on the company."

While Cindy ran the car through a deep turn, Roberta stared ahead and stayed silent. Then she drew a deep breath. "Who fucked us?" she asked flatly.

"You fucked yourselves, Roberta. You fucked *yourselves*."

5

The directors arrived at the track. They ate lunches and waited for a car to come in so that each of them could drive one.

"C'mon," said Betsy to Angelo. "I threw my weight around and got a car. My father's waiting in it."

Loren was in the backseat of a bright red E, slumped and dour. Betsy drove, looking grim and aggressive. Angelo sat in the passenger seat, expressionless, ready for whatever was about to come.

"You owe me one, Father dear," said Betsy.

"I can't imagine how I could possibly owe you anything," said Loren.

"Well, you do. Number One had that videotape of you and Roberta, showing her blistering your bare ass with a belt."

"That's impossible."

"Nothing was impossible for Number One when he made up his mind to do something. Every room in the house in Palm Beach was bugged, and he had hidden TV cameras in the guest bedrooms. He had tape of you and Roberta. He had one of me and Angelo."

"You said you have them. Where? In London?" asked Loren urgently.

"I destroyed them," she said.

"How did you get your hands on them?"

"I killed the old bastard," said Betsy calmly. "He died of a heart attack, but it was while I was smothering him with a pillow, just after he showed me the tape of me and Angelo."

"You say this in front of—"

"Angelo has known for a long time. He guessed it, but I told him."

"If anyone ever asks me," said Angelo, "I'll deny I ever heard anything contrary to the coroner's report on the death of Number One."

"*Why, Betsy?* Why did you . . . ? Oh. I can guess. He was going to change his will!"

Betsy nodded. "Shutting me out. Shutting out my children."

"And you committed . . . *murder*!" Loren screamed.

"Right," she said insouciantly.

"To deprive me of my inheritance! He would have left it all to me!"

"Right."

"And now you, the two of you, have robbed me of what I did inherit," Loren complained bitterly.

"You're still a very wealthy man," said Angelo.

"You should be grateful we took control of XB away from you," said Betsy. "You're not very bright, Father. What is more, you can't control your emotions. Sooner or later you would have destroyed the company, and your stock would have become worthless."

"You think so, do you? At least I'm incapable of killing someone."

"You were capable of having Angelo beaten half to death," said Betsy coldly.

"Thereby winning his undying animosity, which has cursed me for twenty-two years."

Angelo shook his head. "You're wrong about that, Loren," he said. "I thought you were a fool, but I didn't hate you—until last year."

"Last year?"

"Business is business, Loren, and it can sometimes get down and dirty. My grandfather was not just Number One's bootlegger. You know that Joe Warren was your father's lover and was blackmailing him. What you maybe don't know is that when Number One decided to get rid of Joe Warren once and for all, he called on my grandfather, and my grandfather saw to it that Joe Warren was blown away. You do remember that he died in an explosion?"

"I . . . I don't believe it," said Loren.

"I do," said Betsy. "That's what your father was talking about that night at Alicia's, isn't it, Angelo?"

Angelo shrugged. "Suit yourself, Loren. Just business. Maybe even the beating you had done on me was just business, too. But lately you got personal—very, very personal. That changed everything."

"It changed things for me, too," said Betsy. "I was half ready to attempt a reconciliation with you, but—"

"I don't know what you're talking about," snapped Loren.

"Rebecca Mugrage," said Betsy. "You tried to ruin two young people's lives by hiring a hooker to seduce my son. That's *personal*. Damned personal."

"Besides which," said Angelo, "you hired a con man to worm his way into my wife's affections and spy on me. That's personal, too, Loren. It's unpardonable." Angelo looked over his seat back and grinned at Loren. "How are they supposed to say it at the CIA? We turned your spy. There never was a liquid battery. We used Carpenter to feed you disinformation."

"I was trying to defend what was mine," muttered Loren.

"You were playing out of your league," said Betsy without taking her eyes from the road.

"I was trying to defend—"

"Fuck that," said Betsy. "We've done you a big favor. We didn't announce who was guilty of making the fake videotape. We kept you on the board of directors."

"One vote out of nine," muttered Loren.

"And lucky to have it," she said.

Loren spoke to Angelo. "How long you figure the company's yours?" he asked.

"Long enough," he said. "Number One tried to hang in until he was a hundred. Not me. I'm going to step down when the time's right."

"When Loren Number Four is ready?"

"Probably not," said Betsy. "Van is fascinated with law school. Anna wants nothing to do with XB Motors. It has bad associations for her. They may change their minds, but—"

"Then who?" Loren interrupted.

"Maybe Angelo's son John," said Betsy. "He's interested. And maybe . . . just maybe, another John. He's only eleven, so he's got a lot of time to grow up and decide."

"Your son? You mean the child the two of you had?"

"If he wants it," said Betsy. "And maybe he won't. Maybe

the two Johns: John Perino and then John Hardeman, in succession."

"You've got it all worked out."

"And you had better not try to interfere," Betsy said, an unmistakable threat in her voice. "You're outclassed and outgunned. Enjoy your retirement, Father dear. We're going to make your stock worth a whole lot more money."

6

"We're going to the dinner in the Ren Center, and we're going to act like we're enjoying ourselves," Roberta told Loren.

Angelo had reserved a private dining room, where the families would gather: Betsy, her husband and children, Angelo and Cindy with theirs, Alicia with Bill Adams, the Prince and Princess Alekhine, and Loren and Roberta.

"Do I have to let them gloat over me?" Loren asked.

"We're going to act like civilized people. Besides, to stay away would be a hell of an admission."

Loren stared into his Scotch and soda. "I suppose I have to get used to it," he said.

"Right," she said. "The game is over, Loren. We lost."

Loren smiled. "Unless . . ."

"Unless what?"

"Unless his fuckin' car turns out to be a failure like the Super Stallion did. We can hope for that."

7

For the dinner Cindy wore a beaded floral silk chiffon T-shirt dress in gold and green and shades of orange and red. It was a Karl Lagerfeld design and won sincere compliments even from Anne, Princess Alekhine. In the hotel room later she took it off. Without it, she was as spectacular as she had been all evening. Her sheer, dark, thigh-high stockings had bands of black lace around the top, concealing the bit of rubber that held them up without garters. Her black bra was underwired to thrust her up and out, and it was open tipped to bare her nipples. Her tiny

lace panties had no crotch, so her furrow and a narrow
stripe of pubic hair were entirely uncovered.

When he took her in his arms, she whispered in his ear. "I
can compete with any of them."

Angelo nuzzled her throat. "You don't have to," he
murmured.

XXXIX

April 1995

1

The XB 000—officially the E Stallion, but almost always simply called the Stallion—was not prepossessing in its outward appearance: a small black sports coupe with something of the appearance of a Mazda MX-6. It was a solid little car, sitting confidently on a low chassis. In April it set out on a trip from Los Angeles to New York, as a test and a demonstration.

The news media became immediately enchanted with the team of handsome, engaging young people Angelo chose to drive it coast to coast. Loren van Ludwige—Van—was the principal driver, with John Perino to spell him. Sitting in the rear seat were Anna and Valerie Perino. Van was twenty-three years old, John was twenty-two, Anna was twenty, and Valerie was sixteen.

The route was Los Angeles to Flagstaff to Albuquerque to Amarillo to Oklahoma City to Tulsa to St. Louis to Indianapolis to Columbus to Akron and finally across Interstate 80, over the George Washington Bridge and into New York, where the car would be put on display at the Exhibition and Convention Center. The idea was for the four young people to drive like a family of tourists, stopping for lunches, staying overnight in motels. They were to keep the car running at the speed limit or a little above. They were to run the air conditioner when they needed it. They were to play tapes and disks and listen to the radio news. The idea was for them to drive the E Stallion exactly as they would drive a gasoline-powered car.

But, of course, their drive across country could not be exactly that kind of trip. They were followed by a truck carrying the generator they needed to recharge their batteries. Only in Oklahoma City, St. Louis, and Columbus could they recharge in service stations. As the constant flow of news releases from XB pointed out, though, recharging equipment could be added to service stations as readily as diesel fuel once had been—more readily, since there would be a greater market.

The big point was that the E Stallion could be recharged while the drivers and passengers ate lunch, or during their first half hour at a motel. It did not require an overnight charge. In St. Louis, where XB had arranged for recharging equipment to be installed at a McDonald's, Van smiled at television cameras as he plugged the Stallion into the recharger that looked very much like a gasoline pump, and the car was recharged in twenty minutes while the crew ate Big Macs and fries and drank Cokes. Van paid $16 for that charge.

They spent Monday night in a motel outside Akron. The next day they would drive across Pennsylvania to Stroudsburg, where they would spend their last night on the road and be ready to make a triumphal entry into New York by noon on Wednesday.

Anna also shared in the driving. When they stopped in the service area just west of DuBois, she moved into the driver's seat. They waited a few minutes for their service truck to catch up, and Van talked for a minute or two with the crew. The rule was for the truck to stay two or three miles behind them, so it would not be conspicuous or appear in the pictures that were taken of them everywhere. Van climbed into the passenger seat, and Anna pulled onto the highway. She would drive the next hundred miles or so.

Without realizing it, she had chosen one of the most

mountainous hundred-mile stretches of their whole coast-to-coast trip. But she was a skilled driver, and this was an interstate highway. What was more, the Stallion had long since demonstrated its power and reliability on long uphill stretches that often caused internal-combustion engines to overheat. In fact, twice they passed cars with geysers of water and steam shooting from their radiators. They laughed when they noticed that one of them was an old Sundancer.

They crossed a high ridge, and the highway began a descent down the eastern slope of the Appalachians.

Eighteen-wheelers ran fast on long downhill runs, clocking seventy miles an hour or more. Signs urged them to downshift, but few of them did. Their drivers were impatient to regain some of the time they had lost laboring uphill. Truck traffic was heavy, too, as I-80 was a major transportation route.

An immense yellow rig loomed behind the Stallion, its engine roaring. The driver began to blink his lights.

"What the hell does he want me to do, get off the road?" Anna asked.

"Seems to be what he has in mind," said Van.

A red eighteen-wheeler filled the lane ahead of them, this one showing brake lights, slowing down. Anna caught up with it and had to use her brakes to stay a safe distance behind it.

"You're gonna have to pass him. That son of a bitch back of us is too close," John said from the backseat.

Anna turned on her left-turn signal and began to ease out into the left lane to pass, but the yellow eighteen-wheeler jerked abruptly into the left lane and came up beside the Stallion.

"Hey!" yelled Van. "Look at that bastard ahead of us. Look! He's got no license plates!"

Not only that. The identification numbers painted on the trailer had been covered with paper and masking tape.

Anna gripped the wheel grimly with both hands. She glanced to the right. Only a guardrail separated the highway from a long, steep plunge into woodland.

"They're trying to force us into the guardrail," Van muttered.

"Like hell," Anna grunted.

The huge front wheel of the yellow eighteen-wheeler rolled just to the left of the front of the Stallion. Anna eased closer to it, then abruptly rammed the big tire with her front bumper. A puff of smoke issued from the tire, and shreds of rubber flew, hitting the Stallion's hood and windshield. The tire's cords were exposed. She hit it again. The tire exploded.

Anna swerved to the right and applied her brakes. Suddenly the Stallion was behind the eighteen-wheelers, and the one with the shredded tire began to fishtail. Out of control, it rammed into the trailer of the red eighteen-wheeler and drove it against the guardrail. The weight of the rig ripped away a piece of the guardrail. The driver braked and was hit again, this time from squarely behind, by the yellow rig. Finally, the yellow eighteen-wheeler veered wildly to the right, tore away more guardrail, and plunged down the steep wooded slope. It turned over and rolled.

Anna swerved into the left lane and accelerated. She glanced at Van, and her eyes filled with tears. "I think I just killed a man," she said.

"Somebody just tried to kill *us*," said Van. "I wouldn't want to be that person when your father figures it out."

That night in the parking lot of a motel just outside Stroudsburg, the crew of the service truck replaced the front bumper of the Stallion, which was the only damaged part of the car.

News accounts of the collision between the two eighteen-wheelers—and the death of the driver of the yellow one—noted that a small black passenger car had somehow miraculously escaped the trap the two out-of-control rigs had created; but all witnesses had been at least several hundred yards away, and no one had any idea what kind of car it was or where it went.

2

When the four young people checked out of their Stroudsburg motel, Angelo did not know what had happened to them. He had come to Betsy's suite in the Waldorf—for breakfast, she had said.

She lay beside him gleaming with sweat, some of his own mixed with hers. He inhaled the unique, unmistakable odor that human bodies exude while in the throes of rapture.

She was a rare beauty. She had been when he first met her, when she was sixteen. Now she was forty-two, and she was, if anything, even more beautiful: with those memorable, calmly defiant pale blue eyes that had disordered the wits of many a man, still wearing her blond hair long and smooth, her body still as sleek as ever, with smooth bottom and belly. She swam nude and was tanned all over; the sun had even darkened the big and shiny nipples on her big, firm breasts.

"Angelo Perino," she whispered hoarsely, "you're a fuckin' fugitive from Medicare, but you're still the best who ever gave it to me."

He suspected she spoke the truth. "You inspire me," he said.

"That would be a wonderful compliment," she said, "except that I can probably count a hundred other women who've inspired you."

Angelo Perino was sixty-four. In some ways he looked it, and in some he didn't. He was gray only at the temples. Women had always found him handsome, and the lines that had slowly come to his face during the last twenty years had added maturity and had made him handsome in a new way. His flesh remained taut; he had not gone loose the way so many men did. People who had known him when he was a racing driver still recognized him without difficulty.

Two weeks ago he had begun posing for Amanda Finch, nude, as Cindy had asked him to do. It was a stimulating new experience, something he had never thought he could do but was now comfortable with. His and Cindy's pictures would hang side by side in their bedroom.

"You inspire me one hell of a lot, Viscountess," he said.

She sighed. "At least you don't call me Miss Betsy anymore."

He grinned. "It doesn't seem appropriate anymore. Not since . . . Well . . . Miss. No more appropriate than the way we all called the old man Number One."

"He was the only one capable of killing you. And when he found out about us, he would have liked to."

"He did his damnedest," said Angelo.

"Not really. I don't think you ever really understood him. I don't think you ever gauged how completely evil he was, or how vicious—or how much awe and respect he had for you."

"I think I may be the only one who ever *did* understand him—at long last, after painful experience."

"Honey-babe," she murmured, "you got enough left for one more? You have to hurry. You have to get across the George Washington Bridge. A quickie?" She ran her hands over his still-hard-and-muscular body, then seized his half-erect organ. "One more time?"

"To hell with the E. If I haven't got the time for one more, by God I'll *take* the time!"

3

Anyway, he would be *flying* across the Hudson, not crossing the bridge, and he had the time. Forty minutes after he agreed to a final quickie, a small Bell helicopter lifted off from a pad on the riverfront, rose over Manhattan, and crossed the Hudson River at an altitude lower than the tops of the towers of the George Washington Bridge.

No matter how many times he flew in one of these noisy, shaking little choppers, Angelo never ceased to be fascinated and afraid. It was not like flying in a plane, which carried you so high above the landscape that everything below became toylike and unreal. This was how the world must look to the gods: seen from a superior height, yet intimately. He could look into the cars on the GW and see women's skirts drawn back and showing handsome legs. Still, it was scary. The little ship vibrated and was shaken by gusts of wind, also by updrafts and downdrafts. He could see, too, that flying the thing was like rubbing your belly and patting your head at the same time: a daunting exercise in counterintuitive concentration.

Constantly talking on the radio to Teterboro tower, the pilot guided the helicopter across metropolitan New Jersey, keeping for the most part no more than two hundred feet above the rooftops, until he settled down gently on Caldwell-Wright Airport. Interstate 80 was in sight during much of the flight. Angelo had stared at it thoughtfully. It and I-95 were his return route to Manhattan.

He was never willing to leave a helicopter until the rotors stopped turning, and it made him distinctly uncomfortable to see Anna running forward, hand in hand with Van. They ran with their heads ducked to avoid the decapitating potential of the swinging blades. Valerie waited for the blades to stop, restrained probably by her elder brother John.

Television cameras and surging reporters pressed against police ropes. The long lenses of the cameras were capturing every expression of the principals, as Angelo at last stepped down from the chopper and embraced Van and Anna.

Anna asked Angelo to get inside the Stallion with her and Van so they could talk for a few minutes. They told him what had happened on the mountain.

His face turned red and rigid. But he said, "All right, we've got a show to put on. You forget what happened. I'll take care of it."

4

A few minutes later a motorcade pulled away from the airport, led by two New Jersey State Police cars.

The Stallion followed, driven by Van, with Anna sitting beside him.

A sleek family van followed the Stallion. It kept alive the name Sundancer, though officially it was Model 000 V. It, too, was an electric-powered vehicle, driven by Angelo Perino. Cindy sat beside him. In the rear seats were Morris Perino, Mary Perino, and John Hardeman.

A truck loaded with television cameras followed the two electrics, followed by half a dozen cars filled with reporters. Two helicopters hovered over the motorcade, affording television cameras an overhead view. Two more police cars finished the motorcade.

"A triumph," Cindy said to Angelo.

Angelo nodded. "Provided we make the convention center without a breakdown."

She leaned closer to him and said under her breath, "Loren would love that."

"That's why the two vehicles have been guarded by enough security men to fight a small war—with enough guns to fight a big one."

"He wouldn't dare."

"Wait'll I tell you what he's already dared. I'm gonna kill him. I swear I'm gonna kill him."

"It couldn't be that bad."

"No? I'll tell you later."

Angelo turned and looked at this woman who was his wife. She was the mother of his five children. But she was a hell of a lot more than that. The gamine in torn blue jeans who had hung around the racetrack pits had turned out to be a well-educated, sophisticated woman. She loved Angelo. He'd never doubted that. But she had never been dependent on him. Cindy was Cindy: lovely, caring, erotic, yes, but also smart and astute, objective and realistic.

She had aged well. Seventeen years younger than Angelo, she could no longer have wandered the pits as a racetrack groupie, but she could have haunted the docks as whatever a yacht groupie might be called. Race drivers, most of them, would lack the perspicacity to appreciate her. Yatchsmen, more sophisticated in their tastes to begin with, and more mature, would find her delicious. Everything she once had, she still had—including a supremely adventuresome spirit.

Apart from that, she still had a great figure, and the marks of maturity that had come with the years only made her more interesting. He retained his special image of her: tight butt in ragged jeans that might have been painted on, tits hanging loose inside a white T-shirt, the race-driver groupie he had never seen in a dress until he'd known her a year— that image supplemented by the paintings Amanda had done of her.

No marriage was perfect. She remained adventuresome and had her adventures, maybe was having one even now. Okay. He had his. But she was the love of his life. He wouldn't have wanted her any other way.

At the toll plaza for the upper deck of the GW, the New Jersey police cars pulled away, and their stations were taken up by blue-and-white cars of the NYPD. Crossing the bridge, they picked up two more news helicopters.

Still speaking quietly to Angelo, Cindy said, "Anyway,

it's a goddamned *triumph*—and it's a Perino triumph, not a Hardeman triumph."

"Shared," said Angelo. "That's why Van is driving."

"He's Betsy's son," said Cindy, "not Loren the Third's grandson. I wonder if he's a Hardeman at all."

"Don't kid yourself," said Angelo. "He may be a van Ludwige, but he's a Hardeman, too. And so's Betsy."

Cindy shrugged and stared southward toward the World Trade Center and all the rest of Manhattan visible from the upper deck of the GW on a clear day like this.

Turning off the GW, the motorcade made its way down the variously called segments of the West Side Highway to Fifty-seventh Street, then across town to Broadway and down to the crosstown street that led to the Javits Convention Center.

The idea of the circuitous route was to give a few more New Yorkers a look at the E Stallion and the Sundancer van. Few of them looked. To jaded New Yorkers, the motorcade was just another excuse to foul up midtown traffic.

The media people were more easily programmed. They went bug-eyed on cue. As the Stallion and the new Sundancer swept into the Center and to their places on the floor, where they would be on display for a week, strobes flashed and reporters and cameramen surrounded the two vehicles.

What the four young people had to say had been heard a score of times during the trip. Television and newspapers had already reported that the car ran smoothly, that it was comfortable, that it had plenty of acceleration, that it had never come near running short of electrical energy. Now the reporters wanted to hear from Angelo Perino.

"When will the car be on the market, Mr. Perino?"

Angelo stepped up to a group of microphones that had been arranged for answering questions. "Next year," he said. "The first E Stallions will be sold in the Los Angeles area. We've entered into contracts with two major gasoline companies to add recharging equipment to their stations."

"What will it cost to recharge the batteries?"

"A little more than a tank of gasoline. Roughly two dollars more. Driving the electric Stallion will cost about one cent per mile more than a gas-powered car. On the other hand, you never have to change oil or transmission fluid, you have no filters to change, you never have to add antifreeze, you have no spark plugs to burn up, and so on. I think the car will run about as economically as a conventional car—and maybe later, when the oil companies reduce the cost of a charge, it may run cheaper."

"What's it gonna cost to replace the batteries? Isn't that the big question?"

Angelo nodded. "Our test cars have averaged eighty thousand miles on a set of batteries. Then they cost about two thousand dollars to replace. How many conventional automobiles run eighty thousand miles with no more than two thousand dollars in maintenance costs? By eighty thousand miles you're replacing piston rings, valves, carburetor parts, points, coils, water pumps, and so on—not to mention how many sets of plugs you've gone through."

Two security guards opened a path through the reporters, to make a way for Elizabeth, Viscountess Neville: Betsy. With her was Roberta.

"Ladies and gentlemen, here is the Viscountess Neville, great-granddaughter of the founder of XB Motors, and Roberta Hardeman, wife of the founder's grandson."

Betsy rushed to her son Van and embraced him warmly.

As soon as he could, Angelo pulled Betsy and Roberta off to one side. "All right, where is he?"

"Where's who?"

"Loren. *Where is he*?"

Betsy glanced at Roberta. "You didn't tell *me*, either."

Roberta flushed and shook her head. "He went to Florida last night. Palm Beach. He still owns Number One's house, you know. Why?"

"I'm gonna kill him!"

5

Angelo did not appear at the Hardeman house in Palm Beach for a week. Then he arrived, dropped off by a taxi. Loren had revived Number One's old habit of keeping two vicious guard dogs on the premises. As Angelo walked toward the house, they lunged toward him, snarling. He had come prepared for that. He drew a cannister of Mace from his jacket pocket and dropped both dogs in their tracks. As they writhed and howled, he gave each of them an extra shot, to be sure they would not bother him again.

The doorbell was answered by Roberta. She pointed toward the lanai. Betsy was there. Loren sat on a chaise longue, a .38 revolver in his right hand. He was wearing a beach coat. His hairy legs were exposed, and his feet were bare.

"Did you expect me sooner?" Angelo asked Loren.

"I did. Where've you been?"

"I took the trouble to make sure I was right. I didn't want to come here and accuse you until I was sure."

"What the hell are you talking about?"

"The Pennsylvania State Police were having difficulty figuring out how that truck driver got dead and why there were no license plates on his rig and why its various numbers were covered with brown paper and tape and why another rig was in the same condition. That is, they were having difficulty until I gave them the sworn statements of four witnesses."

"Really, Angelo," said Betsy. "What *are* you talking about?"

Angelo spoke to Betsy. "He tried to kill Van and Anna and John and Valerie—three of my kids and one of yours. He hired two truckers to run the Stallion off the road on a steep mountainside. The attempt failed, but one of the truckers was killed."

Loren pointed his revolver at Angelo. "Be careful of how you bandy words about, my wop friend. You know . . . you know, if I shot you, several witnesses would testify that you threatened to kill me. Self-defense."

"What witnesses?" Betsy asked.

"You yourself told me he said he was gonna—"

"Don't count on *my* testifying that he threatened to kill you," said Betsy coldly.

"Can you *prove* this accusation?" Roberta asked, her face flushed and her voice breaking.

"I don't have to prove it. The district attorney of Centre County, Pennsylvania, is going to prove it."

"What lies did you tell *him*?" Loren demanded loudly.

"I haven't even talked to him. The Pennsylvania State

Police are conducting the investigation. The four kids will testify that two big rigs tried to force the Stallion off the highway at high speed. Anna was driving, and thank God she was a skillful enough driver to escape the trap—though she caused the trucks to crash in the process, killing one of the truckers."

"*She* killed him, then. I didn't. And it'll be those kids' word against—"

"The surviving trucker has not been able to explain why his license plates were in the cab with him and why his ICC numbers were covered with paper and tape—the same as the other rig, identification obscured. The trucker's in jail. He knows he's in big trouble, and he's given a sworn statement—on the advice of his attorney."

"Okay, he and the other one tried to run the Stallion off the road. What've *I* got to do with it?"

"Both truckers owned their rigs. Both owed on them. Odd. The mortgages on their rigs were both paid off a week before the accident. With cash—a hundred and fifty-five thousand dollars. The district attorney will be subpoenaing your bank records. You didn't just happen to withdraw a hundred and fifty-five thousand dollars in cash recently, did you Loren?"

Roberta screamed. "*You did this?* You tried to kill those kids? You stupid, drunken, insane—"

Loren grinned. "Murder . . . It didn't bother you before."

Roberta spoke to Angelo and Betsy. "Burt Craddock. He tried to blackmail us." She turned to Loren, her face rigid. "Put that goddamned gun down. You shoot Angelo, you won't have one favorable witness. Not me, for damned sure. And don't forget you're in Florida. Down here they favor the death penalty."

Loren stared at the pistol for a moment, as if maybe he was thinking of putting it in his mouth. Then he shrugged and laid it aside, and Betsy picked it up.

"You better put your toothbrush in a little bag, Loren," said Angelo without a note of sympathy. "A Pennsylvania grand jury is going to return an indictment. Then Pennsylvania will ask for extradition."

Betsy poured a water glass of Scotch and handed it to her

father. "Have a drink, old man," she said scornfully. "That'll make you feel better."

6

Early in the evening of June 24, Anna Perino married Loren van Ludwige. The wedding was held under a red-and-white striped tent on the lawn behind the Perino home. A string quartet played, stopping only during the ceremony itself. All the women wore gowns, some with wide-brimmed hats. The sun still shone, and Amanda Finch remarked that the women in their many colors looked like flowers.

Anna had all the soft, appealing Mediterranean beauty of her ancestry. Her dark eyes were warm and fluid. Twenty years old, she was mature in every respect. Her physical maturity showed through her chaste white wedding dress.

Van was a tall and handsome young man, which was to be expected of a son of Betsy Hardeman and Max van Ludwige. Max was a handsome man, but the genes of the Hardemans predominated in Loren—as they did in every child of that clan. He had inherited his mother's strong simple face and pale blue eyes.

The young couple were conspicuously, touchingly in love.

"Even *I* don't recognize all these people," Betsy said to Angelo. She and the Viscount Neville were sipping champagne. "I can't introduce George."

"Well, everyone's here," said Angelo. "Just about."

Everyone *was* there—all the other children of both families; the eighty-five-year-old Jenny Perino, grandmother of the bride, happily holding court in a peacock chair; a beaming Max van Ludwige and his ever-handsome wife; the supremely elegant Prince and Princess Alekhine; the dignified Alicia Grinwold Hardeman and Bill Adams; Henry Morris and his family, all confused as to who most of the guests might be; a conspicuously impressed Amanda Finch, Marcus Lincicombe, and Dietz von Keyserling; the formally polite Keijo Shigeto, Toshiko, and their children; jolly Tom Mason; a bemused Alexandra McCullough; Signor Giovanni DiCostanzo and an exuberant few members of the local Italian community, who brought generous cash gifts to the bride; and many neighbors and friends and classmates.

"Not *everyone,* thank God," said Betsy. "But for the first time in my life I have halfway human feelings about my father. I mean, *in jail!* That's more of a comedown than you meant for him, Angelo."

"Well, he tried to—"

"Yes, I know. Even so."

"He's going to cop a plea, you know. Six, seven, eight years, he'll be out."

Betsy glanced around. "I'm sorry I mentioned him. I don't want to think about him."

The quartet, which had taken a break, now began to play dance music.

"You should dance," said Angelo. "Since I had the floor put down, you should use it."

The setting sun was still bright. The wind was warm and gentle and fragrant. Van danced with his new wife. Then Angelo danced with his daughter.

"Thank you, Daddy," she whispered tearfully. "For everything. For so very much."

"And thank *you,*" he murmured. "I'm very proud of you. You see, life is good . . . for the good."